The Best
AMERICAN SHORT STORIES 2009

GUEST EDITORS OF
THE BEST AMERICAN SHORT STORIES

1978 TED SOLOTAROFF
1979 JOYCE CAROL OATES
1980 STANLEY ELKIN
1981 HORTENSE CALISHER
1982 JOHN GARDNER
1983 ANNE TYLER
1984 JOHN UPDIKE
1985 GAIL GODWIN
1986 RAYMOND CARVER
1987 ANN BEATTIE
1988 MARK HELPRIN
1989 MARGARET ATWOOD
1990 RICHARD FORD
1991 ALICE ADAMS
1992 ROBERT STONE
1993 LOUISE ERDRICH
1994 TOBIAS WOLFF
1995 JANE SMILEY
1996 JOHN EDGAR WIDEMAN
1997 E. ANNIE PROULX
1998 GARRISON KEILLOR
1999 AMY TAN
2000 E. L. DOCTOROW
2001 BARBARA KINGSOLVER
2002 SUE MILLER
2003 WALTER MOSLEY
2004 LORRIE MOORE
2005 MICHAEL CHABON
2006 ANN PATCHETT
2007 STEPHEN KING
2008 SALMAN RUSHDIE
2009 ALICE SEBOLD

The Best AMERICAN SHORT STORIES® 2009

Selected from
U.S. and Canadian Magazines
by Alice Sebold
with Heidi Pitlor

With an Introduction by Alice Sebold

Mariner Books
HOUGHTON MIFFLIN HARCOURT
BOSTON • NEW YORK 2009

ISSN 0067-6233
ISBN 978-0-618-79224-5
ISBN 978-0-618-79225-2 (pbk.)

Printed in the United States of America

DOC 10 9 8 7 6 5 4 3 2 1

Contents

Foreword

THIS YEAR I read a large number of wonderfully messy, wildly plotted, and/or boldly paced stories. Stories that took risks. I was thrilled to watch so many writers quiet their years of grammar lessons and writing workshop rules about showing and not telling, the evils of emoting, that sort of thing. Let that antsy imp inside have a word or two, and then more. It was inspiring to read stories that pushed voice to some limit, that shirked subtlety and nuance and stripped naked before the reader, even if not all of these stories lifted off in the end.

Of course, to sit before an empty page and dare to fill it with a new truth, to open a blank document and lower one's fingers to that rectangle of keys and attempt to create something of interest and import, are in themselves risks.

In the end, though, how much does a fiction writer actually risk? Does anyone still read fiction? At this time, all sorts of publishing seem destined to disappear, or at least exit from this challenging time enormously scathed. I have talked with editors who claim that literature is dead (editors are a notoriously pessimistic bunch) and agents whose fear is palpable. In search of a different perspective, I began rereading the early *Best American Short Stories,* particularly those published during the Great Depression. In the 1933 volume, series editor Edward O'Brien wrote, "In a time of doubt and uncertainty a nation is wise if it turns to its artists for enlightenment. The artists of a land are its most nearly conscious voice . . . New life always springs from old." Alice Sebold offers equal and eloquent hope in the following pages.

I read dozens of haunting stories this year about the war in Iraq and Hurricane Katrina and poverty, stories that powerfully refracted these difficult times. I was glad to read an unusual number of stories that used humor or structure in innovative ways. Winnowing the thousands that I read down to 120 was no easy task, and Alice Sebold faced a much tougher job in choosing just twenty. Warm thanks are due to her for her thoughtfulness in reading the stacks that I sent her. She read with an open mind and spirit, and I eagerly awaited her honest, insightful, and often hilarious reactions.

Each of these twenty stories is risky in its own way. Steve De Jarnatt locks a drug-addicted veteran in a New Orleans attic during Hurricane Katrina. Eleanor Henderson organizes a horribly mismatched playdate in a poor apartment complex and brings to life the parents' worst fears. Alex Rose juxtaposes one moment in an elderly woman's life with snippets about the history of medicine, the Han Dynasty, and World War I. So much conflict! Too depressing! Doesn't flow! But with stunning voice (De Jarnatt) and dead-on tone (Henderson) and perfect rhythm (Rose), these writers do no less than dramatize the collision of faith and fear, naiveté and cynicism. They demonstrate the human ability to endure crises and to regenerate afterward. There is nothing safe about these stories. In the hands of a talented writer, a gamble managed with just the right touch and emotional volume is exhilarating to behold. I have a strong radar for the literary equivalent of seared sea urchin crepes on a bed of Jell-O, but no rules apply when fiction is written convincingly and ecstatically and with finesse. I think of David Foster Wallace as having written this way, and his work will be missed.

John Updike will also be missed. He was a frequent contributor to this series, as well as a guest editor in 1984 and the editor of *The Best American Short Stories of the Century*. He was generous with his time and spirit, and I can think of few other people as self-reliant and gracious. The literary landscape has changed profoundly with him no longer here.

Thanks are also due to Nicole Angeloro, Ken Carpenter, Chris Castellani, Kate Flaherty, Andrea Schultz, Carla Gray, and Alia Habib.

The stories chosen for this anthology were originally published between January 2008 and January 2009. The qualifications for selection are (1) original publication in nationally distributed American or Canadian periodicals; (2) publication in English by writers who are American or Canadian, or who have made the United States their home; (3) original publication as short stories (excerpts of novels are not knowingly considered). A list of magazines consulted for this volume appears at the back of the book. Editors who wish their short fiction to be considered for next year's edition should send their publications or hard copies of online publications to Heidi Pitlor, c/o The Best American Short Stories, Houghton Mifflin Harcourt, 222 Berkeley Street, Boston, Massachusetts 02116.

HEIDI PITLOR

Introduction

A Necessary Crapshoot: Prizes and Awards in the Literary World

A FEW YEARS AGO I was nominated for an award. Awards are nice; I don't blame people for taking joy in receiving them, or for tearing up and/or becoming inarticulate if they are forced to give an acceptance speech. I now think that's preferable to being loaded to the gills on a generous friend's antianxiety meds.

The ceremony was long, and many awards were given out that night. The occasion was videotaped, as everything now seems to be. As each category was announced from the stage, the nominees' names were read out, and each of us was expected to stand at our place at various groaning tables, flanked by our spouses and friends and those in the publishing industry who I always think of as having drawn the short straw at the office that day. I had had two vodka martinis before the ceremony, and bottles of red and white wine surrounded each table's floral centerpiece. Although I was too nervous to eat, my thirst was endless. My husband recalls my having an unerring sense of when a camera was anywhere near, for in those moments I would heave a glass toward my mouth while he fruitlessly attempted to stay my hand.

Some time later, I won in my category.

I took to the stage gamely (or so I was told) and said something short and ambivalent that was later used as a positive endorsement of the proceedings. For the remainder of that evening I met other award winners and other nominees. We were posed singly or in groups for photographs in which I had my award in one hand and a cocktail in the other. I also seemed to be smoking. People congratulated me: other writers, publishing professionals, strangers who were readers and who had liked my book.

Apparently — and again I know this mostly from my husband — I had only one thing to say.

"You know this is bullshit, right?"

When a happy, better-adjusted award winner would inquire what I was referring to, I would bray while holding up my golden statue: "This. Award. Bullshit. Right?"

Why my fellow award winners and nominees have not kept in touch is beyond me.

I said what I said for many reasons, and not all of them have to do with my own insecurities or the toxic swim of booze and pills that greased the pathway of my thoughts from brain to tongue. Consider, for example, Groucho Marx. If he never wanted to be part of a club that would have him as a member, then my discomfort on awards night most likely has something to do with this same phenomenon.

But there's more. I have long distrusted anything that smacked of a prize, and I still distrust them. Of course, in the end, prizes, awards, scholarships, contests, elections, appointments, best ofs and worst ofs, most hideous sex scene, most overvalued stock, best American city, highest-ranking university, most valued player, best ass, best rack, best book, are subjective measures of one person's or a group's taste against that of another's. Enough of this can breed a culture, and culture, by definition, is inevitably corrupt.

Of course, this distrust is also personal and involves school. Doesn't everything?

When I was a freshman in high school, the state of Pennsylvania decided to institute a program for students deemed gifted. But my joy at lording this status over my more academically talented sister was short-lived. The gifted program chose to focus on one course per year, so that during my sophomore year — the first year of my eligibility — the focus was on math. To put it mildly, this was not my gift. I found myself placed among a small group of students who ever after would be known as "dumb gifteds." Along with six others thought equally hampered, I was segregated from the smart gifteds and put in a special classroom with a wardenlike geometry teacher whose stiff canvas skirts seemed prison issue.

How could you be gifted one day and a moron the next — simultaneously the best of and the worst of? That was our question. Only two of us studied. One of us took such an arcane combination of drugs that he ended up in a coma and woke with permanent brain damage. I got a D. In the regular classes, my sister was doing swimmingly.

Advance nearly twenty years. I am in graduate school. Though I have taught freshman composition as an adjunct for a decade in New York City, I am a teaching assistant now, and I am placed in what the school refers to as a pod. A pod is a group-teaching situation in which four teachers must agree on the grading of student papers, meet weekly for roundtables, share e-mails, and check in with each other on a daily basis. My problem with groupthink makes me bristle. I feel as if I've moved from New York to an ashram, and no one's told me. My fellow teachers are peppy, bright, bossy, and majoring in critical theory. I am frightened.

A Vietnamese student writes a personal essay about being beaten with a wooden spoon daily as a child. Compelling material. But the essay is written poorly and riddled with grammatical and spelling mistakes. I'm thinking C− but, soft at heart or so I think, I propose a C. The pod is horrified. The argument put forth is that in sharing such deeply personal material the student should be judged differently from the rest. In the face of forces greater and more adamant than I, I fold. The final pod-approved grade is a B+. I hand the paper back to my student, and I know we have done her no favors.

I was reminded of the pod one night when I listened to a writer recount his experience as a judge for the National Book Award. Forces both greater and more adamant than he — and with longer publishing histories and greater clout — made him fold and choose a book he did not believe in.

Up until now, I have avoided sitting on awards panels. Since 2000 I have avoided writing book reviews for the same reason many writers don't: writing a book, whether good or bad, is so difficult that standing in judgment is not something I'm comfortable with. I rarely blurb, though admittedly, when the book is terrific or from a small press or an unknown or overlooked author, I feel I must. I do feel a blurb is a moral contract a writer makes with the unknown reader, not something that should be done as a favor to a friend or to your publisher or because maybe his or her spouse writes a column somewhere or is powerful and can/could help you down the line.

In spite of these reservations, I take writing and competition very seriously. I believe that all writers should compete — even if I now know this to be a quixotic quest — on a level playing field.

Why, then, did I decide to take on the job of editing *The Best American Short Stories* of 2009?

I was honored to be asked.

And there you have it: the job is an award. It was also far away. I said yes a full two years before the stories would be passed on to me, having been whittled down from thousands to 120 by Heidi Pitlor, a woman who reads nothing but magazines and literary journals eight days a week. Then the day came when the first pile of stories arrived at the post office and I waited with my little slip for the oversized package. "Heavy," the postman who handed it to me said, and as I walked it home, clutched to my chest like the stack of books it resembled, I realized something. To be chosen for the *Best American Short Stories* annual volume is indeed an award of a kind, and even if the writers whose pages I had not yet seen would not be subjected to the public humiliations of ball gowns and tuxes and might take their poison in peace upon news of their inclusion or exclusion from the final volume, I would be the final arbiter of who did and who didn't make the cut.

I returned home, pet the dog, and threw up.

We are living, as I write this, in the worst economic conditions almost any of us can remember. In the world of publishing, good people have lost their jobs, and more job losses are on the horizon. Whole divisions of venerable publishing houses are falling away. Historic names are disappearing overnight, there one day and gone the next. The individuals who have survived so far are not quite sure why, and spend hours every day doing a job — editing quality fiction — that the powers that be are beginning to deem no longer necessary.

But I think highlighting good fiction is more important now than it ever has been. Because of this, I've also come to feel that now, more than ever, awards are a necessary crapshoot from which, on balance, all of us benefit.

Briefly, in the wake of 9/11 a poetry renaissance occurred, as — clueless about how to survive the hopelessness that immediately followed — many of us turned to poems written in the wake of the world wars for succor. Something in the way Siegfried Sassoon or W. H. Auden could bend the atrocities of the trenches or the invasion of Poland into lyric form and reflect ourselves back to ourselves gave us hope at that time. Often a reflection in the mirror, even if hideously accurate, stands as confirmation of existence, and this mere confirmation then serves as hope — we are still alive in dark times. Old poets, and some new, flared brightly for a time in instantly published anthologies or on ever more muscular blogs. Within weeks, however, we were told by our government to go out and buy new cars or bigger houses; everything, we were assured, would be all right as a result. So we put down the sustaining challenge of the poets and took up our machine-stamped plastic cards that entitled us to be "a member of the club" or "earn points toward a free windjammer."

Here we are encountering another sort of ground zero — this one economic — and my house is stacked with Xeroxed short stories whose paper clips fall to the floor after being decorously pulled at by the tiny teeth of cats. Journals of all different sizes and shapes lean against the wall of my office — anonymous additions to the winnowed pile Heidi Pitlor sends at regular intervals and from which I hope to pull an unknown author. I have gone in a few brief months from being overwhelmed with the burden of this responsibility and even, admittedly, from being a shade cynical about the process to being awed by possibilities and hope for the future.

Narrative, after all, is perhaps the most powerful antidote we have in the face of what at first may appear to be insurmountable odds. If this weren't true, the Incredible Hulk never would have become so popular with so many powerless children, the novels of Orhan Pamuk would not be publicly excoriated yet covertly embraced in his native land, and *The Catcher in the Rye* would not stand, as it still does today, as a timeless, ageless call into the wild abyss.

To say that the twenty stories I chose for *The Best American Short Stories 2009* will save your life, vanquish the collection agents pounding at your door, or return your child, spouse, or cousin from the war is obviously ridiculous. But more than mere solace is to be gained by reading good stories — short stories in particular. Stories provide an endless access into another world, brought forth by an infinite number of gifted minds. A story about grief can comfort; a story about arrogance can shock and yet confirm; a story populated largely by landscape, whether lush or industrial, can expand the realm that we as individuals inhabit.

I read 200-plus short stories this year. The publisher of *The Best American Short Stories* allows for only twenty to be published under that name. Eleven stories were total *yes* moments for me, when I wrote "It's in!" immediately after finishing the last page. Then I had thirty vying for nine spots, and fifteen vying for six, and finally three vying for one. Was the judging process scientific? Not in the least. Does this volume include stories that every writer — being honest — would give his or her eyeteeth to have written? You bet. Are the merits of some stories arguable? Certainly. But I promise you this: every story in the final selection deserves to be read. Deserves to be published. Deserves, in the case of some newer or lesser-known authors, to help lift these authors out of the slush pile when they submit again, and to help these authors — and here is what a prize or a best of can do — find a larger audience in the world.

A hospice worker I know is fond of saying, "A nurse can't be an island," meaning that helping others is impossible if you can't reach them. The same, to me, seems true of narrative. In a busy world of things competing for attention, a lot of them are easier to turn to than a literary journal or even the rare glossy magazine that still prints short stories. Awards and prizes for this form seem important, and editing a best-of collection becomes an imperative. Reading for it, an honor.

As a late-to-publishing person, I have done a 180-degree turn in terms of my experience of being in a bookstore and seeing golden and silver badges on books. I see starbursts and crests, hear of readers' circles and celebrity endorsements, find blurbs on the front covers of hardbacks. If our economy had stayed robust, no doubt someone would have mass-produced Margaret Atwood's remote-control signature arm into a fist that grabbed you by the lapels, shoved a book into your hand, and hauled you to the checkout. All of these things are done in the pursuit of a perfect storm of readers.

A good nurse can't be an island.

Nor can a good story or a best-of collection of stories. They must reach, they must confirm, they must reflect us in both delight and sorrow. Whether this is done through humor or history, from an imagined town or via a series of letters written by an inhabitant of an internment camp, does not matter. Great poetry will always be available to us, and so will good fiction, but what both of them need now, and what an award or a best of might bring them, is more readers.

I will now go pet the dog, feed the cats, and read that National Book Award winner who, even with his golden seal for all to see, I found remaindered at my local bookstore. Here's the catch. His work may survive because of that seal; I can no longer judge this to be a bad thing.

ALICE SEBOLD

The Best
AMERICAN SHORT STORIES 2009

DANIEL ALARCÓN

The Idiot President

FROM *The New Yorker*

WHEN I WAS FIRST out of the conservatory, I did a two-month stint with a theater group called Diciembre. It was an established company that had formed during the anxious years of the war, when it was known for its brazen trips into the conflict zone, bringing theater to the people, and, in the city, for staging all-night marathon shows — pop reworkings of García Lorca, stentorian readings of Brazilian soap-opera scripts, always with a political edge, sometimes subtle, often not at all, anything to keep people awake and laughing through what would otherwise have been the dark, lonely hours of curfew. These shows were legendary among the theater students of my generation, and many of my classmates claimed to have been present, as children, at one or another of these performances. They said that their parents had taken them, that they had witnessed an unholy union of recital and insurrection, of sex and barbarism, and that they remained, however many years later, unsettled and even inspired by the memory. They were all liars. We were, in fact, studying to be liars. It's been nine years since I graduated, and I imagine that these days students at the conservatory talk about other things. They are too young to remember how ordinary fear was during the war. Perhaps they find it difficult to imagine a time when theater was improvised in response to terrifying headlines, a time when delivering a line of dialogue with a chilling sense of dread did not even require acting. But then, such are the narcotic effects of peace, and certainly no one wants to go backward.

More than a decade after the war, Diciembre still functioned as a loose grouping of actors and actresses who occasionally put on a show, often in a private home, to which the audience came by invitation only. Paradoxically, now that travel outside the city was relatively safe, they hardly ever went to the interior, so when a new tour was announced I auditioned eagerly. It was a rare opportunity, and to my surprise, I got the part. Only three of us went — me, a curly-haired actor named Henry, and a short, dark-skinned man who introduced himself as Patalarga and never bothered to give me his real name. They were related, sort of — Henry had, at some point in the distant past, married and then divorced Patalarga's second cousin, a woman named Tania, to whom they alluded with the sort of hushed respect that tenant farmers might use when speaking of the weather. The two men had been friends for a long time, as long as I'd been alive, and I was pleased to be accepted into their company. I figured it would be a chance to learn from veterans.

Henry wrote most of the plays, and for that tour we were doing a subtle piece of invective he called *The Idiot President.* Though its politics were easy to trace, it was very funny, involving a delicate interaction between an arrogant, self-involved head of state and his servant. Each day the president's servant was replaced, the idea being that eventually every citizen of the country would have the honor of attending to the needs of the leader. These included helping him dress, combing his hair, reading his mail, etc. The president was fastidious and required that everything follow a rather idiosyncratic protocol, so the better part of each day was spent teaching the new servant how things should be done. Hilarity ensued. I played the idiot president's idiot son, Alejo, a role perfectly suited to my youthful skills, and over the course of our rehearsals I came to love this buffoonish adolescent in a way that I hadn't expected. He was a boastful lout and a petty thief, who was a great source of pride to his father, despite his many shortcomings. The climactic scene involved a heart-to-heart between the servant of the day and my character, after the president has gone to sleep, in which Alejo lets his guard down and admits that he has often thought of killing his father but is too frightened to go through with it. The servant is intrigued — after all, he lives in a ruined country, subject to the president's disastrous whims, and furthermore has spent the entire day being humiliated by him. The servant probes Alejo's doubts, and he opens up, voicing his concerns about freedom, about the rule of law, about the suffering of the people, until the servant finally allows that, yes, perhaps killing the president wouldn't be such a bad idea. For the sake of the country, you understand. Alejo pretends to mull it over and then kills the startled servant himself, as punishment for treason. He picks the corpse clean, pocketing the man's wallet, his watch, and his rings, and the play ends with him shouting toward the room where the president is sleeping, "Another one, Father! We'll need another one tomorrow!"

Patalarga, Henry, and I left the capital in early March, the day after I turned twenty-one. It was summer on the coast, hot and humid, and we rode a bus up into the rainy mountains to the region where Patalarga was born, a part of the country I'd never seen before. Even at the time I felt certain that I would never see it again. Everything about my life then — every decision I made or failed to make — was predicated on the idea that I'd be leaving the country soon. I expected to join my brother in California before the year was up: my visa was being processed, and it was only a matter of time. This was a very pleasant way to live, actually. It gave me a kind of private strength that allowed me to withstand certain indignities, confident that everything was temporary. We performed in small towns and villages, up and down a wide and gloomy valley, subject to heavy, freezing downpours that were like nothing I'd ever experienced. The skies swirled with blue-black clouds, and when it wasn't raining the winds blew straight through you. We were greeted warmly in each town, with a certain ceremony and solicitousness that I found charming, and every night the audience gave us a standing ovation that made all our efforts seem worthwhile. Sometimes the villages were just a handful of houses dotting endless yellowish gray fields. Our audience might be a dozen people altogether, a few farmers with ruddy faces, their long-suffering wives and undernourished children, who'd approach Henry after the play, never looking directly at him, and say respectfully, "Thank you, Mr. President."

The cold nearly destroyed me. In two weeks I lost three kilos, and one night, after a particularly energetic performance, I nearly fainted. When I recovered, we were invited to a party at a one-room adobe house on the outskirts of town. Henry and Patalarga were both on edge, drinking more than usual, because this was the town where Tania lived; apparently she'd been at the show and might reappear at any moment. I was too ill to worry about that: taking a breath was like swallowing sharp knives, and my head felt as if it might separate from my neck and just float away into the threatening Andean sky. But everyone was exceedingly kind, paying special attention to feeding me and getting me drunk. The liquor helped, and it felt nice to be doted upon. When I started turning blue, the owner of the home, a squat gray-haired man named Cayetano, asked if I wanted a jacket. I nodded enthusiastically, and he rose and walked to the refrigerator, standing before its open door as if contemplating a snack. I thought, He's making fun of me, and I heard Henry and Patalarga snickering. But then Cayetano opened the vegetable drawer and took out a pair of wool socks. He tossed them to me, and when he opened the door a little farther I saw that the refrigerator was, in fact, being used as a wardrobe. There were mittens in the butter tray, sweaters and jackets hanging from a wooden bar nailed to the inside walls. Only then did I notice the few perishables sitting on the counter. In this cold, of course, they were in no danger of spoiling.

The gathered men and women told sad stories about the war and laughed at their own suffering in ways that I found incomprehensible. Sometimes they would speak in Quechua, and then the laughter became much more intense, and also much sadder — or at least that's how it seemed to me. When Tania arrived, everyone stood. She had long black hair, which she wore in a single braid, and an orange-and-yellow shawl draped over her shoulders. Older than me but a little younger than my colleagues, Tania was petite, and yet somehow she gave the impression of great strength. She circled the room, shaking hands with everyone — except Henry, who instead received a floating kiss in the air just beside his right ear.

"Are you still acting," she asked when she got to me, "or are you actually that sick?"

I didn't know what to say, so when someone shouted, "He's drunk!" I was relieved. The room roared, and then everyone sat.

The drinking began in earnest now, and soon a guitar appeared from a corner of the room. It was passed from person to person, making a few laps around the circle before finally Tania kept it. Everyone cheered. She strummed a few chords, then cleared her throat, welcoming the visitors, thanking us all for listening. She sang in Quechua, picking out a complex accompaniment, her agile fingers unrestrained by the cold. I turned to Henry and asked him in a low voice what the song was about.

"About love," he whispered, without taking his eyes off her.

As the night wore on, I found myself appreciating Tania's beauty with greater and greater clarity. Henry and Patalarga watched me watching her, alternately glaring and smiling, in a sequence that was impossible to interpret. Much later, when I was finally succumbing to the cold and the liquor, Tania offered to lead me back to the hostel where I was staying. This was noted with feigned alarm, but she ignored it all. The town was small, there was no possibility of getting lost, and we trudged drunkenly through its streets, both of us wrapped in Cayetano's blanket. "You sing beautifully," I said. "What was it about?"

"Just old songs."

"Henry said you were singing about love."

She had a lovely laugh: clear and unpretentious, like moonlight. "He doesn't speak Quechua," Tania said. "Must have been a lucky guess."

We paused at the door of the hostel. I moved to kiss her, but she just patted me on the head as if I were a little boy. "Drink lots of water," she said, "and get as much rest as you can." And then she walked back to the party.

Inside the hostel, the owner gave me a large rubber bladder swollen with boiling water, and as I prepared for bed I held it in my hands the way one might hold a beating human heart — my own heart, perhaps. I tried to go over my day — what had happened, or what, to my chagrin, had not. But the cold made coherent thought impossible, so I lay down with the bladder pressed against my belly, curling myself around it like a snail. I wondered whether I should have stayed in the city and what my friends were doing at that exact moment. They'd been jealous of me and my tour with Diciembre, and I struggled to remember that. Patalarga and Henry had done this circuit before, were constantly running into old friends. They seemed unfazed by the conditions that were slowly wearing me down. They had lived in the city for decades but did not consider it home.

And it was like this for weeks. In the mornings, weather permitting, we rode to the next town on a rickety bus, or on the bed of a truck piled with potatoes. I'd learned to chew coca leaves by then, had come to enjoy the numbness as it spread over my face, down my neck, and into my chest. The roads were barely wide enough for a horse cart, and often I looked over the face of a crumbling mountain, forcing myself to think of something other than death. Patalarga and Henry recovered from the previous evening with their eyes closed, suspended in deep and peaceful dreams. They were enjoying themselves; me, I was trying to stay alive.

Toward the end of the tour, we arrived at a town called San Germán, which was the remote outpost of an American mining company. The town consisted of a couple of hundred houses that seemed to have been airlifted to the wind-battered top of a desolate mountain, which was surrounded on three sides by even higher, more foreboding peaks. I think it was a silver mine, but it could have been copper or bauxite or something else, and in a sense it doesn't matter: all mining towns are the same. They are pitiless and isolated, often situated in places that might be beautiful were they not so extreme, and defined by a kind of human deprivation particular to the industry. In San Germán, thick clouds hung just above us, and I could smell metal in the air. I had never felt so far away from the world. We were more than four thousand meters above sea level, and the altitude rendered me useless. I spent the first day in the hostel, gripping the sides of the bed as if I were riding a roller coaster. San Germán was a small place, and there was very little to see, but Patalarga and Henry sat by my bedside, regaling me with the invented wonders of the town.

"You must get up," Patalarga said. "You have to see this place."

"There's a replica of the pyramids," Henry told me, "and it shines golden in the sunlight."

I opened my eyes and saw his breath gathering in a cloud.

"A miniature Arc de Triomphe," Patalarga said.

"Cafés, tree-lined boulevards, and the nightlife — you won't believe it! Discos like in Batista's Havana, like Beirut before the war."

I paid them no attention. The room — indeed, my brain — filled with the concussive sound of their voices. I begged to be left alone, and then they disappeared. I closed my eyes again, and for a few hours I didn't move. I just listened desperately to the sound of my own breathing.

When my colleagues returned, they were sullen and angry. I could smell the mud that clung to their boots.

"You tell him."

"No, you tell him."

From my sickbed I could hear them pacing. "Someone fucking tell me," I said. I had intended to shout, but I was weak, and it came out as the raspy plea of a heart patient. I kept my eyes closed. Someone sat on my bed. It was Henry. Bad news. Our first performance was scheduled for the next night, but there was a glitch. There was no electricity, no light. This was not a temporary condition, as we had been told when we checked into the hostel. The only power still running in town went to the homes of the American engineers, on the other side of the mine. "You should see how they live," Henry said, and described how, behind a high fence, they had created a facsimile of American life. Comfortable suburban homes, neatly paved streets, a baseball diamond.

I sat shivering beneath a half-dozen blankets. It sounded nice.

"Don't you have a brother in the U.S.?" Patalarga asked.

"Sure."

"Does he play baseball?"

"How should I know?"

I could barely get the words out. I knew nothing about baseball. In fact, I knew virtually nothing about my brother. He'd left home when he turned eighteen, several years before, and I thought of him only in terms of the visa he was supposed to get for me. It was too cold to waste energy scavenging through childhood memories.

Henry was upset. He spoke quickly, and I could hear the bitterness in his voice. We'd been promised a place to perform for the workers. The workers, the workers — these gallant, dignified men who were our entire reason for existing. We were supposed to do two shows, one for each shift. Our afternoon performance would be unaffected, but the miners on the day shift wouldn't be able to come. If we did a show at night, it would be in the dark — or only for the engineers. The fucking engineers. Henry was getting upset now, as he described men who spent their days nursing daiquiris, pausing only to take turns whipping the noble miners.

It sounded positively feudal. "Are they really that bad?" I asked.

"Never mind him," Patalarga said. "His father was an engineer."

"Fuck you," Henry said, scowling.

"Henry here was a star on the company baseball team."

"Really?"

"Till he started stealing dynamite to give to the rebels."

"You're lying."

Neither would answer me.

A moment later Henry was complaining again; this time he tapped his finger on my forehead as he spoke. It felt like a mallet striking the skin of a bass drum, a strange way of showing affection, and I kept my eyes closed through the operation.

"We've come to this town for nothing. They've made fools of us, and Nelson here is going to die for no reason at all."

They were talking to each other now.

"We've sacrificed a young life — the best this country has to offer! — and we'll have nothing to show for it. Oh, the tragedy of it all! How he has suffered for his art! But what will we tell his mother?"

"You're both very funny," I said. "Seriously."

That night they dragged me out into the dark streets of San Germán, all but carrying me. My head and body ached, and the earth beneath me seemed unsteady. I walked with one arm slung over Patalarga's shoulder, as Henry pointed out the dim yellow lights on the far slope of the hill: those were the engineers' homes. Behind them a treacherous mountain peak disappeared into the clouds. I looked at that miserable little settlement and found it hard to feel much antipathy toward the Americans. Nature could have crushed them, and all of us, in an instant.

"Do you see them?" Henry asked. "Can you believe it?"

"No," I said. "I can't believe it."

I would rather have been poor anywhere else in the world than rich here.

We pushed on through the muddy streets. For the play Henry wore long white gloves, but because of the bitter cold he had taken to wearing them even between performances. They were thin, sateen, probably not very warm, but they looked delicious. Now I noticed Patalarga eyeing them jealously.

"Give me those," he said finally, pointing at the gloves.

Henry held his hands up, wiggling his white, glowing fingers. "These?"

"Those."

"I'm the president," Henry said. "I wear the gloves."

Patalarga considered this for a moment. He turned to me. "I found him in an alley behind the cathedral, huffing glue and talking about how mean his daddy was."

I didn't say anything, nor did I let go of Patalarga. Without him, I would've fallen.

Henry didn't appear to be listening.

"All that change we wanted," Patalarga said. "And still the dark-skinned one plays the servant. And still the dark-skinned one dies in the end. Isn't that something?"

Henry shrugged. "It's because you're so good at it," he said.

We made it to San Germán's only restaurant, and by the light of a kerosene lamp ate food warmed by a kerosene stove, so that everything smelled and tasted of fuel. We were in a sour, helpless mood. Henry and Patalarga weren't talking, and it took all my strength just to keep from slipping off my chair and onto the cold cement floor. Still, after a meal and some tea, I had recovered a bit. We were nearly finished when some old miners walked in, carrying their helmets. Even in the dark, Patalarga recognized them from his days as an organizer. They joined our table and spoke in hushed tones about the conditions underground, which had improved somewhat since Henry and Patalarga's last visit. Better ventilation, better safety. Ten-hour shifts, down from fourteen.

"But no electricity."

The miners shrugged. They had hard, weathered faces. "It's coming, and anyway, the mine is well lit," one of them said. His name was Ventosilla. It was written on his helmet, which he placed on the table. He flicked a switch and the headlamp came on, casting a vivid patch of light on the wall of the restaurant. Ventosilla turned it off and on a few times, and we all stopped to admire it.

He tapped the headlamp with his fingernail. "Halogen."

"And you all have those?" Patalarga asked.

The miner nodded.

My colleagues grinned.

The next night we performed *The Idiot President* in a large tent made of blankets, by the combined lamplight of fifty miners. There were children and wives in attendance as well, and even a few American engineers who deigned to join the fun. I was feeling better, though not yet myself, whatever that means. I hadn't felt like myself since we'd left the city, since the bus had begun climbing into the clouds, but the sight of this makeshift theater, abuzz with expectation, the halogen lights flitting every which way, made me hopeful. Backstage was actually just outside the tent, where the three of us stood, freezing and jittery, unusually excited, peeking in occasionally to see the crowd as it gathered.

When the tent was full, we slipped inside, to the relative warmth of the stage. The view was breathtaking: the crowd sitting on a rickety set of bleachers, a bright field of stars gleaming in the heavens. I turned to Henry and Patalarga, and saw that they were lost in it too. This was the sky we had barely seen, the sky that had been hidden behind thick black rain clouds for the previous six weeks. We were introduced by the local union rep, and this night, like every night, the crowd cheered when they heard the name Diciembre, the lights bobbing up and down as the miners nodded with satisfaction.

I ceded the stage to my colleagues and sat just off to the side. They began. With hunched shoulders and a face racked with worry, Henry imbued his idiot president with a certain deranged gravitas, like Nixon in his last days, or Allende contemplating the tanks surrounding La Moneda. He paced the stage barking nonsensical instructions at his flummoxed servant — and no one has ever owned "flummoxed" as expertly as Patalarga did that night. I knew the whole play by heart, so mostly I concentrated on the miners' headlamps, which together formed a limpid pool of white onstage, shifting ever so slightly as the dialogue ping-ponged from one speaker to the other. When I stood, just before my cue to come on, the lights shifted stage right, so much so that Patalarga, standing opposite me, disappeared briefly in the sudden darkness.

Even in the dim light, I could see him smiling.

Toward the end of the play, we hit a rough patch. We could tell instantly. Henry delivered a line that usually got a laugh, but now it fell flat. We were losing the audience — the lights moved up and down or side to side, wandering, and in an instant we were performing at dusk, when just a moment prior it had been morning. Never before or since has it been so easy for me to read a crowd, to get feedback so transparent and immediate. The failing light energized us, and we rallied. Minutes later, the tent was again quaking with laughter, the stage as bright as a landing strip, and I can note, with not a small amount of pride, that my last lines, the ones I shouted to my sleeping father, the president, were delivered on a fully lit stage, with the complete attention and collaboration of the miners of San Germán and their halogen headlamps. There was no curtain to close, no stage lights to dim, and I stood there for a moment after the play had ended, bathing in the glow, enjoying myself.

Why not?

A few weeks later, I was home again, and for years afterward, when one or another of the productions I was a part of failed, I thought of that night. I was invited on another tour with Diciembre, but it was more out of politeness than anything else. My middle-class life had rendered me unable to handle the rigors of the road. I declined. I'll be leaving soon anyway, I thought, but I never did. Occasionally I performed with Henry and Patalarga locally, and we remained friendly. Whenever I ran into one of them, at a show, at a bar, on the street, we always embraced, shared a laugh, and spoke fondly of that night in San Germán. I knew that they remembered the performance as well as I did, though they had forgotten other details — my name, for instance. They called me Alejo, without shame or apology. I didn't mind. I liked them both. I had learned from them, and could learn from them still. Of course, invoking San Germán was an invitation to philosophize, but that was precisely the point. I would listen, just as I had on that trip, and watch Patalarga's or Henry's chest swell with pride. You make do. You manage. You take what the audience gives you and return it to them, only better, burnished by love and commitment. They give you light, and you give them truth. Etc. I liked hearing Henry and Patalarga talk, because no one my age ever spoke that way. Not about theater, not about politics. Not even about love. It made us uncomfortable.

A few years passed, and one day I found myself hopelessly out of work. I'd made too many enemies, taken everything too lightly. My visa had never come, and I could no longer pretend I'd be young forever. My brother called every now and then, but only at my parents' house, and sometimes months would go by without our exchanging a word. I began auditioning for the soap operas I'd sworn

I'd never do again: jilted lovers, home-wrecking womanizers. But I didn't get any of these parts. I was going broke. I thought about giving up my rented room and moving home, but the idea was too humiliating. My father, for his part, was relentlessly optimistic. "Your brother will send the visa. You'll go to America. You'll go to California. You'll be in the movies. Write to your brother, remind him," he said, but I couldn't bring myself to do it. I don't think even my father believed it anymore. Still, he kept me apprised of the weather where my brother was, as if I needed to know what clothes to pack. "There are forest fires all over California," he said to me one day. "Hundreds of them."

I just stared at him. That night I imagined this place I'd never been, its skies blurred with red-brown smoke, and its sun — which was not our sun — setting against the ashy backdrop of a regional catastrophe. I considered the possibility that what my father wanted was simply to have me out of his way. While I was worried about failing him, perhaps he was simply hoping that I would become someone else's problem.

The following week I found myself reading the script for a small, recurring role on a local soap opera. It was a six-episode run — not bad — after which my character was to be killed, off-camera. He was a police informer, appropriately troubled by the complicated ethics of betraying his friends, a man who lived in the full expectation that these transgressions would cost him his life. The character's name was, to my great satisfaction, Alejo, and suddenly I felt more confident than I had in months. Though this character and the Alejo I had played with Diciembre were two entirely different people, reading the script felt like running into an old friend. How this country has changed, I thought: the son of the president is now an ordinary snitch, a man doomed to look over his shoulder for six one-hour episodes and then die invisibly, his passing just a footnote to a larger drama that has little to do with him.

I was so excited that I told my parents about the audition. I told my friends. Alejo, I thought, we meet again. I even thought of tracking down Henry and Patalarga, though I hadn't seen them in a year or more, just so we could all have a laugh about it. By then Diciembre was on semi-permanent hiatus, and the country had become frankly unrecognizable. It was possible to walk the now bustling streets of my city and forget why I'd ever wanted to leave. Global metal prices were at record highs, and the newspapers were announcing 7 percent growth. All this prosperity was dispiriting; it was the one thing I'd never expected. I'd never been back to those towns I had visited with Diciembre, though some of my peers had — on vacation, during the dry season, with their spouses and overweight kids, to see a bit of the country as it once was. At the first sign of discontent, the government ran television ads showing images of provincial roadblocks, angry campesinos tossing stones at police, the screen stained an ominous and familiar shade of red. The stern voice-over warned the rural poor to be patriotic and not ruin it for the rest of us.

Henry and I met on a winter afternoon at a café in Asylum Downs. It was the day before my audition. He had no phone, no e-mail, and I'd got a message to him through a mutual friend who lived in his neighborhood. He seemed genuinely pleased to see me, and gave me a big hug, clapping my back heartily. We sat at an inside table, protected from the damp. It was great to see him — he hadn't changed at all — but where was Patalarga?

Henry rubbed his eyes and pushed his heavy curls down with his palms. "Our friend," he said in a helpless voice, "is no longer with us."

I was stunned. I sank into my chair. "When?" I managed to ask.

He looked down into his coffee cup. "Nine months ago, ten."

"Jesus."

"I know," Henry said, but then he was laughing. "The jerk moved to Barcelona. Imagine!"

"You asshole," I muttered.

"It's just you and me, Alejito," Henry said. "Father and son." He held out his hand. "Laugh!" he ordered. "You were always such a serious boy."

This was a line from *The Idiot President.* I took his hand and gave him a weak smile. The shock was draining away — Patalarga was alive, after all, and I should be happy. We sipped our coffee.

In any case, there was other news. Henry had a daughter now, and she had changed his life. He saw her two or three times a week, and dedicated everything he wrote to his little girl.

"So you're writing a lot?" I asked.

Henry shrugged. "Some."

I told him about Alejo the snitch. I even took out the script and talked him through the first episode, where Alejo is caught stealing wiring from a construction site and avoids jail time by offering information on a local street gang. The dialogue was good, nice hard-boiled stuff, and I could scarcely contain my enthusiasm. Henry listened carefully, nodding all the while.

"It's glorious," he said. "Written just for you."

"I know," I said. "I really feel like it is."

After a while Henry said that he had a question, but he didn't want to offend me. He made me promise not to take it the wrong way. "Sure," I said.

He tapped his fingers on the wooden table. "Weren't you supposed to go somewhere?" he said.

"What do you mean?"

"Well, it was all you ever talked about out there." He paused. "Every day, constantly. We figured it was the altitude. We could hardly stand it, Patalarga and I."

"Really?"

Henry nodded.

In my recollection of our two months in the mountains, I had barely ever spoken of leaving. I'd carried the notion with me, of course, but had held this private reassurance very close, like a charm or a lucky coin. Knowing that it would all pass was what had got me through.

"We learned to tune it out," Henry said, "because we liked you. We really did. Still do." He reached across the table and pinched my cheek affectionately. "Son," he added. "So why didn't you leave?"

Outside, a phalanx of pigeons had landed in the avenue's concrete median, swirling like a dust storm around an overturned trash can. I stared at them for a while, admiring their hunger.

"Everything got so good around here," I said.

Henry nodded. "Of course," he said. "That's just what I was thinking."

We said goodbye outside the café, on the busy avenue. Henry wished me good luck, and I promised to let him know how it turned out.

I nailed the audition, and waited optimistically for a callback. I measured the passing of time by the progress of the fires in the distant north. My old man gave me daily updates, and I pretended to listen. Five hundred, a thousand, two thousand fires. After a month they had burned out, and I was still waiting.

SARAH SHUN-LIEN BYNUM

Yurt

FROM *The New Yorker*

A YEAR AGO Ms. Duffy, the fifth-grade English and history teacher, had come very close to losing it, what with her homeroom being right next to the construction site for the new computer lab, and her attempts to excise the Aztecs from the curriculum being thwarted, and her ill-advised affair with Mr. Polidori coming to an end. She had come *very* close — or at least that was the general opinion among both the middle- and upper-school faculty, and who was Ms. Hempel to disagree? But now, upon her return, Ms. Duffy looked unrecognizably happy. It was the first week of May, and she was holding court in the teachers' lounge, her hair nearly down to her waist and her big belly protruding over her lap. Above the belly, Ms. Duffy laughed and swayed and gestured freely with her hands, as if to say, "What — this old thing?"

Ms. Hempel couldn't take her eyes off it. It looked as tough as a gourd.

"Yemen is magical," Ms. Duffy was telling the handful of teachers who happened to have fourth period free. "Just unbelievable. The pictures don't capture it at all."

A stack of dun-colored photographs was circulating around the room. After her difficult year, Ms. Duffy had sublet her apartment and struck out for the ancient world. There had been long and poetic e-mails, reasonably free of gloating — they were full of figs, marketplaces, bare feet against cool tiles, shuttered naps at noon. In between classes, Ms. Hempel had stood in front of the faculty bulletin board and read about Ms. Duffy's naps, trying to detect in these messages a note of melancholy, of homesickness. "Miss you all!!" Ms. Duffy would write in closing, but the absence of a subject, as well as the excessive punctuation, made the sentiment seem less than heartfelt. And then the e-mails had abruptly stopped.

Ms. Hempel studied the photograph that had been passed to her: a blazingly bright and empty street with the tiny figure of Ms. Duffy standing at its center. Who had taken the picture — a Yemenese friend? A Yemenan? It seemed important to know a little more about the person who'd stood in the shade of those massive, intricate buildings and pointed the camera. Perhaps this was the first of many foreign transactions that had resulted, so spectacularly, in Ms. Duffy's new belly.

Ms. Hempel waved the photograph in the air. "Anna, where was this one taken?"

But Ms. Duffy was distracted as more of her former colleagues filtered in to embrace her. "You astound me!" Mrs. Willoughby said, pressing her clasped hands to her lips, a gesture she normally bestowed upon seniors who were making their final appearance in the spring choral concert. Ms. Duffy looked triumphant: her face shone; gone was the faint grimace that had once been her habitual expression. This wasn't like the first week of school, when the teachers turned up in shorts and sundresses and still had their summer tans — Ms. Hempel remembered the shock of seeing Mr. Polidori's brown, hairy calves for the first time. The change in Ms. Duffy seemed permanent, irreversible.

"Have you seen your kids?" Ms. Cruz, the assistant librarian, asked. "They'll go crazy."

"They will freak!" Ms. Mulcahy said. "Suzanne, where's the sixth grade now? Are they at lunch?"

"They're in gym," Ms. Sprague said. "That's all I've heard this year: 'Ms. Duffy, Ms. Duffy.' They can't write their own names without mentioning Ms. Duffy."

"I missed them," Ms. Duffy said, vaguely.

"You won't believe how big they are. Huge. Amy Weyland is wearing a bra now."

From his cubicle, Mr. Meacham moaned, "Must we?"

And Mrs. Willoughby, peering into her coffee, said, "That girl's going to have a great little figure."

"Amy Weyland?" Ms. Duffy echoed.

"Yes! Can you believe it?" Ms. Olin, teacher of sixth-grade French, nearly shouted. She appeared slightly feverish; in fact, everyone did, everyone seemed eager and a little overheated. There was so much to tell: Jonathan Hamish had got suspended; Travis Bent had gone on medication; Mr. Peele had agreed to turn on the air-conditioning early. And, oh — the computer lab was finally done! Ms. Duffy needed to be apprised, and ushered back into the world they all had in common. The merry, frantic din of school rose up around them, louder and louder, as Yemen, fascinating and dusty, drifted farther away.

Ms. Hempel placed the photograph back on its pile. She would have a chance to find out more, eventually; she and Ms. Duffy were friends, school friends, in the sense that they were both part of the group of younger teachers who liked to gather at a dark Irish bar as soon as the bell rang on Friday afternoons. Ms. Hempel watched as Ms. Duffy was escorted out of the faculty lounge, in search of her former fifth graders.

"Look who's here!" Ms. Olin cried, leading the way.

The whole display was affecting but naive. Did they all think that Ms. Duffy was back? That once more there would be field trips to Chinatown for soup dumplings, and scavenger hunts in the botanic gardens, and sing-alongs to the Meat Puppets and other college radio stars of the eighties? That the Temple of Dendur would once more be erected in all its cardboard and tempera glory, and the final bittersweet pages of *Tuck Everlasting* read aloud in Ms. Duffy's husky, choked-up voice?

Ms. Hempel knew better. She'd known as soon as she'd seen her: Anna Duffy wasn't ever coming back, not even after her big hard belly had resolved itself into a baby. Most likely, necessity had prompted this visit; she probably needed to empty her locker, or roll over her retirement plan. Didn't the others see? She was no longer one of them; at some point during her year off, she had turned away. Slipped into her civilian clothes and disappeared. And if she was back now, it was only to say goodbye.

Mooney's, the Irish bar, was just a few blocks away from the school. Beautiful Ms. Cruz, who really did lead the fabled double life of the librarian, had discovered it one night while careering through town with a free-jazz drummer nearly twice her age. It had been their last stop. What must Ms. Cruz have thought when they finally left the place, an hour before dawn, and she realized, looking up and down the avenue for a taxi, that she was just around the corner from her desk, her rubber stamps, her little stack of overdue notices? Maybe she thought, How perfect. To feel one's real life rub up so closely, so carelessly, against one's school life — there was no greater enchantment. Or so Ms. Hempel supposed, never having put enough distance between the two to experience it herself. She liked to hear Ms. Cruz talk, in her calm and self-effacing way, about all the old musicians she had fallen for, the hard-drinking drummer included. Ms. Cruz had taken him home with her that night, and the next Friday she had brought the teachers to Mooney's.

The narrow space was illuminated by strings of colored Christmas lights and a glowing clock. A jukebox stood in the back, in between the cavelike entrances to two unisex bathrooms. Battered black tables, high unsteady stools, linoleum floor. The floor was wonderful to dance on. It made Ms. Hempel feel graceful and coordinated, even before she started drinking. All the teachers loved to dance on Friday afternoons. The sticky blinds on Mooney's windows were always pulled shut, so it was easy to forget that it was only four o'clock and the sun was still shining outside. They danced as if it were the middle of the night. They did the hustle. They did the electric slide. They did silly moves they remembered from high school, and they looked good doing them. When Mr. Radovich tried to dance as if he were black, no one minded. They were too happy feeding quarters into the jukebox, shimmying back to the bar. As she bumped hips with Ms. Cruz and sashayed toward the bathrooms, Ms. Hempel realized that an awful mistake had been made: she had actually been meant to spend her whole life dancing, not teaching English to the seventh grade.

For someone who had an abundance of freckles and almost always wore clogs, Ms. Duffy could dance astonishingly well. She tossed back her hair and half closed her eyes and lifted her chin ever so slightly, as if a handsome invisible person were tilting her face up to kiss her. And then she stepped from side to side, with a barely discernible motion in her hips, her spine long and straight, her shoulders faintly twitching. It was the simplest dance in the world, and also the most beguiling, somehow. Other dancers drew close to her, unconsciously. She could often be found in the middle of a spontaneous dance sandwich. One afternoon Mr. Polidori had sprung from his barstool, cracked his knuckles, and slid across the linoleum floor on his knees, arriving breathlessly at her neatly shuffling feet.

Ms. Hempel liked to think that this was the moment that their romance had begun. Of course, she could be wrong; Mr. Polidori performed sudden extravagant gestures all the time — kissing your hand in gratitude, wrapping his fingers around your neck and gently throttling you, draping his arm across your shoulders with comradely affection — gestures that thrilled Ms. Hempel whenever she happened, through luck and proximity, to be the recipient of them. Her skin on fire, she felt how ridiculous it was to be thrilled: you could not, as a rule, take Mr. Polidori seriously. And that afternoon on the dance floor, Ms. Duffy did not appear to do so. When he came gliding toward her, his arms outspread, she merely offered him her hand and hoisted him up, never once losing the beat of her winsome little dance. But what if, as their hands joined, a secret message had been exchanged? A message that had taken them both by surprise? Ms. Hempel sometimes thought of this moment now, as she tried to piece together a story of what had happened. How interesting it would have been to witness the very inception of an affair! She could have hoarded up the image — him on his knees, her swaying above him — to share with Amit when he came home. Often, walking dreamily home from the bar, the afternoon light slanting across the pavement, Ms. Hempel found herself full of marvelous observations and stories to relate to him. But then she went inside and it got dark; she turned up the television and felt a headache coming on, and by the time Amit returned from the lab she couldn't think of anything to say, even when he wrinkled his nose and asked mildly, "How come you smell like cigarettes?"

Ms. Hempel wondered about the father of Ms. Duffy's baby. A sloe-eyed camel driver, singing under his breath? A poet studying English at the university, or maybe a young doctor who had led her through a bazaar? She spent much of the day's final period considering the possibilities. And if in her speculations she caught a whiff of something faintly rotten and imperial, she ignored it. Of all the wonderful novels E. M. Forster had written, *A Passage to India* was her favorite. It made her wonder, were there any caves in Yemen? Caves that Ms. Duffy could have wandered into to explore, and then stumbled out of, dazed and transformed?

At the entrance to the library, Ms. Cruz sat behind her enormous wraparound desk. It resembled a sort of cockpit, its high sides studded with librarian paraphernalia, Ms. Cruz wheeling expertly about the interior in her ergonomic chair. The desk had two levels: the lower level was intended solely for the librarian's use, while the upper level was used by anyone who wanted to stand around bothering the librarian, as Mrs. Willoughby was doing now.

"Did you see?" Mrs. Willoughby turned to Ms. Hempel with excitement. Then she remembered. "Oh, yes, you were there. Isn't she gorgeous?"

Ms. Hempel said, "Gorgeous. And very . . ." She extended her arms.

"I know, I know! Not what we expected. I thought she'd come back with a slide show and some nice scarves. But no! So much more."

She leaned toward Ms. Cruz, resuming: "Thirty-five miles from the nearest hospital. Isn't that madness?"

"There's a midwife. She'll be fine."

"Of course she will be. But still. Out in the middle of nowhere? With your first child? You have no idea."

"She was tired of living here. She said so all the time."

"You girls don't know what it's like. You get so lonely at the beginning. You're tired, your nipples hurt, you can't remember what day it is."

"Roman will be there. And they're building a second yurt," Ms. Cruz said firmly, and then glanced up at Ms. Hempel. "Anna is moving upstate," she explained.

But that explained nothing. "A yurt?" Ms. Hempel asked. "Is that something . . . Yemenese?" She blushed.

"Mongolian," Mrs. Willoughby said. "I had to ask too. Not everybody who teaches here is a walking encyclopedia. It's a big circular tent made out of animal skins. Or, in Anna's case, some fancy state-of-the-art flame-retardant fabric." Mrs. Willoughby conjured up a miniature yurt with her hands in the air. "Not like a tepee — more like a circus tent. Made out of yaks."

"But the father," Ms. Hempel asked. "Is he from Yemen?"

Mrs. Willoughby looked at her peculiarly. "Heavens, no."

For the trip abroad had been cut short. Something in the food had made Ms. Duffy sick, dangerously so. Only two months out of the country and she was doubled over, shitting water. This explained the end of the lyrical e-mails. Ms. Duffy had lost nearly twenty pounds by the time she'd crept onto the airplane and come home to convalesce at her mother's; it was there that, looking pale and otherworldly, she had met Roman. A kite artist.

"He was visiting his mother too," Ms. Cruz said.

"They're neighbors in the condo complex, the one her mother moved to after the divorce," Mrs. Willoughby said. "Anna claims that it's soulless and horrible. But maybe she feels different now."

"Wow," Ms. Hempel said, collecting herself. So the father of Ms. Duffy's baby was an American, whom she'd met in the courtyard of an ugly condominium.

"Being a kite artist — that's his job?" she heard herself asking.

Ms. Cruz nodded. "He's a master. You can find him on the Internet."

"He spends all day making kites?"

"And flying them."

"How wonderful," Ms. Hempel said uncertainly. "I'd like to do that."

"Oh, wouldn't we all?" Mrs. Willoughby said, and took a great breath, and for a precarious moment it looked as if she might sing the chorus of "Let's Go Fly a Kite." But the opportunity passed. "There's family money too, of course. And a big piece of land passed down through the ages. Anna is living on an estate! In a yurt, admittedly, but still. Pretty grand. Isn't this what they call marrying up?"

"She got married?" Ms. Hempel asked, startled. She hadn't seen a ring.

A delicate look passed between the two other women. Ms. Hempel caught it, and felt her skin prickle.

"It happened very quickly," Ms. Cruz said.

"As it so often does," Mrs. Willoughby added. "One minute you're all alone, and the next — boom! — you're standing there in City Hall with the man of your dreams."

"And moving upstate," Ms. Hempel said. "And having a baby."

"Exactly," Mrs. Willoughby said, with a slap of her hands on the top of Ms. Cruz's desk. "That's the trick of life — how much everything can change."

And then, squeezing Ms. Hempel's arm, she asked, "Remember? Anna was miserable."

But Ms. Hempel wouldn't have described her as miserable, and she doubted that Ms. Duffy would have used the word herself. Because didn't misery imply a wallowing sort of wretchedness? And a teacher had no time for that. The curriculum was always marching on, relentlessly: the ancient Egyptians melting into the ancient Greeks, the blur of check marks and smiley faces, the hot rattling breath of the photocopier, book reports corrected shakily on the bus, the eternal night of parent-teacher conferences, dizzy countdowns to every holiday, and the dumb animal pleasure of rest. One could be quite unhappy and never have a chance to know it. Ms. Hempel was sometimes astonished by the thoughts she'd have while walking to work. One morning she looked longingly at a patch of ice on the pavement and realized that if she were to fall and fracture her leg in several places, then she wouldn't have to go to school. And maybe, if the doctors put her in traction, a substitute would be hired for the rest of the year. Perhaps she'd need a body cast. There was a way out, an honorable and dignified way out. All she had to do was undergo a terrible accident . . .

But then her desk would be emptied in her absence, and all her secrets would come scuttling forth: the torn and smelly pair of stockings, abandoned there months ago; the descriptive paragraphs that had taken her so long to grade she'd finally claimed to have lost them at the laundromat; the open bag of Doritos. And, embarrassment aside, she had responsibilities: The volleyball finals were fast approaching — who would keep score? Someone else would have to chair the weekly meetings of the girls' after-school book group and conduct the middle-school assembly on Diversity Day. And who would finish grading the *Mockingbird* essays, adhering to the byzantine rubric she'd devised?

The fact was that no one could.

"Call in sick," Amit would say sleepily, his arm flung over her. "Tell them you caught a cold." He'd kiss her. "You're infected. And extremely contagious. You need to stay in bed, OK?" But she would already be staggering toward the shower.

Had Ms. Duffy ever thought about slipping on the ice? Probably not; her thoughts likely took a more enraged and practical turn. Probably, as she waited for the bus, she drafted letters of resignation in her head, letters that described in withering detail the incompetence of the new middle-school director or the shabby state of the women's second-floor bathroom. Ms. Duffy was so thoroughly good at complaining. She'd begin dryly enough, with a sigh and a little self-mocking smile, but soon the full force of her indignation would take over, and her complaints would build in hilarity until she was magnificent to behold — her whole body radiant with fury. Often her stories ended with poor Mr. Mumford, the head of the middle school, saying, "Now, Anna, *just calm down*" — a phrase that, even when recollected in the yeasty tranquillity of Mooney's, made Ms. Duffy utter a murderous, strangled scream.

"Aaaaaaaaarrrrrrrr!"

From the end of the bar, Mr. Polidori would raise his glass to her. The gesture was perfectly in character: joking, wry, yet also somehow gallant. He would then return his attention to Mimi Gertz, the person whose company he appeared to enjoy more than anyone else's. She ran the art department, and made sculptures out of giant nails. She was fifteen years his senior and went on long bike trips with her girlfriend. Yet he, a teacher of physics, seemed always full of things to say to her. A mystery. But no more a mystery than his affair with Anna Duffy.

Affairs. Flings. Apparently they happened all the time, and between the people you'd least expect.

"You didn't know about me and Phil?" Ms. Cruz asked, leaning forward in her ergonomic chair. Phil Macrae taught life science to the sixth grade. Beardless and cowlicked, he looked as if he himself had only recently completed the sixth grade. Ms. Cruz had also had sex with Mr. Rahimi, the computer teacher, and Jim, who ran the after-school program.

"It got a little weird," she said.

Things had also got weird, Ms. Cruz revealed, for Mrs. Bell and Mr. Blanco — so weird, in fact, that he had had to go teach at another school for a few years, until the conflagration finally died out.

"Julia?" Ms. Hempel cried in dismay. She loved Julia Bell, who taught both remedial and advanced math.

"This was ages ago. Long before you came to us," Mrs. Willoughby said.

"But Daniel?" Ms. Hempel cried. "I thought he was gay."

"Oh, no. No. What ever gave you that idea? He's just Spanish."

And, incredibly, the former lover of Mrs. Bell. With his pointed goatee and his funny little vests? It was very hard to picture. Perhaps in a younger version his ambiguous sexuality had actually been quite dashing. Even irresistible. So much so that Julia Bell — a teacher blessed with pluck and humor and sense — had risked everything to be with him.

"This was before the boys were born?" Ms. Hempel asked.

"Wally was two, I think, and not yet in school. But Nathan had already started kindergarten." Mrs. Willoughby raised her eyebrows. "It could have been a real mess."

Unthinkable, Julia making a mess. Which was exactly why Ms. Hempel adored her: the serene, amused, and capable air; the way she kept an easy sense of order among even the most fractious children; the affection that her sons heaped upon her, tackling her in the middle of the hallway. She also had a plume of pure white hair growing from her right temple — she was the Susan Sontag of eighth-grade algebra. Her husband taught math too, at the state university; they had fallen in love during graduate school. And all this — her world of boys and equations and good cheer — had been hazarded.

And then recovered.

Now she could sit in faculty meetings with Daniel Blanco and not show the slightest sign that he was in any way special. If it weren't for the older teachers like Mrs. Willoughby, who remembered, there would be no trace left of the perilous affair. Ms. Hempel couldn't decide which amazed her more: the sight of Mrs. Bell and Mr. Blanco talking amiably by the coffee urn or the thought of them locked in an urgent, hopeless embrace.

Leaving the library, Ms. Hempel was surprised to find Ms. Duffy standing alone in the vestibule, her hands resting lightly atop her belly. She seemed to have lost her entourage somewhere along the way. She was looking at the enormous bulletin boards that lined the walls and displayed the latest projects generated by the younger grades. Only a year ago she had been responsible for filling such a board, a task that required judiciousness (for not every child's hieroglyph could be hung) and a protracted struggle with crepe paper and a staple gun. But now she was free of that. She gazed at the artwork with the cool eye of an outsider.

"Beatrice," Ms. Duffy said, and Ms. Hempel gave her a hug. "Have you seen this?" She pointed to the fifth-grade bulletin board.

"The projects are overlapping. You can't read them. And he put a staple right through that kid's name."

He being Mr. Chapman, Wall Street trader turned teacher, called in to replace Ms. Duffy for the year, and now, it seemed, quite possibly for good.

"How are we supposed to know who drew the Minotaur?" she asked. "A child spent hours — hours! — working on this, and you can't even read his name."

"The name is kind of obscured," Ms. Hempel agreed, peering at the display.

"My God," Ms. Duffy muttered. "This isn't rocket science." She reached up and pinched the staple between her thumb and forefinger. With a worrying motion, she extracted it, and then flicked it to the ground like a cigarette butt.

The child's name was Lucien Nguyen.

"Much better," Ms. Hempel said, and smiled. She wanted to leave, her curiosity dulled now that she knew Ms. Duffy wasn't harboring a little half-Yemenese baby. But Ms. Hempel's tendency to suggest precisely the opposite of what she actually wished, in the vague and automatic hope of pleasing someone, asserted itself.

"Do you want to walk to Izzy's and get a bubble tea? My treat?"

For a moment it looked as if Ms. Duffy were going to agree. But just as she was turning away from the displays she inhaled sharply and wheeled back around.

Her finger landed on a piece of pink paper, then circled a single word. "Did you see this?"

The text was printed in a computer's version of girlish handwriting: "Persephone picked up the pomegranate and ate four of its' seeds." Ms. Hempel winced.

"Oooph. Not good."

"They're kids," Ms. Duffy said. "They make mistakes. But how are they going to know that they've made mistakes if their teacher hangs them up on the fucking wall? I mean, does he make them do drafts? Does he correct anything?"

Ms. Hempel shrugged weakly. Her own alertness to error had wavered over the years. But maybe all it took was some time away, some time abroad, for one's acuity to be restored, because now, simply standing beside Ms. Duffy, she could feel her powers beginning to return — the mistakes were leaping out at her, the bulletin board lighting up with offenses.

"Upper right-hand corner," she told Ms. Duffy. "Completely random capitalization. Since when is *swan* a proper noun? Or *rape,* for that matter?" Though she had to admit, both choices had their own logic.

She also spotted *Aries* for *Ares, alter* in the place of *altar,* and, there it was again, that old devil *its'*. The real wonder of it all was how these mistakes managed to survive spell check. You had to kind of love them for it, for being indestructible.

Ms. Duffy was pulling Persephone off the wall. "Where's Leda?" she demanded. There was now a naked, pockmarked hole on the board.

"Up there," Ms. Hempel said, a little reluctantly.

Ms. Duffy rose up onto the very tips of her clogs, like a ballerina in toe shoes. Her belly didn't seem to throw off her balance. Up, up, her puffy fingers reached, quivering with purpose. "Got it," she gasped. Down came Leda. Down too came Hera and the peacock, Echo and a weedy-looking Narcissus, Danaë dripping wet in her shower of gold. Down came the Minotaur and Medusa, Hermes, Neptune, Athena leaping bloodily from her father's splitting head.

"Neptune? Wasn't that the name the Romans used?"

"Exactly," Ms. Duffy said.

Ms. Hempel gazed at the pillaged display, felt afraid, and looked down the hallway, in the direction of help. She wondered briefly why she, of all the young teachers who drank too much at Mooney's, had been chosen by Ms. Duffy to share this particular mission. Perhaps it was simply chance. The end of the day, an empty vestibule, a surge of nameless emotion — and then someone emerges, making you not alone anymore. So it had happened, a year ago, with Mr. Polidori. "Out of the blue?" Ms. Hempel had asked Ms. Duffy at the time. "The two of you just . . . ?" She could not believe it then, but now, holding the plundered goods against her chest, it made a sort of sense to her. It was easy to find oneself, without warning or prelude, embroiled. She crouched down and tapped the papers against the floor, neatening the pile, making a crisp little sound, wanting above all to avoid the appearance of untowardness, wanting the whole operation to feel as tidy, as considered, as possible.

*

They agreed, finally, that the best thing would be to return the projects, with a carefully worded note attached, to Mr. Chapman's classroom. "My room" was how Ms. Duffy referred to it, and then she alarmed Ms. Hempel by asking, "You're going to sign it too?" No, she was not, but she didn't have the heart to say so yet, especially now that Ms. Duffy had been seized by some fresh distress. As the fluorescent lights flickered on in the classroom, she looked about her wildly. Things were not as she had left them.

The purple beanbags were still in the reading corner, and the jade plants were thriving, having been faithfully watered by Ms. Cruz. The record player was there too, although it was buried under stacks of handouts, and the Calder mobile still dangled from the ceiling. But the Indonesian shadow puppets were gone, and so were the poems.

"He took down my poems?" Ms. Duffy's voice was small. She had gone to great lengths to procure them, even risking arrest. A few years earlier, the poems had begun appearing on subways and buses, alongside the advertisements for credit repair and dermatologists. As soon as a new poem was posted, Ms. Duffy would devise a plan for obtaining it: scouting out empty subway cars, climbing up onto the scarred seats, easing the poem from its curved plastic sheath, secreting it away beneath her long winter coat. All for the sake of her fifth graders! Every day they could gaze up and contemplate the words. Or not, and therein lay the beauty of osmosis. They passed the year in the company of Whitman and Dickinson, Mark Strand and May Swenson; some of the poetry would penetrate even the most obdurate souls.

Which was probably the thinking of the transit authority as well — but the fact that her fifth grade's edification came at the expense of the citizenry did not seem to give Ms. Duffy pause. And then it became possible to acquire the poems lawfully, by sending off a simple request on school letterhead — but Ms. Duffy, like all the best teachers, had a renegade spirit, and continued to haunt the buses late at night.

Now in the place of her stolen poems hung boldly colored posters urging the class to READ! And pointing out that READING IS FUN! That people everywhere should CELEBRATE READING! Additionally, there was a poster commemorating a Super Bowl win of the Green Bay Packers. All of which, it was obvious, had been obtained through official channels.

Ms. Duffy sank down onto one of the many little tables arranged throughout the room. The fifth graders didn't yet know the isolation of desk-chairs; they still worked companionably at these low shiny tables. She covered her face with her hands and sighed, her elbows digging into the high mound of her stomach.

"I hope he put them somewhere safe," she said.

"You want me to send them to you?" Ms. Hempel asked.

"No, there's no room. I just meant in case he changes his mind."

She glanced over at what had once been her desk, at the piles she was no longer accountable for.

"He has them doing those dumb workbooks?" she asked, but all her earlier outrage was now exhausted.

"It's his first year," Ms. Hempel said, and laid the ransacked myths on Mr. Chapman's desk. "He should take whatever shortcuts he can find."

Ms. Duffy didn't answer. She was still looking around the classroom, at the small ways in which it was now strange, at the names taped onto the backs of the chairs, names she would not recognize.

She said, "I lost Theo McKibben at the Metropolitan Museum. My first year."

"Theo?" Ms. Hempel laughed. "That's easy to do."

"It was a nightmare. My first waking nightmare."

"The first of many," Ms. Hempel said. "But just think: you'll never have to go on a field trip again."

Ms. Duffy smiled slightly. "Never again."

And then Ms. Hempel realized, with a sick feeling, that she had forgotten to distribute the permission slips for next week's outing to the planetarium. Only three days left — not a problem for the organized students, but it didn't allow much leeway for the children you always had to hound. She would have to resort to an incentive plan. Early dismissal? Ice cream?

She paced around the desk mindlessly, and saw it as both hopeful and doomed: the careful stacks beginning to slip; colored pens littered everywhere; memos from Mr. Mumford protruding at odd angles; the plastic in box taken over by trading cards, half-eaten candy bars, extra-credit assignments on the verge of being lost.

"You're brilliant." She turned to Ms. Duffy. "You are. Because we can't leave to make more money — that's despicable. And we can't leave to do something easier, some nice quiet job in an office —

that would be embarrassing! Am I supposed to tell my kids, 'Okay, I'm off to answer phones at an insurance company'? It's impossible. So what can we do? We can —" Ms. Hempel gestured helplessly at Ms. Duffy's belly. "Why didn't I think of that?"

She had imagined a body cast instead.

Again Ms. Duffy gave her a thin smile. It wasn't clear whether she took Ms. Hempel's compliment as such.

"So what's stopping you?" she asked idly. She plucked a long, loose hair from the sleeve of her blouse and dropped it onto Mr. Chapman's floor. Then she seemed suddenly to remember that she was pregnant and undergoing a remarkable experience. She lit up. "You should do it!" she said with abrupt conviction. "You'll love it. You will." She pushed herself off the little table and began moving toward Ms. Hempel. "We think we have all the time in the world, but in reality we don't. And when you've found the right person, you just have to go for it. There's never a good time — it's never convenient. Don't fool yourself into waiting for the perfect moment —"

She stopped. Her hands flew up to her mouth. "I'm so sorry!"

Ms. Hempel touched the fair, freckled arm. "Oh, don't worry. Please, really, don't worry."

"I'm an idiot!" Ms. Duffy cried.

"You're not," Ms. Hempel said. "Because I forget too. After I do the dishes, I get this panicked feeling that I've put my ring down somewhere and now I can't find it." She lifted her bare hand and looked at it. "Everything was friendly, it really was."

Ms. Duffy nodded, her face stricken.

"Amit and I still talk on the phone. And last week he sent me a book." She didn't mention that it was actually one of her books, a book that he had taken with him by mistake. "We're in very good touch," she said.

Ms. Duffy was unconsoled. "What happened?" she murmured. "What made you decide —"

It was hard to keep straight — they had told people different things at different times. There was Amit's fellowship in Texas, which he couldn't turn down; and there was the difficulty of finding time to plan a wedding, not to mention the expense; there was their youth, of course, and the uncertainty that comes with it, the fearful cloudiness of the future (and what a mercy that was, to be considered, at nearly thirty, still hopelessly young). All of which was true, just as all of it was prevarication, and even in the midst of saying these things she was never sure exactly whose feelings were being spared, who was being protected. For whose sake was all this delicacy required? She hated to think that it might be hers.

"It wasn't the teaching, was it?" Ms. Duffy asked.

Oh, no, it wasn't that. At least she didn't think so. But funny how everyone had a theory of her own. "It's not your father, is it?" her mother had asked. Her father had been dead for two years now, but at times she still found herself ambushed by his absence.

She had told her mother no, it wasn't because she missed her father. And she had told Mr. Polidori no, it wasn't because of him, either. She was surprised that he'd even asked. It had been a startling glimpse of vanity, of self-importance. He had cornered her by the jukebox and gazed down at her earnestly — the earnestness itself a surprise.

They had only kissed!

And nuzzled, with some breathless pressing and hugging, in the bathroom at Mooney's. Ages ago, on one of those happy Friday afternoons. After he had ended things with Ms. Duffy but before he had fallen for the gamine younger half-sister of Mimi Gertz. A pause between acts, there in the dark stall at Mooney's, everyone giddy with the rapid approach of summer. She had tumbled into the bathroom and found him, back to the door, penis presumably in hand, and before she could even gasp he had glanced over his shoulder, told her to wait, and then unhurriedly finished, washed his hands, and dried them with a sheet from a roll of gray paper towels, asking her, "Do you hate this song as much as I do?" They had danced, barely able to move. He had lowered the swinging latch into the little round hook by the door.

"Forgot to do that," he'd said, and she'd laughed.

Or had she? She would like to think that she had, that she had kept her wits about her and laughed, kept things floating along lightly, the encounter accidental and jolly. She would like to think that she hadn't swooned. Hadn't shut her eyes and given way, tipped her head and held on. There had been no hesitation — only treachery, only readiness — a perfect swan dive into the dark pool of flings and affairs. Maybe she had let out a little moan. But then the song had come to an end, and he had clasped her bearishly, pecked her on the forehead, and said, "I bet you make all the boys crazy, Ms. Hempel." And, after releasing the latch, he had gallantly held the door open for her.

She'd walked obediently back to her seat at the bar, wondering, What just happened?

Later she would return to this moment, flipping it back and forth like a tricky flash card, one that somehow refused to be memorized. She had asked herself all the boring questions (not pretty enough? odd smell? fiancé?), but couldn't quite manage an answer. Causality kept escaping her. He had kissed her, then he had changed his mind — that was as far as she ever got. But always fascinating to her was the fact that she had felt him changing his mind. Felt it in her muscles and on her skin. Not that he had done anything as obvious as stiffen, and his body hadn't once let go of hers, yet something had shifted — the pressure that was once excited now merely emphatic, the mouth still warm but only reassuringly so, the embrace turning into a squeeze. His body's gracious withdrawal of interest in the very moment that he decided, No, this really isn't for me.

And though many things would reveal themselves in time — the sex of Ms. Duffy's baby, a girl; and her name, Pina, after the bleak choreographer; the name of the woman who worked at Amit's lab, which was Lilly; the right word, the word she'd been looking for, *Yemeni* — still she returned to the bathroom at Mooney's, to its perfect mystery, to the moment when Mr. Polidori had wrapped his arms around her like a bear. That moment in which someone had made a decision. She wanted to remember how it felt.

STEVE DE JARNATT

Rubiaux Rising

FROM *Santa Monica Review*

"NEVER TAKE YOU BACK, son, hard as it break my heart," Aunt Cleoma had told Rubiaux. "This the last you come home like this — we don't break this demon now."

Two weeks ago that was, and since then Rubiaux has sweated away twenty-two pounds of his bedeviled flesh, screaming up in Cleoma's attic where she nailed him shut. A pot chambre to piss in, another to upchuck the cooler of gumbo and crackers he's tried to eat between sieges of nausea. High nineties it's been in the day, just the thing for the bone chills and shivering spasms they both knew came with the territory.

This early morning, as Rubiaux rouses, it is long-dead quiet. Like wads of chawed paper stuck flush back up against eardrums. Just blood rushing nothing in his head. Then blood simmers down, and he can hear gulls squawking on the wind somewhere. He sees gray light squeezing through rippage in the curling tarpaper lining the inside of this well-built roof. Wood is bare, creosoted here and there, but no paint. He has tried to steal an hour of sleep after an unholy night of ceaseless howl and shredding from the fiercest storm this parish has ever seen. How the roof stayed on was miracle indeed, testament to his late Uncle Zachary's carpentry skill. The extra nail he'd always pound, just to be sure. But that craftsmanship has also imprisoned poor Rubiaux here in dire predicament. All night, as the din of the tempest crescendoed again and again, he thought it surely must be the Rapture. But here he is at dawn — left behind — not risen to heaven.

Lord, you have tested, and I remain. You grant me new strength, and I will not forget. I will not succumb again to the sorrows of my flesh, Rubiaux thinks, throat too dry to speak.

Rubiaux has suffered more than one hell. The wounds of war, the subsequent addictions that brought about the necessary cruelty of Cleoma's home-style detox, as well as that Category 5 hurricane last night he still does not even know the name of. But Rubiaux has no idea that another and one far worse than even those is seeping right this moment through a breach at the base of the 17th Street Canal levee.

Rubiaux has been gone two years and came home with much of him gone. All his ample baby fat. An arm at the elbow. A leg midcalf. There is a large temporary titanium plate across the back of his scalp that is long overdue for replacement. In his most desperate hour, he had tried to pawn it, thinking the metal surely worth some long green. Rubiaux still feels whole most of the time, but not because of that phantom feeling phenomenon they talk about. It was the lush veil of constant OxyContin crushing and morphine spiking that kept him unaware of his loss extreme.

Rubiaux was always a kind, self-sacrificing soul. A bit simple, but he had tried to follow a righteous path in life best he could. This justified Aunt Cleoma's repeated troubles to always give him one more chance to pull out from his downward spiral. The boy was large for his age, with a fierce, dormant temper, but never a boulet. In fact, he beat the local bullies down. Could never stand to see the weak advantaged in any way.

When his half-wit cousin Remi went on a two-day binge and got himself hoodwinked by a zealous Marine recruiter, Rubiaux showed up in Remi's stead, taking his name at Camp Lejeune. He bore the burden of boot camp without a solemn peep and, before he could write home, found himself carrying an M60 in a sandy shithole called Al-Najaf.

"The light — the blood and dust — fear's such a human stink here, Aunt Cleoma. You just would not believe!" he would write her later.

Only two months in country and Rubiaux had run through a phalanx of AK and small-arms fire to pull four others from what was left of a Humvee an IED had tunneled a molten hole through. He shook off three sizzling rounds that snapped into his flesh like they were mere bee stings, but a tiny, jagged, crab-shaped shrapnel from the blast was propelled through his skull, deep into some important cleft in his cerebellum. This coma'd him quick as fluid ballooned around his brain. And this was lucky too — he could not feel the catastrophic wounds to his arm and leg from the blast of the second IED. The one meant to kill off those who came in aid.

Rubiaux awoke a month later with slurring speech and a constant liquid fire pumped down his ganglia, searing his tender meridians with such rich, raw, perpetual agony, he prayed to die a thousand times a day.

Back stateside, the tolerance of his dose-to-pain ratio grew exponentially, and as he had tried to heal in one squalid VA outpatient sty after another, he had twice nearly landed in the brig for narcotic theft. Then in testament to true absurdity, Rubiaux, a double amputee with severe brain impairment, was declared AWOL. He still was not officially excused from duty, they were so desperate for human fodder to police the chaos wrought over there in New Babylon.

In the attic Rubiaux watches light pour in — dancing dust around, slow and celestial like the Milky Way. His ears improve with a crack-jaw yawn. What's that high-pitched rushing? Those low knocking sounds like bowling heard outside the alley. And that slow, mean rumble. What is coming this way?

A shock wave hits the house like a dozen Peterbilts crashing one after another into the frame. Beams groan, the whole foundation nearly quaking off its shoulders, nails and screws strain to hold their grip, eeking like mice as wood and metal mad grapple to hold their forced embrace.

A new light shines at the far window, painting the ceiling with golden ripples. Reflection. Water. Water is coming. Water is here.

Rubiaux, who has been through more than anyone should ever have to, tries to remember his comfort song, the one he always hummed in his head on those endless missions, packed sardines inside the furnace of the A2.

"Wingo wheat lariot . . ." He tries to sing the first notes of the refrain again and again like a needle that can't hop a scratch-trap groove. "Wingo wheat lariot — comin' for to — coming for to —

coming to for — for to — to for —" But his addled noggin short-circuits. No sweet chariot can take him home today.

Cleoma had gone to town long before the storm. She left in the truck and swore she'd be back before all hell blew with someone who could help pull the nails up from the boarded barriers. But she has not returned.

And where is Remi? How come he never came to visit even once? Rubiaux took bullets meant for the callous lout and even now has not one ounce of anger toward him, only an ache of wondering.

Rubiaux looks down through the small hole where Cleoma had pushed up his sodas and daily medicine, doled out strict. He can see angry water rising in the kitchen now, pillaging the house without a hint of mercy.

There is no more food in his cooler, and Rubiaux has never been as hungry in his life, but for the first time in two years there is no demon in his veins making him crave sweet oblivion. He looks at what is left of suturing on his arm. He has not looked for months. In the infirmary he could never face the larceny of his limbs. He found that if he made himself numb enough all over, their lack could be forgotten for a spell. Displaced enough from his true axis, he would sometimes reach out with a shadow for a hand, laughing, not connecting to the perversion of his senses — his lying brain believing it was still part of him. He could even snap his ghost fingers and plainly hear the sound. But now he examines that forsaken stump all crossed with purpled scars and enjoys the reddened itching of it.

Rubiaux allows himself to face more remembering. The dust of Al-Najaf. The fear and heat. An adrenal thrall boils up quick to that 'lectric shock that keeps that day so vivid in dream and flash-mare. That day — the one he was blasted from being whole — his unit singing — "The roof . . . the roof . . . the roof is on fire." Boys just like him and boys not at all like him. Laughing, braying, praying — all together, tight as one — then the flash of hellfire somewhere and the devil's sneeze of a concussion that ripped apart the Humvee up ahead like it was a Tonka toy.

He remembers the succession of surgeries, one after another, the caduceus carrion coming to pick at his living carcass. "We can try to save the leg . . . we are unable to save the arm . . . we have to take a little more . . . there's another infection, so sorry . . . just a bit more, son, no other option. . ." He remembers the infinite boredom in between. Most of all he remembers the cruel mind-fucking of Gus Windus, a mean pissant in the next bed, who told Rubiaux again and again how he got off easy.

"Ya hear what them fuckin' rug pilots did to Terry Finnell? Strapped that boy down bareback over this big ole metal box dat wuz chock full o' Baghdad rats. Starved 'em for days, they did. Then they took a blowtorch to the metal. Really lit her up good, roastin' all them rodents. Fuckers ate right up through Terry's belly to get out — path o' least resistance. Poor fucker had to watch 'em all come scramble up through his own guts like that guy in the first *Alien* movie."

Rubiaux forever hated rats — since waking as a child to find a small scourge of them nibbling at the blisters on his feet. Finnell's story shivers him again with a flood of harsh memory — then, like vermin from an upturned rock, they all scatter away to some other dark place. Salt crusts his eyes where tears should be. He has long cried out his life ration of them. Deep, slow breathing brings him back to the sanctuary of the attic.

What Rubiaux really feels now, more than anything, is hunger. Like a panther growling inside him. He has already licked up every crumb he could find up here and is sure he has not missed a one. Then, in the dying of the light, he sees a vision: the silhouette of something hanging just outside the tiny window at the other end of the attic. *Please, do not let this only be a trick of the eye. That trompe l'oeil would be too cruel, the tempt of it,* his mind pleads to no one.

Rubiaux drags himself toward it with all his awkward might, scraping his tissue over the rough surface until he sits beholding it — crimson on crimson in the setting sun — a ripe, obese, heirloom tomato. Five full inches across, ugly and bulging uneven, the way they were born to be before genetic homogenization rendered their cousins into perfect, bland, tasteless orbs. A volunteer vine has crawled itself up the side of the house like that beanstalk in the child's tale just to bring this gift to him. Rubiaux plucks the tomato up quick and ponders it as if he were Eve in the Garden. If eating this will change the world, it can only be for the better, and if not, he really does not care. His belly rules him at this moment. He can smell the fetid, alluvial soil it has grown through — *la terre puant.* He caresses the tension of the tight-stretched circumference, rolls its skin across his cheek, then takes a small bite. The flavor rages through his taste buds, obliterating the stench of the attic. The air outside is no better now, spiced now with uprooted cesspools, floating gasoline, and the occasional whiff of fresh-rotting death. But this primal taste destroys every bit of it. Rubiaux leaps into its abyss, devouring. Juice and seeds flow down his throat and over his chest. Never has a thing tasted so heavenly. The last of its maroon flesh slides down his parched gullet. He pulls on the vine careful as can be, and another misshapen, wine-colored globe lifts up through the tiny window. He looks at the scratches on the wooden frame where, in his cold-turkey madness, he had kicked the fan out and tried to claw his way through the square-foot hole. He pulls up another, then another — drags the cooler near with his good foot, putting six more magnificent, monstrous tomatoes inside.

The creaking of the whole house suddenly amplifies again as the leveled wash begins to seep upward through the cracks and holes in the attic plafonnage. Like a string of dirty pearls, a dozen wet mice come pouring up ahead of filthy gray water that makes separate little flows all over, merging like quicksilver into greater water and rising still.

Rubiaux stacks three large travel cases in this corner near the window. He crawls up top, leaving him not even a foot to the tarpaper ceiling when he sits upright. The water rises and rises quick, inch by living inch.

The sun is sinking fast. Rubiaux realizes he may drown here in darkness, far from his choice of leaving this life. He curls up against the corner. There is a long ledge, a foot wide, high up in the rafters where he can put the cooler and stretch out his good leg. He eats another tomato, savoring every morsel, and he prays to keep the rising at bay — prays the way all have done in the Easy and the bayous forever. Those prayers had always seemed answered, peril postponed till another day, as each storm would somehow graze away from them, sparing their special, voluptuous lives. Till now.

Distant shouting melts with the whistling of the breeze through the cracks. Rubiaux closes his eyes before the light is gone so he can remember it all — then wills himself to sleep.

Rubiaux awakes out of time. In pitch darkness. He scratches his leg where it isn't with his hand that is not there. The water level is now up over the stacked supports, soaking him a good inch. But it has stopped. Prayer has worked, if only partly. But there is something new in the darkness now — breathing, movement. Others. He keeps his own breath steady, feigning slumber, waiting for light to grow in the east.

When he slowly opens his eyes again an hour later he sees them — the unholy menagerie. All down the ledge, crowded near him in awkward proximity, are: a large king snake; two smaller water snakes; four fat nutria; a half-drowned feral cat and two shivering kittens; three pitiful brown rabbits; a soggy raccoon; a dozen Norwegian rats; a clot of huddled mice; along with a teeming mess of spiders, beetles, centipedes, and such. His eyes dart. Theirs do too. All seem to breathe in some strange unison. Waiting a move. Nobody is eating anybody this morning. They share the same fear and confusion — orphan brothers in the storm.

Rubiaux ever so slowly lifts the brim of the cooler. He offers an heirloom to the king snake, which twists itself back into a tighter coil. He rolls it down the rafter toward the nutria, who clutch it up, nibbling through the skin. He tosses another down the ledge toward the rats, but it rolls askew, off into the water, bobbing there in shame. The next one barrels right into the rodents, who share it with the rabbits till the coon takes it away from the both of them. There is a peace here he never thought possible on this earth. Wild beasts together, the lion and the lamb — a living Bible story of some lost Eden.

Then — another mountainful of liquid slams into the house, ending this bliss. The nutria fall into the water and paddle off. The floor has slipped fully off the foundation and is splaying itself down into the weak, muddied ground. Whether the water is rising or the house is sinking it matters not — in minutes Rubiaux will surely drown.

The sound of a Sikorsky is heard, the circular clicking hovering not far off. Rubiaux again tries to claw at the hole of the window, tearing fingernails off, but this hole will never get bigger. Time to die with snakes and rats, his newfound friends. Rubiaux knows that at long last at least he is clean — his mind clear, and he is ready to meet his Maker.

Rubiaux loops his belt around his throat, securing it up over a two-by-four, cinching it tight across his Adam's apple. He wishes not to go by drowning, having nearly done so twice in life. In death he chooses hanging, which someone told him once is fairly quick, and you might even get a raging bone on as you blind out in a red, gruesome rush.

Just before giving himself to gravity, he notices warping patterns of golden light dancing around the roof. This baffles him. He tries to see it straight on, but it keeps moving, always off to his side again. Then he realizes the sun is hitting the shiny, curved, titanium plate on the side of his head. This makes Rubiaux laugh. He squints till it looks to him exactly like an angel floating free above his shoulder. Then, in a flash, he knows what he must do. As if the angel told him.

It takes some prying, tearing the rest of his fingernails to get it loose. Then, using a rusty nail for leverage, he stuffs it up under a gap between the plate and the tender, fibrous growth of his scalp and yanks hard as he can. It comes clean off, falling into the water, gleaming there like a lure. He snatches it up before it fades from view, shaking off the droplets, then trains the convex side sunward, compounding the rays into a blinding hotspot on the roof. In seconds tarpaper bursts into flame, coughing out thick, black hellfire smoke. The rest of his natural guests leave as fast as they can scurry, slither, or hop away. Rubiaux feels bad about this and prays safe passage for them all, even the rats.

When the smoke hugging the ceiling gets too thick to see through, he pulls the cooler down over his head and drops into the water with the brim submerged around him. He holds there as long as he can, safe in the air pocket. Something sinister in the water brushes through between his thighs, then comes back to nibble at his suturing. Oxygen is used up quickly, and he weakens, in danger of not having the strength to lift it away, but then shoves with all he has left and sees there is now a three-foot hole in the roof, encircled with red flame. Through it he can see a helicopter lowering down through the smoke. Rubiaux flashes the angel glint up toward the cockpit window, and the behemoth hovers down, clearing smoke from the attic.

The pilot rubs his eyes several times, not sure of what he is seeing. On the side of the roof, two snakes are stretched out over each other, forming a perfect cross on the burning roof.

This craft is already full up, but one of the bone-tired Coast Guard heroes who have labored valiantly with no rest whatsoever all day descends down in a basket, pulling Rubiaux aboard, strapping them together. They rise up, flying Rubiaux low over one submerged ward after another — to the heart of the drowned Crescent City. Passing over gas fires, families wading chest-high, looters floating plasma televisions, dogs in trees, and so many other sights Rubiaux thought he would never see.

As they set him down on the overpass near the Dome with the huddled bunches of others, Rubiaux knows his suffering is finally over — help and comfort will surely be coming soon.

JOSEPH EPSTEIN

Beyond the Pale

FROM *Commentary*

I LEARNED MY YIDDISH from my grandfather, who came from Montreal to live with us in Chicago for the last four years of his life, after his health failed and he could no longer stay alone. These were the years, just after World War II, when I was between fourteen and eighteen — not at all a bad age, really, for absorbing a new language. A small and somewhat foppish man, my grandfather began each day by wrapping himself in a prayer shawl and tefillin for his morning devotions. After bathing, he would dress in one of his five suits, tailor-made and very well cut, which he maintained with great care and wore in rotation. His shirts were white and starched, his neckties dark. A thick gold watch chain depended from his vest. When he died he left the watch to me, and also, I would later come to realize, a certain standard of seriousness.

In Montreal, where he had spent much of his adult life, my grandfather had been a leading figure in Hebrew education. Oldtimers in that city still remember Raphael Berman as a man of deep learning and wide culture. Living with us in Chicago must have marked a sad coming-down for him. *Immaculate* was the word my mother always used to describe her father-in-law; he, for his part, worried about her following the laws of kashrut, previously foreign to her. After more than eighty years keeping kosher, he feared falling off the wagon at this late stage of his life.

My grandfather still had strong memories of pogroms in his childhood shtetl a few miles outside Berdichev in the eastern Ukraine. He told me how his parents had managed to smuggle him out of Russia to avoid conscription into the czar's army. Although he never said so aloud, he must have been disappointed that none of his four sons — of whom my father, a successful retail furrier, was the youngest — had turned out to be in the least scholarly or even mildly bookish. There was only me, his grandson: a last chance to impart to another generation his love for Hebrew and above all for Yiddish, his sweet, endlessly subtle *mamalosh'n.*

Patiently he taught me Yiddish grammar, syntax, vocabulary, the semantic intricacies of a language whose every word — even, my grandfather joked, the prepositions — seemed at least a triple-entendre. Once we had run through the few available lesson books, he led me gently into the great storytellers, Shalom Aleichem, Peretz, Mendele. Together we also read David Pinski and Chaim Grade and Abraham Reisen, even the problematic Sholem Asch.

At sixteen, I may have been the world's youngest reader of the *Jewish Daily Forward,* still sold in those days at the newsstand at Devon and California, four blocks from our apartment. It was in the pages of the *Forward* that I first came across the stories and serialized novels of Isaac Bashevis Singer, published, in their Yiddish version, under the name Bashevis. And it was there too that I first came across Zalman Belzner, a writer who interested me more than Singer.

Belzner wrote of the struggles of the young Jewish Communists in the early days of the Russian Revolution, and of the plight of young men caught between the traditional Judaism in which they had been raised and the lure of Haskalah, or Jewish "enlightenment" and secularization, in its various early-twentieth-century permutations. Belzner wrote about these things in the most vivid detail. He achieved realism, I remember my grandfather saying, rather cryptically, with none of its accompanying vulgarity.

I was still a kid, had not yet been exposed to Tolstoy or Dostoyevsky, Proust or Thomas Mann, but in Zalman Belzner I already sensed that I was encountering literary writing built to last a very long time. Such writing, it seemed to me then, was the exclusive province of the dead, of whom I assumed Belzner was one. "Oh, he's very much alive and kicking," my grandfather informed me when I inquired. "I believe he lives in New York, with his second wife, a story in herself, if you'll pardon the expression." My grandfather chose not to tell that story, at least not to an adolescent boy, but I could read a fair amount in his raised right eyebrow.

*

My grandfather died the year I went off to college. There were not all that many Jewish students at Yale in the early 1950s, when strict quotas were still in effect, and those few among us did not exactly advertise our Jewishness. I studied English; after my grandfather's influence, I wasn't really good for anything but literature. In the fashion of the day, I was taught to unpack the meanings, often Christological, hidden in English lyric poems, and to comb and curry the symbols from the brooding works of American fiction, an exercise for which, after extended exposure to the power and charm of the great Yiddish writers, I hadn't much taste.

The study of English at Yale convinced me that I did not want to teach, and so, upon leaving New Haven, I took a job at *Time* magazine, where Yalies in those days, even Jewish ones, had an inside track. The work paid well, and many interesting characters were still on the premises, drawing large checks and full of contempt for their jobs, their boss, and the society that forced men of their talent to slave at infusing the trivia of the news with interest and dash. I myself felt lucky to have the job. And then too I met Naomi, my wife, at *Time*, where, after graduating from Radcliffe, she had been hired as a researcher.

Living in New York, I began to read the *Forward* again, every so often buying a copy from the newsstand at Seventy-eighth and Broadway not far from our apartment. In the *Forward* I came upon a notice of a reading by none other than Zalman Belzner at the Rand School, downtown near Union Square. Since Belzner was now in his early eighties and would live who knew how much longer, I felt I couldn't miss it.

Including the rickety woman on two canes who introduced the guest of honor, there were seventeen of us in the audience that Thursday night, twelve women and five men. I must have been the youngest person in the room by fifty years. The crowd reminded me a little of the one that had gathered on a cold February evening in Chicago to mark the death of William Z. Foster, who in 1932 had been the Communist candidate for president of the United States. I no longer remember why I attended that event, but, like the American Communist Party, Yiddish literature in the 1950s seemed to me another, if much more gallant, lost cause.

Zalman Belzner was given an introduction in which he was at one point called the Homer, and at another the Shakespeare, of twentieth-century Yiddish literature. As he slowly approached the lectern, one could see that he was near the end of his trail. He was a large man, and must once have been very handsome. His skin was wrinkled but pinkish, his hair white and still plentiful; in fact, he was in need of a haircut. He had big, fleshy ears, which stuck out. His features, as sometimes happens with people in old age, had become a bit blurry, as if someone had fooled with the contrast button. His hands were large; lifting them seemed to require an effort. His breathing carried a low rasping sound.

Yet as soon as he began reading, passion kicked in and Belzner's age dropped away. He began, in Yiddish, with a series of five poems, recounting the cycle of Jewish hope and disaster that was the great revolution in Russia. He next read, also in Yiddish, from two welcoming letters sent to him by Shalom Aleichem upon his first publications. Next, in somewhat stilted English, he read from what he called "a work in progress," a section from a new novel about a young yeshiva student in Vilna whose passion for a beautiful young leftist catches him up in the intricacies of revolutionary politics. Belzner's strong greenhorn accent made what he read seem all the more powerful. At the end of this excerpt he thanked his wife, Gerda, for her work on the translation.

Applauding, everyone turned to look at a woman sitting in the row in front of mine and a bit to my left. Gerda Belzner looked to be in her late fifties, twenty or so years younger than her husband, small and very thin, with fine bones and emphatic features and hair dyed henna red. She sat with an impressive uprightness; deep pride showed in her bearing. She took the applause, I felt, rather as if she were not the translator but herself the author.

A reception had been set up that reminded me of the small spread after Shabbos services at Ner Tamid Synagogue where I used to accompany my grandfather. Slices of sponge cake and small glasses of Mogen David wine plus, in this case, a samovar with glasses for tea. Belzner was standing; supported by a cane that he hadn't used at the lectern, his wife holding his other arm, he was talking to three admiring elderly women. After they wandered off, I went up to him.

"Mr. Belzner," I said, "my name is Arnold Berman, and I work for *Time* magazine, and I just wanted to tell you that your writing has meant a great deal to me, and I want to thank you for it."

"No, no," Belzner said, extending his hand, "it is I who must thank you. All that a writer can ask for is intelligent and generous-hearted readers. And in you, young man, I seem to have found such a reader. I am most grateful to you." I felt my hand disappear in his large padded paw.

"If you don't mind my asking, Mr. Berman," said Mrs. Belzner, "how did you come to learn about my husband's writing, a man so young as you?" She was less than five feet tall and her eyes, more black than brown, shone fiercely. Her accent was as strong as her husband's but metallic and harsh where his was warm and caressing.

"Through my grandfather, who taught me Yiddish."

"And for *Time* magazine," she said, "what exactly, if I may ask, it is that you do?"

Don't ask me why, but I lied, or at any rate exaggerated. "I write about culture," I said, "mostly things in what we call 'the back of the book.'" In fact, in those days I chiefly wrote the squibs, in the section of the magazine called Milestones, about recent births and deaths and divorces among the celebrated.

Two other women had captured Belzner's attention, and he was expending his charm on them, but Mrs. Belzner stayed with me. "You would like a piece of sponge cake or a glass tea?" she asked.

"Thank you, no," I said. "I really must be going, but I didn't want to leave without telling your husband how much I admire his work."

"He is a great writer, Zalman Belzner," she said, fire in her eye, "and if he wrote in any other language but Yiddish, the world would long ago have known it."

I told her I thought she was absolutely right about this, and excused myself.

The next afternoon at the office, just after I returned from lunch, the receptionist called to say that a large package had been left for me. When I picked it up, I discovered that it contained three of Zalman Belzner's books in Yiddish, all inscribed to me, and a copy, in manuscript, of his wife's translation of *Beyond the Pale,* the book from which he had read the night before. It also contained no fewer than thirty reviews of Belzner's work, almost all of them from the Yiddish press, and, in an emphatic hand, a four-page letter from Mrs. Gerda Belzner.

I'll spare you the florid politesse of her opening and closing paragraphs, which could only have been written by someone whose first or second or even third language was not English and were in a style more appropriate to the eighteenth century than to our own. The main point of her letter was, as she put it, "a simple but felicitous idea" — namely, that *Time* put Zalman Belzner on its cover, with a story, to be written by me, about his travails as a great Yiddish author. She, who knew Zalman Belzner's life better than anyone in the world, would be pleased to fill me in on the facts, perhaps over lunch at the Belzners' apartment on West End Avenue at, she wrote, underlining, *"your earliest permissible convenience,"* adding "maybe next Tuesday." She also noted that she would appreciate my comments on her translation of *Beyond the Pale.*

I waited until the next day to call.

"Mrs. Belzner," I said, lying again, "I talked over the idea of a cover story about your husband with Mr. Luce, our editor in chief, and he said that while he thought the notion had much merit, perhaps the timing was wrong. In any case, we've already run three covers on writers within the last fourteen months. He asked me to thank you for your interest and to congratulate you on the translation of *Beyond the Pale.*"

The truth was that I had never met Henry Luce, having been in the same room with him only once and then was too nervous to introduce myself. Except as the wildest comedy, I certainly could not imagine discussing with him, or with any of the senior editors, a *Time* cover on Zalman Belzner.

"You'll maybe forgive my saying so, Mr. Berman," she said, "but this man Mr. Luce must be an idiot. Zalman Belzner is probably the greatest writer in the twentieth century, and hardly anyone knows about it. *Time* is a newsmagazine, no? If this isn't news, what, if I may ask, is?"

"You're probably right, Mrs. Belzner," I said, "but it's Mr. Luce's magazine, and what he says goes."

"Like I say, an idiot," she said. "But you'll come to lunch anyhow?"

"I'll be happy to," I said.

"Next Tuesday, at one-thirty is good. Zalman Belzner writes from ten till one. You have the address?"

The Belzners' building at 420 West End Avenue was not all that far geographically from where Naomi and I lived, but in certain respects it seemed a different world. Although the West Side was entering a decline that would only get messier and more dangerous as the sixties wore on, most of the large buildings on West End retained their air of solid if shopworn gentility. The side streets were another matter; the thought of the shaky Zalman Belzner on his cane walking those streets was not pleasant to contemplate.

An elderly doorman in a shabby maroon coat, hat slightly askew, informed me that the Belzners lived on the sixth floor. Someone had scratched *Up Yours* on the inside of the elevator door. The interior halls were gloomy and gave off a cabbagey smell. When I knocked, Gerda Belzner came to the door.

"Mr. Berman," she said, "I'm sorry to have to inform you that Zalman Belzner, because of poor health, will not be able to join us for lunch today."

"Nothing serious, I hope," I said.

"With Zalman Belzner, everything is serious," she replied. "He is a sick man."

"What's wrong?"

"The aftereffects of tuberculosis, which, not helped by his having smoked for so long, have turned into emphysema," she said. "Another gift from Mother Russia, the tuberculosis. Zalman Belzner, you should know, is a writer who has been a guest at the Lubyanka prison under two regimes, the czar's and the Communists'."

I hadn't known. Nor did I know, as I would soon discover, that Belzner was acquainted with Babel, Pasternak, Akhmatova, and the Mandelstams. His second wife filled me in on these and other matters. Belzner's first wife, according to Gerda Belzner, was a maniacal Communist. She had tried to convince him to write in the style of socialist realism, to desert Yiddish for Russian, and, later, to take up the editorship of the Yiddish magazine *Soviet Homeland,* which was devoted to the lie that Jewish culture in the Soviet Union was thriving. When Zalman Belzner was able to flee the Soviet Union, she chose not to go with him. She was said to have died in the gulag in 1950, three years before the death of Stalin.

While telling me these stories, Gerda Belzner would frequently interrupt to go to the back of the apartment — to minister to her husband, I assumed. At each return she took up the conversation without missing a beat. She told me that she had met Zalman Belzner after he had defected; he lived briefly in Paris before moving to New York. She was herself originally from Warsaw, a refugee from Hitler. As a young girl, a member of various Jewish literary societies in Warsaw, she had of course read Belzner and admired him greatly. When she met him in New York, she was immediately swept away. "He was," she said, "an even more handsome man than he is today."

"You understand, Mr. Berman," she said, "my life is devoted entirely to the work of Zalman Belzner. It has no other meaning."

She didn't really have to say it. Everything about her underscored the point, not least her inability to refer to her husband except by his full name, as if she were reading it off a title page.

Gerda Belzner served me a bowl of cold and not very good borscht, a platter of cold tongue and hard salami, rye bread, a sliced onion, a tomato, some too-strong coffee, with grapes and an overripe banana for dessert. None of the food seemed quite fresh. But then, neither did anything about the dark and dusty apartment, whose every available flat surface was covered by Yiddish books and newspapers. The windows had not been cleaned for a long time, and the light coming in felt crepuscular, even though it was midday. Every so often I would hear a weak but racking cough from the back. I imagined poor Belzner, sequestered in his room in an old woolen bathrobe in a bed with less than clean sheets. A homemaker Gerda Belzner clearly was not.

"And so, Mr. Berman," she asked, "have you had a chance to read my translation of *Beyond the Pale?* And if you have, what, if I may ask, do you think?"

"It's a wonderful story," I said, "and the translation is excellent, fluent, only a few rough spots."

I was truthful about the story but not about the translation, which was stiff, overly ornate, studded with odd bits of immigrant English, its syntax hopeless, sometimes bordering on the comic. The Yiddish of the Zalman Belzner I remembered from my grandfather's *Forward* was straight, delivered with power and unshowy verbal agility, in staccato, machine-gun-like sentences. Only well after you read a passage did it occur to you to wonder how, in so few strokes, he had managed to bring off the astonishing effects he did. His skill as a pure storyteller deflected your attention from the style that gave his tales their magic.

"I have now sent this translation to nine American publishers, none of whom has expressed any interest whatsoever," she said. "What do you make of this, Mr. Berman?"

"I'm not quite certain what to make of it," I said, "except perhaps that there may be limited interest in your husband's subject matter. We live in sensationalist times. Everything is geared to the contemporary."

"Then how do you account for the success of that pig Singer?" She did not so much pronounce as spit his name.

I. B. Singer was just then beginning to catch on with a large American audience. "Even for Singer I'm told it hasn't been so easy," I answered. "I've heard that when Knopf brought out *The Family Moskat,* they cut the manuscript substantially. It's a hard world, the world of American publishing, with very little sentimentality."

"May I ask a very great favor of you, Mr. Berman? May I ask you to go over my translation once more, with an eye to eliminating the rough spots you mention, and then maybe to think about where next to send the book? More than anything in this life, I want *Beyond the Pale* published while Zalman Belzner is yet alive."

Careful, Arnie, I said to myself. This woman can only be trouble. Besides, I had quite enough going on in my life. There was my job at *Time,* up whose masthead I had at long last begun to climb — I was now an associate editor, and had become the magazine's third movie reviewer. My wife was pregnant with our first child. I had writing ambitions of my own; I was on the lookout for a good subject about whom to write a biography. To take on the polishing of this wretched translation — polishing, hell, a full retranslation was required — was not exactly a good career move.

Of course, there was Belzner himself to consider. However reduced his circumstances, he was a great writer; of that there couldn't be any doubt. And my grandfather, I thought, would have been pleased that his grandson was putting his training to such high purposes. The manuscript of *Beyond the Pale,* in Yiddish, ran to 460-odd pages. A fair portion of it was in dialogue. If I could do two pages a night, with perhaps a little more on weekends, I might have the whole thing done in fewer than six months. Gerda Belzner set off all my warning signals — dangerous, nutty woman, *beware* — but her husband's situation was serious and sad. Never suffocate a generous impulse, my grandfather used to say.

"Let me give it a try," I said. "Working at a full-time job, I can't promise to have it done too quickly, Mrs. Belzner. But maybe, just maybe, I can smooth out the rough spots and make the novel a bit more attractive to an American publisher."

"Tank you, Mr. Berman," she said, failing to pronounce the *h,* "and I know that Zalman Belzner will want to tank you too, and will do so in person once he is again up and around. We are both most grateful to you, please never to forget that."

Leaving the Belzners' apartment, the Yiddish manuscript and Gerda Belzner's translation in a Klein's shopping bag, I thought, Well, kid, you're in the soup now, up to your lower lip. Out on West End Avenue it had begun to rain. On the side street to Broadway a young guy in a tweed jacket three sizes too big for him, a crazed look in his eyes, approached.

"Hey, buddy," he said, "can I have all your change?"

Caught off-guard, I reached into my pocket and gave him what must have been nearly two bucks in silver.

"Thanks, pal," he said. As he walked away, I noted a large tear in the seat of his pants.

This was, apparently, my big day for charity.

After my second session with *Beyond the Pale,* I dispensed altogether with Gerda Belzner's translation, which was, as I discovered on closer scrutiny, crude beyond retrieving. The novel, however, was Zalman Belzner's masterpiece. It recounted the life of a boy, Eliezer Berliner, brought up in strict religious observance, a star pupil at one of the great yeshivas in Vilna, with all the potential to be a great scholar and rabbi, who runs off to Russia, lives among revolutionaries in Moscow where Jews were not allowed, is captured and imprisoned in the Lubyanka, rejoins his comrades on the eve of the Russian Revolution, only to be jailed again two years later by the Soviet secret police, and finally flees to Paris, where he hopes to devote his life to poetry. Belzner had supplied brilliant cameo roles for Lenin and Trotsky, Bukharin and the young Stalin. The book, from what I knew of Belzner's life, was intensely autobiographical. In his taut narrative, Belzner took on the emptiness of formal religion, the hopelessness of radical politics, the vanity of all art that does not ultimately turn one back to religious contemplation, if of a vastly different kind from that ever dreamed of by the Vilna rabbis who trained his protagonist.

Belzner's method in telling Eliezer Berliner's story was pointillism of a sort, a careful setting down of dots, one after another, of precise and synecdochical detail. So perfectly had he linked these dots that one read with the intensity of a dying man racing through a book prescribing hitherto unknown cures for his disease. As a boy I had done translation exercises of a page or two for my grandfather, but nothing so extended as this. I found myself working four hours a day on *Beyond the Pale* — two hours in the early morning before going off to *Time,* another two after Naomi, tired from her pregnancy, had gone to bed. I thought about it at work, in my mind revising English phrasings that weren't quite adequate to Belzner's powerful text. I lingered over it before I fell off to sleep, reformulating sentences, my arm around my wife and my mind in Moscow with the young Eliezer Berliner.

It was only a translation, but I found an immense excitement in the task. By now I knew that in my own life I would never attain to truly creative work; toiling on Zalman Belzner's manuscript was as close as I was ever likely to come to the thing called literature. In getting things right, a great deal — everything, really — was at stake.

I finished two months earlier than I planned and sent the work, along with Gerda Belzner's version, to the apartment on West End Avenue. Four days later she called.

"Mr. Berman," she said, "Zalman Belzner has read your translation of his novel, *Beyond the Pale,* and would like to meet to talk with you about it. When, if I may ask, are you available?"

We settled on Thursday. She suggested lunch at their apartment, once again at one-thirty.

This time Belzner himself answered the door. His largeness filled the doorway. He was wearing unpressed gray trousers, a rumpled white shirt with an ink stain near the pocket, and at his neck a skimpy paisley ascot with a maroon background. His eyes looked more tired than I remembered from our previous meeting at the Rand School.

"Ah, Mr. Berman," he said, full of bonhomie, "is good to see you once more. Do come in. Do come in."

The same table was set — once again for two — in the small living room.

"My wife will not be joining us today," he said, "which is perhaps just as well, since it is about her that we must talk, at least in part."

The meal, already on the table, turned out to be exactly the same as the one Gerda Belzner had served me roughly four months earlier, from borscht to the tired fruit compote. Belzner questioned me a bit about my grandfather and his origins. When I said he came from Odessa, Belzner smiled and said, "Ah, the city of Jewish violinists and Benya Krik, the great Jewish gangster." He told me about his meeting with Krik's creator, Isaac Babel, also of Odessa, and about Babel's craze for literary revision: forty and fifty times he would rework a simple three-page story.

Over the fruit compote our conversation began in earnest. "I wish to speak to you, of course, about your translation of my book. My English is less than perfect, as you can hear even now as I talk to you, but your translation seems to me excellent, highly excellent really, and I am most grateful to you for the care you must have put into it. For a writer in Yiddish, as you must know, a good translator into English is not important merely — it is everything."

"I'm pleased you think well of it," I said, genuinely delighted.

"I think very well of it, but I couldn't help noticing you seem not to have made much use of my wife's work as first translator of the book. Is this not correct?"

"Correct," I said. "I felt it was better to begin from scratch."

"Yes," he said, "from scratch." He stopped to think about an American idiom that was evidently new to him. "From scratch. I see what you mean. What I wonder now is whether I can convince you to share the credit with Mrs. Belzner as cotranslator of the book. It would mean a great deal to her if you were to do so. Meanwhile, in recompense, I am sure some royalty arrangement on the translation could be worked out in your favor."

"It's a little irregular," I said.

"I'm sure it is," Belzner said, "but then, as you may have noticed, so is life and so especially is Mrs. Belzner a little irregular. She is not an ordinary woman, my Gerda, as you will have noted."

"It would be difficult not to note it," I said, trying to sound neutral.

"She, I fear, has maybe a greater investment in her husband than is perhaps normal. But then I owe her everything. More even than I am able to explain to you. She has saved my life, and continues to save it every day that remains to me. Without her, please believe me, I would long ago have been dead." Belzner took a soiled handkerchief out of his back pocket and dabbed at his flushed face.

"I told Gerda," he continued, "that your translation was built on hers, that it was, in the highest sense, a collaboration between two good minds. To do otherwise, you understand, would have been very cruel. And you don't seem to me a cruel man, Mr. Berman."

"I hope not," I replied.

"Excellent," Belzner said. "When my wife returns, I shall tell her that if we are able to get an American publisher, the title page will read, 'Translation by Gerda Belzner and Allan Berman.' She will be pleased."

"Arnold," I said.

"I'm sorry?" he said, cupping his right ear.

"My name is Arnold, not Allan."

"A thousand apologies," he said. "Please to forgive."

Zalman Belzner walked me to the door. He moved as if in slow motion; his footfall was heavy; I could hear his every breath. As we parted, he grasped my hand in both of his and said, "I am more in your debt than you can ever know. I thank you, Mr. Bergman."

Through a connection at *Time,* I was able to get my translation into the hands of Ben Rayburn, a small publisher interested in things Jewish, who quietly brought it out eight months later under his Horizon imprint. I was unable to attend the small publication party for the book. A page-three, highly laudatory review by Irving Howe appeared in the *New York Times Book Review,* with a brief paragraph toward the end commending the "stately translation" of Gerda Belzner and Arnold Berman. *Beyond the Pale* had a modest sale of some 2,700 copies. I never saw a penny in royalties, which was all right with me. I hadn't done it for money. I did it for Zalman Belzner; I did it for my grandfather; who knows, maybe I did it for myself. In any case it was over, and I went back to my regular family life and to my job at *Time.*

Roughly eighteen months after the publication of *Beyond the Pale,* around eleven-thirty on a Tuesday night, I stumbled out of bed to answer the telephone.

"Mr. Berman," said Gerda Belzner, in her unmistakable accent, "my husband Zalman Belzner is terribly ill and needs to be driven to Florida — tonight. Can I count on you to help me drive Zalman Belzner to Miami? We need to leave immediately, within the hour."

"Mrs. Belzner," I said, "can't this wait till the morning?"

"No," she said, "Zalman Belzner must leave for Florida now. There is no time to lose. Can you help me drive him to Florida or not?"

"Mrs. Belzner," I said, "I have a pregnant wife and a young child to worry about. I have a job. I can't take off for Florida at midnight on such short notice."

"Very well," she said. "Thank you anyhow."

"Mrs. Belzner —" But she had hung up.

Two days later I read the six-inch obituary of Zalman Belzner that ran in the *New York Times.* It announced that he had died, of congestive heart failure, on Monday, the day before Gerda Belzner's call, and that he was being buried that day in a private ceremony.

From my office at *Time,* I called Gerda Belzner.

"Mrs. Belzner," I said, "I see in the *Times* that your husband's funeral is today, though no address for a funeral chapel is given. Where is it to take place?"

"I am sorry, Mr. Berman," she said, "but you are not invited. No one is invited who refused to drive Zalman Belzner to Florida with me."

"But Mrs. Belzner," I said, "unless I'm mistaken, when you asked me to drive your husband to Florida, he was, according to the *New York Times* obituary, already dead."

"That," she said, in a cold voice, "is none of your business. You were unavailable when needed. I am inviting to the funeral only those friends of Zalman Belzner who were willing to drive him with me to Florida. Thank you anyhow for asking." She hung up.

I stared into the phone. What was going on here? Another Jewish test? Our religion, after all, almost begins with a test, when God commands Abraham to sacrifice his son Isaac. But this test of Gerda Belzner's, driving a man already dead to Florida, at midnight and on a moment's notice, provided a new twist — this was nuts. In any case, I had failed the test.

But my Belzner connection was not permanently broken. A few months later Gerda Belzner called again. She wanted another meeting. She suggested a dairy restaurant on Broadway near

Eighty-sixth Street. I wanted to say no, but somehow I couldn't bring myself to be cold to this woman, who was now, for all I knew, absolutely alone in the world.

I arrived fifteen minutes early. The crowd in the restaurant was made up chiefly of elderly Jews, most of them immigrants to judge by their speech and dress. The majority must have escaped Hitler or Stalin; some may have had to escape both. They had seen the devil up close. I felt callow in their presence.

When Gerda Belzner walked in, she was wearing a black cloth coat with a black dress underneath, boots with high heels, her henna-colored hair swept up in a bouffant, her makeup at maximum strength, leaving her sharp features in something approaching boldface. She seemed a small, possibly predatory bird. Yet there was also a touch of the regal in her appearance. She was, after all, now the widow of Zalman Belzner.

Along with her purse, she was carrying another of her shopping bags from Klein's. I rose and waved from my table. She saw me and walked over.

"Well, Mr. Berman," she said, "we meet again."

"I thought perhaps we had seen the last of each other."

"Why would you think that?"

"It's been a while," I said, choosing not to mention the funeral from which I had been excluded.

We ordered vegetarian cutlets, small salads, tea. The waiter, an older man, flat-footed, a slightly dirty towel over his forearm, looked and sounded like something straight out of a classic Jewish vaudeville routine. ("Vich of you gentlemen vanted the clean glass?")

"Mr. Berman," she said, getting right down to business, "I have today a proposition to make to you."

"What might it be, Mrs. Belzner?"

"I want you should translate with me six of my husband's as yet untranslated novels. My plan is for us to do them together, as we did with *Beyond the Pale.* I would give you a third of the royalties on each of the books." She passed her shopping bag over to me; it contained copies, in Yiddish, of the books.

"Forgive me for saying so, Mrs. Belzner, but that doesn't finally come to a lot of money. I have a wife and child to support, and another on the way. You realize you're asking for a commitment here of several years on my part."

"Which reminds me," she said, "please give my very best wishes to your Mr. Luce. All right, then, how about half the royalties?"

"That's very generous of you. But the objection remains the same. The truth is, I couldn't afford to do it for all the royalties. Money isn't really the main point here, Mrs. Belzner."

"Then what is?" she asked.

"The main point is that I have to get on with my life. There are literary projects of my own that I would like to work on."

"I don't know what these things might be," she said, "but how can they be more important than seeing that the books of Zalman Belzner, a man who belongs to world literature, find their rightful readers? Let's not kid ourselves, Mr. Berman. What you are going to write for yourself cannot compare with the writing of Zalman Belzner."

This was an argument I had no way of winning — at least not with this intense little woman sitting across the table from me. I told her I would have to think it over. We had rice pudding and coffee. Mrs. Belzner was without small talk, or at least any that she wished to expend on me. She repeated the urgency of getting all of Zalman Belzner's works into good English-language editions as soon as possible. She went into a little tirade against Isaac Bashevis Singer, who had been so fortunate in his translators, but whose filthy writings could not compare with those of her husband.

"Zalman Belzner is a very great writer, as you know maybe as well as anyone in this country, present company excepted," she said. "Someday, with God's help and yours and mine, Mr. Berman, he will have the readership he deserves." She touched my hand as she said this. I looked into her eyes and saw, for the first and only time in all my days, what it meant to have a true mission in life.

When we parted outside the restaurant, I told her I would call her within the next few weeks. I had agreed to take one of her husband's novels home to read, and I now shifted it to my left hand in order to shake her own small, bony, and dry hand. I watched her walk off down Broadway, her thin legs in high-heeled boots, swinging her Klein's bag before disappearing amid a wild assortment of kids in scruffy Afros, elderly Jewish couples, drugged-out hippies, failed hustlers, and who knew how many others with spoiled ambitions and busted dreams, none of whom had ever heard or could possibly ever hear of Zalman Belzner.

I had already made up my mind at the restaurant not to take on the translation of any of these novels. The whole thing was hopeless. At *Time* I had long since been taken off Milestones and been made a general editor. I was doing the occasional book review. I was called in to help edit the magazine's larger culture stories. One of the senior editors let me know that the magazine was soon going to need a new theater critic and asked if I had any interest in the job. In short, it was no time for me to be spending all my free hours sweating over books about old Jews cavorting around Eastern Europe in a culture that had long since been wiped out.

In the cab on the way back to the Time-Life Building, I thought I would write Gerda Belzner a letter in which I would set out my responsibilities to my career, to my family, and to myself, and how I must give these priority. Even she could see that first things came first — that the living have a greater claim on us than the dead. And if she couldn't see it, well, too damn bad.

I didn't have much luck with the letter. I intended it to be less than a page, but it kept running on, in one version to five full pages before I even got to my wife and family. I attempted a second draft and then a third, both unsatisfactory.

A couple of weeks after our lunch, Gerda Belzner phoned.

"Mr. Berman," she began, "I have called to report to you that Zalman Belzner's reputation is in peril."

"In peril?" I asked. "How in peril, Mrs. Belzner?"

"An essay on Yiddish writers appears in a Philadelphia Jewish paper, *The Investigator* — maybe you know it? It pretends to discuss Yiddish literature and yet it makes no mention, none whatsoever, of Zalman Belzner. Mr. Berman, it is incumbent on you to write a strong letter of complaint to the editor. It wouldn't be such a bad idea to do it on your company stationery. In this letter you might say that the failure to mention Zalman Belzner in such an article is not an oversight but an outrage, which no serious student of Yiddish literature can be expected to tolerate."

"Mrs. Belzner," I said, "the absence of mention of your husband is a serious mistake, I agree, but it is not slanderous. I think we'd do best to let it pass."

I scarcely noticed the *we* crossing my lips. "In any case, Mrs. Belzner," I continued, "I don't think a letter of protest would be quite in order. I'm not sure what would be, but let me think further about it."

"You'll call me back?" she said.

"Yes, of course," I said.

Before the week was out, my wife's water broke, at two in the morning. In good sit-com fashion, I woke our daughter and brought her over to our neighbors, the Hoffmans, with whom we had become good friends. And then, forgetting my wife's already packed small suitcase, I called a cab. We were waiting downstairs when I realized my error. Back in the apartment, I remembered that I might be spending hours in the maternity waiting room and scuttled about for something to read. I came up with *Yeshiva Bokher,* the novel in Yiddish that I had taken from Gerda Belzner on the day of our lunch.

Naomi was twenty hours in labor, during which time I finished more than 400 pages of Zalman Belzner's 626-page novel about life at one of the great rabbinical schools in Lithuania in the late nineteenth century. It was brilliant stuff, entrancing, absolutely dazzling. As I read its confidently cadenced Yiddish, all I could think about was proper English equivalents. A fair amount of the material in the novel had to do with complex Jewish texts, mostly legal, about which I knew next to nothing. Any translator would have to be versed in them and in the historical life of the time. Nearly twice the length of *Beyond the Pale, Yeshiva Bokher* was in every way a much denser and more difficult work, requiring at least two years, maybe more, to render into English. A job not likely to be done again soon, if ever, it had to be done supremely well.

To be a translator was to be at best a secondary figure. To be a translator from Yiddish, a language now plundered for its idioms mainly by comedians and spoken by nobody under fifty not wearing a black hat — this was hopeless, to condemn oneself to the periphery of a periphery. Why was I so drawn to it? Even now I can't say. All I can provide by way of explanation, to myself if to no one else, is a line from Keats that I must have picked up at Yale, probably in Cleanth Brooks's class on the Romantics: "so I may do the deed/That my own soul has to itself decreed."

My newborn son weighed seven pounds six ounces. Two days before his bris in our apartment, my wife yielded to my wish to name him Zachariah. Since neither of our families had any relatives with names beginning with the letter *Z*, it was a mystery to everyone in attendance. To everyone, that is, but a small woman with dyed red hair and too much makeup, who, with the look of a fanatic in her eye, stood off in the corner, spoke to no one, and never smiled. She had arrived at the bris without a gift for our new baby but with a heavily laden bag from Klein's, and she departed empty-handed before the food was served.

ALICE FULTON

A Shadow Table

FROM *Tin House*

IN FOX'S SWEET SHOPPE, I once saw a woman take off her shoe, unscrew the heel, and drink from it like a shot glass. I could almost taste the vinegar of home brew mixed with the grit from her lizard pump. "Thirst," I said, "the eighth deadly sin, right after gluttony." And my fiancé, Ray Northrup, smiled between spoonfuls of his ice cream soup.

Frozen treats named for hot places — Hawaii Frappés, Pompeii Phosphates — were all the rage, but Ray was the only one who liked his ice cream cooked. We were leaving that day for Connecticut, where I would meet his family. As he ate, I packed the makings of a special birthday dessert in a cooler. As long as things stayed chilled, we'd be all right.

Stamford was in a different state from Watervliet, and it was a long, cold trip down. Ray said driving made him so hungry he wanted to rip the lid off and eat the dessert ingredients with his bare hands. I knew what he meant. I was a lot hungrier than he was, though I'd never admit it. Starvation is easier than moderation. That's why we had Prohibition instead of temperance and why I'd eaten nothing but tea and crackers for two weeks.

It was a time of boyish silhouettes — corsets that flattened the bosom, dropped waistlines that dissolved the waist. The minute I'd noticed my hips thickening, I'd disciplined myself to thinness. But the more I tried to reduce, the more attracted I became to food. Once I understood how much food meant to me, I began to fear it. Still, I wanted to be around it — to smell it, touch it. That's how I came to be a waitress. I wanted to serve food. And I wanted to serve Ray.

We both were starving. We had that in common. The difference was I tamed my hunger by not eating and Ray tamed his by eating to his heart's content. We were well suited as Jack Sprat and wife.

Working at the Sweet Shoppe, I'd learned you could cook with cold instead of heat. Once, the stove had been the heart of the home. Now it was the icebox. I counted on the draft seeping through the car windows to preserve the dessert ingredients on the way down to Connecticut. To amuse ourselves, we listed anything green we spotted outside. Ray said it would quench our thirst for spring. But on that snowy drive, there wasn't much green to be found — some pine trees, maybe, a child's hat.

Night had fallen by the time we got to Stamford. As we pulled in the driveway, I made out stone fences and a big white house. It was lovely at first sight, even in the dark.

"Someone's coming," I said.

Ray said, "Oh, that must be our maid."

I laughed.

Then I saw she was wearing a white paper tiara like the frill on a lamb chop, and I faltered on the path behind him, distracted.

"Hello, Bridget. Is Mother awake?" His father was abroad on business. "Are there any leftovers?" he said.

Waitressing appeals to people who like to leave a place neater and cleaner than they found it. I felt equal to the responsibilities of the Sweet Shoppe, which included wiping a lot of white marble, humoring customers who wanted their ice cream on top of their topping, and turning a blind eye to the owner's bootlegging business. I think Ray fell for me because I was so unlike any other girl he'd met. He could confide in me and not feel judged, and this meant a lot to him. It meant he could bring up the notion of sweet suppers, for one thing. Just us, he said. Just desserts. Would you? Why, sure I would, I said.

Our sweet suppers took place after hours at the Shoppe. I served sponges, dumplings, puffs, puddings, creams, jellies, delights, supremes, Bettys, gems, jewels, rolls, tortes, tarts, meringues, kisses, and floating islands. Ray feasted while I sipped tea. At first he wanted me to join in, but soon my fasting began to seem natural. He never nagged me to eat or noticed my weight loss, and this made me feel acceptable. Ray was a student of Rensselaer Polytechnic Institute, remember, not a student of human nature. His interests were mechanical, scientific. When it came to people, he was innocent. He wasn't a soul searcher, I knew he'd never delve, and being with him was peaceful for that reason.

Private. It was private.

The other day I came across an old photo album. The pictures show my sisters and me at home, standing in front of broken barbed-wire fences and splintery woodpiles with drainpipes and clotheslines and dead trees growing out of our heads. I could tell which photos were taken by Ray because he posed me between plum blossoms. My family had no sense of background. Some might say we were raised to aim low, but I'd say we chose our disappointments just as others choose their battles. After Catholic High, I'd received a scholarship to St. Rose and turned it down so I could make money and help out at home. My neighbor went to St. Rose and afterward she got a big desk job with the state. A big desk with her name on it.

The Northrups' living room had tall windows and flowers in crystal. It had easy chairs, and bridge lamps that swiveled to throw the light just so, an upright piano and twirling banisters. Wallpaper with a small raised figure. Their dining room suite looked like swans trying to be furniture. Ray introduced me to the maid, who actually did a little curtsy. I did one back, and he laughed and squeezed my hand, but I could tell from her expression that it was the wrong thing to do. I made a mental note: *Do not curtsy to the servants.*

She grabbed the cooler, and Ray asked what birthday dessert I'd planned. He asked in a dreamy way, but my answer was no-nonsense. I said it was one of those unforgiving delicacies that had to be made perfectly the first time; there'd be no second chance. Remember, Ray liked his ice cream cooked. It was hard for him to understand the danger of melting. "Couldn't you refreeze it?" he said. Tinkering with mechanical things, he'd come to believe anything broken could be fixed. "Couldn't you buy more and start again?" Nothing could be ruined for him, you see. He was a hopeless optimist. This meant he saw me through a mist and thought all he had to do was say "Here's Charlotte" and everyone would gasp and say what a find he'd found. I had no such expectation.

When the maid left, he ran his finger down the piano keys and said he'd often thought of me being there. Then he shrugged his shoulders like a little thrill had passed through and said maybe we could have one of our sweet suppers some night after his mother had gone to bed. Now wait a minute, I thought. Making a birthday dessert for his sister was one thing, but sneaking around a strange kitchen, playing with sugar . . . "I don't know," I said. "What if your mother wakes up?" I was eager to meet her and get first impressions over with.

"She won't."

"Reach for a Lucky instead of a sweet." I smiled and offered him a cigarette.

I fully expected our families to have differences. Mother had no patience with la-di-da ladies. All her buddies were men. She felt comfortable bossing them; she liked to hold the reins. Although she couldn't swim, she once ran into Lake George, shoes and all, and saved a child from drowning. She had such confidence. If I married Ray, I'd have to leave her, my family, Watervliet, the Catholic Church, and live in Connecticut the rest of my life. Where was I most wanted? Who needed me most? That's how I thought about it. Sometimes I considered what I'd be giving up either way. I thought about giving up a lot.

I once asked Ray if Episcopals had Lent. Why yes, he said. So I asked if he'd ever given up sweets for Lent. Why no, he said, he'd never given up anything. How could anyone live without abstinence? That was my question.

The church had some odd answers. My aunt, who was a Sister of Mercy, knew them all. She told me if I married a Protestant, I'd be excommunicated and go to hell. If I married Ray, she said she'd pray every night that he would die before me. That way, the marriage would be over, and I could go to heaven. But how could it be heaven without Ray? I asked. Charlotte, you can't change paradise to please yourself, she said. What I wanted wasn't part of the picture. It was easier to think of what I didn't want.

Like the time I didn't want to be a waitress. It happened right after a father came in the Sweet Shoppe with his little girl. She was a beautiful child in perfect health. It must have been a big day because she was all dolled up in dotted swiss and patent leather shoes she kept showing off. The father ordered our Xanadu Special Nut

Sundae for her, and I served it with a smile. I can still see my hands on the dish, handing it over. The next thing I knew, this beautiful child was choking. The father jumped up and called to me for help, but I froze to the spot as everything went topsy-turvy. He turned her upside down and held her by her ankles and shook her till the bow fell from her hair and you could see her drawers, and tears ran into her bangs. He yelled, Hit her, hit her! because he didn't have a free hand to do it himself. Another customer started hitting her, but it didn't do any good, so the father laid her on the floor, where she had a fit. The other customer yelled, Get a spoon, she'll swallow her tongue! I did, but she was still by then.

You can see how flawed I was. Yet people said I was good. Psychology was just getting started, and no one put any stock in it. Everybody came up with their own theories. Mine was: some people are doomed to be good. They can't help it any more than Episcopals can help being Episcopal. Saints don't deserve special credit — they'd be worse if their nature allowed.

Anyway, I was no goody two-shoes. My boss, Harry Fox, saw to that. He had a still in the cellar of the Sweet Shoppe, where he manufactured Father Harry's Medicine for Coughs That Hang On. I thought his slogan, *If Not, Why Not,* made people remember why not. Mother could have come up with something better. She had some catchy sayings: *Don't come home if you get killed. The past is always with us. A move is as bad as an accident. Time won't tell.*

Actually, it was a Sweet Shoppe accident that led to my romance with Ray. I was pouring coffee for him when the chief of police walked in. My boss, Harry Fox, bumped into me as he ran out, and the boiling coffee splashed onto my arm. Ray drove me to the hospital, where they diagnosed a third-degree burn. Don't worry, doll, Harry said when he saw the scar. It's a long way from your heart.

As Ray showed me around his family's home that first night, I noticed everything was imported from afar. They had French scrap baskets, Venetian glassware, Japanese lacquer trays, Dutch silver boudoir lamps, a Chinese dinner gong, and Yorkshire singing canaries. "But nothing from Watervliet till you," Ray said, and I laughed.

"A gift from Mother," he said, handing me a book from an end table. I'd been wondering why his mother hadn't stayed up to greet us. This made me feel more welcome.

"*Honorable Daughter,*" I read.

"It's almost her Bible."

"I'll start it tonight."

"There's an inscription," he said.

"'To Grace, the sweetest child in the world.'" Grace was Ray's sister, the birthday girl. There was a picture of a plum blossom on the opposite page.

"Mother used to read it to us before we went to sleep."

"I hope Grace likes her dessert." Why was Mrs. Northrup giving me her daughter's book?

"Sugar Girl," Ray said. "There's something you should know."

Some people would have demanded the secret there and then, others would have nagged it out gradually, but the author of *Honorable Daughter* would have done exactly what I did. Like me, she'd been taught that questions were unladylike. She had this tendency to bow and scrape and back respectfully out of a room, and a heart that could be killed with shame.

We had a late dinner. The maid had left, so I did her duties. As a waitress, you learn to be attentive to the needs of others. Ray was easy. All he needed was understanding and permission to live a little.

As we sipped our coffee, he asked me to forgive him for something that might seem sneaky but was more a sin of omission. He was worried I'd mistrust him, but I did not share this fear. Something inside me had decided to love him all my life, and I knew he couldn't talk me out of it. You loved someone or you didn't.

He took my hand. "Will you read the book? *Honorable Daughter?*"

Now, I was no reader of books. I liked the newspaper. "Why, sure I will," I said, with a smile.

Ray nodded. He cleared his throat. "Mother and Father lived in Japan for years," he said. "My sister, Grace, died while they were there. I was so young I hardly remember."

"Your sister, Grace?" My voice went loud with shock. "She passed away?"

"I'm sorry I never mentioned it. It's just, I didn't want to be glum." He blushed and fumbled for a cigarette. "Mother still celebrates Grace's birthday every year with a shadow table in her honor. It's a Japanese custom. Do you understand, old pal?" He fanned the smoke away from my face. "Do you?"

"I do," I said.

And we fell silent. We sat there looking out the window at the snow coming down in tatters. The dining room was drafty; it was like being in the car except we weren't going anywhere. I was thinking of the day my brother, James, died. He was two, and I was eleven. He'd had his oatmeal that morning, like always, and put the empty bowl on his head, like he always did, to make us laugh. All gone! he said. It always made us laugh. He had this little cough, nothing serious. Then, about an hour after breakfast, his breathing got raspy, and Mother told me to fetch the Vicks VapoRub. She put some on, but in no time he was struggling. His lips turned blue, but he was too sick to cry the way a baby should. Mother held him in her lap, and that's where he died. It all happened so quickly. I hid in the back kitchen. I'd never seen Mother so upset, and it scared me.

The wake was in our tiny parlor. I recall it very mistily. There were flowers and a plate of divinity brought by a neighbor. Papa led me over and told me to kiss James goodbye. I was shocked by how cold he was, like a baby made of snow. The hearse was pulled by horses with big plumes on their heads and big dark oily eyes and smoke pouring from their noses. Men carried the casket out. It was small and white as a wedding cake. And every Sunday after this, Mother would pack a picnic, and we'd walk to the cemetery to eat and play around James's grave. Of course I understood a shadow table.

In my room that night, I started reading *Honorable Daughter,* as promised. The author, Kikuno Takamoto, wrote about her childhood in old Japan, in a world of propriety and restraint. As a samurai girl, Kikuno had been taught to discipline her mind and body even in sleep. Boys could sleep carelessly outstretched, but girls had to curl themselves into the character *kinoji,* meaning "spirit of control." Like the plum blossom, their bridal flower that bloomed in snow, girls had to bear hardship and injustice without complaint and move without abrupt unceremony. Kikuno said she'd once been scolded for shifting her position slightly during a lesson, and the shame still burned in her a lifetime later.

Reading this, I remembered my boss's daughter, who refused to raise her hand or speak in school. Harry Fox said he'd tried everything from coaxing to whipping. She had been whipped till he declared he would not whip her anymore, as it did not help. He'd threatened to wash her mouth out with soap if she did not speak. What more can I do? he'd asked.

The snow crackled like a fire against the window as I read, and I lost track of time. It must have been after midnight when I came to the true story of the handmaid. She'd committed an unforgivable breach of etiquette by talking alone with a beautiful youth. Suicide was the only honorable option. Accepting her fate, she washed off her rouge, tied her hair with the paper death bow, donned her white death robe, and went to the room where her lord was waiting. There was a ceremony for suicide, and she knew it. She kneeled and bowed deeply to her lord. Then, facing west, she tightly bound her folded knees with her long crepe sash and pressed her dagger to her throat. But instead of dying bravely, she clumsily flung out one arm, staining the wall with her open hand.

Her story reminded me that you could get hurt while serving others. Once my hand got crushed in a swinging door. Another time, while drying dishes, I forced my hand inside a glass and could not get it out. I panicked, the glass broke, and blood went flying.

But my most humiliated moment happened during a sweet supper with Ray. He was eating a burnt sugar cake and I was having tea and crackers. I took a sip of tea and started choking so badly that the tea came out my nose. It was over in a minute, and we tried to go on as if nothing had happened. Ray began talking about a sage who'd cut off his eyelids in mortification after falling asleep during meditation and how the first tea bushes had sprouted from his eyelids. That must have been a sweet sight, I said. And we laughed and never mentioned my disgrace again. Silence is the best medicine, they say.

That night in Connecticut, I dreamed of frozen flowers. I dreamed I was eating them. They were noisy things to eat. In the morning, I saw the picture on the bedroom wall was one Mother had at home, *The Helping Hand.* It shows a little girl and an old fisherman rowing a boat. The little girl looks so honored to be helping. If Harry Fox asked my advice again, I'd say, Honor thy daughter. That's a commandment.

Of course, I felt for Mrs. Northrup over the loss of Grace. And her passion for Japan filled me with awe. I supposed she'd have impeccable manners and want everything just so. Had I packed enough ladyfingers? My dessert seemed even more critical now that I knew about the shadow table.

The next morning Ray had errands in town, so we ate quickly. His mother never had breakfast. After he left, I asked Bridget, the maid, about the food I'd brought, and she led me to an unheated sun porch where the less perishable ingredients had been stacked beside a linen-covered box. She went about her business then, and I began my inventory. Snow rustled against the house, and I thought a blizzard must be brewing.

As I counted the ladyfingers, I glimpsed something moving on the edge of the waxed paper. I focused then and saw a big greenish white caterpillar moseying along, all fat and creamy. I gasped, for I'd never seen a bug so out of this world. It was quaint as a toy. As I backed away, I was startled by a voice. *I see you've met one of my little friends.*

I turned to find a smartly dressed lady in the doorway. "How do you do," I said.

"I've made pets of them." She held out her finger and the bug toddled onto it. It looked like a dollop of whipped cream. "You're not frightened, are you? Because that would be foolish." She moved her finger closer to my face. "They don't have lungs, but they do have a heart. You can see it beating."

"They're like . . . animals," I said.

"They're domesticated insects. *Bombyx mori.* They'll eat out of your hand."

"That sound. I thought it was snow."

"It's their jaws. They nibble constantly. Yet they're dainty about food. One wilted leaf will send them foraging."

She let the caterpillar creep into the box next to my ingredients. Then she opened another container. "They spin these cocoons to protect themselves. But, alas, it doesn't help."

Eager to change the subject, I said I'd like to be useful during my visit. "If there's any cooking I can do . . ."

"You could boil the cocoons," she said. "They have to be boiled alive, poor dears."

The blood drained from my head. They must be a delicacy like lobster. I'd rather drink a pint of gall, I thought. "Why, surely," I said.

"I keep some for the next generation," she continued. "Their eggs can be stored in the refrigerator for years. I have some in there now."

"Do they go for" — I waved at my ingredients — "sweets?"

"Sweets? I should say not! They like mulberry leaves. Though mine are raised on lettuce."

With that, she hustled off, and I plopped into a chair, still gripping the ladyfingers.

When Ray got home, he showed me around the garden, which was planned especially for winter. He lit a candle in a stone lantern designed to hold snow on its roof, and we admired the shadow it cast.

"These trees," he said, taking my hand and leading me over, "were planted to frame that distant steeple. It's called captured scenery. Another Japanese idea." I shivered and he moved closer. Hunger made me feel the cold. "You met Mother's silkworms."

"Silkworms."

"Bridget boils a few cocoons for the thread, but Mother isn't really interested in their silk." He rubbed my hands as if he could start a fire with them. "Mother said you were *wabi*."

"What's that?"

"A compliment."

"Tell me about the shadow supper."

"Shadow supper?" He frowned a little.

"The memorial dinner. On Grace's birthday."

"Oh, the shadow table. It's Mother's version of an old custom. It's also *wabi*."

"Translate, please."

"Genuine," he said, as we walked toward the house. "Good."

We were sitting in the living room, listening to a radio Ray had built himself, when Mrs. Northrup came in. She handed me a blue silk kimono, saying it was a gift and wasn't it a pity no one did such exquisite work anymore. Then she took up some lacework or tatting. Her thread was coiled around a wooden spike in the center of a bucket. Ray, meanwhile, was tuning in a distant station.

"Can you guess what this once was?" She nodded at the bucket.

"An ice cream churn?"

"You must be an expert on those, given your line of work."

"Tell Charlotte about the shadow table," Ray said. He had one ear glued to the radio.

"This was a head bucket," his mother continued. "When a samurai committed suicide —"

"The shadow table," Ray interrupted, "is for an absent family member. Their place is set, and they're served their favorite foods." He turned to his mother. "Charlotte's planning a grand dessert for Grace's shadow table."

"Grace's dessert will be pure snow," his mother said. "Pure snow, fresh from the sky, gathered from a tree, and seasoned with maple syrup. That was her favorite."

"Charlotte went to a lot of trouble —"

"That's okay," I said quickly. "It should be pure snow."

"Snow nothing!" said Ray in exasperation. "Where's my radio map?" And he went off looking for it.

Mrs. Northrup licked her thread. "Raymond is being honored, you know."

I nodded. I hadn't known.

"At the radio awards ceremony tomorrow." And she told me the nominees' dates brought sweets to celebrate their escorts. That was the custom. Rubbing her thread to a point, she said my dressy dessert would be ideal.

"To honor Ray? Why, surely."

"Then it's settled," Mrs. Northrup said, her needle threaded.

I spent the next day splitting, crumbing, mixing, whipping, beating, boiling, standing, draining, pouring, setting, and chilling, in honor of Ray.

That evening we took Mr. Northrup's Packard to the awards dinner. There was no sign saying COUNTRY CLUB. You just had to know about it, like a speakeasy. The grounds were largely snowy fields with green links underneath. A maid was taking the desserts at the door. Please, I said, handing mine over, keep this cold.

Inside, people clustered around setups of White Rock and ginger ale. A girl called out, Old flame! Old sweetheart! She hustled over, dragging her date, and Ray introduced us. They were Pearl and Oliver. Pearl's dress was the last word — black crepe with steel disks. Slashed arms. She had platinum hair and a chinchilla wrap. I could see it was a reversible affair and very costly.

"How is Honorable Mother?" Pearl said. Ray and Oliver were checking our coats. "Still raising her silkworms? Has she tried to bribe you with an old kimono?"

"Bribe?"

"No girl's good enough. Hold out for the jewelry. Did she give you material for an obi?"

"I beg your —"

"A cummerbund made from twelve yards of brocade. You fold it in and fold it in till it's this thick." She measured air with her fingers. "It's a shame to hide such magnificent stuff. I had mine made into a train. Oh, and I still have that queer little book about Japan."

"Honorable Daughter?"

She laughed. "My favorite was the soldier whose enemies didn't lock the prison because they knew he was too polite to leave."

"Too honorable," I said.

"Far too honorable. Ray was raised on that hogwash. It explains a lot."

"Like what?"

"Oh, you know." She wrinkled her nose.

I folded my arms and looked her in the eye. "Ray is good," I said. "He's a prince."

"If you like that kind of thing," Pearl said, as we followed the boys to our table.

Once we sat down, Ray produced a silver flask and poured some in our drinks. He was saying he'd been nominated for a silly prize given to the man whose homemade radio could pull in the most distant station. Pearl pointed her long cigarette holder at me. "You'll be the one to present the prize, as your initiation." Now wait a minute, I thought.

Meanwhile, my dessert had been placed on the table. Oliver said it should be called Mount Everest Surprise because if we ate all that, we'd suffer the fate of the last expedition. And he told how some climbers failed near the summit, and two made the top only to die there of exposure. Or possibly one slipped, and being roped together, the pair fell to their deaths in the eternal ice of the Himalayas. As he was talking, something white flew across the table and hit Ray's lapel.

"Charlotte, your dessert has met with an accident," Pearl said, flinging another spoonful. "It has been injured. Your dessert has suffered. It has been wronged."

Ray shook his head as if she were a spoiled child and dabbed at his tuxedo. Catching my eye, he smiled and licked some whipped cream from his finger with a blissful expression. Another spoonful sailed across then, landing in his hair. He held up his palms, signaling stop, but she scooped up more sugar ammunition. Oliver was laughing and the band was playing hard. Ray mouthed, I'll be back, as he got up and moved off through the smoke and saxophones. Old flame, Pearl called after him, it was entirely my fault, I could just weep with sorrow. Black olives, salted nuts, and peppermints littered the table, the ashtrays were overflowing, and the help had mostly left. I saw my dessert was in ruins, beyond repair.

"Ray looked like he'd been used to wrap a workman's lunch," Pearl said with satisfaction. She took a swig from Oliver's flask. "Let's speak Japanese," she commanded. "Charlotte first."

"I only know one word."

"Tell."

"Wabi."

"What's it mean?" Oliver asked.

"Boring," Pearl said. "Amuse me."

Oliver stuck out one of his legs and tripped a waiter carrying an ice bucket.

"That man nearly fell," I said. Somebody could get hurt.

"I'll leave the fellow a large tip," Oliver said.

The band was taking a break, and someone was playing a ukulele and singing "Show Me the Way to Go Home" under the table next to ours. Pearl leaned over and whispered in my ear: "Why do you want to come here, anyway? No one knows you, and you won't have any friends."

I couldn't sit a minute longer looking at the crumbs and ashes. I began stacking the dirty dishes along my arm, so I could clear the table in one trip. "That's quite a balancing act, Lottie," Pearl said, shoving her slave bracelets higher. "That's quite a stunt. Oliver, look what a good little waitress she is."

I sidled between the drunks and dancers and set the dishes down near the kitchen. Then I saw Ray was back at our table. He kept swiveling in his chair, looking around, and I knew he was looking for me. I could see last summer's freckles on his skin and his lush, lush lips. That contrast always killed me. What else did my Sugar Boy look like? Like every young man in love, I guess, except that he was mine.

Though the band wasn't playing, some couples were dancing.

One group had spread their tablecloth on the floor for a picnic. A girl was bent over double, laughing. Every time she straightened up, she was struck by another bout of hilarity, and so she jackknifed back and forth, like someone bowing or being sick. There was such a din I hardly heard my name being paged for the award presentation. People were throwing sweets at each other, and I was afraid I'd get hit with a pie before I made it to the stage. I knew in Japan silence was the greatest tribute given an accomplishment, yet I wanted applause for Ray; I wanted the lift of pride it would bring.

When I got to the podium, the bandleader handed me an envelope, but before I could open it, a gust of wind hurricaned up from the floor. Later I realized there was a fan hidden under the stage, positioned to perfectly shame. But when it happened I didn't know what was happening. I froze in place, too petrified to move, while my skirt went up like a flame, exposing everything, and the room erupted in wolf whistles and laughter. These mockeries blended with a roaring in my ears. I hadn't eaten all day, remember. I'd only had doctored drinks. I reached toward the mike to steady myself as a powerful weakness surged through me, and I knew I was going before I was gone.

Ray was bending over me when I came to. I heard people saying give her space, air, water, uncut Park Avenue gin. He kept telling me I was all right, and I tried to act that way as we hurried to the car. He said they were asses. He said Pearl was a vampire. I asked who won the award, and he said another fellow, and he was sorry because it would have given him such pleasure to throw it back in their faces.

We got in his father's car, and he took a drink from his flask. When he was upset, Ray liked to talk about things at a distance. Now he brought up bootleg silk — how once upon a time, Persian monks hid silkworm eggs in their walking sticks and smuggled them out of China. I marveled that something so delicate could make it through that long journey alive.

I had a bad headache and felt queasy. I tried to fight it, but my body was in charge. It was frightening to be so out of control. Everything's coming up, I said. Here? he said. Now? He stopped the car and rushed around and opened my door. We were blocking the clubhouse driveway; everyone was in back of us, in their cars, all eyes. No, I said. Not outside. I wanted to be sick in the car, in private. I thought I could use the cooler. I didn't want an audience.

Ray tugged on my arm and tried to help me out of the car. No, I said. Please. He said his parents would never understand, while the people here didn't matter. I knew he wanted to avoid a mess, but the urgency in his voice sounded like annoyance. I knew he was being practical, but I felt forced.

He didn't understand how deeply shaming this would be.

Until that instant, I would have trusted him with my life. Now I felt he'd let me suffer to keep things smooth. I felt sacrificed. But I had no choice. I was in his hands. And when a door is held open, you go through.

Snow filled my shoes, and the scar on the white of my arm from the old accident, the scalding, glowed like a plum blossom in the moonlight. People swerved around us, honking and yelling and hitting me with their headlights as I sank to my knees.

Afterward, he asked if I was all right. My shoe had come off, and he picked it up and shook the snow out. Everyone else had left. He asked if I'd like to go back and get my dessert, so we could eat it at home — because from the little taste he'd had, it was really something, an accomplishment. Sugar Girl, why don't you answer? he said.

He said he knew he was flawed, a letdown, but I was the only unselfish person he'd ever met, he only felt at home with me, and wasn't that the true test of friendship. Then he said he was thirsty and gave his flask a little shake. All gone, he said.

At that moment I wanted nothing more than to wash my mouth out with snow.

As we stood there shivering, he started talking about Japanese lovers, how they never kissed. "How do they express their devotion without kissing?" he asked. "Is it possible?"

It was only because of my education in Connecticut that I knew the answer.

"Why, sure it is," I said. "Don't you remember? In moments of passion, they gently turn their backs on each other." I held out a handful of snow, and he put his mouth to it, cold and pure and burning.

KARL TARO GREENFELD

NowTrends

FROM *American Short Fiction*

WHEN I SET OUT for Chengdu, in the middle of our country, to interview Xiu Xi, I carried in my jacket pocket an envelope full of kwai — I hadn't been told the amount — which I was to hand over to Xiu's manager if I found upon arrival that the starlet was unavailable or noncooperative; her way of saying, Pay me, please. If everything went smoothly and we completed the story and photo shoot without a problem, I was to return to Beijing with the envelope, which I would then hand back to my publisher. At that point, I assumed, the publisher would request from Xiu Xi's manager a payment to place her on the cover.

We are at the stage in our great socialist experiment when we are no longer sure who should pay whom. In the past it was clear: the subject of the story would discreetly, or not so discreetly, hand over an envelope full of kwai to the journalist, and a larger sum would be paid to the publisher. Stories and photos, it was understood, were nothing more than advertising for the person or venture being profiled. But magazines like mine soon discovered that certain prominent cultural heroes — actors, athletes, telecom moguls — actually helped us sell magazines if we put them on the cover. So we began to pay to these subjects their own red envelopes of so-called lucky money. Now, because all parties involved find the issue awkward and hard to broach beforehand, we don't always know upon undertaking a new story which way the money should flow.

Xiu Xi was an emerging actress, as famous for her appearance in a handbag advertisement as for the supporting roles she had played in two films by a Taiwanese director (handbag advertisements, in our country, being more closely scrutinized and discussed than feature films). Her popularity wasn't such that we could be sure she would sell magazines, but it seemed likely she would be a successful cover subject, and so I was dispatched, after her management agreed that she would sit down for an interview. I was a trusted member of our editorial staff, considered politically reliable and perhaps our best-known writer. I had completed Beida and even won a fellowship to a journalism school in America for one semester; that had been a confusing four months spent in a small apartment on Manhattan's Upper West Side and attending lectures where various questions of journalistic ethics were raised. In the United States reporters do not pay for stories. I found this practice to be admirable. When I spent two weeks over the holiday known in the United States as spring break at the offices of a prestigious American magazine in midtown Manhattan, I asked several of the editors there if it was true that they didn't pay their cover subjects, and they all concurred. That was wonderful, I told them. I imagined that a magazine as prestigious as theirs must extract huge fees from those wanting to appear on their cover. They explained I was mistaken. No money changed hands. That seemed to me to be terribly wasteful.

While that American magazine had been founded, many years ago, as a weekly magazine, the magazine I worked for in China had started in the 1980s as a monthly journal of the goings-on of the young bureaucrats — those under sixty years old — of two interministry departments in charge of culture and telecommunications. To comply with PPP regulations, we still bear our original name, *The Journal of Interministry Junior Cadre Affairs,* in small characters beneath the much larger title by which we are better known, *NowTrends.* We have a staff of thirty-six, many of whom work in both editorial and publishing. Our publisher is also our editor in chief, and I have known him since we were at Beida; he was once a very fine writer, perhaps the best in our department, so it was not surprising that he would take over his own magazine and leave writing behind. If you are a creative person, there is only so much you can do in fields like writing or journalism. Business offers more freedom. He has offered several times to promote me to the advertising department of the magazine and seems genuinely disappointed that I have declined. He tells me I could move to a bigger apartment closer to the center of the city, perhaps the third ring road instead of the grubby, smoky little *hutong* that I share with an old couple and a Muslim currency trader. I like my two rooms, though I am quite sure that our little courtyard house has already been earmarked for destruction by some princeling and when it is finally flattened, I will regret not having more money and better connections.

I was looking forward to the trip to Chengdu, to escape the capital for a few days and the frantic Olympic preparations, the strictures against spitting, drinking beer in public, the reminders to queue in orderly fashion. It all seemed so un-Chinese to me that I was beginning to wonder when the antibadminton campaign would begin. Also, an old friend of mine had been living in Chengdu for a few years. He had been a classmate of the publisher's and mine at Beida, another great talent; he would certainly have received the fellowship to study in America if he hadn't been viewed by the professors as politically suspect. After graduating, he became the first of our crowd to become well known when he joined a group of writers and filmmakers, loosely supervised by the PPP, who traveled the country in the mid-nineties, producing a series of ostensibly probusiness documentaries that showed how various entrepreneurs and businessmen were starting to get rich in the new China. Huang had never been a member of the party, of course, and so he had no official role in this troupe, but it was generally known that he had written and conducted most of the interviews for almost the entire ten hours of television. The footage and interviews had been remarkable not because of the portrayal of these new business leaders and their party hack partners but for the poignant and widespread depiction of how China's rural poor were being systematically stripped of their already limited resources and protections. Why the documentary was ever aired on CCTV was a widespread cause for speculation; I believe it was the sentimentality of a few senior leaders who harkened back to the days of the peasant revolution. These nonagenarians would be dead or retired within a few months of the airing of the documentary, and the PPP would subsequently ban the distribution and even the mention of this elegant television production. Huang, of course, could no longer find any work in television, and so he left the capital and moved south, to Guangzhou. For a time he found work at one of the aggressive daily newspapers, before that too was closed and he hit the road again, settling, most recently, in Chengdu.

I had not seen him in a few years, and had always been circumspect in my communication with him because I worried his phone might be tapped and his text messages monitored. He assured me that wasn't the case, that the state security apparatus was not nearly as efficient as it claimed. Then why, I didn't bother to point out to him, was it omniscient enough to blackball him from almost any publication in the country? My boss, the publisher, told me that Huang was a lost cause, a waste of talent. He should have been fabulously wealthy by now, with his brains and his degree. With his talent, there was no limit to how much money he could make in the new China. But Huang, in the publisher's view, was flawed. I could see the publisher saying this as he was stuffing himself with freshwater crab in the banquet room of a Shanghai-style restaurant, using the Chinese word for *flaw,* which has a connotation of a spot of black decay on a perfectly white tooth. (Like most successful Chinese, the publisher never ate in restaurants' main dining rooms anymore; he only ate in private rooms.) I considered for a while whether Huang was flawed, idealistic, or just born in an inauspicious year. It was, I concluded, a combination of all three. The publisher, Huang, and I were all born in 1977. We are all snakes.

Our cities are simultaneously boomtowns and ghost towns. New construction proliferates, yellow cranes extending skyward, steel girder infrastructures jutting out from their unfinished glass-and-concrete sheaths like bones waiting for skin to grow up around them. Once they are completed, however, these new buildings, many of them lavishly fronted and auspiciously named, give the sense of being unoccupied, desolate, despite their strips of shrubbed garden and carefully appointed walkways. For a few hours, in the morning and the evening, the inhabitants emerge from their condominiums to march off to their lucrative jobs, which they might change tomorrow or even today. In America, I had noticed, there was this notion of career, that a young person would join a particular field and then grow old within that sector. Most of my friends change jobs for one reason, money, with little regard for the field they are leaving or entering. This morning's mobile content marketer might be this afternoon's real estate agent and this evening's owner of a Pacific Coffee franchise. We don't find anything strange about that.

Yet these vast new developments are all missing that incessant buzz and thrum of life, the spitting, cigarette smoking, public drinking, and badminton playing that composed the street life of Chinese neighborhoods. The inhabitants here tend to stay home, preferring instead to watch their LCD televisions. I don't know where the children have gone, but they too seem to have disappeared into an endless routine of after-school study programs designed to propel them into the best colleges and then a life of wandering through meaningless, ever higher-paying jobs.

I am to meet Xiu Xi in one of these developments near the center of Chengdu. Many of Chengdu's famous charms — the scholar trees, for example, that somehow were spared the various modernization drives of previous five-year plans — are now finally succumbing to the more ruthless efficiency of capitalism with socialist characteristics. The taxi driver finds the quiver of buildings, which are arrayed along a wide avenue favored by truck drivers heading east. There is a lovely, arched stone bridge over what would be a stream, or moat, I suppose, but is instead dry and into which piles of construction residue — cinder blocks, sand, a twisted metal frame of some kind — have been discarded. The bridge is similar in shape to several I have seen inside the Forbidden City and is intended to lend an air of nobility to this particular conclave of new condominiums. This is the sort of place my friend the publisher has been urging me to buy.

The lobby is vast and attended by two men in black uniforms who sit behind a marble countertop. In their indifference they are identical to the old man who sits at the end of my alley on a overturned bucket and who is supposed to, for a fee of a few kwai a month, "guard" our little house. I tell them where I am going and they point to an elevator that smells strongly of cleaning solvent.

Xiu Xi and her manager are in an apartment near the top of this building, one that offers views over the city, a panorama of more cranes and inchoate buildings just like this one. She appears terribly small at first, delicate, breakable, a physique that is incongruous with her strange posture of slouching down on the brown leather sofa so that she is almost parallel to the floor. Her manager is seated at a glass dining table, talking into a mobile phone about a document that he is reading on a laptop computer screen. The maid who welcomed me into the apartment has vanished back into the kitchen. She reemerges a moment later with see-through plastic cups filled with iced coffee so heavily saturated with milk that it is almost white.

They are here, I will later discover, because Xiu Xi is to become a spokesmodel for this development, her face and lithe figure appearing on billboards throughout the province advertising the virtues of Supreme Confidence Happy Houses. Her manager, a short, slightly chubby man with unkempt hair that hangs down beneath his ears, tells his phone partner that he will be right back and sets down the phone but doesn't bother to stand to greet me.

This is the first time I have ever seen Xiu Xi without makeup, and her face is remarkably plain, nothing more than eyes, nose, and a small, exquisitely shaped mouth that forms a perfect sideways oval with an elegant dip in the center of her upper lip. It is a face, I know, that is easy to fashion with the various tools of the makeup artist into whatever is desired: vamp, ingénue, innocent, hero, victim, star. She can be whoever you need her to be. She acknowledges me with a curt nod and squirms herself into a more upright position, casting a glance at her manager and then smiling at me with closed lips. I sip my milky coffee and stand near the glass dining table, between Xiu Xi and her manager, unsure of where I am supposed to go. This is an awkward moment, and I think for a second about pulling the red envelope from the breast pocket of my jacket but then decide I should wait a moment.

"Welcome to Chengdu," the manager says.

"Thank you."

"You know, they are building a new airport," he says, "another new runway. There will be six flights a day from Hong Kong, a dozen from the capital."

"Exciting," I reply.

"Yes," the manager says, "and the weather, of course, and the food." Chengdu is famous for its putatively spicy cuisine, but as in so many Chinese cities, that cuisine has so quickly been refined and changed over the last few years, it is hard to tell what is a Chengdu dish and what is an imported one. You would have to be a culinary historian to keep track, combing prerevolution texts to really figure out what people were eating in Chengdu before the establishment of the People's Republic. It is a good guess to assume that during the fifties and sixties, the people of Chengdu were eating what the rest of China was eating: nothing. But a rapidly developing city is always quick to latch on to whatever shreds of history it can, and Chengdu loudly celebrates its cuisine.

"Well," I say, "it is certainly a lovely afternoon." I point out the window at the smoggy cityscape.

"Who are you?" Xiu Xi finally says. "Are you from the development corporation?"

"Big sister," the manager intervenes, "he is from the magazine that is celebrating you." She is not his sister, of course. That is just a figure of speech denoting respect and family, but one that is so gratuitously used it now means virtually nothing.

"Sit down," she tells me.

She speaks in an enervated monotone, the vocal equivalent of her blank-canvas face. Her accent is very standard; any traces of the eastern coastal province in which she was born have been flattened out. Her voice, with a little more inflection, some coaching, with the right tonal inflection, could convey worlds, but as it is now, it is as informative as a party boss's speech. Our interview proceeds unevenly, her answers monosyllabic and almost deliberately clichéd. Then Xiu Xi's head drops forward and she falls asleep.

Her manager, who has been behind his computer the whole time, fails to notice her passing out, and so I sit for a while in silence before reaching over and patting Xiu Xi's hand.

"Are you okay?" I ask when her eyes flutter open.

She smiles; this one is real, flared lips, a tiny wrinkle on her neck behind her ear. "You're too handsome to work at a newspaper."

"Magazine," I correct her. "Never mind. Do you need some tea?"

I have been told I have a pleasingly ovoid face — and it does seem that way to me when I look in the mirror, a perfect 0. Those who work at magazines tend not to be the most handsome collection of young men, and so I have been complimented several times when I have gone out on my assignments. I don't dress particularly stylishly, but I do try to at least wear simple clothes, black or white T-shirts beneath black blazers. Still, I am always flattered when I am told I am good-looking. It gives me a feeling that I have options, that a fellow with a pleasing oval face could do whatever he likes in this life.

"Are we finished?" the manager says. He has now risen up and come to stand next to us. "Big sister is very tired."

I don't have enough to fill the pages between the photos, and I haven't even asked the most important question, the one that every interview with a star must lead up to: if you could be any kind of animal, what would you be and why?

"We need to talk a little more," I say.

"Big sister has been working very hard," the manager explains. "Can you call this evening to schedule a time tomorrow?"

I should, I realize, just give them the envelope. But I am petulant about having my afternoon wasted in this manner, so I just nod and bow slightly.

I look at Xiu Xi and she is smiling up at me. She has no idea where she is.

I return to my hotel and leave my briefcase and again call my old friend Huang. A drugged-out starlet is a problem I would like to forget for a few hours, and I am eager to meet him. I texted him and told him I would be arriving in town and that I would call. He never picked up or returned my calls, and now, when I try to reach him, instead of Huang another man answers, saying only, "Who is this?"

"Who are you?" I say.

"I am here with Huang," he says.

"Let me talk to him," I tell him.

"Are you a family member?"

I am about to say I am an old friend but for some reason I instead say, "He is an acquaintance."

"Huang is being detained for his own safety. He has violated state security regulations too numerous to mention," he explains. "I am a state security officer."

"What did he do?" I ask. "Where is he?"

He tells me that Huang is at a police station on the other side of Chengdu. For a fee, I could see him. Also, if I would like Huang to have food and tea, I should bring a small donation. Ask for Officer Hu, he says.

My heart is pounding when I hang up and I wonder if I should call the publisher. I don't know where Huang's family is. I assume they are somewhere in his native Hebei, but Huang has never mentioned them to me. I am surprised that Huang would be detained.

For the past few years, I had thought he was doing part-time work for small advertising agencies, nothing political or even journalistic. Why would they suddenly decide he posed a threat? And these weren't political officers or state security agents, these sounded like local cops.

It is already late afternoon when I take a taxi across town. I am let off in front of what looks like a parking garage. I ask the taxi driver where is the police station and he points into the rows of parked cars. "Back there."

I walk that way, and when I am under the concrete overhang I can see that in the back of the garage there seems to be a bank of windows with men in leisure clothes sitting before them on white plastic chairs. When I approach them and ask if this is the Number Six Sub-Provincial Security Office, there is no response, but when I ask for Officer Hu one of them points into the offices. The pavement here is covered with cigarette butts.

There are two women seated behind a counter, on which placards urge citizens to report suspicious activity and to make sure their vehicles are properly registered and have working brake lights. There are several posters promoting antilitter campaigns and urging that any sellers of counterfeit medicines be reported to the appropriate authorities. Along the wall, seated on the floor beneath the windows, are several men and women in shabby clothing who appear to have been waiting for a long time. There are empty Styrofoam food containers and plastic sweet-tea bottles spread around them. The two women ignore me until I ask them for Officer Hu.

They tell me he is not here.

They do not know when he will return.

"Can you call him?" I ask.

They don't respond.

A woman dressed in a black blouse with a garish flower pattern walks in and rests her gold-jewelry-encrusted arm on the counter. She speaks in a familiar tone in the local dialect to one of the women, who obviously knows her and tells her she can go upstairs. I guess that she is related to an officer, perhaps a wife or mistress.

I look at the line of forlorn citizens resting against the wall and consider leaving the office. Then I remember that Hu had answered Huang's phone and step outside and call the number.

"Yes?"

"I am here to see Huang."

"Ah, you again, with the Beijing accent. Where are you?"

I explain that I am at the Number Six Sub-Provincial Security Office.

"Wait there. I'm having dinner."

So I take my place among my fellow impassive comrades, taking care to lift my jacket up around my waist as my bottom rests on the linoleum floor.

Huang had never been a handsome man, I reflect. He had small eyes and a prominent birthmark on his chin that sprouted a few unsightly, discolored white hairs. (He trimmed them regularly.) In an earlier time, such a feature might have been viewed as lucky. But in our more superficial era, it just seemed impure. Yet his homeliness, I always felt, helped to explain his greater perspicacity; he couldn't rely on getting by on his looks. In college, in our crowded, garlic-smelling dormitory rooms with clotheslines strung across them like a giant cat's cradle, he was the best at mahjong and pai gow, and paid for his meals from his winnings. (He was the only one among us who didn't receive some money from home.) He had always yearned for women who seemed just out of his reach, and while most of us resigned ourselves to the arduous and slow courtship of coeds that was a regular feature of Chinese university life, he condemned this process as pointless and useful only as preparation for marriage, which he dismissed as a trap. We dated our female colleagues but seldom were granted by them any carnal satisfaction; Huang took up with girls from outside the university, some of them dropouts but of high school age. How he managed to keep these karaoke lounge girls happy was a topic of some speculation among the rest of us. Huang finally confessed to me a few years later that he had been using his gambling winnings to pay these companions. Lest I would judge him, he quickly added that a good-looking guy like me doesn't understand how it feels to see that expression of disappointment on every woman he meets.

Anyway, he shrugged, the ends justify the means.

I stand up and bow slightly when Officer Hu appears. I try to appear both confident and supplicating at the same time. One never becomes comfortable dealing with security agents; they are simply too unilaterally powerful, possessing, as they do, the ability to make you disappear. But I am of some use to Officer Hu, and we both know that, so I follow him up a dirty stairwell to his desk, one of four in a smoky, surprisingly orderly office. Above us the ceiling is crisscrossed by thickly painted pipes and gleaming electrical ducts. A rectangular fluorescent light fixture hangs on two chains.

"What is your name?" Hu asks after he has gathered a clipboard holding a form that reads "Relatives and Friends Of," and then, in scribbled handwriting, "863784235."

I tell him a common Chinese name, a surname shared by literally tens of millions.

"Do you have identification?"

I tell him I am sorry but I have forgotten my ID.

"How do you know Huang?"

"He is an acquaintance," I explain. "We know one person in common."

"And who is that?"

I give another very common Chinese name. He knows this is a formality, and that I will avoid giving him any real information about myself. He will tolerate this until he can discern how much money I am willing to sacrifice for my "acquaintance."

Hu has an air of sleepy indifference that fails to hide a seeping, menacing quality that I fear could emerge at any moment. He has a crewcut that is flat on top, a narrow forehead, wide-set eyes, small nose, thin lips, and a large, round chin that makes his face seem flattened, like he is made of rubber and his face has just been pressed against a hard surface and his features have yet to spring back to their usual three-dimensionality.

"Can I see him?" I ask.

Hu shrugs and sips from a clear glass mug of tea that must have been sitting on his desk for hours. Surely it is cold by now. He explains there is a processing fee to visit a detainee, and that the detainee has already run up a bill for the disposable handcuffs that were used to bring him in, the intake processing, and the clear broth he had to drink this morning.

I take ten hundred-kwai notes from my pocket and hand them to him. "This is all I have."

Hu leaves the money on the desk. "Not here," he says. "At the counter. Go downstairs, pay, and then they will tell you what to do."

*

I am told after I pay that I cannot see Huang this evening and that the earliest appointment will be tomorrow morning at 7 A.M. I return to my hotel and sleep fitfully, forgetting to call Xiu Xi's manager. I am back at the station a little before the appointed time and find an ill-formed line of tired-looking people already waiting. We are taken in groups of ten down another stairwell to a long room divided by two steel-mesh fences with a one-and-a-half-meter gap between them. On one side of one of the fences are the prisoners, then there is this gap where a guard sits on a stool near the door; we are herded in to stand on the far side of the other fence. I recognize Huang by his pigeon-toed stance. I am surprised that even his body language is so familiar to me, since I have not seen him in more than three years. It's strange to say this, but he does not seem surprised to see me, though he manages to nod and even attempt a smile.

His birthmark is gone. He must have had it removed while he was living in the south, famous for its cut-rate plastic surgery.

He doesn't look much older than he did a few years ago, perhaps a little thinner, but he is a relatively young man and still seems vital, or at least as full of life as one can look in such a place.

Around us, the family members and friends of the other prisoners have begun chatting noisily in the local dialect, shouting to each other across the open space. When I ask him what happened, he shrugs.

"I took out a personal ad on one of those singles websites, saying I wanted to meet a girl."

"That's it?" I say. "That's not illegal."

"It was what I said."

"What?"

"I said I had something illegal, you know, a substance, and wanted to party and if you were a female and wanted to party, then let's meet."

At first we are both shy about talking so openly, but as it becomes clear that everyone around us is too immersed in their own conversations and that the guard is completely uninterested, he finally lays out what happened. A woman had answered his ad, saying she wanted to take drugs and have sex, so Huang had gotten a taxi, rode across town, and then when he arrived at this woman's apartment, there were two policemen waiting for him. He had the morphine and amphetamines on him. He has been detained for six crimes, and the sentence for opiate possession, he tells me, could be death.

"They made me fill out a form saying I would donate my organs to the Ministry of State Security," Huang says.

The twenty minutes go by quickly, and we never even speak about our old friends or mutual acquaintances. By the end of my visit, Huang seems depressed, as one would expect, and he asks me to leave a little money for him — he promises to pay me back — so that he can eat something besides the broth they serve, which gives him terrible diarrhea. We talk about what might happen and Huang says he doesn't know but that these cases sometimes just go away after a few months if State Security believes there is no money in it for them. This is the hardest part, he explains, when they are trying to squeeze him. He doesn't seem to be taking into account his own past, his suspect political activities, the fact that his name might still excite a higher-level bureaucrat in the capital if it comes to his attention that Huang has been arrested. I assume the party would love to punish Huang and has been looking for a reason.

"How long are you in town?" he asks, his voice suddenly betraying how alone he must feel.

When I am back upstairs I ask at the counter if I can see Hu. They tell me to wait, and a few minutes later Hu appears again, on his way out. I fall in alongside him and ask him what will happen to Huang.

"He will eventually go to trial," Hu says. "But that may take a long time. In these cases, drug cases, we usually recommend a mental health facility."

These institutions for the criminally insane are famously cruel, with the inmates locked into vast wards for years at a stretch. The party, I have heard, runs this system, and for those who end up in them, there is no recourse to the criminal justice system. Huang's life, I now suspect, has been irrevocably lost. As I walk beside the officer, I think back on the young man I knew, so full of promise, as we all were — excellent test-takers, bright, quick-witted — and now Huang ends up here, in a prison cell, waiting for transfer to an even harsher place. Where do lives go? I wonder. So many of them just fizzle away, through bad luck, flawed character, whatever. For a second I want to confide in Officer Hu what a genius Huang once was, a great writer, a visionary, the college classmate the rest of us were sure would make a success of himself, and then he had been the first of us to make a name for himself, to gain a measure of fame. But that would only alert Officer Hu to the political dimensions of Huang, an area I would rather not mention.

Instead, almost without thinking, I remove the red envelope full of kwai from my jacket — the money I am supposed to pay to the actress — and hand it to Officer Hu. "For taking care of Huang," I tell him.

He quickly slides the envelope into his pocket without saying a word.

I see Huang again the next day. Hu has arranged for us to meet in a small office next to his. Huang sits in a white resin chair, another pair of plastic restraints on his wrists. He smells of sweat and feces. I am across from him. He thanks me for the money. I give him a cigarette.

"How much did you give those bastards?" he asks.

I tell him not to worry about it, that the magazine has paid.

He nods and asks about the publisher.

"He's rich," I say.

Huang nods in a way that indicates he is not surprised. "You two were always accommodating," he says.

"What does that mean?"

"Just that you always knew how to get along."

"I'm not like the publisher," I defend myself. "I'm just a writer."

"Writing about actresses," he says.

"So what?" I tell him.

"Nothing," he says.

I am a little surprised he is condescending to me, but I am reluctant to force a confrontation. It seems pointless. And who is Huang to be acting so virtuous? He has been detained for actual crimes, not for any great ideological stance. He was stupid, I think to myself, a fool to have been arrested in such circumstances.

"What is it like in there?" I ask him.

He tells me that there are ten of them in a room smaller than this office. They don't have enough space to lie down simultaneously, so they have to sleep in shifts, five horizontal and five standing. A boy of seventeen died two nights ago; he was suffocated while he slept. Huang suspects it was so there would be more room in the cell. "They haven't removed his body."

He has been getting regular meals of rice and chicken in Styrofoam containers as well as bottles of tea. Then he pauses. "I guess I will die here."

I tell him we will do whatever we can. That I will talk to the publisher and we will call in his connections. Huang perks up for an instant at this thought, but then settles back into his pessimism. "It doesn't really matter," he says. "There just isn't space for a person like me."

"Where? In the cell?"

"Anywhere."

This time Xiu Xi's manager is forthright about asking for a fee when I revisit the condominium they are using. Wearing headphones, Xiu Xi sits on a sofa, flipping through a copy of our magazine. I am unsure for a moment of how to proceed, but then from nowhere, I begin to deliver a small speech about the crooked ethics of my business and the grave costs when the population cannot trust the media. This gradually expands into a subtle condemnation of our whole system of klepto-capitalism, of pay-for-access, of a society so dependent on bribery and corruption that there can never be an honest thought, a pure action. "If the water is too dirty," I tell him, "no fish can live in it." We, our magazine, are making a stand, I explain, are refusing to pay because we want to provide the truth. Our best writers, our best journalists, are quitting because they are so disillusioned at this process. Our finest minds are rotting away in jail, our great artists silenced because they can't tolerate this form of capitalist censorship. "You know," I say, "in America, they don't pay for stories. And American movie stars end up making much more money than anyone in China."

He listens for a few moments and then shrugs, momentarily unsure of how to respond to my ploy. I have surprised even myself with my little speech, by how heartfelt it is, and while I want to believe that it has to do with Huang and his current incarceration, I know that I am just trying to get my story without paying the price.

We are at an impasse, I know. The manager, I suspect, is done with me. Will happily send me back to the capital without his starlet's story. For this is a principle for him as well: you pay to play. If not, how else is she supposed to make a living?

Then Xiu Xi herself speaks up. She has apparently been listening and she says, "I'll do the story."

You can trust an actress to respond to bad acting.

The manager has no choice but to go through with it.

"And the photos?" I say. A photographer is scheduled to arrive tomorrow.

She nods. We sit down and she is alert and cheerful, cooperative, a pleasure. She becomes beautiful to me then, as I watch her precisely featured face move around her mouth as she forms words in her soft accent. I understand her success; when she is sober, when she wants to please, she wins you over.

If she could be any animal, she would be a griffin.

"Why?"

"Because no one eats griffins."

I don't know where the manager has gone, but when we are finished and I am smoking in the darkness with my pants folded neatly over the back of a chair — she carefully arranged them — we are alone in the shadowy condominium. She is very pale, and when she moves in the darkness, it is hard for me to see precisely where she ends and the rest of the world begins.

The last time I see Huang, we are back in the same office as before and he looks very tired. He is unshaven, already thinner, and one of his eyes is red and appears swollen. He tells me it is some kind of infection that he can't shake. The guards gave him an antibiotic cream, bought, presumably, because of the red envelope I gave to Officer Hu. But one of his cellmates stole the cream last night while Huang was sleeping. The infection causes Huang to blink repeatedly. They have already told Huang that as soon as he has his hearing, he will be moved to a provincial mandatory rehabilitation hospital, a fancy name for a prison, but probably better, certainly, than an actual prison. Once he is officially detoxed, however, he will have to stand trial for the six criminal charges.

"I will never come back," he says.

I wish he could be more optimistic, I think to myself, but that has never been Huang's strong suit. He was always a realist, determined to confront the truth of a situation, his own homeliness, the nation's deceitfulness, his friend's duplicity. He will no doubt face this with the same heaviness with which he has gone through life, and as an intellectual, a basically gentle person, he is probably correct in assuming he might never return from prison. Who will send the money every month to bribe the guards, the cooks, the doctors? He will need clothes, heating oil, medicine. Huang isn't a common criminal who can maneuver among that element; he will be out of his depth in there, as he had been out here.

I tell him I have to return to the capital. That my work here is finished. I don't know what to say, so I tell him he'll be fine.

"Forget about me," he tells me.

The publisher and I are sitting down eating Szechuan food in the banquet room of a restaurant on the third floor of a shopping mall near our offices. We are poking our chopsticks through chicken and hot peppers. The article about Xiu Xi has been written, photographed, and will soon be shipped to the printer.

"It's strange," the publisher says, wiping his mouth with a cloth napkin. "When the photographer arrived in Chengdu, he was asked by Xiu Xi's manager for lucky money."

I nod. I have been caught.

"So I wondered," he continues, "would Xiu Xi's manager ask for double lucky money? Or did she somehow never receive the first lucky money?"

"I'm sorry," I tell the publisher. "I gave it to Huang, or to the officer working on his case. It seemed the least I could do."

"I assumed you did something like that."

He has always had a wide smile with broad, clean white teeth. He is not conventionally handsome; instead he looks utterly inoffensive. There is nothing remarkable about the publisher, yet the sum total of his typical features is that he is pleasant-looking. I find myself hating him for his banal appearance.

"I thought you would want to help out, somehow." He smiles. "To feel as if you were helping him."

I assume the publisher will fire me now. I have lied to him, stolen from him. I have proven myself not to be trustworthy.

"So," I say, "am I fired?"

"Little brother," he says, using a term of diminutive familiarity. "People like us, like you and me," he says, "there will always be a place for us."

*

According to a newspaper account, Huang committed suicide while he was in the provincial mandatory rehabilitation center. The story was written in a matter-of-fact tone, but with a certain smugness that an enemy of the party had taken his own life. It is amazing how many of those deemed enemies of the state end up dying by their own hand.

But in this case, I suspect, the newspaper accounts were right.

ELEANOR HENDERSON

The Farms

FROM *Agni*

AFTER MY LITTLE BROTHER DIED, we moved from the house on the lagoon to a two-bedroom apartment near I-95. It was in one of those sand-colored complexes built like a cluster of beach motels — two stories, with cedar shake roofs, cement staircases, and connected balconies the width of a sidewalk. Rusty half-moons from the sprinklers stained the first floors, and if you drove by at six in the evening with your windows down, you could smell sulfur from the well water. On the balconies, you might see a cooler of beer, a cactus plant on a paper plate, or a Florida Gators folding chair. There might be a towel drying on the railing. There would be crosses hanging on the doors and a bowl of wet cat food beside a welcome mat, swarming with flies. Our old house had had a sunroom, a pool with a slide, and a bathroom with two sinks where my brother and I had brushed our teeth side by side.

Now we lived on the second floor. To our left, in the end unit, was a retired couple who had their food delivered each Saturday by a Meals on Wheels minivan. The wife had fallen down the stairs and broken her hip, and the husband left the apartment only to pick up her prescriptions. In the two apartments on our right lived a large Puerto Rican family — aunts and uncles and chubby cousins who rode their scooters in the parking lot between our building and the one across from it. On the second floor of that other building, there was a family of Jehovah's Witnesses, a lady my parents said was a drunk, and the man who bagged our groceries at Publix, who drove a moped with Confederate flags streaming from the handlebars. In 2F, the unit directly across from ours, lived a black woman and her daughters, two skinny little girls she liked to dress in identical outfits, down to the barrettes.

In our old neighborhood there had been a Puerto Rican family too, as well as the Velazquez del Castillos, who hung a Cuban flag from their carport, and whose name I loved to say. But the black kids I went to school with were bused in from Riviera Beach or out in Belle Glade; they had never been my neighbors. In our new building, I watched the woman from 2F fold clothes in the laundry room while her daughters played with a lizard they'd trapped in an empty detergent box. She had a way of whipping a sheet out in front of her, to snap it straight, that kept me from saying hello. "Don't be getting those clothes dirty again," she told the girls. I was tie-dying a T-shirt in one of the washing machines. I didn't have anything else to do.

That fall, the fall I started eighth grade, I took the bus home from school. My dad didn't get home from the office until after six most of the time, and my mother, a special ed teacher, had started working in the kitchen department at Macy's three nights a week. I would walk home alone from the bus stop, let myself in, and do my homework and chores. I'd watch *Donahue.* I'd call my friend Krista, who lived in my old neighborhood, and when her mother answered, she'd talk about how much she missed me, ask how my parents were holding up, and list all the games her daughter and I used to play. While she did this, she hunted for Krista, opening and closing doors. "You don't know where she is, do you?" she'd ask, forgetting that I was the one who'd called.

Andrew had gotten HIV through a blood-factor infusion, and then in the summer he'd caught pneumonia and gone into a coma and hadn't woken up. I didn't know the total of his medical bills, but it was enough to put us in what my dad called, as cheerfully as possible, as though we were on a wacky adventure, "the poorhouse." My brother used to be the one I'd spend afternoons with, playing game show and microwaving things from the freezer. I was supposed to be taking care of him.

On *Donahue* I watched a rerun of the tribute to Ryan White with Elton John, John Cougar Mellencamp, and Kareem Abdul-Jabbar. I was tired of mourning. I was bored.

The first time I saw the girls alone on the balcony across the way, they were sitting against the building with their feet propped up on the railing, the contents of their open backpacks scattered between them. They looked content to be doing their homework in the shade, passing a bag of Skittles between them. I held up my hand as I fit my key into the lock, and they waved back, first the younger one, then, grudgingly, the older.

The second time, a few weeks later, it was raining. It was one of those afternoon storms in South Florida when the rain steamed off the sidewalks. Even under the overhang the girls were getting wet. They stood against the wall, wearing their backpacks over their bellies. This time I didn't wave. I let myself into our apartment, put away the dishes, and opened my algebra book. I'd completed one problem when I peeked through the blinds and saw that they were still there. The rain was getting heavier, a shot of lightning zapping the air pink. The parking lot was almost empty. I grabbed my umbrella, still wet, and darted back out into the rain, down my stairs, and up theirs.

"It's raining cats and dogs," I said. It was something you said to little kids.

The girls eyed me. They were wearing white tank tops with pink polka dots, pink Lycra shorts, and white sandals, all of which were soaked and a little too small. The rain had turned their shirts translucent against their dark skin; their plaits, held in place with white barrettes, were soggy. The younger girl wore glasses like the ones I used to wear, the kind with opalescent plastic frames, and behind the wet lenses her eyes were even more enormous than my own, alighting on me, then her sister, then me again.

"That's a watermelon," she said, pointing to my umbrella. It was pink with black seeds and a green border.

"It sure is. Would you like to hold it?"

The girl looked to her sister for permission and, when she didn't say no, reached for it.

"Where's your mom?" I asked them.

"At work," said the little one. I guessed she was five or six. "Donatella lost the key again." She explained how her sister had taken off the key, which she wore around her neck on a shoestring, to do handsprings on the playground, and had forgotten to pick it up from the grass. "She can do a front or a back. She's fixing to be in the Olympics."

The little one said there wasn't an extra key hiding anywhere and they didn't know their mother's number.

"This watermelon's making me hungry," the little one said. I was hungry too, I realized. I was starving.

"We've got Girl Scout cookies," I said. "Thin Mints."

The note I slipped under their door, printed on a damp sheet from the little one's newsprint tablet, said, *I'm watching the girls in 2B.* Under this I drew a smiley face.

They needed to change into dry clothes, but I didn't have anything small enough for them. I put a chair in front of my parents' closet to reach the boxes of Andrew's clothes. I found two T-shirts, two pairs of shorts with elastic waists, two pairs of socks, and two pairs of underwear. My mother had packaged everything to donate it to the AIDS charity in West Palm, but then she'd decided she wasn't ready.

"These are boys' clothes," the little one objected. She'd told me her name was Bernice. She was in first grade, her sister in fourth. When I told her my name was Meg, short for Margaret, she said, "I never heard that name before."

"I don't know if we should wear these," said Donatella, the older one. It was the first thing I'd heard her say. She had wide-set eyes, delicately carved nostrils, and a jaw full of large white teeth that reminded me of a pony's.

"It's like dress-up," I told them. "Do you guys play dress-up?"

"I know what that is," Bernice said.

"Mama didn't say we could wear someone else's clothes," said Donatella.

"It's like on Halloween," Bernice told her sister. "When you wear a costume."

While they toweled dry and changed into the clothes, I arranged Thin Mints on a plate and poured each of us a glass of milk. When the girls came out, I ran back downstairs and tossed their clothes and the towels in the dryer, using two of my own quarters, and then we sat down at the kitchen table. The clothes were too big on Bernice, but they fit Donatella perfectly. Andrew would have been in fifth grade, but he was small for his age.

"We got on white boy's drawers," Bernice said, crumbs falling from her mouth as she giggled. She was missing one tooth, but with her mouth full of chocolate she looked like she was missing more.

"Shut up, Bernice," said her sister. She spoke in a discreet way, as though trying to keep her mouth closed. Neither of them had asked whose clothes these were.

"They got a hole you can pee out of."

"Drink your milk, girl."

Bernice balanced her nose on the edge of the glass and sniffed. Everything was too big for her — the glass, the clothes, the chair. She said, "It taste like water."

"It's skim," I said. I didn't mind the taste, but now I wondered if I should. "My mom buys it."

"Where's your mama at?" Bernice asked. She wanted to know how old I was, whether I could drive, if I had a boyfriend (I didn't, but I didn't want one), if I was a Girl Scout (I wasn't, but I wanted to be). I liked talking to kids. Around children I was interesting, resourceful, self-possessed, occasionally glamorous. I could find the most obscure hiding places; I could weave a friendship bracelet with five colors; I could make pancakes in the shapes of their initials. When I took my glasses off, they would marvel at my crossed eye, as though it were not a defect but a magic trick, which they would then try to master themselves.

But I didn't baby-sit much anymore. The families in my old neighborhood called Krista instead; they didn't want to drive me. My most recent baby-sitting job, just before school had started, had been for my father's boss, whose regular sitter had canceled at the last minute. He offered to pick me up, but my father insisted on driving me there, to a house in Palm Beach the size of a department store, seashell pink with a Spanish tile roof and a wall of French doors that opened to the ocean. It was raining that night too, the windows black, the angel-faced children asleep. I peeked in on them in their gossamer beds, then walked the dark chambers of the house, opening the pantry, scanning the bookshelves, padding over marble floors and carpet that still showed the path of the vacuum. In the middle of one room, a stone mermaid posed with her head tilted toward the beach, listening with me to the palm trees beating their fins against the glass in the storm.

I'd never baby-sat in my own home before. Now Bernice was the one exploring every corner, heaving open the refrigerator, planting her hands in the kitchen drawers. "Bernice, close that," her sister told her. "Bernice, put that back."

"It's okay," I told them. "You guys know what Girl Scouts do?"

Bernice was operating our can opener like a pair of scissors. "Hey, Bernice, you know what Girl Scouts do? Have you ever been camping?" She dropped the can opener on the floor.

"It's like, you go in a tent?"

"That's right. You know what I've got?"

"I ain't never been in a tent."

"Don't be saying *ain't,* girl."

I fetched the tent from my parents' closet, pushed back the coffee table, and set it up on the pea-green shag carpet. My father had taken us camping up near Gainesville once, and Andrew and I used to pitch it in our old backyard. I turned out the lights and we crawled inside, and with a flashlight under my chin I told them the ghost story my father had told us about a man who was run over by a train, and how he haunted the tracks, and sometimes when you heard a far-off train whistle you could see his empty boots walking along them. I felt sick with meanness telling the story, because for weeks after hearing it myself I had slept between my parents in their bed.

But even with the thunder, the girls were unimpressed. In the glow of the flashlight, Donatella sat with her hands in her lap, her eyes searching for something to stare at. "You forgot the lantern," she said. "Isn't he supposed to carry a lantern?"

I had seen adults court small children, vying for their attention at my father's office parties or in the stands at my softball games, teasing them, winking at them, asking them to do high-fives, trying to get their mothers to say, "He likes you." I had never had to stoop to such methods. I wasn't used to kids resisting my charms. I wondered if Donatella didn't like white people, or if she just didn't like me.

"It's hot in here." Bernice unzipped the flap and stuck out her head. "It looks like nighttime."

I turned the lights back on and collapsed the tent. For no reason except that it was an appropriate thing for kids to do, we continued to sit on the floor.

"What's this?" Bernice asked, lifting the lid off my mother's sewing basket. She picked up the cloth tomato and looked it over. I told her it was a pincushion. There were no pins in it — Andrew had pricked his finger on one once — but Bernice was unbothered by this detail. "You got a watermelon *and* a tomato," she said, flashing me her missing tooth, then traded the cushion for a length of cloth measuring tape, which she belted around her oversized T-shirt. "What's these words say?" she asked, looking at her shirt upside down.

I told her it said *Manatees.*

"That's the smart school," said Donatella, whose shirt didn't say anything. It was cornflower blue with a stain like a birthmark on one sleeve, where Andrew's thumb had smeared barbecue sauce.

"They live in the water, but they're mammals," I said, trying to demonstrate their universal appeal.

"I'm a mammal, right?" Bernice asked.

Donatella and I told her she was.

"All people are mammals," Bernice said.

"That's right."

"These your clothes?" she asked, pulling up her socks.

"Hush, Bernice."

"Whose are they, then?"

"Bernice, I said!"

"It's okay," I said. I didn't mind. I was the only one who wanted to talk about Andrew. Krista, our old neighbors, my teachers, even my parents — everyone tripped past his name, hopped over it in coded silence. Listening to the sternness in Donatella's voice, I wondered now if our new neighbors might be doing the same thing, if we were what they were talking about on their balconies in voices too low for me to hear, and if that was why they refused to meet my eyes before ducking into their cars. Was it possible the girls knew that I'd had a brother, and that he'd died? I said, "They're my brother's."

"Our daddy's dead," Bernice said. "He died in the war." She made her bug eyes even bigger. She had seized the conversation so abruptly — I didn't know if I believed her; she seemed to be a kid who might make things up — that I barely had time to wonder how she'd arrived there.

"What war?" I said stupidly.

"Desert Storm," Bernice said. "What do you think?"

Then, of course, I did believe her. I was only vaguely aware that a war had taken place at all, let alone that people had died in it. Several months before, in the distant epoch of seventh grade, I had cross-stitched a yellow ribbon in home ec, and every once in a while a tank had steered across our television screen before someone changed the channel. Andrew had preferred cartoons, and so had my parents.

"His tank blowed up," said Bernice. "It got blowed up by his own team."

"It's not a *team,*" Donatella said.

"First we lived with our grandma, and now we live in Florida."

"He got a Purple Heart," Donatella said, unable to help herself, "even though it was friendly fire."

"He's in heaven with Grandpap and Jesus and the Lord."

"Shut up, girl. Jesus and the Lord are the same person."

"No, they ain't. Are they?" Bernice looked to me. "What's your name again?"

I told her.

"Are Jesus and the Lord the same person?"

"It depends what you believe," I said. "What denomination you are." I was glad to have this large word handy to put an end to the question. For months I had been dissatisfied by the condolences offered to me, as embarrassed as those giving them, and now I was at a loss to offer anything better. Heaven wasn't something my parents talked about. Andrew's memorial service had been held in our old backyard, and we had scattered his ashes in the lagoon.

"Hey, let's play funeral," Bernice said.

"No, Bernice," said her sister.

"You're dead" — she pointed to me — "and we're alive."

"I don't know if we should play this game," I said.

"No, it's *fun!*" Bernice leapt up and pushed my shoulders back, easing me down to the floor. "Close your eyes." Because I was comfortable there or sleepy or just curious, I did. With my eyes closed, the rain on our roof increased its volume. "You're the mama, and me and Donatella are the daughters."

"I'm not playing, Bernice."

"Fine. I'm the daughter, then. You be in the audience." Bernice placed the pincushion on my chest. Its soft weight bloomed over my heart. "That's your flowers. You're in a casket."

"How did I die?" I asked.

"Cancer," Bernice said.

"That's how Grandpap died," said Donatella.

"What kind did I have?"

When Bernice didn't answer, I opened an eye. She was looking to her sister for help.

I said, "It can be stomach cancer, lung cancer. Any part of the body. Brain cancer."

"Leg cancer," Bernice decided.

I started to protest. Then I just said, "Okay."

"You're my mama and you died of leg cancer. You died three days ago. Your body ain't started decomposing yet."

I expected Donatella to scold her, but she didn't. She was listening with me.

"Mama, you was the best mama a girl could have." I felt Bernice kneel by my casket. "You always loved me and brought me up right. You worked hard to give me a good life and keep me out of harm's way. I don't know how I will go on without my mama. Donatella, now you do the trumpets and fire the guns."

"That's only for the military."

"She was in the military," Bernice said.

"No, she wasn't."

"How do you know? Girls can be in the military."

"She just wasn't. She died of leg cancer."

"That's okay," I said. "I don't need trumpets."

"Shhh," Bernice said. "You're dead."

I complied.

"Donatella, help me say the prayer. We got to lower her into the ground."

"You say it."

"I don't know all the words."

Donatella sighed. There was a shuffle of bodies. A moment later I felt two little pairs of hands slip under my back, one on each side. Donatella was cautious, sparing only two fingers from each hand. I thought of the game my friends and I had played at slumber parties, trying to levitate each other's bodies while we chanted, "Light as a feather, stiff as a board." I had never been levitated, but the words the girls recited now raised me up, up, up over my family's living room, where I hovered, as high as any spirit, even while my body remained flat on the pea-green rug. It wasn't until years later, at church with a friend, that I heard that psalm again. Until then, I half believed that the girls had made it up themselves.

"Now you're in the ground," Bernice said when it was over. I heard her slap her hands together, dusting them off. "Now let's play school bus. I'm the driver, and you're the kids."

"No, Bernice. You can't always be the driver."

I opened my eyes. The girls loomed above me like statues, and outside the rain was still coming down. I could hear the palm trees whipping around in the storm, the same way they had whipped around in Palm Beach, but it seemed impossible that it was also raining there now, that Palm Beach was not on the other side of the world.

Bernice crouched down and hung her magnified eyes close to mine. "You can be alive now," she whispered, as though trying not to wake the still-dead.

"Okay," I said, not getting up. On her breath was the minty, sour smell of chocolate and milk.

"What's your name again?" she asked me.

While Bernice was in the bathroom, her sister and I stood by the door. The hallway was hung with pictures of Andrew and me: riding ponies, wet-haired at the beach, Andrew missing both front teeth. A low rumble of thunder rolled through the building, the storm quieting outside. "She's hyperactive," Donatella apologized. "She's on Ritalin."

Alone, Donatella seemed older, closer to my age than her sister's. Our encounter was charged with all the awkwardness of meeting a stranger in a store, someone your age that you didn't know, while your mothers chatted brightly in the checkout line or outside the dressing room — except with Donatella I wanted to have something more in common than just being kids. I wanted her to find me alluring and charitable, a keeper of secrets.

"My brother was on meds too," I told her. "For practically his whole life he had to have injections to make his blood clot. Then when he got sicker he had to be on *more* meds."

"I don't know about all that," said Donatella.

"He died over the summer. After your dad, I guess. How old are you — nine?"

She gave a defensive little nod.

"My brother was ten."

Donatella did not seem surprised or sobered by this news. Instead she became more animated, relieved that the encumbrance of politeness had been lifted. "My mama said he had AIDS, like the crack hos and junkies in Belle Glade. I didn't know white people could catch it."

Donatella was looking at me with her wide-set pony eyes; they were so far apart that I felt I couldn't look at both of them at once. I'd heard kids say you needed to be gay to have AIDS. I'd never heard them say you had to be black. I stood there trying to figure out who it was that Donatella disapproved of.

"We were supposed to go on a field trip to see the farms, but my mama wouldn't let me."

The farms were in the furthest reaches of Palm Beach County, out by the lake. That was where the AIDS epidemic was: in the sugarcane slum where the Haitians lived. I remembered that place — acres and acres of sea-green fields under the endless, overcast tarp of the sky. It too seemed to be on the other side of the world, as far away now as my brother was.

"I've been on that field trip before," was all I could say.

Bernice waddled out of the bathroom, her shorts hanging past her knees. "I didn't pee through the hole."

"You better not." Donatella yanked up her waistband. "You wash your hands?"

Bernice promised that she had.

Then I turned on the TV. Donatella did her homework on the coffee table while I paged through our atlas with Bernice, who had pulled it off the shelf. She fell asleep sucking her thumb, her puppet legs dangling off the couch, the warm mass of her head cupped in the crook of my arm. Was the scent of her hair, like talcum powder and almonds, from the oil her mother put in it, or was that just the way she smelled? I still don't know.

At first I had wondered if the girls' mother would pay me for my time. I hadn't expected much, just a token of appreciation, an acknowledgment of my good citizenship. For the evening of baby-sitting in Palm Beach, I had received a small fortune: two twenty-dollar bills, which I'd exhibited to my father on the ride home. "Pity money," he muttered, guiding our car over the bridge back to the mainland. It didn't occur to me that pity might not be the only thing our neighbors felt for my family. Years later I would think of this phrase — "pity money" — when the company that had gotten

Andrew sick finally offered my parents compensation. "Blood money," my father said, and then, "No, thank you."

It was hard for me to turn down money. But I decided that, if offered, that was what I would do. True Samaritans went unpaid. All I wanted was for the girls' mother to tell me, "Thank goodness you were home." I didn't anticipate the cold, hard rap on the door and, when I opened it, the set of my neighbor's jaw, as heavy as her firstborn's.

"Donatella. Bernice. Get your things. We're going."

She was wearing a navy skirt suit, a pair of nude-colored pantyhose with a run in the knee, and penny loafers. Around her neck hung a gold cross, and up close I could see that her glasses were also like mine, but they had the opposite effect from her daughter's. Instead of enlarging her eyes, they shrank them, giving her the lost, bleary look of a burrowing rodent. Her eyes never looked at me, only at her daughters, who appeared by my side.

"We was playing," said Bernice. "I went in a tent."

"Get your things. Whose clothes you wearing?"

"I didn't want to," said Donatella.

"Theirs were wet," I said. "I forgot them in the dryer." I ran downstairs to the laundry room, where I fished out two of my mother's towels, two polka-dot tank tops, two pairs of pink shorts, and one pair of white panties, not two. I spun my arm around in the dryer, but there was nothing else there. Donatella was still wearing her own wet underwear.

While the girls changed again and their mother waited out on the balcony, I washed our milk glasses in the sink, soaking my arms up to the elbows. Rush-hour traffic whirred by on the highway. The rain had stopped, but its dusky breath was still on the air, and it was hard to tell whether the gray sky through the kitchen window was left over from the storm or if it was just dark with the settling evening. I didn't know yet that the next summer we would move again, to another neighborhood, to an apartment not much bigger, for reasons never explained to me, or for no reason at all. I wasn't thinking then of what my own mother would say when she came home from work — whether she'd be furious at me for lending Andrew's clothes, or at our neighbor for her ingratitude (she was both) — or what I would do the next time the girls locked themselves out (they never did). I was thinking of all the times I'd administered cootie shots to protect myself from the Haitian boys in my class. I was thinking of all the times, even after I knew better, that I'd refused a hug or kiss from my brother, or a sip from his glass.

When the girls were dressed and their backpacks strapped on, their mother hurried them out the door, down the balcony, and down the steps. "We got the same house," I heard Bernice note for the third time that day, "except it's backwards." Just as they reached the bottom of the stairs, the sprinklers burst on and the girls squealed. Their mother grabbed them by the hands. I watched from the door as the three of them dashed across the parking lot, through the untimely choreography of the place we all lived in, and then up the stairs to safety.

GREG HRBEK

Sagittarius

FROM *Black Warrior Review*

THE LAND SURROUNDING the house is state forest. A dirt road climbs farther up the mountain, where paint-stained bark indicates the direction of hiking trails and orange signs warn off hunters. It is into this wilderness that he has run away. Seven o'clock in the evening. While they were arguing (again) about the surgery, the baby vaulted over the rail of the playpen, as if it were a hurdle to be cleared. They heard his hooves scrabbling on the rubber mat, but were too late to see him jump: tucking his forelegs up, hind legs flexing and thrusting, body tracing a parabola through the air; then the earthward reach of the forelegs, the tucking up of the rear hooves, the landing. They shouted his name in unison. When they reached the sunroom, they saw him bounding out the door. Upper half, human half, twisted in their direction; a look of joy and terror in the infant's eyes. But the equine part would not stop . . . Now he stands in the trees, hominid heart thundering in his chest. Though the twilight air is cold on the bare white skin of his torso, it can't touch him below the waist: his hindquarters are warm under a coat of dark hair. He hears his mother call. "Sebastian!" A flick of the tail, the shuffle of hooves. As he bounds deeper into the maze of trees, night's first star appears in the ecliptic.

◆

The first fear blazing through her mind: someone with a rifle will mistake him, in the mist of dawn, for an animal. No, Isabel thinks. Dawn is ten hours away. We'll find him before then. We'll hear him crying long before that. We have to. Hardly April. The temperature still hypothermic at night. Even if he wanders for a mile, in this silence we'll hear him. Except that his cries, until today, have been so very faint . . . She herself can scarcely speak. When she calls for him, his name seems to catch on spikes in her throat and come out torn. She stops. Sweeps the flashlight through the trees. Listens. All she hears is her husband's voice. Much stronger, more certain than hers. Still, he sounds far away. Each time Martin calls Sebastian's name, he sounds a little more distant, and Isabel feels a little more alone in the dark. It seems very wrong to her, in these moments, to be frightened for herself. But she is. A sense of the future washes through her like the memory of a dream, vague and unreliable but sharp nonetheless — an impression of a place she will be one day. Dark, solitary, cut off from lovers and children. She is thinking only of her baby. Where he is, how to reach him. But every thought of him feels somehow like a thought about herself. As if there's still a cord strung between them, a useless cord that links them but doesn't keep them connected. She stops. Listens. Sweeps the beam through the trees. There's a burning in her chest as the light catches on two yellow eyes. Too big by far, this animal. But for the moment before it bounds across the road, darkness and hope conspire to let her see exactly what she wants. For one blessed moment, it's him. Then it's a fawn darting into the forest — with its mother, chasing behind.

Martin could see, for a short time, the other beam sweeping up the dirt road and his wife's figure delineated in an auroral glow; but the space between them is widening — trees, darkness — and the light seems, from where he stands, to be going out. "Sebastian!" he shouts. He's careful to keep his voice free of anger so his son will not misinterpret his intentions. I don't want to punish you, I just want to help. He does not feel panicked. Worried, yes. Scared. But calm, clear enough to wonder if he might be succumbing to a state of shock. Probably he's been in shock for months already. He and Isabel both. Each in their own way. It's getting darker. Just since they've been out here (can't be more than four or five minutes), the sky has blackened enough to begin showing stars. The buds on the trees haven't opened yet, so the view to the firmament is clear. Martin only glances up, but that one glance is enough to remind him just how much space there is, in heaven and on earth, to get lost in. Again he calls out. Hears only the clicking of crickets and the wind-chime reverberations of traveling starlight. Then noise from up the road, where he thinks his wife is.

"Is it him?" He waits for an answer. "Isabel?"

"A deer, I said."

She sounds shaken. Her voice already tinged with grief.

The boy sits on the couch watching the eyes of the cartoon characters bug out on the television and their tongues unfurl like party favors. Through the cotton of his pajamas, he tugs on his penis. He's three years old. He has never been alone in the house before. Although his parents sometimes threaten to leave him here (if he doesn't hurry up and get dressed or hurry up and get in the car), and though tears sometimes spring to his eyes at the thought, he always understands that the abandonment is not really going to occur. Yet here he is now. Left behind. At first he was able to hear them calling his brother's name. Not anymore. He can't hear anything now. He has touched the remote control and made the voices on television go away. Now he can't hear anything but crickets marching closer and closer in the dark.

◆

Night is nearly done falling. Isabel thinks momentarily of Kaden, back at the house. She has never left him alone, unless you count the time she accidentally locked him inside with all the keys. After breaking in through the bedroom window, she found him sitting on the kitchen floor playing with the salad spinner. She thinks: he can take care of himself. Then her mind returns to the woods and her fears to wild animals. Raccoons, owls, black bear. What is her baby to these creatures? A peer, a brother — or an unknown encroacher? Isn't it all about territory, the cruel mathematics of the food chain? It occurs to her suddenly that this is all her fault. If she hadn't refused after the ultrasound to believe what the screen showed them; if she'd consented to the operation after the birth (at which point she could no longer deny the truth); and if she hadn't brought him out here, just today — only hours ago they'd climbed this very road. If she hadn't shown him the world in all its openness and wildness. What happened today, what's happening even now: doesn't it validate the position she took from the very beginning? Her mind flashes to the first appointment with the orthopedic surgeon. They hadn't even left the hospital yet. The baby was in neonatal intensive care, and there she was in that waiting room, with the magazines fanned out on the tables, those airbrushed cover photos, those mirages of flawlessness. Back in his office, the doctor told them their son would never walk. To increase the slim chances of ambulation, but mostly for the sake of anatomical correctness, he advised the removal of the two forelegs . . .

You mean amputate?

Mmm.

Is that . . . necessary?

Depends, Mrs. Avery, on your definition of necessity.

Martin leans against a tree and feels that some balance is tipping inside him. He closes his eyes, opens them again. Sees plainly, as if it's something caught in the beam of his flashlight, the futility of what they're trying to do. The baby could be anywhere! Abruptly he starts back toward the house (remembering, all at once, his elder son). He intends to call the police, report a missing person. Then decides, with equal impulsiveness, against the idea. What kind of description would he give? How can he explain when he himself does not understand? Even the doctors can't make up their minds. The diagnosis changes every week. Spina bifida, muscular dystrophy, cerebral palsy as the cause of the musculoskeletal deformity; the body hair most likely the result of a condition called congenital hypertrichosis; and the extra legs — they don't have a clue. A genetic mutation, or the vestiges of a twin who failed to fully form. The fact is, no one knows exactly what's wrong with his son. No one knows what he is.

"Sebastian!"

His voice sounds, to his ears, less controlled this time. It's a fact that he, the father, is the cause of this situation. Had he responded differently back at the house, the baby would never have leapt over the rail of his playpen, knocked the back door open, and run away. A knife blade twists in his stomach. Suddenly, sharply, Martin is aware of his conduct. Out here, under the stars, he isn't sure if it made any sense at all . . . My son stood today. My son walked today.

Kaden walks down the hall, crying. Saying, "Where are you, Mom?" He knows they went out the back door. Still, he looks for them in the house. He goes to the bedroom first and speaks into the darkness. Gets no answer. He doesn't know where they've gone, yet their absence is part of a pattern: Kaden let his brother out the back door. His brother ran outside. His father ran through the door, his mother ran through the door. They have all disappeared into the night.

I let them out, he thinks.

Me.

I wanted to see my brother run. My brother is a horse.

◆

Isabel's foot slips. The ground is sloping upward. She realizes she's wearing sandals, and this pathetic detail pushes her to sob. She feels a surge of confusion. Not new. She's been feeling it — a dreamlike gap in logic, a page missing from the book — ever since the night he was born. There is a name for what he is. Why can't she think of it, why can't anyone think of it? After the delivery (which had been both easier and more difficult than Kaden's), she had not seen Sebastian right away. While she'd lain in the bed, her body light as a soul, a phalanx of nurses had spirited the newborn away. Nobody would answer her questions. Not the midwife. Not her own husband, who claimed to have seen nothing in the confusion. He sat beside her, worrying with his fingers on the plastic wrist bracelet printed with his name and the name of their son. He took her hand, but wouldn't look at her. The lack of eye contact, though unnerving, allowed her to maintain a kind of distance. As if they were back in birthing class, watching a video about complications. As if the situation were purely hypothetical, a scenario invented for the purpose of instruction . . . Neonatal intensive care. First, a lobby with a nurses' station and a smaller room off to the side equipped with sinks. Isabel could not, for the life of her, figure out how to turn on the water. There were no handles on the faucet. She wondered then if she was dreaming, anesthetized in the operating room; or still in the birthing suite, drugged even though she'd forsworn the drugs, and now she was hallucinating, succumbing to one of the adverse reactions that their birth-class instructor had warned them about: I can't breathe, I'm going into allergic shock, my heart is slowing, slowing, stopping. Suddenly, magically, water gushed from the faucet. Her husband's foot was depressing a pedal on the floor. Then they were going in. The unit was one large room, very quiet, full of incubators that made her think first of aquarium tanks, then display cases, then — because they were wheeled and curtained — of something else she couldn't quite put her finger on. The babies she could see were tiny, impossibly small, blue and mummified. Sebastian was not one of these. Not premature. Despite the debriefing with specialists, she didn't yet understand what he was. Was there no word for him, or simply no cute word, no word that didn't invoke a darker age? She was afraid, but relieved to feel, underneath the terror, crushed and barely breathing, but there, *there*, a desire to see him, a longing, whatever he might be. They neared his incubator. Positioned in a secluded corner of the room. The curtain was drawn. Monitors overhead displayed fluctuating numbers and jagged inscriptions. Under an impulse that upset her stomach and wrung her heart the way feelings of romance had when she was younger, Isabel moved closer. Yes, she had already fallen in love with him, with the idea of him. She'd made a space in her mind and heart, and now he would step into that shape and fit it perfectly, fill it perfectly. She reached out a hand and pulled open the curtain.

He thinks: my son walked today. Any other parent would be filled with a clear and simple happiness. For Martin, it is all too much. He had come home, half an hour ago, with a bottle of red wine and the honest intention to start from scratch. No made-up minds, no sides. They would talk, really talk. Work things out together. Figure out what to do. Then he walked in the door and his older son grabbed him by the hand and pulled him back into the sunroom where his wife was waiting and beaming with joy; and then he saw the reason — the baby was standing, standing on all four feet — and he couldn't understand why, but his spirits simply collapsed, and all his hopes seemed like a fantasy compared to the concrete fact of the creature in the playpen.

He's standing, Dad.

I can see that.

Not only that, said his wife. He can walk. He got up in the meadow today, on the grass, and walked.

Like a foh-wul, Kaden said.

A what?

Dad, a foh-wul is a baby horse.

He's not a foal.

Isabel continued: He fell down at first. But then he did it, Martin, just like they said he wouldn't.

Martin looked again. No illusion. Surrounded by the trappings of any boy's infancy — a floppy blue teddy bear; a plush baseball with a jingle bell inside; a mobile of the solar system, its planets swaying in a lazy orbit — their disabled son was standing. Eyes wide, hands clapping, he bounced on his four legs, hooves scrabbling on the polyester mat. Martin walked over to him and placed a hand on his head and said, We can't let him do this.

Why not?

He'll get used to it.

She smiled uncertainly. I don't see what you mean, she said.

Yes, you do.

I don't, actually.

He'll get used to standing like this. We won't be able to break him of the habit.

Standing isn't a habit.

Okay.

Nose-picking is a habit. Thumb-sucking, she said, tears coming into her eyes. Christ, even today? Even this? I don't understand you.

No kidding.

How can this be anything but wonderful?

It's only going to make everything harder. The longer we wait, the harder it's going to be. For all of us.

He slipped past her, taking pains to avoid brushing any part of his body against hers. She followed him down the hallway to the stairs. Leaving the two children behind.

You just wish he'd go away, she said too loudly.

Untrue.

Not just half of him. All of him.

Kaden remembers the back door. Wonders what he's doing here, at home, when the rest of them have run away. Back in the sunroom, he stares at the empty playpen. The mobile of the solar system hangs frozen in the darkness. His brother had set it whirling when he jumped. Jump, Kaden had whispered. Down the hall, they'd been saying, Go away. All of him. Kaden opened the back door. Go, brother. Now the boy feels a heat, like a candle burning in his belly. He feels for his sneakers in the pile of shoes beside the door. Pulls them on the wrong feet. Steps into the starry night and onto the road.

◆

Suddenly she thinks, The meadow! Of course. That's where he went. Is now. A realization so sharp, so visual — she can *see* him, a four-legged shadow tracing a lazy path through the grass — as to make her feel clairvoyant. Isabel starts to reach for her cell phone, to speed-dial her husband and tell him where to meet her: she's confident enough now in a happy ending to laugh at the impulse. She runs back down the road. Seeking out the trailhead with the flashlight beam. The memory of the afternoon speeding a dizzy spin in her head.

She hadn't been sure, earlier in the day, if the ground of the meadow would be dry (the last of the snow had melted only recently), yet the world wore the beckoning look of spring. She packed a blanket in a backpack and managed to get him into the front-pouch, his forelegs through the two extra holes she'd cut in the padding. All through the winter, Sebastian had confirmed his doctors' expectations — sleeping excessively, communicating only through weak cries, showing little interest in his surroundings — but now, in the outdoors, he observed everything with wide eyes and squawked like a tropical bird. How beautiful to hear! Isabel felt a strength bubble up from deep inside her. We can get through this, she thought. All of us together. As she carried him through the woods, she felt strangely blessed. As if this improbable child, as he appeared right now, were the fulfillment of some secret wish. They found the meadow golden with sun. The flaxen grass long and dry enough. Isabel freed the baby from the carrier, laid him down on the blanket. Immediately he started struggling. A seizure, an allergic reaction? She was about to sweep him up again and rush down the trail, back to the house and the telephone, when she realized there was something methodical, something conscious about his movements. The knobby hairy legs stretched and slipped, stretched and slipped. Then the bones momentarily straightened and locked, and his body almost lifted from the ground. He tried again. Again and again. To hoist himself up. To balance. The closer he got, the more violently his legs trembled. So frail, she thought. Like they might snap under his weight. Scary; but she gently urged him on, supporting his underbelly with a hand. She shaking too — and feeling, too, that she was rising somehow. It took an hour, maybe more; yet the day was far from over, the sun still warm and high overhead when she heard herself say, in a broken whisper, Look at you, little man. Look at you standing up.

Now, searching for the trailhead, she again feels weightless with thanks. Yes, everything's going to be all right. She calls out to her husband. "Martin! Can you hear me?" But a vehicle, a pickup truck, is coming down the mountain, tires rasping against the dirt road, columns of halogen light careering through the trees and blinding her as she moves out of the way.

Martin can barely admit it to himself, but his wife is right. He does sometimes wish the baby would disappear. Not half of him. All of him. Now it's happening. And if they don't find him — if they do and it's too late . . . His mind projects a scene: his return to the house in the gray light of dawn, exhausted and empty-handed. It comes to him like a psychic flash, crisp and definite, this picture of himself. Followed by another that's simply unbearable: their second child dead on a carpet of last autumn's rust-colored leaves. Not the first time he has imagined such a thing. Ever since the doctors started talking about life expectancy, Martin has been fighting off dark imagery. We can't be sure (they say), we need more neuromotor assessment, and intelligence tests are a year away, but the fact is, physical deformities this severe suggest associated malformations of the brain; and if the muscle disease is degenerative, as it almost certainly is — well, it's only a matter of time before it reaches the heart, which is, in the end, just another muscle . . . What would be worse? Losing the boy tonight (just a baby, five months in the world and already gone from it) or losing him thirteen years from now? No, he doesn't want his son to vanish. He just wants him to be normal. He wants fatherhood to be free of pain and paradox.

Suddenly his hands are breaking a fall. Fucking rock, fucking root of a tree. He hits the ground, pant leg tearing on something. Kneeling now on the forest floor, ankle possibly sprained, he becomes aware of an open space ahead. Dark, but lighter than the woods.

The meadow.

For a moment the father can hear something in the grass. A tiny voice. Musical and human. Very small, very clear. There — then gone. Canceled by the sound of a car or truck bounding down the mountain road.

Kaden feels his way along the road. For a few yards, before the trees get thick, the night is like a picture in a storybook: the road faintly glows, but on every page it gets a little blacker. The boy stops, looks back. Focuses on a window of the house pulsing with television light. Figures out, finally, why his feet are hurting. He sits on the rocky dirt. Taking sneakers off is one thing, trying to put them back on in the dark another. He remembers one time in the car (he had no brother yet and his seat faced backward) seeing through the window a girl with dark glasses and a long silver wand which showed her where to go. He needs a wand. Without a wand, he will never, ever find them. He holds a sneaker up to the sky, eyes squinting and blinking. Slowly the object comes clear to him. The red stripes, the contour of the toe. Not until the light grows bright enough to reveal the terrain of the road and to make the trunks of trees leap out from the forest does Kaden wonder about the source of it, turning his head, imagining that such radiance could only come from a friendly, enchanted star.

◆

She glimpses the trailhead (the little tin marker, stick figure with walking stick, nailed to the tree) and hears, at the very same moment, the panic of wheels going into a skid, treads clawing violently at dirt and rock, then the collision — crush of metal, bleat of a horn — and the harmonics of breaking glass. Isabel freezes. Same as when she wakes in her bed, having heard something that may have been nothing. Running down the road now is like all the times she has moved through her home in the dead of night. This is something, this is nothing . . . Isn't that also what she told herself in the days after the ultrasound? On that screen they had seen the ghost of an impossible fetus. Six limbs. Two arms and four legs, each foot badly twisted and missing toes. She saw the images with her own eyes (the technician had printed enough pictures to fill a scrapbook). She heard everything the doctors said in the days afterward about how and why and what to do about it. Still, a patchy fog obscured her vision. Static broke on her eardrums like ocean waves. A few months later she reached for that curtain in the NICU, fearing suddenly that she might be about to suffer a crippling blow. But no. As she pulled the curtain aside, her body felt no shock from without, only a sweet confirmation from within. Not like other boys. And not entirely human. But why all this grave talk of abnormalities and deformities, when anyone can see he is exquisitely formed? A beautiful boy from the waist up, and from the waist down, a beautiful horse . . . Now she runs, as on a tightrope. Each time she blinks, a film of tears spreads evenly over the surface of her eyes, and through this aqueous medium, the light down below (dim; one headlight bulb must have burst on impact) looks like an aura suffusing the scene of the accident. No, no, no. A voice in her head, hers but not hers, keeps saying the word, as if refusing to find something horrible is to omit it from reality. When she reaches the foot of the hill, feet skidding, her lungs crumple and contract. No room for air. The truck is sunk front-first in a ditch at a forty-five-degree angle, rear wheels in the air, hood reshaped by a tree trunk. The driver, ejected from his seat and halfway through the windshield — lower body in the cab, upper on the glass-spangled hood — isn't moving. "Oh God," the mother says aloud. Then starts calling for her baby. Shining the light into the ditch; into the trees; finally onto the road, where it finds first a tiny red-striped sneaker, then her other son, her human son, sitting in the dirt, staring, mesmerized by the wreck.

Though Martin hears the crash, he is also deaf to it. In the peace that follows, there seems to be only one sound in the universe: it comes from the heart of the meadow. "Uh-boo-boo-bah. Uh-voo. Uh-bah-bah-bah-bah-bah." Martin can see him — a four-legged shadow moving through the grass — and as the father emerges from the trees, the sky above the child expands. Not the first time he's been out here after dark. Last summer he made love with his wife under this blown-glass sky. Still, the place feels like a new discovery to him. Never has he seen a thicker spread of stars. Beneath all those dots of light, the baby continues to murmur in a private dialect. When Martin comes within a few yards, he stops and whispers:

"Sebastian."

The boy turns. Neither startles and runs off, nor comes rushing into his daddy's arms. It's as if the parent has been present all along, as if there's nothing extraordinary about the situation. Again he thinks, My son is walking. Only this time the idea, the sight of it, gives him a shiver of amazement. He crouches down and watches. He watches his strange son walk. Emotion twists once more like a knife in his belly. If it were up to Martin alone, the surgery would have been performed long ago. The forelegs lopped off. After that, an operation to alter the angle of the femur, another (involving the embedding of metal hooks and wires) to straighten the spine. Six weeks in a cast. Then laser hair removal. Genital reconstruction. The doctors call it medical necessity. He can't stay like this. He will never walk. He never will — But he is. Ever since the birth, Martin has been praying he'll wake up. Wake up to find that the world is really a mundane place. Now, under the zodiac sky with this infant, he sees the absurdity of the notion; and with a trembling inside, he thinks to turn away from it. The insight seems part of the night, part winter and part spring, something he can breathe in and keep breathing in. Very slowly, he stands and moves closer. Places a hand on the boy's body, on his bare back, the root of his spine, where soft white skin grades into a coat of hair.

◆

He will fall asleep now: here, in his father's arms, long before they reach the house, before they come upon the accident. Breathing the sweet fumes of pine needles. Feeling through the father's flesh the warmth of flowing blood, which is his blood too. When Martin starts to run, Sebastian's eyes will flutter open. He will glimpse the light, the vehicle, the body slumped over the hood. But he won't remember. He won't remember and he'll never forget the night he ran away and his father brought him home. It's the kind of impossible story that holds a family together. You tell it over and over again; and with the passage of time, the tale becomes more unbelievable and at the same time increasingly difficult to disprove, a myth about the life you carry.

ADAM JOHNSON

Hurricanes Anonymous

FROM *Tin House*

NONC PULLS UP outside Chuck E. Cheese's and hits the hazards on his UPS van. The last working cell tower in Lake Charles, Louisiana, is not far away, so he stops here a couple of times a day to check his messages. He turns to his son, who's strapped into a bouncy chair rigged from cargo hooks, and attempts to snag his cell from the boy, a two-and-a-half-year-old named Geronimo.

"Eyeball," Geronimo says into the phone. "Eyeball."

It's one of the boy's few words, and Nonc has no idea what it means.

"Trade?" Nonc asks as he raises a sippy cup of chocolate milk. "For some gla-gla?"

Geronimo has puffy little-boy eyes, white nubby teeth, and an unfortunate sunburn.

"Eyeball" is all the boy will say.

Nonc next waves his DIAD, the electronic pad customers use to sign for their packages. It's got GPS, Wi-Fi, cellular, and Bluetooth capabilities, though most of that is worthless since the hurricane. The kid goes for it, and Nonc steps down into the parking lot, which is a checkerboard of green and blue tents.

The boarded-up Outback Steakhouse next door is swamped with FEMA campers, and a darkened AMC 16 is a Lollapalooza of urban camping. It's crazy, but weeks after losing everything, people seem to have more stuff than ever — and it's all the shit you'd want to get rid of: Teflon pans, old towels, coffee cans of silverware. How do you tell your thin bed sheets from your neighbor's? Can you separate your yellowed, mismatched Tupperware from the world's?

And there are mountains of all-new crap. Outside the campers are bright purple laundry bins, molded-plastic porch chairs, and the deep black of Weber grills, which is what happens when Wal-Mart is your first responder.

Inside, the place is packed, everyone looking sunburned and glassy-eyed in donated T-shirts and baggy-ass sweats. Nonc heads for the restroom, but when he opens the door, a loafy steam rolls out that makes it clear a hundred people have just taken a dump, and even Nonc — a guy who has lately improvised toilet paper from first-aid compresses, a miniature New Testament, and the crust of Chuck E.'s own pizza — even he backs out.

Nonc steals all the plastic spoons and napkins, then checks his voice mail, trying not to focus on the people around him — they're so clueless and pathetic, sitting around Chuck E. Cheese's all day, a place that's only open because it's a Christian outfit. Sure, Nonc shouldn't point fingers — he's had some mosquito problems lately and his wraparound sunglasses have given him a raccoon tan line. But nobody gave him free clothes and prepaid calling cards after he was evicted last year and all his possessions were auctioned by the sheriff.

First, there's a text message from his girlfriend Relle: *411+XXX.*

Then there's a message from a doctor in L.A. about his father. Nonc's old man is a garden-variety scoundrel, and on the scale of bad dads, he probably rates only a medium, but because of his ability to write vicious and unrelenting Post-it notes, he was one of the most avoided characters in Lake Charles, right up to the day he stole Nonc's car and left town. Nonc's father can't speak, so once or twice a year Nonc gets a call from somebody who's been suckered into the task of reading a stream of Post-its.

The doctor's text message is this: *Your father is very ill and not expected.* Nonc's dad has had cancer before, so the diagnosis isn't exactly news. There's something right about it, though. A man spends his life "not expected" — isn't that how it should end?

Nonc steps up on one of the kiddie rides, a paddy wagon driven by a singing rat. From this height, he can see that the evacuees are all wearing orange FEMA bracelets and the same cheap-ass white sneakers. Eating pizza all day, watching TV. It's true these folks had it bad — got hit by Katrina, then evacuated to Lake Charles, only to get hit by Rita three weeks later. But Rita has passed, and it's high time to get their shit tight. Someone needs to tell them that they're better off without their coffee tables and photo albums. Some person is going to have to break it to them that their apartments weren't so great, that losing track of half their relatives is probably for the best. Some shit, though, you got to figure for yourself. Nonc lifts a hand.

"Does anybody know Marnie Broussard?" he asks them, yet again. "She's a white girl from Treme, in New Orleans. She's the mother of my boy."

Soon Nonc's UPS van is grinding toward the top of the Lake Charles Bridge. The bridge cuts the city in two, and it has this weird way of making you forget. Nonc goes over it like ten times a day — parts for the petrochemical plants, drops at the riverboat casinos, a million foam coolers of crawfish to the airport — though he never really thought about the power of the bridge till the hurricanes came. This morning Nonc delivered sausage casings to the hog lots in Lacassine and Taser batteries to the Calcasieu jail, but once he's climbing the bridge, suddenly there's no more pig squeal in his ears and his clothes don't stink of louse powder and prison okra. There's just the clean smell of rice barges, oyster shale in the sun, and that sandwich spread of ocean, twenty miles south.

For the bridge to work, there's only one thing you got to not think about, and that's how this lady from New Orleans tossed her kids off last week. She lined those tots up for the old heave-ho, and when the deed was done, when it was her turn to splash, she chickened. The bridge is no stranger to jumpers, and Nonc has driven past exhaust-blackened wreaths and *we miss you so-and-so* spray-painted down the guardrail. What gets Nonc is that in his experience, parents abandon you slowly, bit by bit, across your entire youth. Even after you get over being ditched, they keep calling to remind you. So the thought of casting off your children in one stroke is unnerving and new. He's used to thinking of his boy as being out of reach, but out there somewhere, New Orleans probably, able to be found if need be. He looks over at the boy on the seat, his faraway stare visible even through eyes squinted against the wind. But nothing to get misty about. Nonc knows exactly how it will play out for that mom: they'll blame the hurricane and put her in a halfway house for a year, then she'll move to Vegas or something and live on dollar-ninety-nine prime rib. Maybe Marnie will be there too, living all high-hog on baby back ribs.

Nonc coasts down the backside of the bridge before turning onto Lake Street, where the fat homes are, with their long docks and boathouses. Because the rich folks are still poshing it up wherever rich folks evacuate to, this will be the last section of town to get service restored. Sections from downed oak trees have been rolled like old tires in the ditch, and Nonc's van lumbers over sprays of brick from fallen chimneys, making Geronimo's yellow boom box skip.

"Grow-grow," the boy shouts.

"Easy there, hot rod," Nonc says, forwarding through the CD tracks — there's Ernie and Bert singing "Elbow Room" and then there's "Batty-Bat," which the Dracula puppet does. He turns it up when Grover starts rapping the ABC's.

It took him a week to figure out the boy was trying to say "Grover." Nonc's had "custody" of him since the day after Katrina. New Orleans was being evacuated, buses coming in by the caravan, and the city was already overrun with tuffdicks from the offshore rigs. Nonc was making a FEMA delivery, which meant wading into a casino parking lot filled with thousands of people, looking for anyone wearing a tie. He emerged to find Geronimo in his van with a yellow boom box and a bag of clothes.

Marnie didn't even leave a note. Do you brush a toddler's teeth? What do you do when a boy stays awake all night staring at the roof of the van? Nonc would give anything for a vocabulary sheet. What does *bway* mean? And the initials MO? So far Nonc's figured out a couple dozen words — *back, bed, mess, broke* — things like that. *Gla-gla* is chocolate milk. When he needs help, he says, "Up, up." And then there's *eyeball,* which he says clear as a bell — why, what the hell for?

Relle taught the boy *hug* and *kiss.* You can say, "Baby kiss van," and though you can tell he doesn't want to, he'll go like a robot and put his lips on the dusty fender. Relle is always saying, "Baby hug chair," and it kills her it's so cute. Geronimo goes into this seek-and-destroy mode, and the next thing you know he's got to third base with the nearest barstool. And it was Relle's idea that the boy should call him Nonc rather than Randall, his real name.

Nonc and Relle call him Rascal, G, G-Ron, Nimo, things like that, because he can't understand his full name, let alone say it. That should tell you what kind of guy Nonc was back when Marnie told him she was pregnant. "Geronimo," he said, in that fuck-it way, like someone jumping from a plane. He didn't say it in a birth-certificate way; at least he thinks he didn't. Marnie moved to New Orleans, had the boy there, and once she figured out how to garnish Nonc's wages, there wasn't much need to talk. Yet here they are, one mean delivery team — Nonc belted the boy's highchair to the jump seat, and the changing station folds down from the rear doors. So Nonc's surviving. It's been five weeks already, and Marnie's vacation from parenthood can't last forever. Hurricane or no, there are only so many places to hide in Lake Charles.

The utility crews have cut a primitive path down Lake Street. The shrubs have been trimmed by sheets of flying glass and the trees are shot through with the cotton candy of insulation.

Up ahead are a few City of Tulsa trucks and a command van. Some linemen are working their way down the street in a halo of sawdust and two-stroke smoke, while the electricians, T-shirts on their heads, sit in fold-up fishing chairs in the shade of a sailboat on its side. You can tell these guys have been living out of their rigs — milk crates of rations are everywhere, half-washed clothes flap from the outriggers of a boom truck. It's easy to live out of your vehicle, though. Once you accept your situation, your shit gets tight real quick.

The package they're delivering isn't some exotic engineering part or anything. When Nonc pulls the box off the shelf, the label reads *Amazon*. Nonc climbs down with it while Geronimo follows with the DIAD — it's his job to get the signatures. An electrician wearing a flipped-up welder's hood descends in a cherry picker to direct them toward a man sitting on the only surviving dock, reading blueprints.

He's an older guy, in his fifties probably, wearing a green boonie-rat hat and some serious binoculars, the kind with orange lenses. Nonc and the boy make their way over, Nonc calling out the address label, "Bob Vollman, City of Tulsa utilities, care of Lake Charles, Louisiana."

"That would be me," Vollman says. "Thank God for Amazon — and UPS, of course."

With a folding knife, he unwraps *Snyder's Guide to the Birds of the Gulf Wetlands.*

"People mostly shoot at birds around here," Nonc says.

Geronimo holds up the DIAD, and the engineer takes notice of him, pulls off his hat. With his hand, like a puppeteer, he makes the floppy hat talk like Yoda. "A signature is wanted, hmm?" the hat asks. "And here we have what, hmm, a child, a boy child, have we, yes?"

Geronimo nears the hat and stares into its folds as if trying to determine its intentions.

Yoda scrunches his face. "Serious, this one is, hmm. Much turmoil has he seen." The engineer glances at Nonc for confirmation. "All around is uncertainty." The puppet looks up and down the street, but Geronimo doesn't follow. "Broken are many things, yes, and not in their proper places." Vollman has the puppet take the stylus and, mumbling, as if its mouth were too full to talk, sign the DIAD. That gets a laugh.

"Got a boy exactly his age," Vollman says. "Two kids off to college, and then along comes Henry."

"Cajuns call that lagniappe," Nonc says. "It means getting more than you were bargaining for."

"I tell you," Vollman says, tousling Geronimo's hair. "It sure is hard to leave them."

Nonc has tried to imagine that moment Marnie put the boy in the van — if only he could think up what she said to him when she left, maybe he'd know where she went, when she might be coming back for him.

"What did you tell him," Nonc asks, "you know, when you left?"

"Henry?"

"Yeah."

"I said, 'I'll be right back.' Kids this age, they don't understand time. They don't know what a month is. Plus, they don't remember. I made some mistakes, parentwise, believe me. At this age, you got some wiggle room."

"This is all just temporary," Nonc says. "The boy's going back with his mama soon."

"The hurricane turned some lives upside down," Vollman says. "Obviously you two are in some kind of situation, but seriously, the boy can't be running around in his jammies. Look at the glass and nails. He needs some boots and jeans, something."

The pajamas are actually a custom tracksuit that Relle made for the boy, but Nonc doesn't say anything.

Vollman lifts up his new field guide. "Amazon has tons of kid stuff."

At the sight of the book, Geronimo says, "Bird."

"That's right," Vollman says. "Let's check out a Tweety Bird." He lifts the binoculars and invites Geronimo to share, each of them peering through one of the lenses. Squinting, they do a sweep of the lake. "Saw a blue macaw this morning," Vollman says. "Not exactly Louisiana wildlife, but quite a sight. He was sitting on an upturned barge, right out there on the water, a big bell pepper in his beak."

"Macaw," the boy says.

"That's right," Vollman says.

"Big bird."

"That's right, she was one big bird."

Standing above them, Nonc too looks out on the water. With the outbound tide, all the refuse in the lake is dog-paddling back toward them, across three miles of brown chop. Shielding his eyes, Nonc makes out roof timbers, recycling bins, logged couch cushions, and all the garage-filling crap a human can own. Out there slowly turning, as if from a logroller, is a black septic tank, and from the water, like a shark, a boat hull rises, flashes its keel, and vanishes. Nonc was picturing those kids from New Orleans falling into blue lake water. He imagined their eyes open, their hands reaching for one another, the knowledge that at least they had each other. But here it is, dark, entangling, a roil of propane tanks, plywood sheets, and fifty-five-gallon drums.

Nonc takes the long way around the lake to the southwest Louisiana visitors' center, which is where Relle works. Instead of handing out brochures for the "Cajun Riviera," Relle now spends her time drawing maps for relief workers to where towns like Gueydan and Grand Chenier used to be. Hurricane or no, the state is flush from gaming, so everybody still gets a souvenir bottle of Tabasco, a Sportsman's Paradise ball cap, and a string of Mardi Gras beads draped on by a pretty girl. Relle is the pretty girl.

Through the window, Nonc can see her talking to some government types, guys with that carefree look that comes from being able to walk away. They're wearing like six strings of beads each, and they're all smiling and laughing, with Relle pausing at their punch lines to fan herself with a coupon book. Nonc flashes his lights at her, points across the street to a roadhouse that Marnie used to haunt back in the day. He flips across the street, hits his hazards, and jams a straw into a juice box. "Baby drink juice," Nonc tells the boy and snags his cell. "Nonc be right back."

Geronimo lifts his arms and strains at his bouncy chair.

"Bway," he says. "Bway."

"Look," Nonc says. "Nonc's got business."

Inside the roadhouse, Nonc does a quick survey, then checks out a wall of beer mugs. If you hang out long enough, they put up a mug with your name on it. The wall's a regular *Who's Not Who* of south Louisiana, but no Marnie. The bartender looks like a tuffdick on leave from an oil rig. He asks what'll it be, and when Nonc says, "Nothing, thanks," the bartender raps the bar twice with his knuckle, which is what riverboat dealers do to point out a lack of gratuity.

All casual, Nonc asks, "You know a Marnie Broussard, ever see her come around?"

"You trying to make some kind of small talk?" the bartender asks. "You want a drink or what?"

"This girl," Nonc says. "She used to come in here, got dark hair, deep-set eyes."

The bartender drafts a beer, sets it in front of Nonc like it's the last one on earth. "Hurricane relief," he says. "On the house."

Nonc opens his phone, finds a weak signal, and scrolls to the doctor's number. He doesn't really know what he's going to say to the guy, but he calls. Just when it seems like no one's going to answer, the phone picks up, but no one's there. And then Nonc can hear the valve in his father's trach tube clicking. Nonc hears that thing in his sleep. The history of that sound, of its wet, wheezy rhythm, is like a country song. It's "The Battle Hymn of the Republic."

If that doctor's right, Nonc's dad's going to die for sure this time. But the truth is it's just an event. Life's full of events — they occur and you adjust, you roll and move on. But at some point, like when your girlfriend Marnie tells you she's pregnant, you realize that some events are actually developments. You realize there's a big plan out there you know nothing about, and a development is a first step in that new direction. Somebody drops a kid in your lap

— that's a development, you've just been clued in. Your ex–old lady disappears — you can't shrug that off. It's a serious development. Sometimes things seem like bigtime developments — you get your wages garnished, your old man takes your car when he leaves town, you get evicted, your possessions seized — but in time you adjust, you find a new way and realize they didn't throw you off course, they didn't change you. They were just events. The truth is the hurricane didn't change Nonc's life one bit. Neither will the death of his father. The tricky part, Nonc has figured out, is telling the difference between the two.

Nonc's just kind of sitting there, staring at the phone, when Relle walks into the bar. She always wears these sexy tracksuits — satiny, falling across her body — that she sews herself.

"Who you talking to?" she asks.

"It's my old man," he tells her.

Startled, she says, "I thought he was dying."

Nonc shrugs.

"Did you call him, or did he call you?" she asks, but she can see the answer on his face. "What did you tell him?"

"I don't know. What's there to say?"

"What's there to say? You hardly shut up about him."

"Me? You're the one who always brings him up. You never even met him."

"I don't need to meet him." She reaches for the phone. "I know all about him."

Nonc knows he shouldn't hand it over — in Relle there is a cold, truthful streak — but he does.

Just to be sure, she asks Nonc, "You're positive he can't talk, right?" When Nonc nods, she smiles. "Mr. Richard," she says into the phone. "I'm Cherelle. I'm a friend of Randall's, and I'm going to tell you a story. Once upon a time, there was a man who lived only for himself. He used up his family, making the most of them the way you'd make the most of a single square of toilet paper. He stole his son's car, and finally he was gone, which is the happy ending. What could he possibly want now?"

When she hurts his father for him, Nonc feels a shiver of fear and satisfaction.

Still, he says, "Ouch, did I mention he's fucking dying?"

She flips the phone shut. "Where's the G-Man?" she asks.

"He's chillin' in the rig. I can't believe you just said that shit. You were talking to my dad, you know, not yours."

Relle takes ahold of the beer, has a drink. "He had his chance."

Nonc takes a drink too. "You think they'll cremate him?"

"Who's they?" she asks.

"You know, California."

"Like the state government? No way, sunshine. That shit's expensive. You're going to have to go all the way out there and bring him back. You got to have a funeral, it's the law."

"You know what I'd love to do?" Nonc asks. "I'd love to take his ashes and scatter them on my mother's lawn. Wouldn't that freak her shit out?"

"I think your only chance is to go out to California, and when they lift the sheet, when you have to identify him, you say it's not your dad. Then it's the government's dime."

Nonc takes a hard look at Relle. "Where do you get this shit?" he asks her. "This isn't about money."

He can tell she wants to say something smart about that, about how Marnie garnishes his wages, but Relle checks herself. By way of sympathy, she says, "You'll never see that car again."

"I know," he says. It was only a Toyota, but those things run forever.

Then she pulls out a photograph, a color copy of one at least, and slides it to him. It's a blurry image of a woman on a table.

"You checking morgues now?" Nonc asks.

"No," she says. "FEMA's got a cadaver book you can flip through."

"Sorry to break it, but this isn't Marnie."

"Did you look at it? Five foot four, bottle blonde, bit of fetal alcohol to the eyes."

"Don't say shit like that."

"Did Marnie have a C-section?"

"How should I know?" he asks.

"Look, I don't want this to be her," Relle says. "Nobody wants nobody dead. I mean, that little boy needs a mom bigtime."

"Marnie's not dead," Nonc says. "She's on a little vacation from parenthood, that's all. Actually, this is just like her, pulling something like this."

Relle shrugs. "Then why not go to Beaumont and see? If it's not her, great. Nothing's changed. If it is her, nothing's changed, except now you can plan, now you can take steps."

Nonc slides the picture back. "You don't know Marnie. She's not the kind to drown in a Quick Mart in Texas. She's going to come out of this hurricane better than ever."

"Lighter, at least," Relle says.

"She probably got some FEMA money and is living it up. When that's gone, she'll be back."

"Who ditches their kid in the good times and comes back in the bad?"

Nonc doesn't have an answer for that.

Relle opens her purse and digs inside. "Why don't you want to find her?" she asks.

Nonc takes one more drink and sets the beer aside. "I'm looking just as hard as you."

From her purse Relle removes a big Q-tip sealed in plastic. "I almost forgot," she says.

"Forgot what?"

"Open wide," she tells him.

"What for?"

"Just open up," she says, removing the wrapper.

When Nonc does, she jabs the thing in his mouth, right in his gums, and twirls it.

"What the hell was that?"

"It's a swab."

"A swab of what?"

Relle takes a slug of beer and puts the swab in a plastic tube.

"We better check on the little man," she says. "'Cause I have to roll."

Outside, crunching through the bottle caps and shale of the parking lot, they can hear Geronimo in the van. He's saying, "Up, up." When Nonc sticks his head inside, he can see that the boy's managed to get the lid off one of the foam coolers. There are crawfish running around everywhere, and Geronimo, in terror, is dancing in place.

"Whoa," Relle says. "Party for one."

She moves to climb inside, but Nonc tells her, "It's okay. I got this."

"You pissed off?"

"No," he says. "We'll talk about it tonight."

"At AA?"

The boy is trying to climb the cords of his bouncy chair.

"Where the hell else?" Nonc says. "Look, I gotta take care of this."

But instead of leaving, Relle steps inside the van. "He is so adorable," she says. "One day we're going to have a little boy just like him." Then she sticks a swab in his mouth.

"What the fuck are you doing?"

"It's just a test," she says, then scrambles out of the van. "FEMA does it for free, to reconnect family members."

Nonc comes after her. "Are you crazy?" he asks. "This is my boy. Right here, he's mine."

"You don't know that," she says, and then, in her tracksuit, she bolts across the frontage road.

When Nonc climbs in the van, the crawfish are all clicking their pinchers, and he realizes Geronimo has the hiccups, which he gets when he freaks. "Up, up," the boy says. He's kicking his legs and straining the cords of the bouncy chair.

It gets Nonc to see him like that. "Hey, hot rod," he says. "Don't be scared of those guys. Nonc's here, okay. Nonc will protect you."

He unhooks the cords, and the boy latches on. He's totally shaking, snot all over his face.

Even though he's not dirty, Nonc takes him into the back of the van for a diaper change. That always soothes him. "Relax, relax," Nonc whispers and lays him back on his changing pad. The boy's still looking around for the crawfish, eyes going this way and that.

"Nonc's back, okay. Nonc always comes back." But there's no way to explain it to the kid. Right now, when he's afraid, he thinks fear lasts forever, that it is everything.

Nonc shimmies off his pants, then unfastens the diaper. He tosses the thing away, even though it's perfectly fine. Geronimo starts to chill when Nonc slides a fresh diaper under him. Nonc keeps saying "Hush," and when he asks the boy to lift his legs, Geronimo quietly obeys, holding them up and keeping them there. That's when Nonc does his favorite part. He takes the baby powder and raises it high. Very lightly he lets it snow down. The stuff is cool and sweet-smelling. He shakes the thing, and his son's eyes follow the dusty white powder as it slowly floats down. The boy can watch it forever.

The UPS yard is almost empty, its skeleton crew of drivers out on the road. Nonc docks the van so they can clean and fuel it before heading out again. Geronimo grabs the hose, and as Nonc sweeps the crawfish out onto the pavement, the boy sprays them into the storm drain. He seems to relish the way they skitter against the beam of water, but when they've all finally disappeared, when they've slipped through the grate for good, he looks lost.

UPS lets Nonc keep all his food and milk in the refrigerated cargo bay, so he can bootstrap up a few PB and J sandwiches and reload the sippy cups between runs. UPS is the coolest company that way — they let Nonc take the van at night, the way a cop brings home a squad car, and they look the other way about Geronimo riding shotgun. As long as you don't fuck up and get your name in the paper, Brown is on your side. One driver got drunk and ran his van into a ditch. UPS just towed it out, no questions. Got him some counseling, sent him back on the road.

Nonc downloads a new manifest to the DIAD, which diagrams the optimal route — right away he sees that one of the stops is his own address, or old one, the place on Kirkman Avenue he was evicted from. He heads there first. On his street a pair of white oaks has blown down, letting a new light fall on the fourplex, so that he almost doesn't recognize it when he pulls up. All four doors have been kicked in, and on the porch some crows are taking turns poking their heads in a cereal box.

Nonc enters to see his old TV on its stand, his couch blooming with mold, his table and chair dusted with broken glass. The rest of the stuff isn't his — the dishes on the floor, the broken picture frames, the bicycle on its back by the door. These things used to mean something to him. When did he find time to sit on this couch? He feels like the person who owned that couch is just as much of a stranger as the person whose family photos litter the floor.

That's when Nonc looks at the package and sees that it is addressed to himself, Randall Richard, from his father. Nonc picks up a piece of glass and slits open the box. Inside is a note, one of his father's unmistakable notes: "Aside from killing me, California has been okay. These are my effects. They asked what I wanted done with them, and I didn't know."

Nonc turns the note over to see if there's more, but there isn't. Inside are his father's clothes, his pants, shirt, belt, and ball cap. Nonc's pretty okay with the man's death, but the notion that he'll never get dressed again, that he's to die in a gown, seems strange and impossible. There's also a wallet. Tooled into the leather is NONC, short for N'Oncle, a Cajun term for *uncle* that's used for close family friends. It's what he called his father when he was a boy, before he started calling him Harlan. It suddenly occurs to Nonc that he never called his father Dad, and now, weirdly, neither does his own son.

Inside the wallet are a Costco membership, some cash, and a handwritten list of Internet casinos with ID numbers and passwords. There is a California driver's license with an address in L.A. that he could map with his DIAD, and there's an ancient, laminated doctor's note stating that he is a mute. Nonc picks up a key chain, a large one with all manner of car keys, Toyota, Ford, Hyundai. One of the keys is for a boat, a Grady-White, which is the best kind. And there's a packet of white hankies, which his father used to clean his trach tube. All this stuff is just sitting on Nonc's lap. It feels like he's rifling through it, like his dad might walk in at any moment and catch him. It feels like his father died long ago, and these are relics. He brushes it all onto the couch — the keys, the cash, LSU ball cap. He stands and takes a last look around. He tries to separate the different owners of all this stuff, tries to put them together. He tries to close the door behind him, but it is broken.

To get a break from Geronimo, Nonc and Relle attend AA meetings at the Presbyterian church, where an old maw-maw provides free child care. For two hours a night they get to drink coffee and listen to other people's problems. Tonight Nonc arrives first, and after dropping off the boy, he grabs a piece of king cake and sits in the half-empty circle.

The regulars start arriving. Even though it's "anonymous," Lake Charles isn't such a big town, and Nonc's knocked on just about every door. Linda Tasso shows up, the oldest daughter of the mayor. She manages to find a new rock bottom every week, goes on and on about it. Jay Arceneaux brings this giant truck-stop thermos of iced tea. He used to run a reptile zoo out by the interstate, snakes and gators galore. He sobered up when they slapped him with animal-cruelty charges after they caught him adopting too many kittens and puppies from the pound. Some folks from New Orleans show up — you can spot them right away, that look of wearing someone else's clothes, those faraway eyes.

Finally Relle strolls in — she's got a chocolate and maroon tracksuit on, and she takes a chair across the circle from Nonc. She slouches in her seat, which pulls the fabric of her pants tight enough that you can see the shadow of her pussy. The girl has really taken a shine to AA meetings, and not just because it's the only time they're free of the boy. She seems to love the idea that normal-looking people, people with careers and houses, are actually, according to their own testimony, weak and susceptible. Relle was the one pretty girl in high school who was never popular, so she loves standing in their group at break, being among the chitchat, bumming cigarettes, laughing when they start to laugh. And then there's that moment when the break is over and everyone heads back inside for the second hour, that moment when she takes Nonc's hand and leads him into the van.

She's even become a talker at the meetings. She loves to discuss the state of their relationship, out loud, in front of witnesses. Tonight she starts right in. One of the evacuees from New Orleans stands up. "My name is James B.," he says, "and I am an alcoholic," and then Relle is off and running. But Nonc's still staring at James B., who's wearing a brand-new Chuck E. Cheese's T-shirt, and the crispness of the white makes the rest of him look battered, like some shit has truly befallen him.

"My boyfriend," Relle says, and looks toward the ceiling as if nobody knows who that might be. "My boyfriend's real strong, but so is his problem. There are struggles ahead and he can't see them. A funeral's on the horizon, travel. I'm trying to help him. I'm offering my hand, but I'm afraid he's not going to take it."

Bill Maque, the guy who runs Game and Fish, says, "Tell your boyfriend that he needs to find a meeting before he travels. Trust me, they need to be expecting him."

"A funeral," Linda Tasso volunteers. "Send in the shrinks, that's a guaranteed spiral."

Nonc's job is to figure out what "problem" Relle's really talking about. Last night she said, "Nobody should have to handle two people's problems," which was code for the position Marnie had put them in, and that, hell or high water, that girl had to be found. But Nonc can't tell if tonight's problem has something to do with Marnie or that paternity test, either of which could result in major developments. Your baby's mama is dead? Your baby's not your baby? Those things are as irreversible as a kid thrown from a bridge, and if Nonc knows anything, it's that you want to minimize developments in life — a few are going to happen, sure, but don't go looking for them, and you sure as shit don't cause them.

"I can't speak for your boyfriend," Nonc says, "but maybe he's thinking, Thanks for the hand but he's on top of it. Maybe he doesn't need any help right now."

Even though it's anonymous, everyone turns to look at Nonc. He can read their minds — *Dude,* they're thinking, *take the help.*

Astonished, Relle says, "You saying my boyfriend doesn't want my hand?"

"Take the hand," James B. calls out. He looks up. "Lord, help him take that hand."

It's clear the man is imploring the Creator himself, and it puts weird gravity in the room.

Nonc says, "I'm just saying maybe your boyfriend's doing okay. He's surviving, right? He's putting one foot in front of the other, he's making it."

Linda Tasso chimes in with a "One day at a time."

"Maybe that's what my boyfriend thinks," Relle says. "But he's stuck, and going nowhere is going backward. I'm making plans, you know. I'm trying to bring him with me."

"What makes you think you know what's best for him?"

"Because he's in my heart," Relle says. "And because I know him better than he knows himself."

Wearily, people turn to look at Nonc. They've had about enough of tonight's episode of the Cherelle Show, but Nonc doesn't care. "If this guy's in your heart," he says, "then so are all his mistakes, you know — so is his kid."

Relle leans forward in her chair. "I am making you," she says. She looks into Nonc's eyes. "Nobody ever made you, no one ever cared enough. Take my hand, let me make you."

That's when James B. points toward the rafters. "The roof is weak," he says, and everybody looks up. "Lord, let it be weak, let me find where."

There is a silence and James B. stands. He really doesn't look very good.

"I used to plot out every single drink," he says. "I used to plot the liquor store. Now you got to plot away from it, from the glow of it. Why would the Lord make a liquor store glow? Now you got to plot out a folding chair, a cup of coffee." He looks at his coffee like he's never seen coffee. "You got to plot a toilet, a bus, a single slice of pizza. Take the dogs off the chain."

Nervously, Jay Arceneaux says, "Okay, I think we've all been where James has been."

"Seize the knife from that table, you will need it," James B. says, and he is talking like a man from a Bible story, like he is one of the guys spelled out in the stained glass above.

Jay Arceneaux stands. Fake laughing, he says, "Hey, no knives, please." He looks at Bill Maque like he should stand too. "James B., we can hear your hurt," Jay says. He has a Bible. He opens his arms. "Would you like some personal fellowship?"

"Prepare for the dark," James B. says. "The water's at your feet, your knees, ribs. All day long I used to breathe for a drink. Close my eyes, and I'd still see the glow — Budweiser blue, Coors yellow. Take your knife to the ceiling, plot your way through the attic. Beware, that insulation floats. A bottle you hid long ago. Take the dogs, please take my dogs off the chain. In that small space, insulation will swarm you. You got to plot the roof. Please let it be weak. Cut till you see the glow, in the dark water look for the glowing. Make yourself small, scrape through. Lord, unhook the chain off the porch or else they do drown."

After the break, Nonc has Cherelle's legs high, and he's inside her. The van smells of baby wipes and crawfish. And from the chapel come the sounds of scales on the organ. The notes are aimless and mechanical, someone trying and trying to do better. Relle's thing is that she looks right at you when you're doing it, that she never unlocks her eyes. It's kind of unnerving, but Relle says she can't help it, and she reminds Nonc that she comes every time. She reminds him how well their bodies fit, the fold of his arms around her shoulders, the way her legs figure-four his waist. Sometimes, though, Nonc gets the distinct feeling she's trying not to come, like she doesn't want to let go of something. Maybe it's more like she's trying to delay it, be in control of it for as long as she can. Nonc can feel her fight what's building, and when she finally gives in, when she lets herself be swept, that's when she closes her eyes.

The result is that, with her glaring at him, Nonc tends to close his own eyes, and that puts him in his own world. Then it's easy for your mind to wander. It's easy to start thinking about James B. and what happened to those people in New Orleans. He'd been imagining Marnie freeloading a ride into town to drop off Geronimo in some kind of vacation from parenting. But it's suddenly clear that some shit went down in N.O., to Marnie, to the boy.

Relle reaches down, grabs his hips, and stops him. Sometimes when she's in a bad mood she'll stop him and make him put on a condom, right in the middle. But she doesn't seem mad.

"You heard what I said in there, right?" she asks. "I'm trying to put myself in your heart."

"You're already there."

"Then I need you to act," she says. "Act that way."

"Okay, I'll go to Beaumont — I'll go see if it's her."

Relle reaches into her bag. "It's not her," she says. "I called after lunch. Turns out it was some other dead girl." Relle pulls out a powder-blue debit card from FEMA. "I'm acting," she says. "I'm making a future for us. The thing is, as decisions need to be made, as options materialize, I need to know you're with me."

Nonc's seen a thousand of these cards; all the evacuees have them. The trouble is, they don't help you survive, because there's nothing for sale — the only thing they'll buy is your way out of Louisiana. "Where'd you get this?" he asks.

"There's five grand on it," she says. "It's a small-business grant. They're giving 'em away."

"Small business?"

Relle reaches into her bag and pulls out a brochure for *Nonc's Outfitters.* On it are images of bird dogs and ducks, along with a scan of Nonc's high school photo and, on the back, a Google map to some property her father owns, to the south. "Not bad, huh?" she asks. "I made it on the computer at work. All those hunting dogs and shit? I pulled those pictures off the NRA website. We spend the money on a four-by-four, and there you have it, there's our business. Maybe we'll build a hunting lodge someday. Or whatever, we can spend the money on whatever."

Nonc could remind her that he doesn't know anything about duck hunting, and neither does she. He could mention that her father raised greyhounds, not bloodhounds, that this is technically a crime, that his wages are already garnished. But it's his picture he can't stop thinking about. In it, his smile is a mix of optimism and relief, as if now that high school is over, the hard part is done. It's the sucker's look on people's faces when they got off the buses from Katrina, when they didn't know Rita was on the way.

"At the visitors' center," Relle says, "I get all these calls looking for hunting guides. I'm supposed to take turns recommending the guys on the list. And then it hits me. The answer is right there."

"This kind of shit doesn't bother you?" he asks.

"What?" Relle asks. "The hunters are stockbrokers and shit. We just drive them out there. They've got fancy rifles and gold-plated whistles."

"Shotguns," Nonc tells her. "You hunt birds with shotguns. And you know what I'm talking about."

"You wanna know what bothers me?" she asks. "I'm bothered by living with crazy people for my room and board. I'm bothered by having to go to AA to get a date with you."

He looks at the map to the property Relle's father owns. The guy used to run a racing kennel there. The whole thing was a fiasco, and everybody knows, though nobody will say, that there are dogs buried everywhere. Whenever Nonc feels bad about having his loser dad skip town, he just thinks of Relle and what it's been like to have hers stay. The truth is that Relle's not about schemes and money, but wiping her slate. For someone who grew up the way she did, Relle's the best possible version of herself.

"Just as long as you know how fucked-up this is," he says.

"Please," she says. "I mailed this brochure to four people today — they're sending in their deposits. One of them lives in Hollywood."

She massages him, pulls him inside again, though he can tell she's got the sex cordoned off, like there's a velvet rope between her and what's happening below. Then she's looking at him, a narrowed, questioning gaze. It's not an angry look — he's just being read. He closes his eyes, sees a roadhouse he and Marnie used to go to, the place where they met, actually. It was called the Triple Crown, out on Highway 90. He recalls this one night they went out — hadn't known each other too long — and no, Marnie suddenly says, she doesn't feel like drinking tonight. That was okay with Nonc, he understood, but he had a feeling, and looking back, he knows that what seemed like an insignificant event was a major development. He wouldn't know then for a month, but that was the day Marnie knew she was pregnant. Developments can happen right in front of you like that, you don't even see them.

When it's time, they pick up Geronimo in the annex.

At the door, they pause. Through the little window they can see the maw-maws inside, arms folded as they confer with one another. Relle says, "These ladies give me the creeps."

"Just don't talk to them," Nonc tells her.

"I don't get old ladies," she says. "Who are they, what do they want from you?"

Nonc feels the same way. Old women look all innocent and goody two-shoes, but then they level some all-knowing eyes on your ass. Plus, they look alike — Nonc can't even be sure if these are the same old ladies as last week.

Inside, Geronimo is sitting in a small plastic chair. He's wearing a smock, tied at the waist, and he's real serious about some clay that he's rolling out. He doesn't even notice when they enter. Nonc stares at the boy, his round forehead and long eyelashes. When Geronimo reaches up to rub his ear, Nonc knows he's sleepy.

"Come to Nonc," he calls out and crouches to receive him.

But the boy doesn't move.

The maw-maws walk to Geronimo. One takes his hand. "Such a sweet child," she says.

"Unbearably sweet," the other adds, as she pulls the smock over his head.

When they bring him to Nonc, he can see they've given the boy a haircut, and they've applied a thick cream to his sunburned face. He's in a hand-me-down set of coveralls from the auxiliary.

"You give him a bath?" Nonc asks.

"We cleaned him up a little," one says, then adds, "Geronimo is such a special name."

"Synonymous with resilience and determination."

"In the Apache language, 'Geronimo' means 'fiercely loyal.'"

"One of the books we read together was *The Last Palomino.*"

The women go on and on about all the books they read and activities they did, enunciating everything like they're hosting an event, like Geronimo's a grand guest and Nonc and Relle are being introduced to him for the first time.

One of them takes a drawing of some yellow swirly lines and pins it to the boy's coveralls. The drawing is captioned *Macaw.* "A disaster can be a trying time," she says.

"Especially for a child," the other adds. She holds out a brown paper bag, its top neatly rolled up. "Here are the child's pajamas."

Nonc can feel Relle wince. "Those aren't pajamas," he says. "That's a custom tracksuit, with piping and everything. It's tailor-made with fabric from —"

"Morocco," Relle says.

"From Morocco."

There is a pause. In it, the old ladies give Nonc that look.

"You were right to come here," one of them says. "Geronimo is always welcome here. All of you are. What a perfect age he is."

"A difficult age to be separated from a parent."

"Such a trauma that can be."

"Maybe I'm the boy's parent," Relle says. "Did you think of that? Do you know that I'm not her?"

Outside, it's dark. Nonc fires up the van and heads to Relle's halfway house. He doesn't prowl roadhouses or cruise Charity looking for Marnie. He steps on the gas to blow out the mosquitoes, and they go.

As soon as they arrive, Dr. Gaby opens the door, which means that Nonc won't be sleeping on clean sheets with Relle and Geronimo, that there will be no hot shower and toilet in the A.M. When Geronimo sees Dr. Gaby, he runs and leaps up onto her wheelchair, which makes Nonc cringe because Relle has told him that Dr. Gaby uses a piss bag, that you'd never know it but it's under her clothes.

Dr. Gaby throws Nonc a dubious look. "You cut his hair," she says.

Relle says, "How do you know I didn't give him a haircut?"

Dr. Gaby doesn't respond to this. She turns the boy's face right and left, inspecting the sunburn. "It's better," she says, and throws Nonc a look of true distaste. Then she goes through her routine:

she takes the boy's earlobe and peers inside. She runs a finger along his teeth. With a thumb, she pulls down his eyelid to inspect the white of the eye. She's not a real doctor, though — she was a psychiatrist before she retired because of her condition.

"Haircut itch?" she asks Geronimo.

Geronimo rubs his neck. "Itchy," he says.

Dr. Gaby blows the stubble off his neck, then wheels an about-face and rolls inside.

Nonc and Relle follow. It's not really right to call it a halfway house. There are four residents with permanent problems and they live here permanently. Once you come to this place, you don't go anywhere. Relle doesn't have any training, so her job is more like baby-sitting, and you can believe she has a rule for everything.

Then, in the wake of Katrina, the dream team arrived. They got off a bus from the Superdome holding hands, eight adult men. Dr. Gaby thinks they have entrenched autism, but she doesn't know — they came from an unknown facility without files, medical records, case histories, or full names. Wherever they were housed, they were housed together, accustomed to staying up to ungodly hours and damned if they didn't get their nightly video. Tonight, as Nonc and Relle pass, they are in the living room, drinking diet sodas in the blue glow of a Robin Williams movie.

"They give me the willies," Relle says.

Nonc looks at their uncomprehending faces, at the sodas in their thick hands.

"So pathetic," she adds. "Can you imagine being like that, stuck watching whichever TV show is played for you, living in whatever town the bus plops you in?"

In the kitchen, racks of cookies are cooling, and the smell is overpowering. The counters are custom-made for a wheelchair, so they're just the right height for a little boy. Geronimo, on Dr. Gaby's lap, sits before a large mixing bowl. Dr. Gaby places an egg in Geronimo's hand, then wraps hers around his. Together they crack an egg on the rim. Dr. Gaby then splits the egg, letting the yolk flop into the bowl. Without a word she hands the next egg to Geronimo. He taps it on the rim, then hands it to Dr. Gaby, who splits it.

Relle grabs a cookie. "God, oatmeal," she says with her mouth full. "Someday our kids are gonna live on cookies."

To Relle, Dr. Gaby says, "Those are for the volunteers. And tomorrow's list is on the fridge." Then she turns toward Nonc. "You've gathered that your girlfriend's not too touchy-feely. I must say, though: give the girl a list, and have mercy, she can procure."

Nonc asks, "So nobody's come forward to claim the dream team?" He knows he shouldn't call them that. It's Relle's term, and she calls them the dream team only to get under Dr. Gaby's skin.

"Hundreds of thousands of people are displaced," she says. "I know your famous position that the hurricane is no skin off your nose, but for the rest of us, it's a different matter."

"What if nobody ever comes to get them?" Nonc asks.

"What if," Dr. Gaby says and shrugs. "And before we get too chatty, I can't let you stay tonight, Randall. I know it happens, and I can't control what goes on when I'm not here, but these people, they're vulnerable right now, they need stability. Plus, I need to think of the child."

"Don't you worry about the boy," Nonc says. "He gets taken care of just fine."

"I don't want to imagine," Dr. Gaby says, "where this child spends his nights. But I'm talking about the boy's well-being in this facility. I don't know these men's backgrounds, what they're capable of. Telling right from wrong, that's a luxury of the able-minded. I'd have to take a host of precautions to have that boy safely sleep here." Dr. Gaby lets Geronimo dip a finger in the batter. "Where do you sleep?" she asks him.

Geronimo lights up. "Van," he says. "Baby kiss van."

"That's a sentence," Dr. Gaby says. "I don't want to know what it means, but he's talking in sentences already."

"I taught him that," Relle says.

"We sleep in a fat house by Prien Lake," Nonc says.

Dr. Gaby throws him a look that says, *I bet.*

"Oh God," Relle says to Nonc, "I totally have to show you something." She takes off upstairs.

"So, how's parenthood treating you?" Dr. Gaby asks Nonc. "What have you learned from fatherhood so far?"

"I don't know," Nonc tells her.

She gives him a look.

"You trying to make me uncomfortable? Just go ahead and tell me something I'm doing wrong. I got the boy his shots, okay? Just like you told me."

"Dr. Benson, at the clinic?"

Nonc nods.

"That's good, Randall. That's a step. Have you ever seen a child with rubella? My Lord, and this is when it happens, after a disaster. Classic distribution potential."

Randall takes a cookie. "If these guys could be dangerous, what about you, what about your saftey?"

"Oh, that's not a concern," she says. "There is something I'm concerned about, though. In life, a lot of important decisions are made for us."

It's clear to Nonc that she's about to give a speech, like the one she gave a couple of weeks ago about child development. The truth is that he has discovered, at the age of twenty-six, that he loves being lectured. Never before has someone spoken to him, at length, with the sole purpose of making him better.

"I wouldn't have chosen to live in Lake Charles," Dr. Gaby says. "My marriage didn't work out as I would have wished. My illness, I didn't choose that. Similar things must be true for you, right? You're adaptive, though, very flexible. It's one of your attributes. But when it comes to things like that boy, you can't ever bend. You have to choose him — then you have to be one hundred percent. Don't think of it as making a choice, but obeying one. Determine what you want, and be obedient to that. You can't stay here tonight, because I've chosen these people and nothing will let me compromise that. You've got to create family, Randall. You choose them and you never let go. Blood, it doesn't mean anything. Your kin, and I know of them — you don't owe them anything. Cherelle, she's talking like that little boy isn't yours, that there's a test that will say that. Do you think that matters to a little boy? Do you think these men are my kin? I'm not even positive of their names. But I chose them, Randall. And I don't let go."

There's a look on Dr. Gaby's face that says she has more to administer, but Relle comes downstairs with a painting of a duck. It's floating above the water, breast-high, wings out, ready to land. It makes you wince to look at it — you can just feel the trigger that's about to be pulled.

"What the hell is that?" Nonc asks.

"I got this at the Salvation Army," Relle says. "It's for the lodge. Our hunting lodge."

*

On the south side of Prien Lake, out at the end of the point, is the foundation of a house that was blown away by Hurricane Audrey, fifty years ago. The footings are brick, and the cement is mixed with lime shale, which glows eerily in the moonlight. Nonc used to park his van out there nights, pull right up like he was home from the office and string his hammock from the van to a lone fireplace stack. Now Nonc has the pick of the litter: Rita's storm surge floated all these houses out into the channel, where the tides broke them up.

In the dark, Nonc approaches a cement slab in the headlights. He muscles the van up onto the foundation, parking in the living room. Then he and Geronimo begin their bedtime routine. They stand on the cool of ceramic kitchen tiles, the wind from the lake rattling their clothes as they brush their teeth and stare out at the green and red channel markers of the shipping lanes and, farther off, the blinking derricks of oil platforms. There is a solitary toilet, the structure's only survivor, but when Nonc cautiously lifts the lid, it has already been fouled. Nonc pisses in the bedroom, then fastens a new diaper on the boy. When he grenades the old one into the marsh grass, the frogs go quiet.

The cargo racks fold up, the foam mat unrolls, and a father and son bed down for the night. Geronimo is on his back, looking up at the dome light. Nonc is on his side, looking at a boy whose breathing is untroubled for all he's been through, though there's a lack of shine in his eyes, as if the little light in him might someday go out. His breath is clean and perfect, though, sweet-smelling. While the boy might not look much like Nonc, there's a knit to his brow, one that suggests an uncertainty and reproof that is unmistakably Harlan's. And those deep brown eyes, streaked with wheat, are pure Marnie.

"Where's Mama?" Nonc asks him.

The boy looks at the light.

"Eyeball," he says. He says it with clarity and certainty, but not emotion.

"Eyeball?" Nonc says.

"Narc," the boy says.

"Nonc?"

"Eyeball," the boy says.

Nonc sees that there's clay gunked under the boy's fingernails. He takes a hand and, with a pen cap, uses a half-moon motion to scrape them clean, one nail at a time. Geronimo shifts his eyes and, with a blank relaxation, watches his father work. The boy's nails are soft and smooth, perfect somehow. Dr. Gaby said you can tell when a kid's had poor nutrition by the streaks on his fingernails — Geronimo's nails were proof that Marnie had fed him well. Nonc had visited the boy a couple of times before she moved him to New Orleans. Under Marnie's ever-suspicious eye, Nonc ate pudding with the boy and played along with games like "I'm Going to Grab Your Sunglasses and Throw Them on the Ground and There's Nothing You Can Do About It." But Nonc had to admit that he had one eye on the apartment, looking to see how Marnie was spending the money. He never really saw the boy, how perfect he was, how utterly unspoiled. Nonc knows that someday, after Marnie takes Geronimo back and the boy grows older, he won't remember these moments, the way they showered early at the Red Cross, foraged for their morning pizza, roamed the countryside together in a brown panel van. It's probably a good thing, Nonc tells himself. Developmentally, it's got to be good for him. He strokes the boy's hair.

There's a ring — California — and Geronimo eyes the phone with great apprehension. Nonc takes the call. It's a woman's voice.

"I'm calling on behalf of Harlan Richard. Is this Randall Richard?"

"It's Ree-shard," he says.

"You may not be aware of this," she says. "But your father has lost the use of his vocal cords. He's asked me to read a note."

"Are you a nurse?" Randall asks.

"Nurse's aide."

"Is he dying?"

"They don't exactly write that on the chart," she says. "But this is hospice."

"Nobody leaves hospice, right?"

"I wouldn't say that."

"How long have you known my father?"

"I just came on shift," she says, then begins reading the note in a clipped, mechanical voice. "I know I haven't given you much, Randall. I haven't always had much to give. It's funny. All the things I have to say to you are all the things you already know. I have some things to transfer to you. You may find them useful. The doc says —"

"Put him on," Nonc tells her.

"It may take some getting used to," she says. "But he's lost the ability to speak."

"Please," he says. "Hand him the phone."

When Nonc hears the wheeze and click, he says, "Here's your grandson," and hands the phone to Geronimo. "It's your grandpa," he tells the boy, but the boy just sits there, the blue buttons of the keypad casting a glow on his cheek. He doesn't even say "Eyeball." *Grandpa* is a word, Nonc realizes, that the boy's probably never heard. Nonc whispers, "It's Grover."

"Grow-grow?" the boy asks. "Grow-grow?" Then he starts mumbling his way through the entire Grover ABC song. His eyes stare blankly into space as he singsongs, and it suddenly occurs to Nonc that the boy may never have seen the *Sesame Street* characters, just heard their voices on that one, endless CD.

After a while Nonc takes the phone back. "You got to talk to your grandson — that's not too shabby, huh? Not every grandpa gets that. Look, Dad, you should know there are no grudges here. There's no blame in me. I want you to tell yourself you did your best — then let things go. When the time comes, don't be looking over your shoulder, okay?"

Nonc closes the phone and pulls the cargo door shut. Then he kicks his leg out from under the sheet and leaves it exposed to lure mosquitoes away from his son, and before the timer on the dome light has extinguished the glow, Geronimo is snoring his baby-fat snore, and they are out.

The next morning is a blur of Brown know-how. After saddling up some sippy cups and sandwiches, Nonc swings them east through Welsh, Iowa, Lacassine, where the newly emptied hog lots speak of the sausage plant's return to glory. There is a shipment at Chennault airfield, then they turn toward the Calcasieu Parish jail, passing the equipment dealers and the boys' home, finally turning off where the bail-bond trailers line the road.

The Calcasieu jail is operating at triple capacity with all the prisoners from New Orleans, and in the parking lot the evacuated families of evacuated prisoners have set up camp outside the perimeter fence, which is serving as temporary visitation room: in the bare sun, a line of parents and wives lock fingers in the fencing, while on the other side, under guard, the inmates keep their distance and do what inmates always seem to do — affirm and reassure, make the future seem doable. Prisoners, visitors, and officers alike are surviving off Red Cross kits, so they all have the same Scope breath, the same hotel-soap smell, the same ring of aluminum around their armpits. Nonc has delivered everything from video games to wedding tuxedos to this jail, but today, as he wheels a hand truck around folks strewn on the sidewalk, he brings quick cuffs, stab vests, and a box from a company called SlamTec.

Waiting in line for security, Nonc leans against those boxes and checks out an inmate tracking station the jail has set up. For the hell of it, maybe — he can't put it into words — he walks up and says he needs to see Marnie Broussard, that he's her brother, Dallas. The guard fingers through stacks of tracking sheets, makes a call on the radio. "If they've got her," she says, "they'll bring her out." Nonc finishes his delivery, buys a soda, then waits in the van with Geronimo, reading the newspaper while that one CD loops. There is an article about the lady who threw her kids off the bridge. It says that there's no record of the kids, no birth certificates or anything. She probably had them at home, it says, in the projects, and then never took them to school or even a doctor. The weird thing is that she claims not to remember their names. For the life of her, she just can't come up with them. Nonc wonders if that's possible, that there could be no record somebody ever existed. Maybe if your life is screwed up enough, maybe if you're living way out on the edge.

Finally, through the windshield, he sees Marnie led out, hands up against the bright light. All kinds of people have been shuffling around in different-colored jumpsuits, but when he sees her in one, it's a shocker.

"Lo and behold," Nonc tells his son, then steps down from the van and crosses the lot.

When Nonc too clasps the fence, Marnie shakes her head at the sight of him. "I should have known," she says. "My brother would never come see me."

"What the hell are you doing here?" Nonc asks. "I've been looking for you."

"How's my boy?" she asks.

"He's fine," Nonc says. "So, what happened to you?"

"This is all a mistake, this is going to get cleared up."

"What did you do?"

"Nothing, I said it's a mistake."

"Did you try to scam FEMA or something?"

Marnie holds up a hand. "Hey, step off. You know what it's like in here? Half of New Orleans in here. There's no showers, I'm sleeping on a cafeteria table. Men and women are together in here, Randall, fags and rapists. They sent our asses to Jena state medium for a while." She stares at him to let that sink in. "There were some freaky bitches out there."

Beside them a convict father is trying to reassure his wife and daughter, who, Nonc realizes, are listening with great trepidation to Marnie.

"What is happening?" Nonc asks.

"Look," Marnie says. "I was with this guy, and I didn't know what he was into. And they caught me up in that. I'd be out right now except for the backlog, there's like a thousand cases before me. I haven't even been arraigned."

"Arraigned for what?"

"I told you, nothing. I didn't do anything."

"I'm here every day, Marnie. You could have let me know. I could have used your help."

"You're doing fine, and I'll be out before you know it. He's a good kid, no instructions necessary."

"Oh yeah," Nonc says. "Tell me what *bway* means."

She laughs. "Are you serious? What do you think it means?"

"I have no idea."

"It's the magic word, Randall. *Bway* is *please*."

"The boy says *eyeball*— what's that mean?" Nonc asks.

"He says *eyeball?*" she asks. "Why would he say that?"

Nonc shakes his head. "What about the initials MO?"

"Jesus, Randall, are you shitting me? Try reading to him. I left a book called *Elmo's Big Vacation*."

"He said the word *narc*."

"You better fucking believe it," she says.

Nonc can feel a vibration in the cyclone fence. He turns and looks past the hands of other visitors. In the distance a team of trustees is using a backhoe to straighten sections of the fence leaned over from Rita.

Nonc asks, "You think it's best for him to see you like this?"

"He's here? You got my boy, and you been keeping him from me?"

"I've got some questions, Marnie, and I got to know the answers."

"Don't be a prick," she says. "Where is he?"

Nonc just stares at her.

"You're a prick," Marnie says. "The only thing I did wrong was let Allen use my phone. That's it, I swear. He was into some shit, and I didn't know about it."

She keeps trying to put her hands in her pockets, but she doesn't have any pockets.

Nonc and Marnie didn't date but two months, though he remembers clearly a gaze she'd sometimes get that he thought spoke of possibility. She gets that look now, only it's so obvious that she wasn't looking toward the future but away from the past.

"Look, they think I was the person who delivered the stuff. Like I got all night to be driving eightballs of speed around. I've got a kid. I got responsibilities. I never even touched an eightball." Marnie covers her eyes, as if to shield herself from some great absurdity. "Jesus Christ, Allen is so stupid. I should have stuck with you," she says, and then laughs a miserable, self-reproaching laugh that says this would be the only way to make her life more wretched.

Nonc thinks of James B. and the way he shook. Of the way James B. couldn't believe God would make a liquor store glow.

"I got a question," Nonc says. "And no games, okay? Is Geronimo his real name?"

"What are you talking about?"

"I'm asking what's the boy's birth name?"

"Are you kidding?" she asks. "You named him."

"I never saw a certificate or anything."

"Where do you come up with this shit?"

"I was just thinking about that woman," he tells Marnie. "You know, the one who threw her kids off the bridge. She's probably in here. Hell, you probably know her."

"Oh my God," Marnie says, laughing away pain. "You fucking prick."

"What?"

"I can't believe you. You asshole. I love that boy more than you will ever know."

"What'd I say?"

"I know what you're getting at, and you're a prick for it. Just go ahead and say it. Say what you're thinking."

Nonc backs away. He backs toward the van, where he takes up the boy, strokes his hair. Nonc puts the drawing of the macaw in his hand, says, "Give this to Mama." They start to walk across the lot, but before long the boy breaks into a run. Nonc holds up, keeps his distance. He watches his boy clasp the fence. He can see Marnie start crying, wiping the tears with shaky fingers. It's a pure thing, it's anguish. It's not a woman who thinks she's seeing her boy in a week, it's the opposite of that, and it's suddenly clear to Nonc that he's going to have that boy a long time.

Chuck E. Cheese's is filled with body odor and booth campers, yet there's no place else to go. The little light inside Geronimo is dim, so Nonc puts him on all the rides, making a slow loop of the playroom. The ghostly thing, the thing Nonc can't get out of his head as he drops token after token into the hoppers, is that he doesn't know who put the boy in his van. It didn't really sink in until he was driving away from the jail, but the thought of a stranger's hands, it makes the pizza burn in his stomach.

Nonc kneels down to Geronimo — perfect cheeks, wide-set teeth, eyes bayou black — going like one mile an hour on a chuckwagon ride. "Who brought you to me?" he asks the boy.

Nonc lifts his hand and passes it through the boy's gaze, but Geronimo will not track it. It's as if by not focusing, he doesn't see the place where his mother constantly isn't. Nonc touches the child, on the earlobe, looks in his eyes. If the kid would just cry, Nonc would know what to do. When a kid cries, you give him an affectionate shake and then swat him on the butt.

Nonc pours some tokens into the ride, then calls Relle.

When she answers, he says, "Are you serious about this outfitter thing, about making that work? Because I need to know — no bullshit."

"What's wrong?" she asks. "Did something happen?"

"Tell me this lodge thing is for real, tell me that's going to happen. Raising my son in the back of a van, this has got to end."

"Of course it can happen, if you want it to. You've seen the geese out there. It's ducks galore. We get a vehicle, then we turn the kennel into a lodge, and the next thing you know we have a chef and a sauna. Before you know it, people are coming for their honeymoons."

"I can get a four-by-four, but if this is some move of yours —"

"People are sending their deposits," she says. "And when have I not been on your side? I'm the only one in the world on your side."

Nonc watches Geronimo for a moment, slowly spinning in a teacup. "No more talk of DNA tests, okay? He's my son, that's final. And I don't want to hear about Marnie ever again."

"You're right," Relle says, "I shouldn't have done that test. That kid's your blood, it's obvious. The thing about blood is that your kid's always going to be yours, no matter what happens to you, no matter where you go."

"That's more like it," Nonc says. "I'm going to make a call, and you need to pack."

"What about the boy?"

"From now on, we do everything right."

Nonc wipes his face with water from a red plastic cup. He puts his wet hand on the shoulder of the boy, then dials California. When his father answers, Nonc says, "Get somebody. We need to talk."

In a minute an orderly is on the phone. *"Hola,"* he says. *"Esta Enrique aquí."*

"Enrique," Nonc says. "Can you help me talk to my father?"

"Hey," Enrique answers. "You the guy who had his girlfriend call? Because I heard about that. That business is cold-blooded."

"That was somebody else," Nonc says.

"Good, good," Enrique says, "'cause your old man cracks me up. My dad, he was one crusty hombre, you know. But your dad reminds me of him."

"How's he doing?"

"He's dead," Enrique says.

"He's dead?"

"Yeah, died last year. Wait, are you talking about my dad or yours? I thought you were asking about my old man."

"You fucking with me?" Nonc asks.

Enrique doesn't answer. Nonc hears him call out, "It's your boy, he wants to know how you doing." Then Enrique tells Nonc, "We gotta wait while he types."

"What's he got, a laptop?"

"The hospice ward is Wi-Fi," Enrique says. "On the computer he can talk, you know." Then Enrique reads slowly, as Harlan types: "Saw the hurricane on the TV. All okay?"

Nonc's not sure who *all* is supposed to be, but he says, "Yeah, tell him a lot of folks are missing, but we made it through."

Enrique repeats this, then reads again. "Very hard on a boy. I was six when Audrey struck. They said that's what stunted my growth. That year after Audrey."

Nonc's heard all the old-timers talk about Audrey, the storm surge pushing in twenty miles, right to the ball sack of Lake Charles, how there was no warning, how the alligators slept under the trees, waiting for the bodies to rot out of the branches. But Harlan has never mentioned it.

"If I'd have stayed in Lake Charles," Enrique reads, "the storm would have taken me. That's where I should have been. That's how a Cajun's supposed to go."

"Tell him I got his package," Nonc says.

Enrique passes this along, then responds, "The numbers in my wallet are Internet poker accounts — that's my bank. No taxes, no traces. Wire cash in, wire it out."

"Ask him," Nonc says, "does he have a four-by-four?"

"Hey," Enrique says, "how about some small talk? You guys are acting like next of kin instead of family."

"What's his answer? Does he?"

Enrique asks, then reads the response: "What'd you name the boy?"

"Geronimo," Nonc says.

"You named your kid Geronimo? That's fierce. You're going to have a fierce kid. Names are destiny that way. My real name is Maximilian."

Nonc says, "Ask him is it an SUV or pickup, you know, what's the mileage?"

Enrique asks, then comes back. "I got a few cars — whatever they're worth, they're yours. I was gonna leave 'em for the lepers."

That's a phrase Nonc hasn't heard since he was a kid, back when people used to leave old furniture out on the docks for the supply vessel to Carville Island, where the leprosarium was. Harlan would joke that you never really owned anything — the lepers just let you borrow it a while. Harlan hasn't laughed since he lost his vocal cords — all that remains is a widening of the eyes, a thinning of the lips — but Nonc remembers him laughing with affection at the fate of the lepers, as if they were the closest to the Cajuns on the evolutionary tree.

"He doesn't sound like he's dying," Nonc says. "You think he's dying?"

"You ask him," Enrique says. "He wants to talk to you."

"What?"

"He's been practicing his talking."

"On the computer?"

"No, talking talking. You can't understand him, but you get what he's trying to say."

Nonc steadies the phone, speculates on what his father wants to talk about — battles he ran from, how he'll be remembered, where he should be buried. But when Harlan comes on the phone, when Nonc hears a hoarse, wet crackle from deep in the esophagus, he can tell it's about the boy. Nonc imagines his father's mouth open, like the door to one of those roofless houses, and though the sound is nothing Nonc can make out, he knows it's about a grandson, a hurricane, and the year ahead.

Nonc drives to his old house, where he grabs the keys and the cash and the wallet off the couch. He notices, amid the junk on the floor, a small pair of binoculars, like you might take to a football game, and all the way to Dr. Gaby's, the boy stares at the world through a single lens. When Nonc pulls up and parks on the grass, the dream team is assembled in folding chairs on the porch, with Relle slowly reading them the entire membership roster of the Louisiana Psychological Association. She reads a name, studies their faces for a reaction, then reads it again before moving on. Geronimo races from the van and joins them in an empty seat.

The day has become stagnant, baked over with clouds, and all of them listen expectantly to Relle's voice as if she were calling their names, as if at any moment they will be chosen to join the ranks of the known.

Nonc walks up the wheelchair ramp. Relle stands, she drops the printout on her chair. "I thought you'd never get here," she says. "Mississippi's psychological association is next."

"Are you ready?" he asks.

"Are we really going?" As if to test reality, she adds, "I mean, what about your job? Won't you get fired?"

"Maybe," he says. "Maybe they'll blame it on the hurricane."

She gives him a measured, appraising gaze. "Okay," she says.

Inside, they find Dr. Gaby in the kitchen, folding an assembly line of sandwiches into plastic wrap. Geronimo fetches a mixing bowl from the cupboard, waits expectantly by it.

As if she knows why Nonc is there, Dr. Gaby doesn't turn to face him.

Dr. Gaby asks Relle, "Any response from the list?"

"They don't even know your name," Relle says.

"They don't have to know any names," Dr. Gaby answers. "Just recognize them."

Nonc speaks up. "We're going to California," he tells her.

"When are you leaving?" Dr. Gaby asks.

"Right now."

"And how are you getting there?"

"The van."

"You're taking your work truck to California — they're okay with that?"

Nonc shrugs, but Dr. Gaby doesn't see this. She's carefully placing each sandwich in the center of a plastic square. She folds one side, then the other, then twists the ends together.

"You can't take the boy," she says. "Not in a stolen van. You don't even have a car seat."

"I know," Nonc says. "That's why I'm here."

She wheels round to look at him.

"Dr. Gaby," he says, "I did what you said, I chose. I chose, and I'm going to be the right kind of father. All my dad's bullshit, all that he did to people, there's a chance to make something good of that. I'm only asking for a week. It's not in the boy's interest to take him. I knew that's how you'd think about it, what's in his interest."

Relle says, "We're going to bring back a four-by-four."

Dr. Gaby asks, "Do you know what you're getting into? You'll have to get a death certificate, out-of-state registration, insurance, and that's just for a title transfer. God forbid there's probate."

Nonc says, "We're going to get there before he dies."

Dr. Gaby turns to Relle. "Is she going to drive this vehicle back? What if it's a stick shift? Will she drive the van?"

"This is about more than a four-by-four," Nonc says.

Relle says, "Quit trying to undermine this. We haven't even got out the door."

Dr. Gaby hands Relle the sandwich platter. "Please, will you pass out lunch?"

Instead Relle goes upstairs to finish packing.

"Helping with the child, that's not the issue," Dr. Gaby says. "I have a heart for the boy. The issue is this: name one person who left Louisiana and came back."

"Me," Nonc says. "I'm coming back."

"Are you listening to yourself? You don't commit to a child by leaving him."

"It's only a week," he says.

Dr. Gaby thinks about this. She wheels to the fridge for milk, then pours Geronimo a Dixie cup of vitamin D. "You know my philosophy on these matters, right? You understand that if you leave this boy with me, I'll have to do what's best for him. That's what will make the decisions."

"That's exactly what I want," Nonc says. "That's why I'm here."

"Did you find the mother?"

"She's in the Calcasieu Parish jail, ma'am."

Dr. Gaby takes a breath and looks at the boy. "Can you give me a contact out there? If your cell phone breaks or loses service, is there someone I can get ahold of?"

"No," he says.

"And can you tell me exactly when you'll be back?"

"I'm figuring a week. Two days out, two days back, two days for the paperwork. A day for unknowns."

"I'm sorry I have to be like this, Randall. Can we agree on an exact time of your return?"

Nonc looks at her with sudden distrust. "Well, the situation is fluid. There are unknowns. I suppose no is the answer, if you're being exact."

"I'm going to have to make a note of that, okay, that you can only guess at your return?"

Nonc lowers his brow in a look of betrayal.

"Randall," Dr. Gaby says. "Do you know what you're doing? You don't have to go, you know. You have a job, I can help you. Do you want me to choose you? I will. I'll do that."

"Come on, Dr. Gaby," Nonc says. "It's just a week."

Dr. Gaby sets a blank sheet of paper on the counter, then searches for a pencil. "You'll have to write me a note, giving me guardianship. If there's an emergency or a medical decision has to be made, I'll need that."

"Temporary guardianship."

"Of course," she says. "Temporary."

Quietly, Dr. Gaby pulls out a small cooler for their trip. While Nonc writes the note, she puts sandwiches and diet sodas inside, with some blue ice to keep them cold. She wraps cookies in foil while Nonc writes. The words come easy for him, but when he's done and tries to read them, his mind can't put them together.

"You must watch her," Dr. Gaby says, handing him the cooler. "I've always believed Cherelle's capable of goodness, though honestly, I haven't seen much sign of it."

When they head outside, they can see Cherelle crossing the lawn. In a waddle, like she is pregnant with it, Relle carries her heavy-ass sewing machine toward the van.

"What are you doing?" Nonc calls to her. "We're going to be right back."

Grunting, Relle says, "I don't go anywhere without my sewing machine."

Dr. Gaby looks up at Nonc. It's the look the old ladies at the church gave him.

"What?" he asks.

She keeps looking at him. "Nothing," she says.

Nonc goes to the van to get Geronimo's yellow boom box and the rest of his stuff, which is still in the same bag Marnie used. It feels like there should be a bunch of things Nonc has to do to prepare for the trip, but really there aren't. He comes back and sets the gear on the porch. Geronimo is sitting on the ramp, with his feet hanging off the side, holding the binoculars up. He's looking through only one lens, so Nonc can look through the other.

"Big bird," Geronimo says to him.

Nonc lowers himself to the boy. "Nonc's got to go," he tells him. "But he'll be right back. Nonc always comes back, remember that." Then he takes his DIAD and hands it to Geronimo. "This thing has a GPS chip in it. No matter where you go or what happens to you, I can find you with this thing. If anything goes wrong, I'll talk to my friends at UPS, and this is how I'll track you down." Nonc kisses the boy on the forehead. "You remember that Nonc's your real father," he says. "And that he'll be right back."

Before he can say goodbye to Dr. Gaby, she wheels inside.

When Nonc climbs in the van, Relle is already sitting shotgun. She unhooks the bouncy chair that hangs between the seats, then pulls out lots of material she's downloaded from the Internet. One printout is called "The L.A. Apartment Hunter's Bible."

"What?" she says when he looks at it. "You can't sleep in a van in L.A."

Things are going okay, Nonc thinks as he fires up the rig. This part went easier than he'd figured. Nonc was afraid that saying goodbye to Geronimo would flatten him, that the boy would fall apart, and then he would fall apart and everything would start off wrong. But things are working out. "We got to make some time," he says as they pull out of the drive. Nonc makes a last wave out the window — the dream team observes him without judgment, without response; his boy looks back at him with one eye. Through those binoculars, Nonc thinks, he must be magnified, he must be the boy's entire field of view.

They turn onto Lake Street, and the plan is in motion. For once, instead of things happening to Nonc, Nonc is making things happen, and that is a new feeling, a good one. The plan is going to take his best, he knows that. It's going to take everything he's got.

Relle starts changing the presets on the van's radio. "Some people say New York is the fashion capital," she tells him. "But really it's L.A."

Nonc's thinking about the one time he went out to Relle's father's property. He kept visualizing where all the dogs were buried. He could imagine a bubble of greyhounds below his feet wherever he walked. But he's got to change that kind of thinking. They have those A-frame lodges that come in a kit, that you set up anywhere you want. He's got to be visualizing that kind of thing.

"You know who would make a good chef," he says. "Donny Trousseau's brother. That guy can cook anything."

"Yeah, that guy's great," Relle says. She opens the cooler and takes out two sodas. Then she grabs the sandwiches. "I have eaten a thousand of these," she says, and throws them onto the road.

Nonc watches them tumble in the rearview mirror. He suddenly remembers that he was going to make a vocabulary sheet for Dr. Gaby.

"Aw, shit," he says. "I was going to write down instructions for the boy."

"Don't worry," she says. "Dr. Gaby's a pro."

"I suppose you're right."

"Of course I'm right," she says. They hit the on-ramp for the I210 bridge. "And you got to relax a bit, okay? Ease up on yourself. Your dad's not going to mess with you — he's almost dead. And it doesn't matter if we're a day late coming back, or even a week. What's Dr. Gaby going to do, roll the boy up in a carpet and put him on the curb? No, she loves him. So if something comes up, everything will be okay. If I got to make a pit stop in Denver, everything will be okay."

"You got to make a pit stop in Denver?"

She takes his hand. "See, you're not relaxing."

Climbing the Lake Charles Bridge, Nonc can see the muscles and elbows of the petrochemical plants, their vent stacks blowing off maroon-blue flame. Below are the driven edges of a brown tide, and everywhere is the open abdomen of Louisiana. At the top of the bridge, there is no sign of what happened here, not a sippy cup in the breakdown lane, not a little shoe. Nonc looks out on the city. It looks like one of those end-time Bible paintings where everything is large and impressive, but when you look close, in all the corners, some major shit is befalling people. Nonc shifts into fourth, and even doing that feels like a development, like it's the first step in a plot so big you can't imagine. The smallest thing now feels like a development, a turn signal. You kiss your son on the crown of his head, and no doubt, no denying, that's a serious development. You turn the ignition and drop the van in gear, and you know this is no ordinary event. You crest the Lake Charles Bridge, headed west with the wind in your eyes, and even flipping down your sunglasses feels charged with forever.

VICTORIA LANCELOTTA

The Anniversary Trip

FROM *The Gettysburg Review*

THEY ARE SITTING in a café on the Boulevard Saint-Germain, not far from the Odéon metro stop, three of them sitting, the wife with her husband, the husband with his mother, not inside the café but at one of the tables on the sidewalk where the prices are exorbitant but the view of the passing crowd is almost enough to counter this. It is November, and Paris should be cold, damp, the sky a low gray sheet, but instead it has been sunny and too warm for the cashmere and corduroy they packed. Their collapsible umbrellas have been useless. The wife — Monica — is damp with an unpleasant sweat most of the time, wet skin cooling at the small of her back and between her breasts every time she stops moving.

It is close to four in the afternoon, and they are drinking: red wine (*vin rouge,* Monica thinks, corrects herself) for Elizabeth, the mother; *un express* for her son, Martin. She herself is sipping an Evian, though what she really wants is a bourbon and soda, Jack Daniel's, please, but she is in no way brave enough to order such a thing, such a crass American drink, at one of these cafés, in the presence of her husband's mother, of Elizabeth.

The older woman finishes her wine and lights a cigarette, gestures to the waiter. *"Encore,"* she says, smiling, lifting her empty glass for him. He takes it and rushes off.

Elizabeth is angular, her cheekbones jutting, her mouth wide, lips glossy red and thin. She wears her silver hair in a neat bob, pulls it up and off her face — her cheekbones — with enameled combs. She is more beautiful now, in her sixties, than her son's wife has ever been, or will be. Monica recognizes this and accepts it. Her husband does not notice or, noticing, does not comment. Or at least has not commented, not in the five years they've been married or the five of on-again, off-again dating before that.

Monica has never quite been able to think of Elizabeth as a mother-in-law, as someone for whom birthday greeting cards are designed with stamped gilded roses and unctuous sentiments in pastel script.

"I should've ordered a half carafe instead," Elizabeth says as the waiter returns with another small glass and a new ticket he slides under her ashtray. "You would've had a glass, Martin?"

He shrugs, eyes his wife's bottle of Evian. "Are you sure you don't want anything else?" he says, and she shakes her head. "Maybe I'll stop on the way back to the hotel for some wine to keep in the room," he says to his mother.

"Darling," she says, "do whatever you like. If you'd rather drink in the room than go down to the lounge, that's perfectly fine with me." She pulls at the cigarette — *How is her skin still so lovely?* Monica wonders — and tilts her head back to exhale against the awning above them. "You can drink from those awful bathroom glasses and Monica and I will go down for apéritifs and pâté." She reaches for her daughter-in-law's hand and squeezes, her grip firm and cool. "Don't you think, my dear?"

They are on this trip to celebrate an anniversary of sorts: it has been just over a year since Martin's father died of pancreatic cancer, six months from diagnosis to death. The perfect length of time, Elizabeth pointed out at the reception after the funeral, long enough for the two of them to say their goodbyes but short enough that there was no protracted decline, no months or even years of false hopes and setbacks, no extended physical humiliation or dementia. He was an efficient man, and he was efficient in his dying. He had been a professor of acoustics, retired but for the occasional dissertation advice for a particularly promising doctoral student. His son, Martin, has a beautiful singing voice, an ease and grace with stringed instruments. Monica herself is tone-deaf, as unmusical as it is possible to be. When she confessed this at one of her first dinners with Martin's family, his mother had laughed in delight. "Finally, someone like me," she said, and raised her glass to Monica. "My dear, you have no idea how happy I am to hear that." Even now it is hard for Monica to imagine how two women could be less similar than she and Elizabeth.

So they are in Paris for two weeks on a trip that Elizabeth planned and booked and paid for, a trip that Martin and Monica would not quite have been able to afford on their own. Their hotel is small but elegant, close to the Seine and the Musée d'Orsay. On their own they might have afforded five nights there, seven if they ate from markets. To manage two weeks they would have had to stay in one of the outer arrondissements, by the *périphérique,* in a hotel with toilets in the rooms and communal showers down the halls. Their budget is not unforgiving, but it does not have room for extended or luxurious travel.

"I don't want an argument about this," Elizabeth said after a dinner of grilled shrimp and salad one hot night in August, when she handed them their tickets and itineraries. "This is something I promised your father I would do," she told Martin, her voice free of unsteadiness or sentiment. "We had planned to go to Paris for our fortieth anniversary," she explained to Monica, "which was obviously impossible under the circumstances. So I told him I would go anyway, but I don't relish the idea of traveling alone at this point."

"I don't know what to say," Monica said, and looked at Martin, whose face was impassive, his eyes focused out beyond the hedges in his mother's backyard.

"I think I'll be having apéritifs with you," she says to Elizabeth now. They have all finished their drinks, and Elizabeth tucks bills under the ashtray, stows her cigarettes in her bag, and arranges her shawl over her shoulders. It is a lovely piece of fabric, purple and brown paisley shot through with gold, rich and exotic. No one guesses she is American until she speaks, and even then her imperfect French charms waiters and taxi drivers. "Dinner is at nine tonight," she says. "I have a few shops I want to browse in the meantime, but you two go along. Take some time alone." She smiles at her son, a smile Monica recognizes, distant, chill. "Find something spectacular for your wife, Martin." She slips through the narrow space between tables, the fabric of her slim black trousers whispering. *"À bientôt,"* she calls to the waiter, who salutes as he rushes past. *À bientôt.* Monica will remember this.

"I wouldn't mind just heading back to the hotel for a nap," Martin says, watching his mother as she crosses the street. "You don't have to come with me," he says. "You can do whatever."

Monica waits for him to finish his sentence — *whatever you want, whatever you feel like* — but he does not. To find the right words would fatigue him, as many such efforts have since his father died, since long before that. As many efforts always have. They both stand and sidle along the neat narrow row of chairs, each one turned to face the street. She looks for their waiter but cannot find him; she imagines him pouring wine and uncapping bottles of Stella Artois somewhere in the dark interior of the café. Martin kisses her cheek and moves off in the direction of their hotel, his head down. She stands on the corner, out of the way of the waves of people moving past, and tries to decide what to do. The sun is dipping behind rooftops, and she finds herself in sudden shadow, though the light ahead of her is still gold and long. She will walk to the river, stroll back to their hotel along the quay. She wants to be sure, these two weeks, of seeing the Seine at every time of day, in every available light. She'd known before she came that Paris was beautiful, but she had not been prepared for how merciless that beauty was, how overwhelming. She had been struck by the lack of what she understood as *charm:* it was not a charming city because it did not need to be.

She chooses a street she has not walked before and starts toward the river and falls into a peaceful near-absence of thought, a calm she associates with childhood. She does not know when, exactly, she became unable to love her husband. She knows only that she woke one night and looked at him, at his face, lovely as his mother's but grave even in sleep, and thought, *I am finished. I am empty. I have nothing left for you.*

She reaches the quay and draws her coat more tightly around her. At this time of day, she cannot tell which looks deeper, the Seine or the sky.

Monica's own mother is not beautiful. The most Monica can say honestly about her, looking through old photo albums and clumsily framed snapshots, is that at one time she was pretty enough. She lives alone in a ranch house with a finished basement that she paid for outright with her settlement from the divorce. Monica sees her once a year, or once every other. She has been in Elizabeth's presence only a handful of times, and each time Monica is tense, alert, watching for the signs that her mother has had one beer too many: the incessant brushing of imaginary crumbs from her lap, the damp-sounding exhale of breath, somewhere between a sob and a sigh. On these occasions Elizabeth has smiled and sipped at her wine and smoked many more cigarettes than is usual while Monica's mother has eaten peanuts from a glazed ceramic bowl, a wedding gift from one of Elizabeth's friends. "These are really good peanuts," Monica's mother has said, or "Aren't peanuts just so good with a nice cold beer?"

She pauses at the window of a narrow shop along the quay. Crowded in the doorway are spinning wire racks of postcards and flimsy chiffon scarves, magnets on easels and tote bags stamped on their sides with disproportionately squat images of the Eiffel Tower. All of these items are helpfully priced in both euros and dollars. She can hear nothing but American accents coming from the shop and is moving away from the door, embarrassed, when she sees that some of the magnets are in the shape of pretty little baguettes, webbed *saucissons,* and surprisingly realistic cheeses, and she smiles in spite of herself. She loves her mother, and her mother would love one of these magnets, probably more than she would love to actually be here, eating food that Monica is certain she will never have the opportunity to eat. She waits until the group of Americans has left before slipping inside the shop. She will be sure to say *à bientôt* when she leaves.

Martin dresses for dinner in neat gray trousers and a jewel-blue shirt. "You look very handsome," Monica says. It has become easier to compliment him with every day that passes, with every day closer to her leaving.

"I bought a few little souvenirs for my mother today," she says. She sees that he did buy wine; there are four bottles lined up neatly on the desk she has been using as a vanity. Her leaving: to where? She has not allowed herself to think of this yet.

"Have you bought anything for yourself yet? You should pick something out — you know better what you like than I do."

She has not. But she has, wrapped in fragile tissue and tied with black silk cord, a package tucked into the corner of her suitcase, a pair of jade and sterling cufflinks she bought for him the day they arrived. They struck her as exactly the sort of gift Elizabeth would have chosen for her own husband, striking in their anachronism. What Monica's mother would call a conversation piece. The elderly shop owner had complimented Monica on her taste as he wrapped them, his English as archaic as his merchandise, and for a moment she was proud of herself: of finding the shop, of going in alone, of counting out euros. She has no idea when she will give them to Martin, and only after she had got them back to the hotel and hidden them away did she become convinced that he would be disgusted with her, that he would think she meant them as some sort of awful consolation prize.

"Are you coming down for drinks with us?" she says. She has dressed carefully, in a simple black dress and red shoes, the shoes bought as a surprise by Elizabeth earlier in the week. "No woman should have to go through life without a spectacular pair of red shoes," she said, handing the bag across the table where they'd met for lunch. "If they don't fit we can exchange them," she said, but when Monica tried them on in the hotel later, the fit was perfect.

"In a bit. I might have a glass here first," Martin says, and gestures toward a pile of academic journals on the nightstand. "There's an article I've been wanting to finish."

Monica nods and takes up her satin purse. "Then we'll just be down in the lounge. We should get our cab by around quarter till." She knows better than to try to coax him out. She knows enough to leave him to whatever abstract imperative he has decided upon.

In the hallway by the elevator is a narrow mirror. Monica stands in front of it and waits. She is thirty-four years old; since high school she has always looked her age, or older. Her mother is fifty-two. When Monica was in her twenties, they were often mistaken for sisters. Her mother was delighted by this; after her divorce she went out every Friday night, and every Friday night she asked Monica to join her. "Why don't you put your party clothes on?" she liked to say. "Let's have a girls' night out on the town."

The elevator arrives, and she tucks herself into the tiny space. Her mother was divorced at forty; "Free as a bird," she liked to say. Monica imagines she herself will be able to say the same by thirty-five.

"My son won't be gracing us with his presence?" Elizabeth asks. A cigarette is burning in the crystal ashtray, and she lifts it to her lips, inhales once, and stubs it out.

"He wanted to get some reading done." Monica settles on the sofa — *chaise longue?* — next to her and crosses her legs so that one pretty shoe is visible. Elizabeth lays a warm hand on the ankle.

"Lovely," she says. "Really. They suit you — you shouldn't be shy about wearing beautiful things, my dear," she says. She fishes in her purse and draws out a tiny vial of perfume, presses it into Monica's hand. "And this I think will suit you as well — a sample from a little *parfumerie* I found today. If you like it, we'll go back and buy some tomorrow." She finishes the drink in front of her, and the waiter appears immediately. "I think we're ready for that champagne now," she says, and the waiter bows, collects her glass and ashtray, and turns on his heel. "Reading," she says, and shakes her head. Her hair is loose tonight, spun silver. Amethyst drops sparkle at her neck. "Why would a man want to read when he could be sipping champagne with his wife?"

"I'm leaving him," Monica says, and once she speaks she is amazed, ashamed by how delicious the words taste to her, exotic and heady like the truffle shavings on her *galette* at dinner last night. "I'm leaving him. As soon as I can — he doesn't know yet," she says. She is racing to get the words out before Martin appears; she feels as though she is running for a train she cannot afford to miss.

The waiter returns and sets the champagne flutes down with a flourish, and Elizabeth says, *"Merci bien, monsieur,"* and picks up the glasses and hands one to Monica. She does not speak, not yet. Her face is still, open and waiting. Monica takes the glass. "I need you to help me," she says to her husband's mother, though she has no idea what kind of help there could possibly be.

Monica was twenty-five when she met Martin.

A serious student, a quiet man, educated, intelligent, everything about him exotic to her, seductive. So dedicated, not yet thirty and a doctoral student in the philosophy department where she worked as a receptionist. He smiled infrequently, and she thought him intense, reflective; she had been smiled at all her life by friendly neighbors in the small town where she'd grown up, by schoolteachers and shopkeepers, by her reckless father and barely grown mother; she had had her fill of smiles.

She was the one to initiate. She was the one to stay at her desk until his Thursday seminar broke at 5:15, to pretend to sort through phone messages and interdepartmental mail until he zipped his coat and shouldered his bag and nodded at her on his way past the desk.

"Martin," she said, and he turned, surprised.

So then: drinks late that Friday afternoon, informal, noncommittal. He was reticent; he talked with comfort about only his research. But he reciprocated the invitation, and she was surprised: a foreign film matinee the following Sunday, then drinks again, then lunch, weeks of quiet meetings — dates? she was never quite sure — for an hour or three and then, *then,* finally, a Friday night that bled into Saturday morning and Saturday afternoon, his apartment dark, shades drawn throughout; his bedroom small and kempt and severe, his body also small and kempt and severe. His mouth unyielding, his skin so too, somehow. He was nothing like the boys and men she'd known growing up, affable in their baseball caps and worn jeans, their coolers of beer and soda on the porch or in the truck bed, ready for anyone who might happen along. They were expansive; they were as undemanding as a soft May sky.

When Martin kissed her she felt a weight of gravity she had not felt before. When he touched her she felt, somehow, solemnified.

The question she finally asked herself was not *Do you love him?* but *Can you love him? Will you love him?*

Yes. I will be able to do that.

So then.

"There are some promises," Elizabeth says, still holding her glass aloft, "that will ruin you. If you keep them past the point of —" She stops, searching, and Monica can see the echo of her son in the upward glance of an eye, the slight tension of the jaw as she thinks. "I don't know," she finally says, laughing. "If you keep them past their own point, I suppose. Past their point of usefulness."

"I tried," Monica says, desperate, close to tears. "I can't even tell you how long —" but Elizabeth shakes her head, silver hair and amethyst earrings swinging, and holds up a hand to stop her.

"A toast," she says, "to my son, who was your husband for longer than I expected him to be." She touches her glass to Monica's and sips, sets the glass down and leans forward to rest her hands on Monica's knees. "I know Martin," she says, "and I believe you did the best you could. Drink, my dear," and Monica does. The lounge is filling, couples dressed for an evening out and a few single men in narrow dark suits, but Martin is not among them, not yet.

"It's difficult to imagine now," Elizabeth says, "but this is not a tragedy. Not for you, certainly, but not for Martin either." She smiles. "And I think you know this, don't you?"

Monica nods. She is still watching the staircase for Martin, for the lovely peacock blue of his shirt. She will give the cufflinks to Elizabeth to give to him as her own gift; they are beautiful enough that Martin will not doubt his mother chose them, and she allows herself another moment of pride in this.

"Then I want to ask you something," Elizabeth says. "A favor," and although Monica cannot imagine what she could possibly do for a woman like Elizabeth, she does not hesitate before saying, "Of course I will."

"I want you to wait, if you can," Elizabeth says. She touches Monica's cheek with a soft fragrant hand, and Monica imagines for one moment that the two of them are in this city alone; that they found each other independently of Martin, of anyone; that there is all the time in the world for Elizabeth to teach her how to be someone completely different from who she is. "Wait until we get home to tell him — think of the rest of this week as a gift to me. Can you do that, my dear?" and Monica nods, lays her hand over Elizabeth's, closes her eyes, and thinks, *I would wait as long as you asked me to, so please ask for longer,* and when she opens her eyes, she sees Martin on the staircase, sees her husband, his face pale and solemn above that lovely shirt as he walks toward them.

He never pretended to be anything he wasn't. I did. I am guilty of that.

Elizabeth stands to greet her son, and Monica does as well. He kisses both of them on the cheek and accepts a glass of champagne from the waiter before they all sit again and touch glasses — "To happiness," Elizabeth says — and they drink, and Elizabeth speaks easily, casually, of an exhibit she is interested in seeing. The room is warm and candlelit and filled with the bright ring of crystal on glass and the low rush of laughter, and Monica sips her champagne, and though it is not something she has been in the habit of doing recently, it seems right to take her husband's hand, slip her fingers through his. He neither resists nor responds. She remembers that first night with him, how cool the tips of his fingers were against her collarbone, how light their touch, as though he were somehow surprised to have found her there, naked and breathing in front of him.

The last man Monica dated before Martin was an old acquaintance, someone she'd known vaguely in high school and met again much later, after graduating from the small college she'd driven ninety minutes each way to attend but before taking the job at Martin's university. She was working in a stationery store when he came in to buy a birthday card for his current girlfriend.

"I remember you," he said as she took his money. "Weren't you a few years behind me in school?" He did not have to specify which school. There was one high school in that town and no university.

His name was James — "But call me Jimmy," he'd said — and in addition to the girlfriend, he had a three-year-old daughter by a woman he no longer dated but whom he still counted as a friend. The daughter's name was Polly, and that day he bought her a tiny stuffed rabbit, pink and yellow. This was James: a man who remembered birthdays and marked them with cards, a man who bought his daughter gifts for no reason, who found excuses — wrapping paper, masking tape, felt-tip pens — to come to the store during Monica's shifts. A man who made sure to tell her, one day a few weeks after that first meeting, that he'd stopped seeing his girlfriend, that he wanted to ask her out properly. She said yes. And at the end of that first date, after a steak dinner and a stop for ice cream, when he asked her out again before he'd even got her back to the house she still shared with her mother, that was also James: a man who understood exactly what was possible for him and was happy with that, a man who had no need of exceeding his reach. Monica was within his reach. And later that year, when she told him she'd found another job and would be moving, he was genuinely puzzled: "But why would you leave? You *belong* here," he said, gesturing as if to take in the entirety of that town where he lived, where everyone he knew lived, smiling, happy, and Monica could not disagree. *That is the reason why, exactly.*

When, eventually, Monica talks to her mother about Paris, she will not even realize how completely it has slipped away from her, has become again what it was before she saw it herself, the images hazy and lucid all at once in the way of any vivid dream. She will sit in her mother's kitchen drinking coffee and describing the soft facades of buildings, white and gray and taupe, the faded red awnings of cafés, the boulevards and gardens and cathedrals, everything warm and inviting and unreal. She will mention Martin only offhandedly and Elizabeth not at all, and when her mother finally tires of feigning interest, she will be secretly glad, relieved that time is passing, that Paris is again becoming nothing more than a word she might see on the cover of a glossy magazine or hear on a cable travel channel, certainly not a place where she once spent a few breaths of her life, and she will hardly remember the way the Seine sliced the city in half, a radiant curving knife, merciless and perfect.

YIYUN LI

A Man Like Him

FROM *The New Yorker*

THE GIRL, unlike most people photographed for fashion magazines, was not beautiful. Moreover, she had no desire to appear beautiful, as anyone looking at her could tell, and for that reason Teacher Fei stopped turning the pages and studied her. She had short, unruly hair and wide-set eyes that glared at the camera in a close-up shot. In another photo she stood in front of a bedroom door, her back to the camera, her hand pushing the door ajar. A bed and its pink sheet were artfully blurred. Her black T-shirt, in sharp focus, displayed a line of white printed characters: "My father is less of a creature than a pig or a dog because he is an adulterer."

The girl was nineteen, Teacher Fei learned from the article. Her parents had divorced three years earlier, and she suspected that another woman, a second cousin of her father's, had seduced him. On her eighteenth birthday, the first day permitted by law, the daughter had filed a lawsuit against him. As she explained to the reporter, he was a member of the Communist Party, and he should be punished for abandoning his family, and for the immoral act of taking a mistress in the first place. When the effort to imprison her father failed, the girl started a blog and called it A Declaration of War on Unfaithful Husbands.

"What is it that this crazy girl wants?" Teacher Fei asked out loud before reaching the girl's answer. She wanted her father to lose his job, she told the reporter, along with his social status, his freedom, if possible, and his mistress for sure; she wanted him to beg her and her mother to take him back. She would support him for the rest of his life as the most filial daughter, but he had to repent — and before that, to suffer as much as she and her mother had.

What malice, Teacher Fei thought. He flung the magazine across the room, knocking a picture frame from the bookcase and surprising himself with this sudden burst of anger. At sixty-six, Teacher Fei had seen enough of the world to consider himself beyond the trap of pointless emotions. Was it the milkman? his mother asked from the living room. Milkmen had long ago ceased to exist in Beijing, milk being sold abundantly in stores now; still, approaching ninety, she was snatched from time to time by the old fear that a neighbor or a passerby would swipe their two rationed bottles. Remember how they had twice been fined for lost bottles? she asked as Teacher Fei entered the living room, where she sat in the old armchair that had been his father's favorite spot in his last years. Teacher Fei hadn't listened closely, but it was a question he knew by heart, and he said yes, he had remembered to pick up the bottles the moment they were delivered. Be sure to leave them in a basin of cold water so the milk does not turn sour, she urged. He stood before her and patted her hands, folded in her lap, and reassured her that there was no need for her to worry. She grabbed him then, curling her thin fingers around his. "I have nothing to say about this world," she said slowly.

"I know," Teacher Fei said. He bent down and placed her hands back in her lap. "Should I warm some milk?" he asked, though he could see that already she was slipping away into her usual reverie, one that would momentarily wash her mind clean. Sometimes he made an effort, coaxing her to walk with baby steps to exercise her shrinking muscles. A few years ago, the limit of her world had been the park two blocks down the street, and later the stone bench across the street from their apartment; now it was their fifth-floor balcony. Teacher Fei knew that in time he would let his mother die in peace in this apartment. She disliked strangers, and he couldn't imagine her in a cold bed in a crowded hospital ward.

Teacher Fei withdrew to the study, which had been his father's domain until his death. His mother had long ago stopped visiting this room, so Teacher Fei was the one who took care of the books on the shelves, airing the yellowing pages twice a year on the balcony, but inevitably some of the books had become too old to rescue, making way for the fashion magazines that Teacher Fei now purchased.

The black-clad girl taunted him from the magazine lying open on the floor. He picked her up and carefully set her on the desk, then fumbled in the drawer for an inkpot. Much of the ink in the bottle had evaporated from lack of use, and few of the brushes in the bamboo container were in good shape now. Still, with a fine brush pen and just enough ink on the tip, he was able to sketch a scorpion in the margin of the page, its pincers stabbing toward the girl's eyes. It had been six years since he retired as an art teacher, nearly forty since he last painted out of free will. Teacher Fei looked at the drawing. His hand was far from a shaking old man's. He could have made the scorpion an arthropod version of the girl, but such an act would have been beneath his standards. Teacher Fei had never cursed at a woman, either in words or in any other form of expression, and he certainly did not want to begin with a young girl.

Later, when Mrs. Luo, a neighbor in her late forties who had been laid off by the local electronics factory, came to sit with Teacher Fei's mother, he went to a nearby Internet café. It was a little after two, a slow time for the business, and the manager was dozing off in the warm sunshine. A few middle-school students, not much older than twelve or thirteen, were gathered around a computer, talking in tones of hushed excitement, periodically breaking into giggles. Teacher Fei knew these types of kids. They pooled their pocket money in order to spend a few truant hours in a chat room, impersonating people much older than themselves and carrying on affairs with other human beings who could be equally fraudulent. In his school days, Teacher Fei had skipped his share of classes to frolic with friends in the spring meadow or to take long walks in the autumn woods, and he wondered if, in fifty years, the children around the computer would have to base their nostalgia on a fabricated world that existed only in a machine. But who could blame them for paying little attention to the beautiful April afternoon? Teacher Fei had originally hired Mrs. Luo for an hour a day so that he could take a walk; ever since he had discovered the Internet, Mrs. Luo's hours had been increased. Most days now she spent three hours in the afternoon taking care of Teacher Fei's mother and cooking a meal for both of them. The manager of the Internet café had once suggested that Teacher Fei purchase a computer of his own; the man had also volunteered to set it up, saying that he would be happy to see a good customer save money, even if it meant that he would lose some business. Teacher Fei had rejected the generous offer — despite his mother's increasing loss of her grip on reality, he could not bring himself to perform any act of dishonesty in her presence.

Teacher Fei located the girl's blog without a problem. There were more pictures of her there, some with her mother. Anyone could see the older woman's unease in front of the camera. In her prime she would have been more attractive than her daughter was now, but perhaps it was the diffidence in her face that had softened some of the features that in her daughter's case were accentuated by rage. Under the heading "Happier Time," Teacher Fei found a black-and-white photo of the family. The girl, aged three or four, sat on a high stool, and her parents stood on either side. On the wall behind them was a garden, painted by someone without much artistic taste, Teacher Fei could tell right away. The girl laughed with a mouthful of teeth, and the mother smiled demurely, as a married woman would be expected to in front of a photographer. The father was handsome, with perfectly shaped cheekbones and deep-set eyes not often found in a Chinese face, but the strain in his smile and the tiredness in those eyes seemed to indicate little of the happiness the daughter believed had existed in her parents' marriage.

Teacher Fei shook his head and scribbled on a scrap of paper the man's name and address and home phone number, as well as the address and number of his work unit, which had all been listed by the girl. A scanned image of his resident's ID was displayed too. Teacher Fei calculated the man's age, forty-six, and noted that on the paper. When he went to the message board on the girl's website, Teacher Fei read a few of the most recent posts, left by sympathetic women claiming to have been similarly hurt by unfaithful husbands or absent fathers. "Dearest Child," one message started, from a woman calling herself Another Betrayed Wife, who praised the young girl as an angel of justice and courage. Teacher Fei imagined these women dialing the father's number at night, or showing up in front of his work unit to brandish cardboard signs covered with words of condemnation. "To all who support this young woman's mission," he typed in the box at the bottom of the web page, "the world will be a better place when one learns to see through to the truth instead of making hasty and unfounded accusations."

"A Concerned Man," Teacher Fei signed his message. A different opinion was not what these women would want to hear, but any man with a brain had to accept his responsibility to make the truth known. A girl among the group of middle schoolers glanced at Teacher Fei and then whispered to a companion, who looked up at him with a snicker before letting herself be absorbed again by the screen. An old man with wrinkles and without hair. Teacher Fei assessed himself through the girls' eyes: bored and boring, no doubt undesirable in any sense, but who could guarantee the girls that the flirtatious young man online who made their hearts speed was not being impersonated by an equally disgraceful old man?

Later that evening, when Teacher Fei had wrung a warm towel to the perfect stage of moistness and passed it to his mother, who sat on another towel on her bed, a curtain separating her partly undressed body from him, he thought about the two girls and their youthful indifference. One day, if they were fortunate enough to survive all the disappointments life had in store for them, they would have to settle into their no longer young bodies.

"Do you remember Carpenter Chang?" Teacher Fei's mother asked from the other side of the curtain. Three times a week, Mrs. Luo bathed Teacher Fei's mother, and on the other evenings Teacher Fei and his mother had to make do with the curtain as he assisted her with her sponge bath and listened to her reminisce about men and women long dead. Half an hour, and sometimes an hour, would pass, his mother washing and talking on one side of the curtain, him listening and sometimes pressing for details on the other side. This was the time of day they talked the most, when Teacher Fei knew that although his mother's body was frail and her mind tangled by memories, she was still the same graceful woman who, with her unhurried storytelling, knew how to take the awkwardness out of a situation in which she had to be cared for by a grown son who had remained a bachelor all his life.

Having his mother as his only companion in old age was not how Teacher Fei had envisioned his life, but he had accepted this with little grievance. He enjoyed conversations with her, for whom things long forgotten by the world were as present as the air she shallowly breathed: two apprentices pulling a giant paper fan back and forth in a barbershop to refresh the sweating customers, the younger one winking at her while her grandfather snored on the bench waiting for his daily shave; the machine her father had installed in the front hall of their house, operated by a pedaling servant, which cut a long tube of warm, soft toffee into small neat cubes that, once hardened, were wrapped in squares of cellophane by her and her four sisters; the cousins and second cousins who had once been playmates, fed and clothed and schooled alongside her and her sisters when they were young, but who later claimed to have been exploited as child laborers by her capitalist father; her wedding to Teacher Fei's father, attended by the best-known scholars of the day and lamented by most of her relatives, her mother included, as a bad match.

Teacher Fei's father had been the oldest and poorest of his mother's suitors. Twenty years her senior, he had worked as a part-time teacher in the elite high school that she and her sisters attended, and when she rejected him a renowned scholar wrote to her on his behalf, assuring the sixteen-year-old girl of what was beyond her understanding at the time: that Teacher Fei's father would become one of the most important philosophers in the nation and, more than that, would be a devoted husband who would love her till death parted them.

Teacher Fei had always suspected that his mother had agreed to see his father only to appease the scholar, but within a year the two had married, and afterward, before Teacher Fei's father found a university position, his mother used her dowry to help her husband support his parents and siblings in the countryside. Unable to become pregnant, she had adopted a boy — Teacher Fei — from the long line of nephews and nieces who lived in close quarters in her husband's family compound, which had been built and rebuilt in the course of four generations. She had never hidden this fact from Teacher Fei, and he remembered being saddened after a holiday in his father's home village when he was eight and finally understood that he alone had been plucked from his siblings and cousins. His relatives, his birth parents included, had treated him with respect and even awe. It was his good fortune, his mother had said, comforting him, to have two pairs of parents and two worlds.

Poor man, she said now, and for a moment, lost in his reverie, Teacher Fei wondered if he had told her about the avenging daughter. Then he realized that his mother was still talking about the carpenter, who had once carved five coffins for his children, all killed by typhoid within a week. The carpenter's wife, who had been hired as a wet nurse for Teacher Fei when he first left his birth mother, had returned to the house years later with the news. Even as a ten-year-old, Teacher Fei could see that the woman had been driven out of her mind and would go on telling the story to any willing ears until her death.

It's the innocent ones who are often preyed upon by life's cruelty, Teacher Fei replied, and when his mother did not speak he recounted the girl's story from the magazine. He paused when his mother, dressed in her pajamas, pulled the curtain aside. All set for the dreamland, she said. He did not know if she had heard him, but when he tucked her in she looked up from the pillow. "You should not feel upset by the girl," she said.

He was not, Teacher Fei replied; it was just that he found the girl's hatred extraordinary. His mother shook her head slightly on the pillow, looking past his face at the ceiling, as if she did not want to embarrass him by confronting his lie. "The weak-minded choose to hate," she said. "It's the least painful thing to do, isn't it?"

She closed her eyes as if exhausted. Rarely did she stay in a conversation with him with such clarity these days, and he wondered whether she had chosen to neglect the world simply because it no longer interested her. He waited, and when she did not open her eyes he wished her a night of good sleep and clicked off the bedside lamp.

"The weak-minded choose to hate," Teacher Fei wrote in his journal later that night. For years he'd had the habit of taking notes of his mother's words. "I have nothing to say about this world," he wrote, the line most often repeated in the journal. Twenty-five years ago, his father, after a long day of musing in his armchair, had said the same thing, his final verdict before he swallowed a bottle of sleeping pills. Teacher Fei's mother had not sounded out of sorts when she had called him that evening to report his father's words, nor had she cried the following morning on the phone with the news of his father's death. Teacher Fei suspected that if his mother had not been an active accomplice, she had, at the least, been informed of the suicide plan; either way it made no difference, for the border between husband and wife had long been obscured in his parents' marriage. What surprised Teacher Fei was his mother's willingness to live on. He visited her daily after his father's death and within a year had moved in with her. He recorded and analyzed every meaningful sentence of hers, looking for hints that the words were her farewell to the world. He was intentionally careless about his pills, and hers too, as he believed she must have been in his father's final days — they had always been a family of insomniacs — but by the fifth anniversary of his father's death Teacher Fei had stopped waiting. She had nothing to say about the world, she told him that day, more out of amusement than resignation, and he knew then that she would not choose to end her life.

The message that Teacher Fei had left on the girl's website was not there when he checked the next day at the Internet café. Why was he surprised? Still, his hands shook as he composed another message, calling the girl a manipulative liar. A young couple, seventeen or eighteen at most, cast disapproving glances at Teacher Fei from another computer, seemingly alarmed by his vehement treatment of the keyboard.

The chat rooms he normally frequented held little attraction for him today. He was leaving on a business trip abroad, he told a friend in one chat room who called herself Perfume Beauty, and then repeated the news to similarly named women in other chat rooms, knowing that they would find other idling men to flirt with. The night before, he had imagined the reaction of the girl and her female allies to his message, and had composed an eloquent retort to throw at these petty-minded women. But no doubt the girl would again erase it, and he could not stop her, nor could he expose her dishonesty. Teacher Fei logged off the computer and watched the boy sneak a hand under the girl's sweater and wiggle it around, perhaps trying to unhook her troublesome bra. She looked at the screen with a straight face, but her body, moving slightly in cooperation, betrayed her enjoyment.

The girl noticed Teacher Fei's attention first and signaled to her boyfriend to stop. Without withdrawing his hand, he mouthed a threat at Teacher Fei, who lifted his arms as if surrendering and stood up to leave. When he walked past the couple, he raised a thumb and gave the boy a smile, as if they were conspiring comrades; the boy, caught off guard, grinned disarmingly before turning his face away.

Teacher Fei had never cupped his hands around a woman's

breasts, and for an instant he wished that he possessed the magic to make the boy disappear and let him take his place next to the girl. What stupidity, Teacher Fei chided himself, after he had gulped down a can of ice-cold soda water at a roadside stand. It was that angry girl and her fraudulence — that was what was depriving him of his peace. He wished that he had been his mother's birth son, that he had her noble and calm blood running through his veins, guarding him against the ugliness of the world.

The good fortune that his mother had once assured him of had not lasted long. At eighteen he had been an ambitious art student about to enter the nation's top art institute, but within a year his father, an exemplary member of the reactionary intellectuals, was demoted from professor to toilet cleaner, and Teacher Fei's education had been terminated. For the next twenty years Teacher Fei's mother had accompanied his father from building to building, one hand carrying a bucket of cleaning tools and the other holding her husband's arm, as if they were on their way to a banquet. Yet in the end even she could not save her husband from despair. Teacher Fei's father had killed himself two years after he was restored to his position at the university.

The next day Teacher Fei saw that his second message to the girl had also been confiscated by the cyberworld. A different message, left by a woman who hailed the girl as a guardian of the morality of modern China, taunted Teacher Fei in bold type.

He hastily composed another post and then spent twenty minutes rephrasing it in a calmer tone, but a day later, when that message had also been deleted, his rage erupted. He called her a "scorpion girl" in a new message, saying that he hoped no man would make the mistake of his life by marrying her and succumbing to her poison; he took great pity on her father, since an evil daughter like her would make any father live in a hell.

Her father . . . Teacher Fei paused in his typing, as the man's unhappy face in the photo came back to him. He decided to call the man's work unit, an institute affiliated with the Ministry of Propaganda, from a phone booth in the street. A woman answered, and when Teacher Fei asked for the man by name she inquired about the nature of his business. An old school friend who has lost touch, he said, apologizing that he did not have another number for him and so had to make the initial contact through the work unit.

The woman hesitated and then told him to wait. When the phone was picked up again, Teacher Fei was surprised by the voice, which sounded as though it belonged to a much older man. It didn't matter what his name was, Teacher Fei replied when the girl's father asked for it; he was merely calling as a man who was sympathetic to a fellow man's situation. He then asked if there was a chance that they could meet in person. The line clicked dead while he was in midsentence.

When Mrs. Luo came the next day, Teacher Fei begged her to stay till later in the evening. He would pay her double for the extra hours, he said, and Mrs. Luo, after complaining about the inconvenience, agreed, adding that a man like Teacher Fei indeed deserved an occasional break from caring for an elderly woman. Mrs. Luo had not lowered her voice, and Teacher Fei glanced at his mother, who sat in the armchair with her eyes fixed on a square of afternoon sunshine on the floor. She was obedient and quiet in front of Mrs. Luo, who, like everybody else, believed that Teacher Fei's mother had long been lost in her own world of dementia.

A man like him. In the street, Teacher Fei pondered Mrs. Luo's words. What did that mean — a man like him — a bachelor without a son to carry on his blood, a retired art teacher whose name most of his students had forgotten the moment they graduated from elementary school, a disgraceful old man who purchased fashion magazines at the newsstand and wasted his afternoons alongside teenagers in a cyberworld, making up names and stories and sending out romantic lies? What did he deserve but this aimless walk in a world where the only reason for him to live was so that his mother could die in her own bed? There must be places for a man like him to go, inexpensive foot-massage shops where, behind an unwashed curtain, a jaded young woman from the countryside would run her hands where he directed her while she chatted with a companion behind another curtain. Or, if he was willing to spend more — and he could, for he had few expenditures beyond his magazines and the Internet café, and had long ago stopped buying expensive brushes and paper and pretending to be an artist — one of the bathing palaces would welcome him into its warmth, with a private room and a woman of his choice to wait on him.

*

It was a few minutes after five when Teacher Fei arrived at the institute, betting that the girl's father was not the type to leave work early, since there would be little reason for him to hurry home. While Teacher Fei waited for a guard to inform the man of his arrival, he studied the plaque at the entrance to the institute. THE ASSOCIATION OF MARXIST DIALECTICAL MATERIALISM, it said, and it occurred to Teacher Fei that had his father been alive, he would have said that it was the parasites in these institutes who had ended hope for Chinese philosophers.

"Please don't get me wrong. I am a serious man," Teacher Fei said to the girl's father when he appeared. "A man most sympathetic to your situation."

"I don't know you," the man said. Had Teacher Fei not known his age, he would have guessed him to be more than sixty; his hair was more gray than black, and his back was stooped with timidity. A man closer to death than most men his age, Teacher Fei thought. But perhaps he would have more peace to look forward to in death.

A stranger could be one's best friend just as one's wife and daughter could be one's deadly enemies, Teacher Fei replied, and he suggested that they go out for tea or a quick drink. A small group of workers, on their way from the institute to the bus stop across the street, passed the pair of men; two women looked back at them and then talked in whispers to the group. The girl's father recoiled, and Teacher Fei wondered if the daughter knew that her father already lived in a prison cell, its bars invisible to the people in the street.

They could go to the man's office for a chat, Teacher Fei offered, knowing that this was the last thing he would want. The father hurriedly agreed to go to a nearby diner instead. He was the kind of man who was easily bullied by the world, Teacher Fei thought, realizing with satisfaction that he had not sought out the wrong person.

At the diner, the girl's father chose a table in the corner farthest from the entrance, and in the dim light he squinted at the bench, wiping off some grease before he sat down. When the waitress came, Teacher Fei asked for a bottle of rice liquor and a plate of assorted cold cuts. He was not a drinker, nor had he ever touched marinated pig liver or tongue, but he imagined that a friendship between two men should start over harsh liquor and variety meats.

Neither spoke for a moment. When their order came, Teacher Fei poured some liquor for the girl's father. A good drink wipes out all pain for a man, Teacher Fei said, and then poured a glass for himself, but it soon became clear that neither of them would touch the drink or the meat, the man apparently feeling as out of place in the dingy diner as Teacher Fei did.

"What are you going to do?" Teacher Fei asked when the silence between them began to attract prying glances from the middle-aged proprietress of the diner, who sat behind the counter and studied the few occupied tables.

The man shook his head. "I don't understand the question," he said.

"I think you should sue your daughter," Teacher Fei said, and immediately saw the man freeze with hostility. Perhaps someone had approached him with a similar proposition already. Or perhaps that was why the young girl had sued her father in the first place, egged on by an attorney, a manipulative man using her rage for his own gain.

Not that he could offer any legal help, Teacher Fei explained. He had been an art teacher in an elementary school before his retirement. He was in no position to do anything to hurt the girl's father, nor did he have the power to help him in his situation. It was only that he had followed his daughter's story in the media, and when he had seen the family picture he had known that he needed to do something for the girl's father. "'How many people in this world would understand this man's pain?' I asked myself when I saw your picture."

The girl's father flinched. "I am not the kind of man you think I am," he said.

"What?" Teacher Fei asked, failing to understand his meaning. He was not into other men, the girl's father said, so could Teacher Fei please stop this talk of friendship. The proprietress, who had been loitering around the nearby tables checking on the soy-sauce bottles, perked up despite the man's hushed voice.

It took Teacher Fei a moment to grasp what the man was hinting at. Nor am I who you think I am, he thought of protesting, but why should he, when he had long ago made the decision not to defend himself against this ridiculous world?

The proprietress approached the table and asked about the quality of the food and drink. When the man did not reply, Teacher Fei said that they were very fine. The woman chatted for a moment about the weather, and returned to her counter. Only then did the man insist that it was time for him to go home.

"Who is waiting at home?" Teacher Fei asked, and the man, taken aback, stood up and said he really needed to leave.

"Please," Teacher Fei said, looking up at the man. "Could you stay for just a minute?" If he sounded pathetic, he did not care. "You and I . . . ," he said slowly, glancing over at the entrance to the diner, where a pair of college students, a girl and a boy, were studying the menu on the wall. "We are the kind of men who would not kick our feet or flail our arms if someone came to strangle us to death. Most people would assume that we must be guilty if we didn't fight back. A few would think us crazy or stupid. A very few would perhaps consider us men with dignity. But you and I alone know that they are all wrong, don't we?"

The man, who was about to leave some money on the table, tightened his fingers around the bills. Teacher Fei watched the college students take seats by the window, the boy covering the girl's hands with his own on the table. When the man sat back down, Teacher Fei nodded gratefully. He did not want to look up, for fear that the man would see his moist eyes. "When I was twenty-four, I was accused of falling in love with a girl student," he said. *Pedophile* had been the word used in the file at the school, the crime insinuated in the conversations taking place behind his back. The girl was ten and a half, an ordinary student, neither excelling among her classmates nor falling behind; one often encountered children like her in teaching, faces that blended into one another, names misrecalled from time to time, but there was something in the girl's face, a quietness that did not originate from shyness or absent-mindedness, as it usually did in children of her age, that intrigued Teacher Fei. He envisioned her at different ages — fifteen, twenty, thirty — but there was little desire in that imagining other than the desire to understand a face that had moved him as no other face had. "No, don't ask any questions, just as I won't ask whether you indeed kept a mistress while being married to your wife. It doesn't matter what happened between your cousin and you, or my girl student and me. You see, these accusations exist for the sake of those who feel the need to accuse. If it wasn't your cousin, there would have been another woman to account for your not loving your wife enough, no?"

The man took a sip from his glass, spilling the liquor when he put it down. He apologized for his clumsiness.

"My mother used to say that people in this country were very good at inventing crimes, but, better still, we were good at inventing punishments to go with them," Teacher Fei said.

When he and his cousin were young, they had vowed to marry each other, the man said; a children's game mostly, for when the time came they had drifted apart. She was widowed when they met again, and he had tried to help her find a job in the city, but she had never been his mistress.

"You don't have to explain these things to me," Teacher Fei said. "Had I not known to trust you, I would not have looked for you." The man could say a thousand things to defend himself, but people, his own daughter among them, would just laugh in his face and call him a liar. The crime that Teacher Fei had been accused of amounted to nothing more than a few moments of gazing, but one of the other students, a precocious eleven-year-old, had told her parents of the inappropriate attention the young teacher had paid to her classmate; later, when other girls were questioned, they seemed to be caught easily in the contagious imagination. He had just been curious, Teacher Fei said when he was approached by the principal. About what, he was pressed, but he could not explain how a face could contain so many mysteries visible only to those who knew what to look for. His reticence, more than anything, caused fury among the parents and his fellow teachers. In the end he chose to be called the name that had been put in the file: a man's dirty desire was all his accusers could grasp.

"One should never hope for the unseeing to see the truth," Teacher Fei said now. "I could've denied all the accusations, but what difference would it have made?"

"So there was no . . . proof of any kind?" the man said, looking interested for the first time.

"Nothing to put me in jail for," Teacher Fei said.

"And someone just reported you?"

"We can't blame a young girl's imagination, can we?" Teacher Fei said.

The man met Teacher Fei's eyes. It was just the kind of thing his daughter would have done, the man said. "She'd have made sure you lost your job," he added with a bitter smile, surprising Teacher Fei with his humor. "Count yourself a lucky person."

Teacher Fei nodded. He had won the district mural contest for the school every year, his ambition and training in art making him a craftsman in the end, but shouldn't he consider it good fortune that his ability to paint the best portrait of Chairman Mao in the district had saved him from losing his job? The time to think about marriage had come and then gone, his reputation such that no matchmaker wanted to bet a girl's future on him. Still, his parents had treated him with gentle respect, never once questioning him. But as cleaners of public toilets, they could do little to comfort him other than to leave him undisturbed in his solitude. Indeed, he was a lucky man, Teacher Fei said now; he had never married, so no one could accuse him of being an unfaithful husband or a bad father.

"Unwise of me to start a family, wasn't it?" the girl's father said. "Before my divorce, my daughter said there were three things she would do. First, she would sue me and put me in prison. If that failed, she would find a way to let the whole world know my crime. And if that didn't make me go back to her mother, she would come with rat poison. Let me tell you — now that she has done the first two things, I am waiting every day for her to fulfill her promise, and I count it as my good fortune to have little suspense left in my life."

Teacher Fei looked at the college students paying at the counter, the boy counting money for the proprietress and the girl scanning the restaurant, her eyes passing over Teacher Fei and his companion without seeing them. "I have nothing to say about this world," Teacher Fei said.

Neither did he, the man replied, and they sat for a long time in silence till the proprietress approached again and asked if they needed more food. Both men brought out their wallets. "Let me," Teacher Fei said, and though the man hesitated for a moment, he did not argue.

In the dusk, a thin mist hung in the air. The two men shook hands as they parted. There was little more for them to say to each other, and Teacher Fei watched the man walk down the street, knowing that nothing would be changed by their brief meeting. He thought about his mother, who would be eager to see him return, though she would not show her anxiety to Mrs. Luo. He thought about his girl student: fifty-two she would be now, no doubt a wife and mother herself, and he hoped that he had not been mistaken and she had grown into a woman like his mother. She — the girl student, whom he had never seen again — would outlive him, just as his mother had outlived his father, their beauty and wisdom the saving grace for a man like him, a man like his father. But for the other man, who would be watching the night fall around the orange halo of the street lamps with neither longing nor dread, what did the future offer but the comfort of knowing that he would, when it was time for his daughter to carry out her plan of revenge, cooperate with a gentle willingness?

REBECCA MAKKAI

The Briefcase

FROM *New England Review*

HE THOUGHT HOW STRANGE that a political prisoner, marched through town in a line, chained to the man behind and chained to the man ahead, should take comfort in the fact that this had all happened before. He thought of other chains of men on other islands of the Earth, and he thought how since there have been men there have been prisoners. He thought of mankind as a line of miserable monkeys chained at the wrist, dragging each other back into the ground.

In the early morning of December first, the sun was finally warming them all, enough to walk faster. With his left hand, he adjusted the loop of steel that cuffed his right hand to the line of doomed men. His hand was starved, his wrist was thin, his body was cold: the cuff slipped off. In one beat of the heart he looked back to the man behind him and forward to the man limping ahead, and knew that neither saw his naked red wrist; each saw only his own mother weeping in a kitchen, his own love lying on a bed in white sheets and sunlight.

He walked in step with them to the end of the block.

Before the war this man had been a chef, and his one crime was feeding the people who sat at his tables in small clouds of smoke and talked politics. He served them the wine that fueled their underground newspaper, their aborted revolution. And after the night his restaurant disappeared in fire, he had run and hidden and gone without food — he who had roasted ducks until the meat jumped from the bone, he who had evaporated three bottles of wine into one pot of cream soup, he who had peeled the skin from small pumpkins with a twist of his hand.

And here was his hand, twisted free of the chain, and here he was, running and crawling until he was through a doorway. It was a building of empty classrooms — part of the university he had never attended. He watched from the bottom corner of a second-story window as the young soldiers stopped the line, counted 199 men, shouted to each other, shouted at the men in the panicked voices of children who barely filled the shoulders of their uniforms. One soldier, a bigger one, a louder one, stopped a man walking by. A man in a suit, with a briefcase, a beard — some sort of professor. The soldiers stripped him of his coat, his shirt, his leather case, cuffed him to the chain. They marched again. And as soon as they were past — no, not that soon; many minutes later, when he had the stomach — the chef ran down to the street and collected the man's briefcase, coat, and shirt.

In the alley, the chef sat against a wall and buttoned the professor's shirt over his own ribs. When he opened the briefcase, papers flew out, a thousand doves flailing against the walls of the alley. The chef ran after them all, stopped them with his feet and arms, herded them back into the case. Pages of numbers, of arrows and notes and hand-drawn star maps. Here were business cards: a professor of physics. Envelopes showed his name and address — information that might have been useful in some other lifetime, one where the chef could ring the bell of this man's house and explain to his wife about empty chains, empty wrists, empty classrooms. Here were graded papers, a fall syllabus, the typed draft of an exam. The question at the end, a good one: "Using modern astronomical data, construct, to the best of your ability, a proof that the Sun revolves around the Earth."

The chef knew nothing of physics. He understood chemistry only insofar as it related to the baking time of bread at various elevations or the evaporation rate of alcohol. His knowledge of biology was limited to the deboning of chickens and the behavior of *Saccharomyces cerevisiae,* common bread yeast. And what did he know at all of moving bodies and gravity? He knew this: he had moved from his line of men, creating a vacuum — one that had sucked the good professor in to fill the void.

The chef sat on his bed in the widow K——'s basement and felt, in the cool leather of the briefcase, a second vacuum: here was a vacated life. Here were salary receipts, travel records, train tickets, a small address book. And these belonged to a man whose name was not blackened like his own, a man whose life was not hunted. If he wanted to live through the next year, the chef would have to learn this life and fill it — and oddly, this felt not like a robbery but an apology, a way to put the world back in balance. The professor would not die, because he himself would become the professor, and he would live.

Surely he could not teach at the university; surely he could not slip into the man's bed unnoticed. But what was in this leather case, it seemed, had been left for him to use. These addresses of friends; this card of identification; this riddle about the inversion of the universe.

Five cities east, he now gave his name as the professor's, and grew out his beard so it would match the photograph on the card he now carried in his pocket. They did not, anymore, look entirely dissimilar. To the first man in the address book, the chef had written a typed letter: "Am in trouble and have fled the city . . . Tell my dear wife I am safe, but for her safety do not tell her where I am . . . If you are able to help a poor old man, send money to the following post box . . . I hope to remain your friend, Professor T——."

He had to write this about the wife; how could he ask these men for money if she held a funeral? And what of it, if she kept her happiness another few months, another year?

The next twenty-six letters were similar in nature, and money arrived now in brown envelopes and white ones. The bills came wrapped in notes — was his life in danger? did he have his health? — and with the money he paid another widow for another basement, and he bought weak cigarettes. He sat on café chairs and drew pictures of the universe, showed stars and planets looping each other in light. He felt, perhaps, that if he used the other papers in the briefcase, he must also make use of this question. Or perhaps he felt that if he could answer it, he could put the universe back together. Or perhaps it was something to do with his empty days.

He wrote in his small notebook: "The light of my cigarette is a fire like the Sun. From where I sit, all the universe is equidistant from my cigarette. Ergo, my cigarette is the center of the universe. My cigarette is on Earth. Ergo, the Earth is the center of the universe. If all heavenly bodies move, they must therefore move in relation to the Earth, and in relation to my cigarette."

His hand ached; these words were the most he had written since school, which had ended for him at age sixteen. He had been a smart boy, even talented in languages and mathematics, but his mother knew these were no way to make a living. He was not blessed, like the professor, with years of scholarship and quiet offices and leather books. He was blessed instead with chicken stocks and herbs and sherry. Thirty years had passed since his last day of school, and his hand was accustomed now to wooden spoon, mandoline, peeling knife, rolling pin.

Today his hands smelled of ink, when for thirty years they had smelled of leeks. They were the hands of the professor; ergo, he was now the professor.

He had written to friends A through L, and now he saved the rest and wrote instead to students. Here in the briefcase's outermost pocket were class rosters from the past two years; letters addressed to those young men care of the university were sure to reach them. The amounts they sent were smaller, the notes that accompanied them more inquisitive. What exactly had transpired? Could they come to the city and meet him?

The post box, of course, was in a city different from the one where he stayed. He arrived at the post office just before closing, and came only once every two or three weeks. He always looked through the window first to check that the lobby was empty. If it was not, he would leave and come again another day. Surely one of these days a friend of the professor would be waiting there for him. He prepared a story, that he was the honored professor's assistant, that he could not reveal the man's location but would certainly pass on your kindest regards, sir.

If the Earth moved, all it would take for a man to travel its distance would be a strong balloon. Rise twenty feet above and wait for the Earth to turn under you; you would be home again in a day. But this was not true, and a man could not escape his spot on the Earth but to run along the surface. Ergo, the Earth was still. Ergo, the Sun was the moving body of the two.

No, he did not believe it. He wanted only to know who this professor was, this man who would, instead of teaching his students the laws of the universe, ask them to prove as true what was false.

On the wall of the café: plate-sized canvas, delicate oils of an apple, half peeled. Signed, below, by a girl he had known in school. The price was more than three weeks of groceries, and so he did not buy it, but for weeks he read his news under the apple and drank his coffee. Staining his fingers in cheap black ink were the signal fires of the world, the distress sirens, the dispatches from the trenches and hospitals and abattoirs of the war; but here, on the wall, a sign from another world. He had known this girl as well as any other: had spoken with her every day, but had not made love to her; had gone to her home one winter holiday, but knew nothing of her life since then. And here, a clue, perfect and round and unfathomable. After all this time: apple.

After he finished the news, he worked at the proof and saw in the coil of green-edged skin some model of spiraling, of expansion. The stars were at one time part of the Earth, until the hand of God peeled them away, leaving us in the dark. They do not revolve around us: they escape in widening circles. The Milky Way is the edge of this peel.

After eight months in the new city, the chef stopped buying his newspapers on the street by the café and began instead to read the year-old news the widow gave him for his fires. Here, fourteen months ago: Minister P —— of the Interior predicts war. One day he found that in a box near the widow's furnace were papers three, four, five years old. Pages were missing, edges eaten. He took his fragments of yellowed paper to the café and read the beginnings and ends of opinions and letters. He read reports from what used to be his country's borders.

When he had finished the last paper of the box, he began to read the widow's history books. The Americas, before Columbus; the oceans, before the British; the Romans, before their fall.

History was safer than the news, because there was no question of how it would end.

*

He took a lover in the city and told her he was a professor of physics. He showed her the stars in the sky and explained that they circled the Earth, along with the Sun.

That's not true at all, she said. You tease me because you think I'm a silly girl.

No, he said, and touched her neck. You are the only one who might understand. The universe has been folded inside out.

A full year had passed, and he paid the widow in coins. He wrote to friends M through Z. I have been in hiding for a year, he wrote. Tell my dear wife I have my health. May time and history forgive us all.

A year had passed, but so had many years passed for many men. And after all what was a year, if the Earth did not circle the Sun?

The Earth does not circle the Sun, he wrote. Ergo, the years do not pass. The Earth, being stationary, does not erase the past nor escape toward the future. Rather, the years pile on like blankets, existing all at once. The year is 1848; the year is 1789; the year is 1956.

If the Earth hangs still in space, does it spin? If the Earth were to spin, the space I occupy I will therefore vacate in an instant. This city will leave its spot, and the city to the west will usurp its place. Ergo, this city is all cities at all times. This is Kabul; this is Dresden; this is Johannesburg.

I run by standing still.

At the post office, he collects his envelopes of money. He has learned from the notes of concerned colleagues and students and friends that the professor suffered from infections of the inner ear that often threw his balance. He has learned of the professor's wife, A——, whose father died the year they married. He has learned that he has a young son. Rather, the professor has a son.

At each visit to the post office, he fears he will forget the combination. It is an old lock, and complicated: F1, clockwise to B3, back to A6, forward again to J3. He must shake the little latch before it opens. More than forgetting, perhaps what he fears is that he will be denied access — that the little box will one day recognize him behind his thick and convincing beard, will decide he has no right of entry.

One night, asleep with his head on his lover's leg, he dreams that a letter has arrived from the professor himself. They freed me at the end of the march, it says, and I crawled my way home. My hands are bloody and my knees are worn through, and I want my briefcase back.

In his dream, the chef takes the case and runs west. If the professor takes it back, there will be no name left for the chef, no place on the Earth. The moment his fingers leave the leather loop of the handle, he will fall off the planet.

He sits in a wooden chair on the lawn behind the widow's house. Inside, he hears her washing dishes. In exchange for the room, he cooks all her meals. It is March, and the cold makes the hairs rise from his arms, but the sun warms the arm beneath them. He thinks, The tragedy of a moving Sun is that it leaves us each day. Hence the Aztec sacrifices, the ancient rites of the eclipse. If the Sun so willingly leaves us, each morning it returns is a stay of execution, an undeserved gift.

Whereas: if it is we who turn, how can we so flagrantly leave behind that which has warmed us and given us light? If we are moving, then each turn is a turn away. Each revolution a revolt.

The money comes less often, and even old friends who used to write monthly now send only rare, apologetic notes, a few small bills. Things are more difficult now, their letters say. No one understood when he first ran away, but now it is clear: after they finished with the artists, the journalists, the fighters, they came for the professors. How wise he was to leave when he did. Some letters come back unopened, with a black stamp.

Life is harder here too. Half the shops are closed. His lover has left him. The little café is filled with soldiers.

One afternoon he enters the post office two minutes before closing. The lobby is empty but for the postman and his broom.

The mailbox is empty as well, and he turns to leave but hears the voice of the postman behind him. You are the good Professor T——, no? I have something for you in the back.

Yes, he says, I am the professor. And it feels as if this is true, and he will have no guilt over the professor's signature when the box is brought out. He is even wearing the professor's shirt, as loose again over his hungry ribs as it was the day he slipped it on in the alley.

From behind the counter, the postman brings no box but a woman in a long gray dress, a white handkerchief in her fingers.

She moves toward him, looks at his hands and his shoes and his face. Forgive me for coming, she says, and the postman pulls the cover down over his window and disappears. She says, No one would tell me anything, only that my husband had his health. And then a student gave me the number of the box and the name of the city.

He begins to say, You are the widow. But why would he say this? What proof is there that the professor is dead? Only that it must be; that it follows logically.

She says, I don't understand what has happened.

He begins to say, I am the good professor's assistant, madam — but then what next? She would ask questions he had no way to answer.

I don't understand, she says again.

All he can say is, This is his shirt. He holds out an arm so she can see the gaping sleeve.

She says, What have you done with him? She has a calm voice and wet brown eyes. He feels he has seen her before, in the streets of the old city. Perhaps he served her a meal, a bottle of wine. Perhaps, in another lifetime, she was the center of his universe.

This is his beard, he says.

She begins to cry into the handkerchief. She says, Then he is dead. He sees now from the quiet of her voice that she must have known this long ago. She has come here only to confirm.

He feels the floor of the post office move beneath him, and he tries to turn his eyes from her, to ground his gaze in something solid: postbox, ceiling tile, window. He finds he cannot turn away. She is a force of gravity in her long gray dress.

No, he says. No, no, no, no, no, I am right here.

No, he does not believe it, but he knows that if he had time, he could prove it. And he must, because he is the only piece of the professor left alive. The woman does not see how she is murdering her husband, right here in the post office lobby. He whispers to her: Let me go home with you. I'll be a father to your son, and I'll warm your bed, and I'll keep you safe.

He wraps his hands around her small, cold wrists, but she pulls loose. She might be the most beautiful woman he has ever seen.

As if from far away, he hears her call to the postmaster to send for the police.

His head is light, and he feels he might float away from the post office forever. It is an act of will not to fly off, but instead to hold tight to the Earth and wait. If the police aren't too busy to come, he feels confident he can prove to them that he is the professor. He has the papers, after all, and in the havoc of war, what else will they have the time to look for?

She is backing away from him on steady feet, and he feels it like a peeling off of skin.

If not the police, perhaps he'll convince a city judge. The witnesses who would denounce him are mostly gone or killed, and the others would fear to come before the law. If the city judge will not listen, he can prove it to the high court. One day he might try to convince the professor's own child. He feels certain that somewhere down the line, someone will believe him.

JILL MCCORKLE

Magic Words

FROM *Narrative Magazine*

BECAUSE PAULA BLAKE is planning something secret, she feels she must account for her every move and action, overcompensating in her daily chores and agreeing to whatever her husband and children demand. *Of course I'll pick up the dry cleaning, drive the kids, swing by the drugstore.* This is where the murderer always screws up in a movie, way too accommodating, too much information. The guilty one always has trouble maintaining direct eye contact.

"Of course I will take you and your friends to the movies," she tells Erin late one afternoon. "But do you think her mom can drive you home? I'm taking your brother to a sleepover too." She is doing it again, talking too much.

"Where are *you* going?" Erin asks, mouth sullen and sarcastic as it has been since her thirteenth birthday two years ago.

"Out with a friend," Paula says, forcing herself to make eye contact, the rest of the story she has practiced for days ready to roll. She's someone I work with, someone going through a really hard time, someone brand-new to the area, knows no one, really needs a friend.

But her daughter never looks up from the glossy magazine spread before her, engrossed in yet another drama about a teen star lost to drugs and wild nights. Her husband doesn't even ask her new friend's name or where she moved from, yet the answer is poised and waiting on her tongue. Tonya Matthews from Phoenix, Arizona. He is glued to the latest issue of *Our Domestic Wildlife,* his own newsletter to the neighborhood about various sightings of wild and possibly dangerous creatures — coyotes, raccoons, bats. Their message box is regularly filled with detailed sightings of raccoons acting funny in daylight or reports of missing cats. Then there's the occasional giggling kid faking a deep voice to report a kangaroo or rhino. She married a reserved and responsible banker who now fancies himself a kind of watchdog Crocodile Dundee. They are both seeking interests outside their lackluster marriage. His are all about threat and encroachment, being on the defense, and hers are about human contact, a craving for warmth like one of the bats her husband fears might find its way into their attic.

Her silky legs burn as if shamed where she has slathered lavender body lotion whipped as light as something you might eat. And the new silk panties, bought earlier in the day, feel heavy around her hips. But it is not enough to thwart the thought of what lies ahead, the consummation of all those notes and looks exchanged with the sales rep on the second floor during weeks at work, that one time in the stairwell — hard thrust of a kiss interrupted by the heavy door and footsteps two floors up — when the fantasy became enough of a reality to lead to this date. They have been careful, and the paper trail is slight — unsigned suggestive notes with penciled times and places, all neatly rolled like tiny scrolls and saved in the toe of the heavy wool ski socks in the far corner of her underwear drawer, where heavier, far more substantial pairs of underwear than what she is wearing cover the surface. It all feels as safe as it can be because he has a family too. He has just as much to lose as she does.

And now she looks around to see the table filled with cartons of Chinese food from last night and cereal boxes from the morning, and the television blares from the other room. Her son is anxious to get to his sleepover; her daughter has painted her toenails, and the fumes of the purple enamel fill the air. Her husband is studying a map showing the progression of killer bees up the coast. He speaks of them like hated relatives who are determined to drop in, whether you want them to or not. Their arrival is as inevitable as all the other predicted disasters that will wreak havoc on human life.

"Where did you say you've got to go?" her husband asks, and she immediately jumps to her creation. Tonya Matthews, Phoenix, Arizona, new to the area, just divorced. Her palms are sweating, and she is glad she is wearing a turtleneck to hide the nervous splotches on her chest. She won't be wearing it later. She will slip it off in the darkness of the car after she takes Gregory to the sleepover and

Erin and her friend to the cinema. Under the turtleneck she is wearing a thin silk camisole, also purchased that afternoon at a pricey boutique she had never been in before, a place the size of a closet where individual lingerie items hang separately on the wall like art. A young girl, sleek, pierced, and polished, gave a cool nod of approval when she leaned in to look at the camisole. Paula finally chose the black one after debating between it and the peacock blue. Maybe she will get the blue next time, already hoping that this new part of her life will remain. Instead of the turtleneck, she will wear a loose cashmere cardigan that slides from one shoulder when she inclines her head inquisitively. It will come off easily, leaving only the camisole between them in those first awkward seconds. She tilts her head as she has practiced, and with that thought all others disappear, and now she doesn't know what has even been asked of her. Her heart beats a little too fast. She once failed a polygraph test for this reason. She had never — would never — shoot heroin, but her pulse had raced with the memory of someone she knew who had. Did she do drugs? Her answer was no, but her mind had taken her elsewhere, panicked when she remembered the boy who gave her a ride home from a high school party with his head thrown back and teeth gritted, arm tied off with a large rubber band while a friend loomed overhead to inject him, one bloody needle already on the littered floor.

You can't afford to let your mind wander in a polygraph test — or in life, as now, when once again she finds herself looking at her husband with no idea of what he has just said. Her ability to hold eye contact is waning, the light out the window waning, but the desire that has built all these weeks is determined to linger, flickering like a candle under labored breath. Somewhere, her husband says, between their house and the interstate are several packs of coyotes, their little dens tucked away in brush and fallen trees. The coyote is a creature that often remains monogamous. The big bumbling mouthful of a word lingers there, a pause that lasts too long before he continues with his report. He heard the coyotes last night, so this is a good time to get the newsletter out, a good time to remind people to bring their pets indoors. Dusk is when they come out, same as the bats, most likely rabid.

The kids are doing what they call creepy crawling. Their leader picked the term up from the book *Helter Skelter.* They slip in and out behind trees and bushes, surveying houses, peeping in windows, finding windows and doors ajar or unlocked. Their leader is a badly wounded boy in need of wounding others, and so he frightens them, holds them enthralled with his stories of violence or murder. They might not believe all he says, but they believe enough to know he is capable of bad things. As frightening as it is to be with him, it is more frightening not to be — to be on the outside and thus a potential victim.

To the kids he looks tough with his tongue ring and tattoos, his mouth tight and drawn by a bitterness rarely seen on such a young face, some vicious word always coiled on his tongue and ready to strike those who least expect it — though he has to be careful when bagging groceries at Food Lion; he has been reprimanded twice for making sarcastic remarks to elderly shoppers, things like *You sure you need these cookies, fat granny?* He has been told he will be fired the next time he is disrespectful, which is fine with him. He doesn't give a shit what any of them says. Dirt cakes the soles of his feet, like callused hooves, as he stands on the asphalt in front of the bowling alley, smoking, guzzling, or ingesting whatever gifts his flock of disciples brings to him. He likes to make and hold eye contact until people grow nervous.

When Agnes Hayes sees the boy bagging groceries in the market, her heart surges with pity, his complexion blotched and infected, hair long and oily. "Don't I know you?" she asks, but he doesn't even look up, his arms all inked with reptiles and knives and what looks like a religious symbol. Now she has spent the day trying to place him. She taught so many of them, but their names and faces run together. In the three years since retirement, she has missed them more than she ever dreamed. Some days she even drives her car and parks near the high school to watch them, to catch a glimpse of all that energy and to once again feel it in her own pulse. She still drives Edwin's copper-colored Electra and has since he died almost two years ago. She would never have retired had she seen his death coming, and with it an end to all their plans about where they would go and what they would do. One day she was complaining about plastic golf balls strewn all over the living room, and the next she was calling 911, knowing even as she dialed and begged for someone to *please help* that it was too late.

The school is built on the same land where she went to school. She once practiced there, her clarinet held in young hands while she stepped high with the marching band. Edwin's cigar is there in the ashtray, stinking as always, only now she loves the stink, can't get enough of it, wishes that she had never complained and made him go out to the garage or down to the basement to smoke. She wishes he were sitting there beside her, ringed in smoke. Their son, Preston, is clear across the country, barely in touch.

Sometimes creepy crawling involves only the car, cruising slowly through a driveway, headlights turned off, gravel crunching. There are lots of dogs. Lots of sensor lights. Lots of security systems, or at least signs *saying* there are systems. The boy trusts nothing and no one. He believes in jiggling knobs and trying windows. When asked one time, by a guidance counselor feigning compassion and concern, what he believed in, he said, "Not a goddamn thing," but of course he did. Anyone drawing breath believes in something, even if it is only that life sucks and there's no reason to live. Tonight he has announced that it is Lauren's turn to prove herself. She is a pretty girl behind the wall of heavy black makeup and black studded clothing. She wants out of the car, but she owes him fifty dollars. He makes it sound like if she doesn't pay it back soon he'll take it out in sex. She is only here to get back at the boy she loved enough to do everything he asked. She wants him to worry about her, to want her, to think about that night at the campground the way she does.

The leader reminds her often that he was there for her when no one else was. He listened to her story about the squeaky-clean asshole boyfriend, feeding her sips of cheap wine and stroking her dyed black hair the whole time she cried and talked and later reeled and heaved on all fours in a roadside ditch.

"He's an asswipe," the boy had said. "He used you." And then later when she woke just before dawn with her head pounding and her body filled with the sick knowledge that she had to go home and face her parents, he reminded her again how much she needed him, couldn't survive without him. "I didn't leave you," he said. "Could've easily fucked you and didn't."

And now she is here, and the boy who broke her heart is out with someone else or maybe just eating dinner with his parents and talking about where he might choose to go to school. He is a boy who always smells clean, even right off the track where he runs long-distance, his thigh muscles like hard ropes, his lungs healthy and strong. He might be at the movies, and she wishes she were there too — the darkness, the popcorn. She wishes she were anywhere else. She had wanted her parents to restrict her after that night, to say she couldn't go anywhere for weeks and weeks, but they did something so much worse; they said how disappointed they were, that they had given up, how she would have to work really hard to regain their trust, and by *trust* it seems they meant love.

The leader is talking about how he hates their old math teacher. "And I know where she lives too." He circles the block, drives slowly past a neat gray colonial with a bright red door, the big Electra parked in the drive. "What's the magic word?" he mimics in a high southern voice and reaches over to grab Lauren's thigh, then inches up, gripping harder as if daring her to move. He motions for her to unzip her jeans, wanting her to just sit there that way, silver chain from her navel grazing the thin strip of nylon that covers her. Lower, he says, even though there is a boy in the back seat hearing every word. She feels cold but doesn't say a word. Her shoes and jacket and purse are locked in the trunk of his car. "For safekeeping," he said. She is about to readjust the V of denim when he swings the car off the side of the road behind a tall hedge of lagustrum, where they are partially hidden but can still see the house. "Like this," he says and tugs, a seam ripping, and then he slides across the seat toward her, his mouth hard on hers as he forces her hand to his own zipper. The boy in the back seat lights a cigarette, and she focuses on that, the sound, the smell; she can hear the paper burn.

Erin and her friend, Tina, sit in the back seat, and Gregory is in front with his Power Ranger sleeping bag rolled up at his feet. Paula will drop him off at the party and then go to the cinema, and then she will still have time to sit and collect herself before driving seven miles down the interstate to the Days Inn, where he will be waiting. The children have said that this car — their dad's — smells like old farts and jelly beans. They say he saves up all day at the bank and then rips all the way home. Gregory acts this out, and with each "Ewww" and laugh from the girls, he gets a little more confident and louder. He says their grandmother smells like diarrhea dipped in peppermint and their grandfather is chocolate vomick. They are having a wonderful time, mainly because it's daring, the way he is testing Paula, the way they all are waiting for her to intervene and reprimand, but she is so distracted she forgets to be a good mother. When he turns and scrutinizes her with a mischievous look, she snaps back.

"Not acceptable, young man, and you know it," she says, but really she is worried that they are right and that *she* will smell like old farts and jelly beans when she arrives at the motel. Her cell phone buzzes against her hip, and she knows that he is calling to see if they are on schedule, calling to make sure that she doesn't stand him up again.

"Aren't you going to answer that?" Erin says. "Who is it, Dad looking for underwear? Some lame friend in need of a heart-to-heart?" The laughing continues as Paula turns onto the street where a crowd of eight-year-olds and sleeping bags are gathered in the front yard of a small brick ranch.

"One of my lame friends, I'm sure," she answers, but with the words pictures him there in the room, maybe already undressed, a glass of wine poured. They have already said so much in their little notes that it feels not only like they have already made love but like they have done so for so long that they are already needing to think up new things to do. Her pulse races, and she slams on the brakes when Gregory screams, "Stop!"

"Pay attention, Mom," Gregory says. "See, they're everywhere," and she thinks he means her lame friends, or kids at the party, but he picks up one of those little gourmet jelly beans, tosses it at his sister, and then jumps from the car. "Thanks, Mom," he says, and Paula waves to the already frazzled-looking mother who has taken this on. Thank you, Ronald Reagan. That's when the jelly bean frenzy started, and then after her husband said something cute and trite about sharing the desires of the president since he was now a vice president at the bank, all his workers gave him jelly beans because what else can you give someone you don't know at all who has power and authority over you? He got all kinds of jelly beans. And now if people hear about the neighborhood wildlife, it means many more years of useless presents — coyote and raccoon and bat figurines and mugs and mugs and more mugs. She will write and send all those thank-you notes. She will take all the crap to Goodwill.

Sometimes Agnes watches television in the dark. She likes a lot of these new shows that are all about humiliating people until they confess that they are fat and need to lose weight or that they are inept workers who need to be fired or bad members of a team who need to be rejected and banished from the island. Her pug, Oliver, died not long after Edwin did, and she misses the way he used to paw and tug and make a little nest at the foot of her bed. She misses the sounds of his little snorts in the night. How could there have been a moment in life when she wished for this — the quiet, the lack of activity and noise? The clock ticks, the refrigerator hums. She could call Preston. She could give him an apology, whether or not she owes it. What she could say is that she is so sorry they misunderstood each other. Or she could call him and pretend nothing ever happened. She keeps thinking of the boy at the grocery, trying to place what year she taught him. Who were his parents? What is his name? Some children she gave things to over the years — her son's outgrown clothes and shoes — but then she stopped, dumping it all at the church instead, because the children never acted the same afterward, and that bothered her. They never said thank you, and they never looked her in the eye, as if she had never made a difference in their lives, and that was what hurt so much when she thought of Preston, how easily he had let a few things make him forget all that she had done for him in his life. She stated the truth, is all. When Preston planned to marry Amy, she told him how people might talk about them, might call their children names.

Right after Edwin's funeral, he called her Miss Christian Ethics, Miss Righteous Soul. He told her he wished he could stay and dig into all that ham and Jell-O but that Amy was at the Holiday Inn waiting for him. "They let dogs stay there too," he said and lingered over the prize rod and reel of his father's she had handed to him, only to put it back and leave. She hasn't seen him since. Now her chest is heavy with the memory, and her head and arm and side ache.

The parking lot stretches for miles, it seems, kids everywhere in packs, snuggly couples, the occasional middle-aged, settled-looking couple Paula envies more than all the others. The Cinema Fourteen Plex looms up ahead like Oz, like a big bright fake city offering anything and everything, a smorgasbord of action and emotion as varied as the jelly bean connoisseur basket her husband's secretary sent at Christmas, a woman Paula has so often wished would become something more. Wouldn't that be easier?

"He's here," Tina says, and points to where a tall skinny kid in a letter jacket is pacing along the curb. "Oh, my God. Oh, my God."

"Puhleeze," Erin says, sounding way too old. "Chill out. He's *just* a *boy.*" And then they collapse in another round of laughter and are out of the car and gone. Paula's hip is buzzing again. Buzzing and buzzing. What if it's Gregory and the sleepover is canceled? Or he fell on the skate ramp and broke something or needs stitches and her husband can't be found because he's out in the woods with a flashlight looking for wildlife? Or maybe her husband really does need her. He just got a call that his mother died. Does she know where he put the Havahart trap? And when is the last time she saw *their* cat?

Lauren is feeling frightened. The other boy, the one from the back seat who is always quiet and refuses to talk about the bruises on his face and arms, has announced he's leaving. He can't do this anymore. The leader slams on the brakes and calls him a pussy. The leader says that if he leaves that's it, no more rides, no more pot, no more anything except he'll catch him some dark night and beat the shit out of him. "I'll beat you worse than whatever goes on in that trash house of yours," he says, but the boy keeps walking, and Lauren feels herself wanting to yell out for him to wait for her. She has always found him scary and disgusting, but now she admires his ability to put one foot in front of the other. He says he's bored with it all — lame amateur shit — but she sees a fear in him as recognizable as her own. "Let him go," she whispers. She is watching the flicker of television light in the teacher's upstairs window. "Please. Can't we just ride around or something?"

"Afraid you won't get any more tonight?" he asks, and leans in so close she can smell his breath, oddly sweet with Dentyne. The lost possibility of his features makes her sad, eyes you might otherwise think a beautiful shade of blue, dimple in the left cheek. He pulls a coiled rope from under the seat. "You gonna stay put, or do I need to tie you up?" She forces herself to laugh, assure him that she will stay put, but she makes the mistake of glancing at the key in the ignition, and he reaches and takes it.

She cautions herself to keep breathing, to act like she's with him. "Next one," she says. "I need to collect myself."

"Well, you just collect," he says. "I'll be back to deal with you in a minute." She doesn't ask what he plans to do. His outlines of all the ways such an event might go are lengthy and varied, some of them tame and pointless and others not pretty at all. He has already said he wants to scare the hell out of the old woman, let *her* know what it feels like to have someone make you say *please* and *thank you* every goddamn day. The girl watches him move into the darkness, numb fingers struggling to finally zip her pants back up, to pretend that his rough fingertips never touched her there. She will get out and run. She will leave the door open and crawl through the hedge until she reaches the main road. She will call her parents, beg for their forgiveness. There is no way now to get her shoes or phone, but she moves and keeps moving. She thinks of her bed and how good it will feel to crawl between clean sheets, to stare at the faces of all the dolls collected before everything in her life seemed to go so bad. Now all the things she has been so upset about mean nothing. So what if she let the handsome, clean-smelling track star do everything he wanted to do? She liked it too, didn't she? Not making the soccer team last year, being told on college day that she had no prayer of getting into any of the schools she had listed, most of them ones he was considering if he could run track. But losing or getting rejected — that happens to a lot of people, doesn't it? She can still find something she's good at, go *somewhere.* Right now she just wants to get home, to shower herself clean with the hottest water she can stand, to soap and scrub and wrap up in a flannel robe. She once watched her uncle skin a catfish, tearing the tight skin from the meat like an elastic suit, and she keeps thinking of the sound it made, a sound that made her want to pull her jacket close, to hide and protect her own skin. She feels that way now, only there's nothing to pull around her, the night air much cooler than she'd thought — and she keeps thinking she hears him behind her, so she moves faster. She is almost to the main road, the busy intersection, the rows of cars heading toward the cinema. Her foot is bleeding, a sliver of glass, and she is pinned at a corner, lines upon lines of cars waiting for the light to change.

*

Paula's cell phone buzzes again, and she takes a deep breath and answers. "Where are you?" he asks. She can hear the impatience, perhaps a twinge of anger, and his voice does not match the way she remembers him sounding in the stairwell. When she pictures his face or reads his tiny penciled scrawl, it's a different voice, like it's been dubbed.

"Almost there," she says and tries to sound flirtatious, leaving him a promise of making up for lost time. Then she glances out her window and sees a girl she thinks she recognizes. Shirt torn and barefooted. They certainly won't let her in the theater that way. The girl is so familiar, and then she remembers — her daughter's school, story time in the library. But that was years ago, when the girl's hair was light brown and pulled up in a high ponytail. She knows exactly who she is. This is a girl parents caution their *good* girls against. She is rumored to be bulimic. She locks herself in the school bathroom and cuts her arms. She once tried to overdose on vodka and aspirin and had to have her stomach pumped. She gives blow jobs in the stairwell of the high school in exchange for drugs. She has blackened ghoulish eyes and jet-black hair, silver safety pins through her eyebrows and lip. Paula has heard parents whispering about her at various school functions. They say, "Last year she was perfectly normal, and now this. She was a B student with some artistic talent and a pretty face, and now this." She is the "Don't" poster child of this town, the local object lesson in how quickly a child can go bad.

Agnes is trying to remember what exactly it was she said to anger Preston so. She had tried to make it complimentary, something about skin like café au lait. She had often seen black people described that way in stories, coffee and chocolates, conjuring delicious smells instead of those like the bus station or fish market across the river, which is what a lot of people might associate with black people. Her maid once used a pomade so powerful-smelling Agnes had to ask that she please stop wearing it, but certainly Agnes never held that against the woman; she couldn't help being born into a culture that thought that was the thing to do.

"Sometimes it's not even *what* stupid thing you say," Preston shouted, the vein in his forehead throbbing like it might burst. "It's *how* you say it. So, so goddamned *godlike.*" He spit the word and shook all over, hands clenched into fists. But now she wants him to come back and be with her. She didn't know coffee would be insulting. She is going through her phone numbers, she has it somewhere. That same day she reminded him that even the president of the United States said things like that. The president had once referred to his grandchildren as "the little brown ones," and why is that okay and chocolate and coffee are not?

It's your mom, she practices now. *Please talk to me, Preston.* She is dialing when she hears something down on her front porch. The wind? Her cat? There was a flyer in her mailbox just this evening saying how she should not leave the cat outside.

Lauren shivers as she stands there on the corner. She expects to hear his car roar up any second and wonders what she will do when that happens. She will have to tell her parents that she lost her purse, that it got stolen, and her shoes and jacket. She shudders with the thought of the boy pawing through her personal things, a picture of the track star cut from the school newspaper, a poem she was writing about the ocean, a pale pink rabbit's foot she has carried since sixth grade when she won the school math bee with it in her pocket. The light is about to change, and she concentrates on that instead of imagining her parents' reaction. Just once she wishes one of them would pull her close and say, "Please, tell me what's wrong," and then she would. She would start talking and not stop, like a dam breaking; she would tell them so many things if there were really such a thing as unconditional love. But instead they will say, "What is wrong with you? Why are you doing this to us? Do you know what people are saying about you?"

"Do you need a ride?" A woman in an old black Audi leans out the window and motions her to hurry. "I know you from school."

She does know the woman, the mother of a girl in her class, a girl who makes good grades and doesn't get into trouble. Not a popular girl, just a normal girl. A nice girl who smiles shyly and will let you copy her notes if you get behind. Erin from Algebra I freshman year. This is Erin's mother.

She hears a car slowing in the lane beside her and runs to get in with the woman just as the light changes. "Thank you."

"My daughter goes to your school," the woman says. She is wearing a low-cut camisole with a pretty silver necklace. Her black sweater is soft and loose around her shoulders. The car smells like crayons and the woman's cologne. "I'm sorry my car is so messy. My husband's car, that is." Her cell phone buzzes in the cup holder, but she ignores it. "Where are you going, sweetheart?" she asks. "It's too chilly to be out without shoes and long sleeves." Something in her voice brings tears to the girl's eyes, and then her crying is uncontrollable. The woman just keeps driving, circling first the cinema and then many of the neighborhoods around the area. The girl sinks low in her seat when they pass the teacher's house, that old Pontiac still parked behind the hedge. She can't allow herself to imagine what he is doing, what he will do when he finds her gone. They drive out to the interstate and make a big loop, the woman patting her shoulder from time to time, telling her it's okay, that nothing can be that bad. Every third or fourth time the woman asks for her address, but for now the girl just wants to be here in this car riding. The woman's cell phone keeps buzzing and buzzing. Once she answers it to the loud voice of her daughter from the movie lobby saying she will need a ride home after all. "Are you mad, Mom?" the girl screams. "Is that okay?" And the woman assures her that it is okay. It is fine. She will be there. Then she answers to say she saw their cat early this morning. And then, apologizing when it rings again, she answers and says little at all, except that so much has happened, she just might not get there at all. "In fact," she whispers, "I know I can't get there." And Lauren knows there is a good chance that she is part of what has happened, but the heat is blowing on her cold feet and the woman has the radio turned down low with classical music, and her eyelids are so heavy she can barely keep them open. When she was little and couldn't sleep, her parents would sometimes put her in a warm car and drive her around. Her dad called it a "get lost" drive, and he let her make all the choices, turn here, turn there, turn there again, and then she would relax while he untangled the route and led them back home, by which time she would be nearly or already asleep. There was never any doubt that he could find the way home and that she would wake to find herself already tucked in her bed or in his arms being taken there.

Preston's answering machine comes on, and Agnes is about to speak, but then she hears the noise again and puts down the phone. She wishes she would find Preston there — Preston and

Amy, waiting to embrace her and start all over again. Preston in his letter jacket like he was all those nights she waited up for him and said, "Where have you been, young man?" And Edwin would be in the basement smoking, and Oliver would be rooting around at the foot of her bed.

Her chest is tight with the worry of it all. She swallows and opens the door. Nothing.

"Here, kitty," she calls in a faint voice. She steps out on the stoop into the chilly air. The sky is clear overhead, a sliver of a moon. There is a car parked way down at the end of her drive, just the front bumper showing beyond the hedge. It wasn't there when she came home. Perhaps someone had a flat or ran out of gas. She calls the cat again and hears leaves crunching around the side of the house. She waits, expecting to see it slink around the corner, but then nothing. There is more noise beyond the darkness, where she can't see. And it is coming closer, short quick sounds, footsteps in the leaves. She is backing into the house when she thinks she sees something much larger than the cat slip around the corner near her kitchen door. She pulls her sweater close and pushes the door to, turns the dead bolt. The flyer talked about coyotes and how they have been spotted all over town.

The girl finally tells Paula where she lives, a neighborhood out of town and in the opposite direction from the motel. Paula's cell phone beeps with yet another message, but now she ignores it. She doesn't want to hear what he has to say now that he has had time to shape an answer to her standing him up yet again. She parks in front of a small brick ranch. The front porch is lit with a yellow bulb, all the drapes pulled closed.

"I'm happy to walk you up," Paula says, but the girl shakes her head. She says thank you without making eye contact and then gets out, making her way across the yard in slow, careful steps. Paula waits to see if a parent comes out, but the girl slips in and recloses the door without a trace.

Paula sits there in the dark as if expecting something to happen. And then she slips off the cardigan and pulls her turtleneck over her head. The message is waiting. He might be saying this is the last time he will do this, he has wasted too much time on her already. "Why are you fucking with me?" he might ask. Or, "Who do you think you are?" The chances of him saying he understands completely and they will try again some other, better time are slim. She imagines him there in the room, bare-chested and waiting, already thinking about his other options, his better options. And she imagines her own house and her return, sink full of dirty dishes, purple nail polish and Power Ranger figures everywhere. A litter box that needs scooping and clothes that need washing and an empty pantry that would have been filled had she not been out buying lingerie all day.

She saw a coyote just last week, but she didn't report it. She was standing at the kitchen window and glanced out to see a tall, skinny shepherd mix — except just as her mind was shaping the thought about someone letting a dog run loose in the neighborhood, it came to her that this was not a dog. It was wild and fearful-looking, thin and hungry, and she felt a kinship as they stood frozen, staring at each other. Everyone wants something.

The leader can see her in there, old bat, holding her chest and shaking. She looks like a puppet, her old bitch of a body jerking in time with his jiggling the knob. "I wore your fucking boy's shirt," he will say. "Thank you so much. That little polo fucker really helped turn my life around." She lifts the phone and pulls the cord around the corner where he can't see her, so he jiggles harder, leans the weight of his body against the door. "Loafers! Neckties! *F* in fucking math." He creeps around and climbs high enough on a trellis to see that she is slumped down in a chair with the receiver clutched against her chest. "Say the magic word," he says and covers his fist with his shirt before punching out the window. "Say it."

When Paula pulls up to the theater, Erin and Tina are waiting. A tall, thin boy in a letter jacket trails alongside Tina, his hand in her hip pocket in a familiar way, and then they kiss before the girls get in the car. Paula is about to mention the girl she picked up but then thinks better of it. She wants to say things like, "Don't you ever . . ." but the sound of her daughter's laughter makes her think better of it.

"I can't believe you, like, ate face in front of my mom," Erin says, and Tina blushes and grins. She is a girl with cleavage and braces, betwixt and between.

"Jesus, Mom, let some air in this stinkhole car," Erin laughs, and then the two girls talk over the movie and everyone they saw there as if Paula were not even present. Paula can't stop thinking about the girl and how she came to be on that busy corner with no shoes, how she looks so different from that clean-faced little girl in a library chair, and yet she is one and the same. And what will she write and slip to her coworker on Monday, or will she avoid him altogether and pretend nothing ever happened, that she never ventured from her own darkened den in search of excitement? She imagines the coyotes living as her husband has described, little nests under piles of brush, helpless cubs curled there waiting for the return of their mother.

"I'm sorry if I messed up your time with your lame friend," Erin says sarcastically, and then leans in close. "Really, Momsy, I am." She air-kisses Paula and smiles a sincere thanks before turning back to her friend with a shriek of something she can't believe she forgot to tell, something about cheating, someone getting caught with a teacher's grade book. She has licorice twists braided and tied around her throat like a necklace, and her breath is sweet with Milk Duds.

The old woman is dead or acting dead, the recorded voice from the receiver on her chest telling her to please hang up and try her call again. It's one of those houses where everything is in place, little useless bullshit glass things nobody wants. She looks as miserable dead as she did alive. It makes him want to trash the place, but why bother now? He didn't kill her. He didn't do a thing but pop out a pane of glass. He searches around and then carefully, using his shirt so as not to leave a print, takes a golf ball from the basket beside the fireplace and places it down in the broken glass. Television is too big to lift, no purse in sight, not even a liquor cabinet. She gives him the creeps, and so do all the people looking out from portraits and photographs. He'll tell the girl that he just scared the old bitch, threatened to tie her up and put a bullet in her head until she cried and begged for his mercy and forgiveness. He'll say he left her alive and grateful.

The moon is high in the bright clear sky when Paula ventures outside to look for their cat. She pulls her sweater close and steps away from the light of the house, the woods around her spreading into darkness. Her husband is sleeping, and Erin is on the phone. There were no messages other than the one on her cell phone, still trapped there and waiting. She hears a distant siren, the wind in the trees, the bass beat from a passing car. *Please,* she thinks. *Please.* She is about to go inside for a flashlight when she hears the familiar bell and then sees the cat slinking up from the dark woods, her manner cool and unaffected.

KEVIN MOFFETT

One Dog Year

FROM *Tin House*

JOHN D. ROCKEFELLER is hungry. On the high dunes, with a nice open view of the ocean, he sits in a wheeled wicker chair, waiting for the airman to arrive. Next to him is Pica, his groom, and below him a crowd of a few hundred has gathered on the hard-packed sand. The mood is high. Men stand with men and ladies with ladies. Children splash in the shallow water, chasing sandpipers and gulls. Every so often the crowd grows silent in response to some distant clatter. First it is a pair of low-slung racecars lurching toward the gathering on the hard sand. When a marching band comes through, the crowd lithely adjusts itself and forms a passageway.

John D watches the ten-man band marching down the beach. Bugles, cornets, drums: happy music, no doubt about it. But its sound is leashed to something easy and sad. Happiness approaching, overtaking, passing him by. Time, time. John D is eighty-six years old.

Yesterday someone saw him up on the wing, a man is saying. Playing the fiddle. The plane was flying itself.

He sits beneath a diamond-shaped sunshade. His wig is pinned into a straw hat and he wears a collarless shirt, a loose vest made of Japanese paper, and trousers, the pockets filled with dimes. He is no longer the hale viper who was booed by a crowd of women. Who wore tight undergarments to investors' meetings to stay alert. He now measures himself only against himself.

In Florida, he hibernates among palms and oleanders in a gray-shingled house with four dozen casement windows. Two decades earlier, before Cettie died, he forfeited every strand of hair on his body and it never grew back. He resembles an old, scabby seal. He bobs and slips away from worry, the long-standing injuries, the tawdriness, the undiluted stupidity of crowds. He practices sustained ameliorative forgetting. He takes potassium bromide for melancholy and bathes off-river in the oxbow lakes of memory. He brightens his own light daily.

He often imagines himself young and on the prow of a ship. Holding on to a mast, steadying himself against the perpetual volatility of the sea, winning, winning . . .

Early on, his father made him draft a list of goals. John D thought of two: amass one hundred thousand dollars and live for one hundred years. Simple, symmetrical.

You will fail, his father told him. He wanted John D to be a cobbler's apprentice, then a cobbler. A cobbler! To spend perpetuity staring at the soles of shoes.

He is now worth one hundred and eighty million dollars.

His man Pica places a tray over his lap. Pica has been his groom for twenty years. He's seen John D through his most abject days — Tarbell's book, the public backlash, the antitrust proceedings — has dressed him and bathed him and brushed his mangled cuticles with scented emollients. He serves him eight meals a day, always the same: a few steamed crucifers and a glass of fitness juice. Good for the heart, good for the mind. John D is a living machine.

Enjoyable, John D says after each swallow. But it isn't enjoyable — it is bland fuel. His doctor, who is responsible for the diet, insists he will absorb more nutrients if he takes pleasure in what he eats. And John D wants nutrients. He also wants crab claws, a London broil, chowder, a fried egg, pecan pie.

He scans the beach as he chews, watching the crowd wait for the airman. For the past three days he has been buzzing over town, dropping yellow handbills from his biplane. One of them landed in John D's lap while he was sleeping in his garden. THE ALARMING ACE II WILL PERFORM DEATH-DEFYING FEATS FOR YOUR ENTERTAINMENT. BACK FROM EUROPE AND THE GREAT PLAINS. SEE HIS FAMOUSE DEADMAN DROP! ONE DAY ONLY.

Air travel has long interested him, with its steady progression from novelty to verity. Since the handbill landed in his lap he's dreamed a sky of benign clouds with men and women cutting through. Their arms extended, they call to people on the ground. Come on, come join us. In the dream John D is on the ground. How awful it is to be on the ground.

In the dream he thinks that. Awake, though, atop the dune, he is able to turn all he surveys into joy. A woman eating fruit: miraculous. Bicycles: a near-perfect invention. Children: he loves children. Loves their necks and their sluggish awe. Every so often a child approaches his shaded chair, and John D reaches into the pocket of his trousers and pulls out a dime. You have two choices, he says, handing a dime to a ruddy boy. You can save it or you can spend it. What do you think I would advise?

Save it, the boy says.

Of course, of course. You have wonderful throat tendons, do you know that?

I didn't, sir.

And how long do you mean to save this dime? A month, a year?

Until I have as much money as you, sir.

Good boy, John D says. He reaches into his pocket and gives the boy another dime. And is sorry the moment he does it. You have doubled your fortune, he says.

He takes another bite of food while watching the boy retreat. The boy, studying the two winged heads on the dimes, is probably mad at him for the promise he extracted.

John D pushes the plate forward, and Pica, standing behind him, leans in to clear it.

Not yet, he says, taking hold of Pica's sleeve. I want to sit here and enjoy the finishing for a little while. Look, pelicans.

Pica and John D watch a quartet of dust-colored birds fly over the shore. One of the birds stops and plunges into the ocean as if shot. After a few seconds, it ascends with something silver flashing in its mouth.

Hunger, John D says. It rubs out all other urges.

I believe I'm going to start writing down everything you say, Mr. John.

I'm still hungry. Write that down.

Pretty soon I'll have an entire book.

You can take away my plate, John D says. And scratch between my shoulder blades. I have an itch.

While Pica scratches, the old man closes his eyes. Bits of food are caught between his dentures, and John D roots them out with his tongue. These are his old dentures, the ones that remind him of twilight and providence's warm paw.

Last year they were stolen while he slept, during his stay with the governor in a hotel in Miami. The teeth are made of porcelain mounted with gold springs and swivels to twenty-four-karat gold plates. They are exceptional. The plates give liquids a cool freshwater taste and the porcelain is smooth and shiny. The thief must have reached in between the slats and grabbed the teeth, soaking in aseptic on a nightstand, in the middle of the night.

A divine act, he told the governor the next day. The Lord was telling me he can take what he wants *when* he wants. He can pluck it like a berry from a bush.

Please kill me, the governor thought, before I get so greedy for more years. Dump me in the ocean, let the sharks have my organs, let eels nest in my rib cage.

John D tried to be charitable — a man who'd steal another man's teeth must need them for *something* — but after a while he could not help but fantasize about finding the thief and guiding his wrists through a pedal-driven band saw. What use could anyone have possibly made of the teeth? You melt down the gold plates and you have a single cufflink, maybe. A bitty angel charm. The porcelain was worthless. What use, what *use,* he asked Pica.

It was an intimate crime, and it left him feeling scornful and inept. The dentist made an exact replica of the old teeth, but they were not the same. They didn't fit right. They made a clicking noise on words like *stop* and *pest.* Food now tasted like . . . food.

He quit wearing teeth around the house. He sat in a wingback rocker, reading inspirational verse and running his tongue along the slick ribbed turtle shell of his palate. What does *numinous* mean? he called to Pica.

Pica looked it up in the dictionary, settled on the fourth entry. Of or relating to numina, he called back.

This did him no good. Without teeth he felt prepped for the tomb. Every night he and Pica circled around his garden listening to the distant insuck of the ocean. It was a sound that reminded John D of blood and his stubborn insides. At the edge of his zinnias he felt weakened by it. He said to Pica, Could you please carry me. And Pica leaned down and cradled him and lifted him up. He was as light as a bird, scooped out and brittle-boned. Pica carried him through the servants' entrance, up the stairs, to his bedroom.

As Pica was leaving, John D said, Come here. Pica walked over to the bed and John D said, Closer. Pica leaned in and the old man kissed him once, delicately, on the cheek. Thank you, he said.

Then, a few weeks ago, a package arrived. Inside was a set of teeth wrapped in purple crepe paper and a warbly written note: *Behave or I might steal them again.*

When Pica presented him with the teeth, John D had to blink back tears. Pica washed them in aseptic and John D put them into his mouth. He smiled, tacked his top molars against his bottom molars, and said, Stop. Pork chop. Pest.

Excuse me? Pica said.

Still clicking. They must have been roughhoused in the mail.

John D touched each tooth with his tongue. Molar, incisor, canine. Welcomed each one back hello, hello, hello. Miraculous, John D said. I'd like you to get me a steamed artichoke, some crab claws, and a glass of fitness juice.

Again John D began wearing the teeth around the house. He wore them during morning tea, during his daily laughing exercises. He even wore them to bed, against doctor's orders. He wasn't worried about choking on one of the gold springs or swivels. These were his *teeth.* He wouldn't allow them out of his sight again, not for a minute.

John D hadn't noticed that when the stolen teeth were returned, the replacement teeth had disappeared. He was too pleased. Pleased with himself, pleased with humankind. So pleased that he failed to notice that the package had no postmark and the handwriting on the note resembled Pica's, even though Pica had tried to disguise it with his left hand.

The old man felt lucky but diminished. He had been regarding time with the same stubborn miserly purpose with which he regarded money for so many years. But time, contrary to the old saying, is not money. Time is time. It is nontransferable. John D has started wondering what all the straining — the naps, the diet, the laughing exercises — will amount to. What it is worth. A week? A year?

And the teeth? The teeth are a lesson. At times he thinks the lesson is *Life is just.* At other times: *Get prepared.* The old man has been around so long and has touched so many, he cannot help but think he has a shorter conduit to the Almighty. He feels twilight all around him: in flowers wilted on their stems, in mosquitoes telegraphing along porch glass, trying to sketch their way inside, in high clouds, in balloons, in his bones, in the ocean, in shadows, in crowds, and now, especially now, in the constant click-clicking of his new old teeth.

Pica is still scratching. He thinks John D has fallen asleep and he has. Good boy, Pica says. The old man's wig is slightly off-center. Pica sings one of his secret songs about him. He has about a dozen. This one goes, A mending must come at the ending. But Mr. John's not ready for sending.

He listens to John D's shallow breathing, like a comb through a sandstorm. Seven years left, he sings. Maybe more, maybe less. One dog year in which to protest.

John D's eyes dart open the second Pica takes his hand away.

Has he come and gone? he asks.

Not yet, Pica says. Someone said he often arrives late. To let the anticipation build up. He's a showman.

Were you talking to me while I was asleep?

To be honest, Mr. John, yes I was.

I knew it. Have I told you how I feel about that?

You'd rather I didn't.

No good can come of it. I feel all jumbled now, like I left something behind. Are those boys waving at me?

I believe so, sir.

John D calls to them and the two boys, one skinny, one stout, slowly scale the dune. Neighbor John, the skinny one says. John D, heartened by the young voice, asks the boys a few questions and then hands each a dime. Take care, take extreme care, he says. I want you to invent better ways of doing things.

We will, sir.

You boys are messengers. You are envoys to a time I won't see.

The boys regard him with ebbing enthusiasm. If they linger for a few minutes longer, John D is sure he will extract something useful from them, but he can think of no casual way to hold them. You look like some type of forlorn dog, he says to the stout boy, who acts like he doesn't hear him.

As they leave, the skinny boy drops his dime. Pica, squinting in the sun next to the old man's shaded chair, watches as he falls to his hands and knees to comb through the loose sand. His friend stands by and waits, doesn't even pretend to help search for it.

John D stands up from his chair, extends his elbow to Pica, and together they sidle down the dune. He says, Now where did it go?

Over here, I think, the skinny boy says.

John D and Pica and the two boys prospect through the soft sand. John D closes his eyes, listens to a voice that sounds like his own — a dime is worth more than a dime, it says — reaches his hand into the dune, roots around, and plucks out the coin. It is perhaps the most satisfying thing he has ever done.

I'm sorry, sir, the boy says.

John D hands him the dime and says, Don't waste another day.

A few minutes later, as Pica is straightening the blanket over John D's legs, his doctor and two nurses visit him. The nurses have come to help him with his daily laughing exercises. Laughter, it was recently discovered, prolongs life. John D laughed very little during his working years, so he is trying to gain ground on men who have laughed all their lives.

One of the nurses reads from a book of witty apothegms while the other contorts his face in a variety of ways. The doctor, a young man blurred by politeness, kneels in the sand with his scuffed black instrument bag by his side. There once was a servant, reads the first nurse, who indulged in spending sprees, and who was advised by his master to save against a rainy day. Some time later, the master wanted to know if the servant had amassed any savings. Yes. Indeed I have, sir, the servant said.

Good man, John D interrupts.

The second nurse crosses his eyes and fishes out his lips.

The first nurse hesitates, then reads on, The servant said to his master, But, sir, unfortunately it rained yesterday and now all the money's gone.

John D looks at the second nurse, who has resorted to hitting his palm against his own forehead, and tries to laugh. But he is confused. Why is the money gone? What did the servant spend it on? An umbrella? Did someone steal the money while the servant was drying a wet porch or something and the servant didn't want to tell his master because the master, like some masters, is cruel and the servant, like most servants, is afraid?

The first nurse says, I'm mute.

You don't say, says the second.

John D's laugh comes out heh heh heh. Craggy, mirthless. He laughed so little during his working years because he found so little to laugh about. Every story, true or not, hangs bitter with implication, forward, reverse. Every pill is recalled by an aftertaste.

When the nurses leave, the doctor stands up and reaches beneath John D's crinkled vest to check his heart rate, blood pressure, then his ears, nose, eyes, throat, temperature, joints, scalp, spine, and basal metabolism. John D has promised the man fifty thousand dollars on his, John D's, one hundredth birthday.

The doctor jots illegibly into his notepad. His patient has eczema, bad kidneys, pleurisy. The doctor isn't writing this down. He is making notes for a love letter to another patient, an old woman. *You are the worm in my aorta,* he writes. *You are my delirium tremens.*

John D uses a lever to recline himself in the shaded chair. The high sun turns the white sunshade orange. He says, What ails me today, doctor? Speak to me, tell me my fortune.

On *speak,* his teeth click.

Only good news, the doctor says. The diet seems to be working. Just look at you, sir. You are the living reward of a life well lived.

I am a prize, aren't I? A living trophy.

Exactly.

Nonsense. All these crucifers. This laughing and fitness juice and hanging on. It's ignoble. I might just fall down dead tomorrow and where would that leave me.

Heaven, the doctor says.

But you aren't a betting man, John D says. Ever since that handbill landed in my lap, I've been dreaming of men with wings. Are men ever born with wings, doctor?

Sure, the doctor says. And tails and fins, gills. Happens frequently in the Orient. It's all the ocean matter in their diet.

John D sighs. Sometimes it sounds like you don't know a heart from a headstock, he says. It used to be my business to fix other people's faulty connections. I was never the smartest man in the room, or the handsomest or the nicest or the meanest, but I was always the least afraid. What are you writing? Are you drawing a picture of me?

No sir, the doctor says. He writes: *You are a terminal condition. My trough has been poisoned.*

The doctor has quick, pristine hands. John D looks at his own hands: pecked, abraded, danced on by age. He says, I'm no more afraid of dying than of being reborn. Do you know that? Would you kindly look at me when I'm speaking to you?

You are my living end.

The doctor meets his gaze. The old man, fleeced but hardy, looks like some nightmare mascot ready to tunnel to the center of the earth. He looks hungry for a soul.

I am firing you, John D says. You can keep the instruments I bought. Use them on someone else.

The doctor consults his notepad again, as if for a second opinion. Page after page of love notes, of beseeching and woe and heart sauce. He needs a marathon enema and perhaps a vacation in a place where none of the women speak English. He collects his things and zips his bag, brushes the sand from its glossed surface. Is that all? he asks the old man. John D answers, Yes. Until the next thing.

The doctor sidesteps down the dune and nearly bumps into Pica. Aren't you going to stay for the airman? Pica asks him.

There's a woman, another patient, who needs me, he says.

He carries John D's wretched voice with him down the beach. Death, the doctor thinks, is not a thing like birth. Birth is a dream, spontaneous and innate. Death, on the other hand, is a slow, false, divine calamity. It is like love.

An opening, an isthmus between clouds. From above, everything on the ground looks precarious. Tiny lakes and streams blend with foliage until the sun catches them and they shiver and glint like mercury. The swampland resembles an old green floor mat, torn and soaked through in places. Tidy farm plots resemble sewn-on patches. In the ocean, past the crowd waiting on the tan belt of beach, past the downy breakers, monsters rove in shipwreck shadows underwater. The airman is ready.

He arrives low and from the west, towing a heavy rumbling sound that causes the crowd to unanimously turn and raise their chins. John D, immobile on the soft sand, watches the crowd watch the sky. For a moment he thinks they are saluting him, showing admiration, but they are just using their hands to visor their eyes from the sun. Perhaps he would have given them each a dime had they been saluting him. But they aren't. They are protecting themselves, awaiting their spectacle. He would have told them to line up and receive their reward. He would have loved that.

The airplane streaks by, dips lower, lower, almost kisses the ocean. Just like the hungry bird. The crowd roars. The airplane arcs and corkscrews back, now moving horizontally to the shoreline. It is a snub-nosed biplane painted gunmetal gray, with two letters on the fuselage: AA II. It flies with impossible grace. It rolls and peaks and buzzes and swerves and herds the crowd like wind herds wheat. It is beautiful, it is irrefutable. It makes John D sleepy.

After a while he stops tracking the plane altogether and is content to watch the crowd. Gathered all together, what are they? They are harnessed parts, a machine manipulated by a smaller, more efficient machine. The input is spectacle, the output is laughter, ecstasy.

Here comes the Deadman Drop! yells a boy in the crowd.

The engine is silenced and the plane flies vertically downward. At the last moment, the engine chugs back to life and the plane pulls up.

Outstanding, Pica says. He's playing a game with us. To be honest, he reminds me of you, Mr. John. How you were able to outmaneuver whole *systems*. Bypassing and circumventing and pulling up just in time. Leaving us all breathless. Even now, especially now. I bet you're enjoying this, Mr. John.

Yes, John D thinks. He has fallen asleep, though, so he does not reply. Beneath the sunshade, his paper vest blows, a dry bug husk clamped to a branch.

The crowd is nearly insane with admiration for the airman. They are having difficulty finding a suitable way to express it. Husbands kiss their wives, a young girl runs around saying, A toast. A toast. A toast.

Pica reclines John D in his shaded chair. On the brink of time when he stands at last, he sings. When his sun has set, and his work is past.

A minute, maybe an hour later he is awoken by a gentle tugging on his wrist. There is a phrase on his lips, pulled from a muddled dream. As Pica and a young man in a leather helmet come into focus, standing before him, John D utters it: deadman drop.

The crowd stands below the dune at a respectful distance while the airman gives his regards to John D. The airman is tall and deeply handsome in his airman outfit. Fur collar, denim pants, twenty-eyelet boots. He looks like someone from the future dressed as someone from the past. He gestures with his hands, laughs, pats Pica on the back. The crowd feels his hand on their backs. He is describing his travels to John D, tailoring his story to what he thinks the old man wants to hear. God, beauty, order, magic. The airman is down to his last twenty-five dollars.

Up there, he is saying, you see the real sense and beauty of the world. Everything's touched by God. Dirt is a hundred different shades of brown. Lakes and rivers, they wink at you. Time stretches, shrinks, loses definition — hours pass like seconds, seconds like hours, but all of it, you know, vaccinates you. Is that the right word? Rebaptizes. Years from now, there won't be any reason to stay on the ground. We'll all be kings of the sky.

John D, groggy from his nap, likes the sound of this. He likes the space this man occupies. When the airman asks if he's ever ridden in an airplane, John D nods and answers, No.

Would you like to? And I only ask because some of the main —

Yes, I would, John D interrupts. Pica, please help me up.

And with that the decision is made. The airman usually has to do more convincing, has to move from the spiritual to the mechanical to convince would-be patrons to fly with him. But John D is awake now. He is not afraid. He stands up from his chair, ducks nimbly around the sunshade to be next to the airman. He clears his throat.

I will now take to the air, he announces to the men and women below the dune. It is something he once heard an acrobat say before a high-wire act. The crowd is subdued, but once they see the old man and the airman and Pica shuffling down the dune, they begin to cheer. John D reaches into his pocket and scatters the rest of his dimes among the crowd like birdseed, not bothering to wait for an outstretched hand.

Pica gently plucks a sandspur from the back of the old man's vest and drops it into the sand. He whispers, It gets real cold up there, Mr. John. The air, he says, isn't as habitual. It's thin. You sure you want to put yourself in jeopardy like this, undo all your hard work? If you want I can go up there for you.

I need you to watch me from down here, John D says. You will wave and I probably won't see you. Make sure everyone else waves as well.

What if there's an accident? Pica says.

Keep waving, John D says.

Down the beach, away from the crowd, the airman pats the airplane's fuselage and says, Hello, Pearl. He opens the latch under the bulkhead and presents the old man with a jacket, helmet, and goggles. Pica helps him remove his wig and replaces it with the helmet. It feels taut and vivified, like a second skin. He is lifted into the cab, latched tight and tucked in with blankets. He is fiercely content: he is on the cusp of something. He moves his legs to make sure they are still there.

Before going through his preflight ritual, the airman hands John D a piece of candy in a wrapper. For your ears, he says. You chew it.

John D opens the wrapper and puts the candy in his mouth. It is powdery, then sweet, then soft. Involuntarily he chews, his false teeth clicking with every third or fourth bite. It tastes like a peach's secret seed. He continues chewing, resisting the urge to swallow it.

It's made from trees, the airman says. He starts the engine, slips into his shoulder harness, tacks the aileron twice. He plans to take off, bank right, and make an easy, easy circuit over the ocean. No tricks, nothing more complicated than a staggered ascent. He will land on the hard-packed sand and gently ask the millionaire for a contribution. Make a joke about a sky tax. A sky monopoly.

Chewing the gum, John D remembers a day more than seventy-five years past, when he and his mother took a trip to the doctor. He can't remember why they were there, but he can still envision the brightly colored cuckoo clock in the waiting room and a boy sitting on his mother's lap greedily licking an amber piece of candy on the end of a small white stick. The doctor kept a jar of them and John D was given one before he left. He saved it until he returned home and then saved it until the following day. He saved it through the next week and through summer and autumn and winter. He saved it until the candy broke into pieces in his bureau drawer. Then he saved the pieces.

You might be the most discreet boy who ever was, his mother used to say.

If he had eaten it, he would have enjoyed it for five minutes. Instead he enjoyed it for five years.

So went his logic at the time. Now, pinned beneath blankets in the plane, which has begun moving, he wonders what he was saving it for, what squirrel impulse made the idea of eating the candy outrageous. In the cab of the plane John D feels something like impatience. He chews the candy, which hasn't yet lost its flavor, with more and more fervor.

The plane taxis past and Pica and the rest of the crowd wave. Pica thinks: I will wave until kingdom come. I will be the last thing he sees when his eyes shut for good.

The airman adds and subtracts in his head. The wind has picked up and is blowing the biplane closer to the shoreline. The airplane taxis down the beach, bucking and swaying, and the airman knows he is going to have to tell the old man that they can't risk taking off. For now he keeps going. From the sound of it, the old man is having a fine time of it.

He is chewing and chewing and chewing, greedily mashing out any patch of sweetness he can find.

It's remarkable. It's the finest thing I have ever tasted, John D says, past the boardwalk, past the dunes, long after it has ceased to be true.

RICHARD POWERS

Modulation

FROM *Conjunctions*

DO

FROM EVERYTHING that Toshi Yukawa could later determine, the original file was uploaded to one of those illegal Brigadoon sites that appeared, drew several thousand ecstatic hits from six continents, then disappeared traceless, twelve hours later, compressing the whole arc of human history into a single day: rough birth, fledgling colonies, prospering community, land grabs and hoarding, shooting wars, imperial decay, and finally, much gnashing of teeth after the inevitable collapse, which seemed to happen faster each time through the cycle. The kind of site that spelled *music* t-u-n-z.

Yukawa — or the artist formerly known as free4yu — was paid to spend his days trawling such sites. When he was twenty-six, the Recording Industry Association of America surrounded his apartment, coming after him to the tune of $50,000 and four years in prison. He was now twenty-eight, out on parole, and working for his old enemies. His job was to study the latest escalations in the arms race that kept a motley army of hackers, crackers, and slackers running roughshod over a multibillion-dollar industry, and then to develop the next counteroffensive to try to reclaim file-sharing no man's land.

By Yukawa's count, the average illegal file server could satisfy half a million happy customers across the planet before being shut down. Most looters rushed to grab this week's tops of the pops. But even files with no identifying description could rack up hundreds of downloads before the well went dry. Much later, Yukawa guessed that the infected track might have installed itself onto as few as fifty initial machines. But as his friends in digital epidemiology were quick to point out, all it took to start a full-fledged epidemic was a single Typhoid Mary surprise package slipping through quarantine.

DI

A week before the music changed, Brazilian journalist Marta Mota was grilling a strike brigade attached to the Second Infantry Division near Baqubah in the explosive Iraqi province of Diyala. She was looking for a story for the *Folha de S. Paulo,* some new angle in the endless war that hadn't already been done to death. The stress the combatants had lived with for years had broken her in three days. All she wanted was to get back to her apartment in Tatuapé and write some harmless feature about local rampant corruption.

On the day before she left Baqubah, she interviewed a young American specialist who called himself Jukebox. He described, in more detail than anyone needed, how part of his informal job description involved rigging up one of the M1127 Stryker Reconnaissance Vehicles with powerful mounted speakers, in order to pound out morale-boosting music for the unit during operations. "What does this music do?" Marta asked the soldier, in her lightly accented English. The question bewildered him, so she asked again. Jukebox cut her off, somewhere between impatience and amusement. "What does it *do?* That depends on who's listening." When she pressed for details, Jukebox just said, "You *know* what the hell it does."

At his words, Marta Mota snapped back in time to Panama, listening as American Marines tried to flush Manuel Noriega out of his bunker with massive waves of surround-sound Van Halen. That was two decades ago, when she was still a fledgling journalist in her twenties, absolutely convinced that the right story could change the conscience of the species. Since then, in combat zones on three continents, she had written up far more soul-crushing sounds.

She asked what music the Stryker vehicle pumped out, and Jukebox gave a rapid-fire list: the soundtrack of the globe's inescapable future. She asked for a listen. He pulled out something that looked like those slender, luxury matchboxes set out on the tables in her favorite Vila Madalena jazz club. She inserted the ear buds and he fired up the player. She yanked the buds out of her ears, howling in pain. Jukebox just laughed and adjusted her volume. Even at almost mute, the music was ear-stabbing, brain-bleeding, spine-crushing stuff.

"Can you copy some of these tracks onto my player?" she asked, and fished her device out of her bag. She would write up the musical recon operations later, in Frankfurt, while on her way back home.

The sight of her three-year-old player reduced Jukebox to tears of mirth. He pretended to be unable to lift it. "What does this beast weigh, like half a *pound?*"

RE

On the campus of a midwestern college dead center in one of the I-states, in the middle of a cornfield that stretched three hundred miles in every direction, a recently retired professor of ethnomusicology walks through a dusting of snow across the quad to his office in the music building to begin his permanent evacuation. Jan Steiner was supposed to have vacated back in August, to surrender his coveted space to a newly hired junior faculty member; it's now mid-December, the semester over, and he's still not started culling.

Born in the late twenties to a German-speaking family in Prague, Steiner came to the States just before half his extended family was rounded up and sent east. He moved from a Czech enclave in Queens to Berkeley and Princeton, and from there he went on to change the way that academics thought about concert music. He has taught at his privileged college for as long as anyone alive, and he has occupied his office one semester longer than the college allows.

He follows the stone path through a break in a hedge and comes alongside the Doric temple to Harmony. For the first time in years, he notices the names chiseled into the building's limestone frieze: Palestrina, Bach, Mozart, Beethoven, Schumann, Brahms, and — after decades, he still can't help smiling — Karl Maria von Weber.

It could've been worse; there's a University of California music building that celebrates the immortality of Rameau and Dittersdorf. His parents revered these names above any humanitarian's; beyond these names, they said, the rest was noise. Steiner's father went to his grave holding his son partly responsible for the twilight of these gods.

Once, at the peak of the iconoclastic sixties, Jan Steiner suggested that all these names be unceremoniously chiseled out of their limestone and replaced by thousands of names from all places and times, names so numerous and small they would be legible only to those willing to come up close and look. Like all his writing from those heady days, his jest had been deadly serious. The whole sleepy campus was outraged; he'd almost been driven to finding work elsewhere. Now, a third of a century on, when the college would probably leap at such a venture, Jan Steiner no longer has the heart to propose it again.

Before Steiner and his like-minded colleagues set to work, scholars wrote about music mostly as an aesthetic experience, masterpieces to be celebrated in religious terms. After his generation's flood of publications, music took its place among all other ambiguous cultural work — a matter of power relations, nationalism, market forces, class contestation, and identity politics.

Jan Steiner gazes up at the Doric temple's entablature, circa 1912, and squints in pain. Could he still tell Palestrina from Allegri, in an aural police lineup? When did he last listen to anything for pleasure? If this building were to collapse tomorrow, what would he advocate, for the replacement frieze? Just spelling out the solfège syllables of the chromatic scale smacked of Eurocentrism.

He lets himself into the building's side door and makes his way up to the second story. Even on a snowy December Sunday, the practice rooms are going full tilt. He walks past the eight cubicles of baby grands — *Pianosaurus rex* in full, eighty-eight-key sprint. The repertoire has certainly expanded in his half a century on campus. The only fragment of sound in the whole polychordal gauntlet he can name is the John Cage emanating from the empty cubicle on the end.

Other voices, other rooms: he's given his life to promote that, and the battle is all but won. Scholarship has discovered the 98 percent of world music it hitherto suppressed. Elitism is dead; all ears are forever opened wide. So why this pall he's been unable to shake for these last several months? Perhaps it's the oppressiveness that Paul Hindemith once attributed to Bach in his last years in Leipzig: the melancholy of accomplishment.

He unlocks his oaken office door and flicks on the light. The tomb is overflowing. Every flat surface, including the dark linoleum floor, is piled with precarious paper towers. Monographs bulge off the shelves. Folders and collection boxes stack almost to the fluorescent lights. But he can still put his finger on any desired item, in no more than a few minutes. The problem is desire.

Now he must judge every scrap. There's too much to save, but it would stop his valve-repaired heart to throw any of it out. Five decades of iconoclasm. The college library might sift through it and keep anything of value. But who in the last five years has set foot in the college library?

He drops into his desk chair and stares again at the awful severance gift from his retirement party. The department presented the mobile device to him in a teary ceremony: a clock, calendar, appointment book, phone, web browser, and matter transporter, but mostly a bribe to get him to quit quietly. The thing also, incidentally, plays music. Even the name sounds like *Invasion of the Body Snatchers*. He should have known, half a century ago, that music, like the most robust of weeds, would eventually come in *pods*.

And this one came preloaded with every piece of music he has ever written about, recorded, or championed. Turkish hymns and Chinese work-camp songs, gamelan orchestras and Albanian wedding choirs, political prisoners' anthems and 1930s radio jingles: his entire life's work arranged for an instrument that everyone could learn to play without any effort. What were his colleagues thinking, giving him his own back? What he needs is music he hasn't yet discovered, any sound at all that hasn't disappeared into the oversold, derivative, or market branded. He grabs the device, flips it on, and blunders through the menu screens, looking for a song he might somehow, by accident, have blessedly forgotten.

RI

On the night before the exploit launched, Mitchell Payne was on his way from Los Angeles to the Sydney 8-Bit Chiptune Blowout. The first humans to grow up from infancy on video games had stumbled inadvertently into young adulthood, a condition that left them stricken with nostalgia for the blips and bleeps of their Atari childhood. And where there was nostalgia, there were always live concerts. The Sydney event was Mitchell's third such extravaganza. The chiptune phenomenon had hit North America ten months ago, which meant it would soon erupt into mass consciousness and be dead by this time next year. But until such demise, Mitchell Payne, leading Futurepop composer and perhaps the greatest real-time Roland MC-909 Groovebox performer of his generation, had found another way to help pay off his Sarah Lawrence student loans.

The one-hundred-and-fifty-grand debt didn't worry him so much. What bothered him, as he hunkered down over Palmyra Atoll for the next hour's installment of in-flight entertainment from the Homeland Security Channel, was the growing conviction that at twenty-three, he no longer had his finger on the pulse. He had lost his lifelong ability to keep one measure ahead of the next modulation. He'd recently scored only 72 percent on an online musical genre test, making stupid mistakes such as confusing acid groove, acid croft, acid techno, and acid lounge. He blamed how busy he had been, trying to master the classic eight-bit repertoire. He told himself that he had just overthought the test questions, but in reality, there was no excuse. Truth was, he was slipping. Things were happening, whole new genres crossbreeding, and he was going to be one of those people who didn't even hear it until the next big thing was already in its grave and all over the cover of *Rolling Stone*.

But he had more pressing worries. In Sydney he'd be up against some classic composers, the true giants of the international chiptune movement. Without some serious art on his part, they'd laugh him off the stage. Fortunately, his material was beyond awesome. He pulled his laptop out of his carry-on and fired up the emulator. He flipped through his sequences again, checking tempi, fiddling with the voicing of chords. Then he peeked again at the climax of his set, an inspiration he still couldn't quite believe he'd pulled off. He'd managed to contrapuntally combine the theme from Nintendo's Donkey Kong with Commodore 64's Skate or Die, in retrograde inversion. The sheer ecumenical beauty of the gesture once more brought tears to his eyes.

When he looked up again, the in-flight entertainment had graduated to that new reality show, *Go for the Green,* where ten illegal alien families compete against each other to keep from getting deported. He watched for a few minutes, then returned to his hard drive's 160 GB of tracks. But before he could determine where he'd gone wrong in discriminating between epic house, progressive house, filtered house, and French house, the stewardess was on the sound system asking everyone to turn off and stow all portable devices in preparation for landing in Sydney.

MI

Toshi Yukawa took too long to realize the danger of the virus. He'd seen the chatter on the pirate music discussion boards, the reports of files that downloaded just fine, then disappeared from the receiving directory. Some guy named Jarod would complain that his file count was broken after syncing with his Nano. Some guy named Jason would report that the same thing was true on his Shuffle. Another guy named Justin would confirm for his Zen. Then another guy named Dustin would chime in, "Get a Touch, you freaking noobs, it's been out for weeks."

Any file that hid itself was trouble. He ran some tests on the twelve machines behind his router firewall: five subdirectories were compromised. He could discover nothing else until he synchronized these machines with portable devices. After syncing, three different handhelds — a music player, a pocket PC, and even a cell phone — showed flaky file counts. Yukawa realized that he was looking at something technologically impossible: the very first backdoor infection of multiple music players.

The ingenuity of the code humbled Yukawa. The main file seemed to figure out what kind of mobile device was attached to the host computer, then loaded in the appropriate code. But the ingenuity got better, and worse. On next check, Yukawa's five suspicious desktop directories had multiplied to twelve. The malicious payload was attaching itself to other files.

What kind of person would want to punish music traffickers? There were the geek hacker athletes, virtuosi like Toshi had been, simply giving their own kind of concert on their own astonishing instruments, regardless of the effect on the audience. There were always the terrorists, of course. Once you hated freedom, it was just a matter of time before you hated two-part harmony. But when he saw how this new virus could spread, Toshi Yukawa wondered if he wasn't being set up. Maybe some of his colleagues at the Recording Industry Association had developed the ultimate counterstrike for a world where 200 million songs a day were sold and even more were borrowed. And maybe his colleagues had simply neglected to tell him about the new weapon.

Some days he wasn't even sure why the RIAA had hired him. So much music could be had by so many for so little that Toshi should have long ago been driven into honest work, say eclectic format disc-jockeying for Starbucks. There was pay what you want and genetic taste matching and music by statistical referral. Customers who liked Radiohead also listened to Slipknot. If you like Slipknot, you may also like the Bulgarian Women's Chorus. The vendors had your demographic, and would feed it to you in unlimited ninety-nine-cent doses or even free squirts that vanished after three listens. He owed his job to saltwater syndrome. Drinking made you thirsty. Buffets bred hunger.

And some kind of strange musical hunger had bred this virus. Whoever had made the payload had made something beautiful. Yukawa had no other word for it, and the way the thing worked scared the hell out of him. Three days into his hunt, he discovered that four other computers behind his firewall were now infected. These boxes had gone nowhere near an illegal download site. The virus had somehow uploaded itself back up to shared music service software, and was spreading itself through automatic synchronization onto innocent bystanders.

A sick and brilliant mind: that's what Toshi Yukawa was fighting. He felt a wave of disgust for anyone who couldn't put such gifts to better use. Then he remembered himself, just four years ago: a collector so obsessed with liberating music that he'd all but stopped listening to it.

FA

Marta Mota woke up in her economy hotel on the Schönstraße near the Frankfurt Hauptbahnhof with a tune in her head. Not a tune, exactly: more like a motif. She couldn't altogether sing it, but she couldn't shake it, either.

It lasted through her hot shower — a marvelous indulgence, after Iraq. It persisted through the heavy black breads and sausages of German breakfast. It was still there as she handled her e-mail and filed another story with *Folha* on the Diyala campaign. She had contracted what the Germans called an *Ohrwurm,* what Brazilian Portuguese called *chiclete de ouvido:* a gum tune stuck in her relentlessly chewing brain.

As earworms went, this one wasn't bad. She'd spent an hour yesterday listening to the testosterone storms that the American soldier had copied for her. She'd needed two hours of Django Reinhardt and Eliane Elias to drive that throbbing from her mind. What she hummed now, she felt sure, was nothing she'd heard in the last five days.

She Skyped her mate Andre at the appointed hour. He was consulting, in Bahrain. The world was insane, and far too mobile for its own well-being. She only thanked God for dispensing Voice over Internet just in time.

Andre asked about Iraq. There was nothing to say. Everyone knew already, and no one could help. She told him about the earworm. Andre laughed. "Oh yes. I had that for three months once. Kylie Minogue. I thought I was going to have to check into a hospital. You see? The Americans will get us all, one way or the other."

She told him she thought Kylie Minogue was Australian.

"Alabama, Arizona, Australia: it's all a World Bank thing, right?"

He asked how the tune went. She tried to describe it. Words were as effective at holding music as smoke was at holding water.

"Sing it," he commanded.

She swore colorfully. "Sing it! Here? In public?"

The man seemed to do nothing but laugh. Wasn't there grimness enough, out in Bahrain?

"The Internet is not public," he told her. "Don't you know that? Everything you do on the Internet instantly disappears."

She tried to sing a few notes, but it was hopeless. The earworm wasn't even a motif. It was more a harmony, a sequence of magical chords that receded when she focused on them.

"Where do you think you heard it?"

She had no clue.

"I read an article about why this happens, but I can't remember it. Would you like the garbled version?"

She said yes. That was the beauty of free communication. They could be as silly as if they were lying next to each other in bed. Andre recounted his jumbled article, something about a cognitive itch, some combination of simplicity and surprise, the auditory cortex singing to itself. He thought he remembered something about the most common stuck tunes coming from the first fifteen years of a person's life.

"You need an eraser tune," he told her. "A good eraser tune is as sticky as the original, and they cancel each other out. Here's the one that worked for me." And into his tinny laptop computer microphone in Bahrain, in a frail but pretty baritone she hadn't heard for way too long, he sang a few notes that rematerialized in her Frankfurt hotel as the theme song from *Mission Impossible.*

It didn't help, and she went to bed that night with the phantom chords taunting her, just out of reach.

FI

Jan Steiner sits in his windowless office, listening to his life's work. It isn't bad, as life's work goes. But all these sounds have become so achingly predictable. He can't listen to anything for more than thirty seconds without hearing political agendas. Somebody preserving their social privileges. Somebody else subverting them. Groups of people bonding together with branded tunes that assert their superiority over everyone with different melodies.

He has recorded hundreds of hours of what people now call world music, and written about thousands more. He always paid the performers out of his modest grant money and gave them any rare recording profits. But he has never taken out a single copyright. Music belonged to everyone alive, or to no one. Every year, in his "Introduction to Music" lecture, he told his freshmen the story about how the Vatican tried to keep Allegri's *Miserere* a trade secret, refusing even to show the score but insisting that for the full mystic aura of the piece, one had to come to Rome and pay top dollar. And the protectionism worked until the fourteen-year-old Mozart, in Rome for a concert, transcribed it perfectly from memory, freeing it for performance everywhere. And every year Jan Steiner got his freshmen cheering the original bootlegger.

The idea was simple: put your song out in the world, free of all motives, and see what other people do with it. When his scandalized colleagues asked how musicians were supposed to make a living, he pointed out that musicians in hundreds of countries had eked out a living for millennia without benefit of copyright. He said that most music should be amateur, or served up like weekly cantatas knocked out for the glory of God alone.

He sits on his green padded office chair, tipped back on the cracked linoleum, under the humming fluorescent lights, listening. He listens to a traditional Azerbaijani mourning song, as personal a lament as has ever been put into tones. He found it gut-wrenching when he first recorded it, two decades back. Now all he can hear is the globally released feature film from a year ago that used the song as its novel theme music. The movie seemed to be mostly about potential residuals and the volatile off-screen escapades of its two stars. The soundtrack made more money in six months than any Azerbaijani musician had made in a lifetime, and the performers on his track — the one that had brought the haunted melody to North America — had seen not a penny.

Just to further torture himself, he switches to his other great recent hit: an ecstatic Ghanaian instrumental performed entirely on hubcaps and taxi horns that only six months before had been turned into an exultant commercial for global financial services. This one also made a mint as a cell-phone ring tone.

He has no one to blame for these abuses but himself. All music was theft, he has maintained over a lifetime of scholarly writing, since long before sampling even had a name. Europe used to call it *cantus firmus*. Renaissance magpies used to dress up millennium-old Gregorian psalmodic chants in bright polyphony. Whole musical systems — Persian dastgāhs and Indian ragas — knew nothing about ownership and consisted entirely of brilliant improvisations on preexisting themes. The best songs, the ones that God wanted, were the ones that someone else transposed and sang back to you, from another country, in a distant key. But God hadn't anticipated global financial services jingles.

Back in the 1970s Steiner had predicted that the rise of computing would save music from death by commodity. Armed with amazing new ways to write, arrange, record, and perform, everyone alive would become a composer and add to the world's ongoing song. Well, his prediction had come true. More music of more variety was being produced by more people than any ethnomusicologist would ever be able to name again. His own illiterate grandson was a professional digital musician, and Jan Steiner finds the boy's every measure unbearably predictable.

He works his way through the towering stacks of offprints, pitching mercilessly. While he works, he leaves the player on shuffle, letting it select his life's tracks at random. By the time he leaves, hours later, he has thrown out two large garbage bins, and it's made no visible dent on the office. He stashes the player in his coat pocket as he leaves the building and heads back toward the snowy quad. Outside, it's night, and silent, the only track he can bear.

But as he rounds the corner of the Georgian psychology building, a tune comes back to him. *Comes back* isn't quite right, since this one is nothing he's listened to this evening. He can't quite say whether he's ever heard it before, or even what scale or mode or key it wants to be in. As far as he can tell, this track — if it is a *track* — has gotten away safely, innocent, never repackaged, let alone heard by anyone.

SOL

In Sydney, Mitchell Payne felt a song coming on. It had banged around his head since deplaning. This was dangerous: when melodies came to him out of the blue, it usually meant he was ripping someone off. He wasn't alone. There were only so many notes — twelve, to be precise — and they could be combined in only so many sensible ways. Someday soon a garage band out in Cos Cob was going to string together the last viable melody, and music would be pure plagiarism and mash-ups from then on.

The industry was already pretty much there anyway. Covers and remakes, quotations and allusions, homage, sampling, and down-and-dirty five-fingered discounts. A Korean kid covering a Taiwanese kid whose arrangement imitated the video game Pump It Up whose soundtrack mimicked an old Brian Eno performance uploads an electrifying guitar video of Pachelbel's Canon in D, already the most hacked-at piece of the last three hundred years, and immediately people from Panama to Turkmenistan post hundreds of shot-perfect recreations, faithful down to every detail of tempo and ornament . . .

The melody nibbling at Mitchell's brain as he set up his loopers, shifters, sequencers, and MPCs on the stage of the small Haymarket theater might have come from anywhere. It was at once oddly familiar and deeply strange. He cursed the snippet, even as it haunted him. He couldn't afford stuck tune syndrome just before performing. He had to settle into the chiptune groove, that quantized trance that the children of Mario demanded.

But by the time he finished testing the gear, Mitchell was flipping. He stood inside the circle of banked electronics, his Mission Control of waveform generators, wanting to pull the plug on everything and crawl off to a Buddhist monastery until the monster tune scratching at his brain either came forward and said what it wanted from him or left him for dead.

While the house filled, Mitchell sat backstage in the green room answering questions from an editor of New South Wales's most prestigious online chiptune zine. What was the most influential mix he'd ever listened to? What would be the most important developments in the eight-bit scene over the next few weeks? If he could put only one video-game soundtrack into an interplanetary spacecraft, which would it be? He could barely hear the questions over the stunning harmonic tension in his head. The stage manager had to call him twice before he heard.

Nerves almost doubled him over as he jogged out of the wings in front of a restive crowd already clapping in frenzied, synchronized downbeats. He had that sick flash of doubt: *Why do I put myself through this? I could retire to something safe, write a music blog or something.* But as soon as he got the backing tracks looping, the MSX emulator bumping, and his Amiga kicking out the MIDI jambs to the principal theme from the old blockbuster game Alternate Reality, he remembered just what face-to-face was all about, and why nothing would ever replace live performance.

SI

By the time Toshi Yukawa realized he needed help from coders beyond himself, it was too late. He'd taken too long to isolate the virus and even longer to break-point and trace the logic, trying to determine exactly what the multiple payloads meant to do to the hundreds of thousands, perhaps even millions of music players already infected. The code was so idiosyncratic and original that Toshi couldn't understand it, even as it stared him in the face. The weapon was cryptic, evanescent, awful, awesome, protean, full of fearsome intelligence and unfathomable routines: a true work of art. He isolated a subroutine devoted to hijacking the player and beaming out music in subaudible frequencies. Yukawa didn't get it: why spend such incredible intellectual effort to take over millions of devices, just to play a tune no one could hear? That had to be just a private amusement, a warm-up act for the headline show. Yukawa dug deeper, bracing for the real mayhem. A person who could write such code could sow destruction on an operatic scale.

Then Toshi stumbled onto a portion of the initializer that made his blood run cold. It checked the host's time zone and adjusted another routine that made continuous calls to the music player's clock. A timed detonator: the code was going to launch a synchronized event to go off at a single moment across all the world's time zones. But what event? The code was inscrutable assembly language. Deleting songs at random? Scrambling the firmware or flash memory?

Yukawa logged in to the best professional discussion board for tracking the thousands of viruses, worms, Trojans, and assorted malicious code in the wild. There it was: growing chatter about something already code-named *counterpoint*. Yukawa posted his discoveries, and four hours later, one of the big boys at Norton found the trigger date for Yukawa's detonator routine. A day obvious after the fact: *counterpoint* was set to premiere on December 21, the winter solstice. The day after tomorrow.

Time had run out. In two days many, many people were going to be walking around earbudless, their billions of dollars' worth of portable media centers bricked. Personalized music would never be safe again. People would be thrown back on singing to each other.

A South American journalist reporting on the eternal hackers' arms race had once asked Yukawa what would happen if the white hats lost. He'd laughed her off, but here it was. Toshi sat back in his Aeron chair, gazed out his window down the glens that hid the unsuspecting venture capitalists along Sand Hill Road, and gave up. Then he did what any artist would, faced with imminent destruction: he turned back to study the beauties of the inscrutable score.

He worked on without point, and all the while, unconsciously, under his breath, in the key of hopeless and exhilarating work, he hummed.

LA

São Paulo did not help Marta Mota. In fact, the relative safety of home only worsened her earworm. It got so bad she had to take a few days' leave from *Folha*. Andre actually suggested she get help. Only the fact that several friends were also suffering from a barely audible *chiclete de ouvido* running through their minds kept her from losing hers.

More confirmation awaited her online. She turned up hundreds of posts, each one plagued by unsingable music. A reporter to the end, she traced the blind leads. She found herself in ancient backwaters, Krishna's healing flute, Ling Lun's discovery of the foundation tone, Orpheus raising the dead and animating stones, the Pythagoreans with their vibrations the length of a planetary orbit, the secret music that powered the building of the Pyramids, the horns that felled Jericho, the drumming dance of Ame no Uzume, the rain goddess, luring the sun goddess, Amaterasu Omikami, from out of hiding in the rock cave of heaven. She read about African maloya, outlawed because of its power to stir revolution. She found a fantastic article by an old Czech-American musicologist tracing the myth of sublime sound, from Ulysses, tied to the mast to hear the Sirens, through Sufi mystics, Caedmon's angel-dictated hymn, and on into songs on all continents that yearned for the lost chord. God's own court composer seemed to be baiting her for a libretto.

On the solstice, Andre was consulting in Kamchatka. Marta worked late, too wired to sleep. She drew a hot bath, trying to calm down. Her player was docked in the living room, whispering soft, late Vinicius de Moraes, one of the few human-made things capable of temporarily curing her of the human-made world. Right at a key change, the music stopped, plunging her into the night's silence. Then another tune began, one that, in four measures, lifted her bodily out of the water. She sprang from the tub and dashed into the living room, nude and dripping. By the time she reached the player, the harmonies were done.

She fiddled with the interface in a naked daze, but the tune had erased its tracks. Whatever had visited was gone faster than it came. She shut her eyes and tried to take down that sublime dictation before it faded, but could make out only vague hope, vaguer reassurance. What was left of the tune said, *Keep deep down; you'll hear me again someday.* She stood on the soaking carpet, midway between bitter and elated. The song had ended. But the melody lingered on.

LI

Mitchell Payne was deep into a smoking rendition of The Last Ninja that was burning down the house when the music died. The backing track piped out by his 160 GB classic simply quit. The iPod brought down the master sequencer, which in turn crashed the Roland, a chain reaction that pretty much left Mitchell noodling away clueless on a couple of MIDI controllers in the empty air. The silence lasted no longer than it takes to change a track, an onstage eternity.

His first thought was that his old partner in crime, free4yu, had come back to wreak electronic revenge on Mitchell for walking away scot-free when their trading concession got rounded up by the federales. But before Mitchell had the presence of mind to power anything down, the iPod started up again.

The thumping audience fell silent and listened. The harmonies passed through a series of changes, each a strangely familiar surprise. Afterward, no two people described the sequence the same way. It was the weaving antiphony of a dream, the tune your immigrant nanny made you laugh with, the unsuspecting needle dropping onto a virgin *Sgt. Pepper,* a call to desert prayer, an archaic fauxbourdon, that tape you tried to make with your high school garage band, the last four measures of something amazing on the radio that you could never subsequently identify, highland temple bells, an evening sing-along, the keys you pressed chasing after your grandmother's player piano, a garbled shortwave "Happy Birthday" from the other side of the planet, a first slow dance, a hymn from back when you were just setting out on the game of consciousness, all resonance, sphinxlike, aching with possibility, a little incandescent phrase transporting all listeners back into timeless time.

That's how the world described it the next day, those who were lucky enough not to rip their buds out of their ears or fiddle with their rebellious players. The nations' blogs resounded with endless variations on one simple theme: *OMG — did you hear that?*

The world on that day had half a billion music-capable mobile devices. If a tenth of those were infected and turned on when the tune got loose, then more people heard the ghost tune at the same time than were alive when music was first recorded into the Samaveda. And here it was again, after an eternity away: a tune that sold nothing, that had no agenda, that required no identity or allegiance, that was not disposable background product, that came and went for no reason, brief as thunder on a summer night.

For his part, Mitchell heard the song he'd been hallucinating for the last two days. And in that instant before the crowd broke out into stunned applause, Mitchell Payne thought, *This is it — a totally new genre.* The first person to transcribe the thing was going to make a fortune. *Bow, you sucker, bow!*

TI

The quad is dark and empty, the snow gathering. Flakes pour out of the woolen air. The sky above him is a lambent orange, scattering the lights of the town. Jan Steiner takes the long diagonal path toward the neoclassical English building. The phantom tune still nags at him. The harmonies take an amazing turn, he calls out in surprise, his foot slips on the icy walk, and he slams to the pavement. Hot current shoots through his brain. Pain such as he has never felt tears up the fuse of his spine and he blacks out.

When he comes to, he feels nothing. Some part of him understands: shock. He tries to stand but can't. His right thigh comes through his hip in a way that it shouldn't. The front part of his pelvis is as powdered as the snow.

He lies on his back, paralyzed, looking up into the rust of night. He calls out, but his voice doesn't carry much beyond the globe of his body's warmth. He always was a feeble little tenor, even in the prime of life. Those who can't sing, teach.

He rolls his head to the left, the empty Colonial anthropology building. He rolls to the right, the abandoned Brutalist auditorium. He can't see past his body to the music building, with the seven names on its confident pediment. Winter's first night. The college is closed, evacuated for the holidays. He'll lie here until morning, undiscovered. The temperature is falling and the pain starts a vast, slow crescendo. He can't imagine how the piece will end.

He's amazed that this fate has been lying in wait his entire life. He looks up into snowy emptiness, recalling the words of the stunned Mozart, when the natives in provincial Leipzig forced him to listen to their old Capellmeister's archaic motet they'd kept alive like some forgotten relic: *What is this? Here at last is something one can learn from.*

Then he remembers: invasion of the pod phone players. By a mighty effort of will, he manages to crane his shattered right hand around into his coat pocket. He shovels the device out onto the pavement in little Lego pieces. No saving call. Not even a diverting tune while waiting to go numb.

He inserts the buds anyway, to keep the warmth from leaking out his ears. World's smallest earmuffs. Snow is falling on the wool of his coat and his cotton cap. Snow falling on concrete, on frozen earth, freezing skin, snow on snow. In the hush, his ears sharpen. Through the dead buds, he hears the crushed device whisper a vast and silent fantasia: the wired world recovering a theme it long ago misplaced.

He lies still in the ravishing dark, listening to a need as big as lust or hunger, an urge with no reason on earth ever to have evolved. The only fundamental human pleasure with no survival value whatsoever: music . . .

> Music for a while,
> shall all your cares beguile.

A few measures more, and the cold returns him to *Do.*

ANNIE PROULX

Them Old Cowboy Songs

FROM *The New Yorker*

Archie and Rose, 1885

ARCHIE AND ROSE MCLAVERTY staked out a homestead where the Little Weed comes rattling down from the Sierra Madre, water named not for miniature obnoxious flora but for P. H. Weed, a gold-seeker who had starved near its source. Archie had a face as smooth as a skinned aspen, his lips barely incised on the surface, as though scratched in with a knife. All his natural decoration was in his red cheeks and his springy waves of auburn hair, which seemed charged with voltage. He lied about his age to anyone who asked — he was not twenty-one but sixteen. The first summer, they lived in a tent while Archie worked on a small cabin. It took him a month of rounding up stray cows for Bunk Peck before he could afford two glass windows. The cabin was snug, built with eight-foot squared-off logs tenoned on the ends and dropped into mortised uprights, a size Archie could handle himself, with a little help from their only neighbor, Tom Ackler, a sun-dried prospector with a summer shack up on the mountain. They chinked the cabin with heavy yellow clay. One day Archie dragged a huge flat stone to the house for a doorstep. It was pleasant to sit in the cool of the evening with their feet on the great stone and watch the deer come down to drink and, just before darkness, see the herons flying upstream, their color matching the sky so closely they might have been eyes of wind. Archie dug into the side of the hill and built a stout meat house, sawed wood while Rose split kindling until they had four cords stacked high against the cabin, almost to the eaves, the pile immediately tenanted by a weasel.

"He'll keep the mice down," Rose said.

"Yeah, if the bastard don't bite somebody," Archie said, flexing his right forefinger. A faint brogue flavored his sentences, for he had been conceived in Ireland and born, in 1868, in Dakota Territory, of parents arrived from Bantry Bay, his father to spike ties for the Union Pacific Railroad. His mother's death from cholera when he was seven was followed a few weeks later by that of his father, who had guzzled an entire bottle of strychnine-laced patent medicine that was guaranteed to ward off cholera and measles if taken in teaspoon quantities. Before Archie's mother died, she had taught him dozens of old songs and the rudiments of music structure by painting a plank with black and white piano keys, sitting him before it, and encouraging him to touch the keys with the correct fingers. The family wipeout removed the Irish influence. Mrs. Sarah Peck, a warm-hearted Missouri Methodist widow, raised the young orphan, to the great resentment of her son, Bunk.

A parade of saddle bums drifted through the Peck bunkhouse, and from an early age Archie listened to the songs they sang. He was a quick study for a tune, and had a memory for rhymes, verses, and intonations. When Mrs. Peck died, caught in a grass conflagration she had started while singeing slaughtered chickens, Archie was fourteen and Bunk in his early twenties. Without Mrs. Peck as a buffer, the relationship became one of hired hand and boss. There had never been any sense of kinship, fictive or otherwise, between them, and Bunk Peck fumed over the hundred dollars his mother had left Archie in her will.

Archie McLaverty had a singing voice that once heard was never forgotten. It was a straight, hard voice, the words falling out halfway between a shout and a song. Sad and flat and without ornamentation, it expressed things that were unsayable. He sang plain and square-cut, "Brandy's brandy, any way you mix it, a Texian's a Texian any way you fix it," and the listeners laughed at the droll way he rolled out *fix it,* the words surely meaning castration. He could sing every song — "Go 'Long Blue Dog," and "When the Green Grass Comes," "Don't Pull Off My Boots," and "Two Quarts of Whiskey," and at all-male roundup nights he had endless verses of "The Stinkin Cow," "The Buckskin Shirt," and "Cousin Harry." He courted Rose by singing, "Never marry no good-for-nothin boy," it being understood that the boy was himself, the *good-for-nothin* a disclaimer. Later, with winks and innuendo, he sang, "Little girl, for safety you better get branded."

Archie, advised by an ex-homesteader working for Bunk Peck, used his inheritance from Mrs. Peck to buy eighty acres of private land. It would have cost nothing if he had filed for a homestead twice that size on public land, or eight times larger on desert land, but Archie feared the government would discover he was a minor. Since he had never expected anything from Mrs. Peck, buying the land with the surprise legacy seemed like getting it for free. Archie, thrilled to be a landowner, told Rose he had to sing the metes and bounds. He started on the southwest corner early one morning and headed east. Rose walked along with him at the beginning and even tried to sing with him but got out of breath from walking so fast and singing at the same time. Nor did she know the words to many of his songs. Archie kept going. Late in the afternoon he was on the west line, drawing near and still singing, though his voice was raspy, "an we'll go downtown, an we'll buy some shirts . . . ," and slouching down the slope the last hundred feet in the evening dusk so worn of voice she could only just hear him breathily chant "never had a nickel and I don't give a shit."

There is no happiness like that of a young couple in a little house they have built themselves in a place of beauty and solitude. Archie had hammered together a table with sapling legs and two benches. At the evening meal, their faces lit by the yellow shine of the coal-oil lamp, whose light threw wild shadows on the ceiling, their world seemed in order.

Rose was not pretty, but warm-hearted and quick to laugh. She had grown up at the Jackrabbit stage station, the daughter of kettle-bellied Sundown Mealor, who dreamed of plunging steeds but because of his bottle habit drove a freight wagon. The station was on a north-south trail that connected hardscrabble ranches with the blowout railroad town of Rawlins after the Union Pacific line went through. Rose's mother was gray with some wasting disease that kept her to her bed, sinking slowly out of life. She wept over Rose's early marriage at barely fourteen but gave her a family treasure, a large silver spoon that had come across the Atlantic.

The stationmaster was Robert F. Dorgan, affable and jowly,

yearning to be appointed to a position of importance and seeing the station as a brief stop not only for freight wagons but for himself. His second wife, Flora, stepmother to his daughter Queeda, went to Denver every winter with Queeda, and so they became authorities on fashion and style. They were as close as a natural mother and daughter. In Denver, Mrs. Dorgan sought out important people who could help her husband climb to success. Many political men spent the winter in Denver, and one of them, Rufus Clatter, with connections to Washington, hinted that there was a chance for Dorgan to be appointed as the territory's surveyor.

"I'm sure he knows a good deal about surveying," he said with a wink.

"Considerable," she said, thinking that Dorgan could find some stripling surveyor to do the work for a few dollars.

"I'll see what I can do," Clatter said, pressing heavily against her thigh, but tensed to step away if she took offense. She allowed him a few seconds, smiled, and turned away.

Back at the station in the spring, where her rings and metallic dress trim cast a golden aura, she bossed the local society and gossip, saying that Archie McLaverty had ruined Rose, precipitating their youthful marriage, but what could you expect from a girl with a drunkard father, an uncontrolled girl who'd had the run of the station, sassing rough drivers and exchanging low repartee with bumpkin cowhands, among them Archie McLaverty, a lowlife who sang vulgar songs? She whisked her hands together as though ridding them of filth.

The other inhabitant of the station was an old bachelor (the country was rich in bachelors), Harp Daft, the telegraph key operator. His face and neck formed a visor of scars, moles, wens, boils, and acne. One leg was shorter than the other, and his voice twanged with catarrh. His window faced the Dorgan house, and a black circle that Rose knew to be a telescope sometimes showed in it.

Rose both admired and despised Queeda Dorgan. She greedily took in every detail of the beautiful dresses, the fire-opal brooch, satin shoes, and saucy hats so exquisitely out of place at the dusty station, but she knew that Miss Dainty had to wash out her bloody menstrual rags like every woman, although she tried to hide them by hanging them on the line at night or inside pillow slips. Beneath the silk skirts, she too had to put up with sopping pads torn from old sheets, the crusted edges chafing her thighs and pulling at her pubic hairs. At those times of the month, the animal smell seeped through Queeda's perfumed defenses.

Rose saw Mrs. Dorgan as an iron-boned, two-faced enemy, her public sweetness offset by private coarseness. She had seen the woman spit on the ground like a drover, had seen her scratch her crotch on the corner of the table when she thought no one was looking. Believing that she was a superior creature, Mrs. Dorgan never spoke to the Mealors, nor to the despicable bachelor pawing his telegraph key, or, as he said, seeking out constellations.

Every morning in the little cabin, Rose braided her straight brown hair, dabbed it with drops of lilac water from the blue bottle Archie had presented her on the day of their wedding, and wound it around her head in a coronet, the way Queeda Dorgan bound up her hair. She did not want to become like a homestead woman, with skunky armpits and greasy hair yanked into a bun. She hoped that their children would get Archie's auburn waves and his red-cheeked, handsome face. She trimmed his hair with a pair of embroidery scissors dropped in the dust by some lady stagecoach passenger at the station years before. But it was hard, keeping clean. Queeda Dorgan had little to do at the station except primp and flounce, but Rose, in her cabin, lifted heavy kettles, split kindling, baked bread, scrubbed pots, and hacked the stone-filled ground for a garden, and hauled water when Archie was not there. They were lucky their first winter that the river did not freeze. Her personal wash and the dishes and the floor took four daily buckets of water lugged up from the Little Weed, each trip disturbing the ducks who favored the nearby setback for their business meetings. She tried to keep Archie clean as well. He rode in from days of chasing Peck's cows or running wild horses on the desert with a stubbled face, mosquito-bitten neck and grimed hands, cut, cracked nails and stinking feet. She pulled off his boots and washed his feet in the dishpan, patting them dry with a clean feed-sack towel.

"If you had stockins, it wouldn't be so bad," she said. "If I could get me some knittin needles and yarn, I could make stockins."

"Mrs. Peck made some. Once. Took about a hour before they was holed. No point to it, and they clamber around in your boots. Hell with stockins."

Supper was venison hash or a platter of fried sage hen she had shot, but not beans, which Archie said had been and still were the main provender at Peck's. Occasionally their neighbor Tom Ackler rode down for supper, sometimes with his yellow cat, Gold Dust, riding behind him on the saddle. While Tom talked, Gold Dust set to work to claw the weasel out of the woodpile. Rose liked the black-eyed, balding prospector and asked him about the gold earring in his left ear.

"Used a sail the world, girlie. That's my port ear and that ring tells them as knows that I been east round Cape Horn. And if you been east, you been west first. Been all over the world." He had a rich collection of stories of storms, violent williwaws, and southerly busters, of waterspouts and whales leaping like trout, icebergs and doldrums and enmeshing seaweed, of wild times in distant ports.

"How come you to leave the sailor-boy life?" Rose asked.

"No way to get rich, girlie. And this fella wanted a snug harbor after the pitchin deck."

Archie asked about maritime songs, and the next visit Tom Ackler brought his concertina with him, and for hours sea chanteys and sailors' verses filled the cabin, Archie asking for a repeat of some and often chiming in after a single hearing.

They say old man your horse will die.
And they say so, and they hope so.
O poor old man your horse will die.
O poor old man.

Rose was an eager lover when Archie called, "Put your ass up like a whippoorwill," and an expert at shifting his occasional glum moods into pleased laughter. She seemed unaware that she lived in a time when love killed women. One summer evening, their bedspread on the floor among the chips and splinters in the half-finished cabin, they fell to kissing. Rose, in some kind of transport, began to bite her kisses, sharp nips along his neck, his shoulder, in the musky crevice between his arm and torso, his nipples, until she felt him shaking and looked up to see his eyes closed, tears in his lashes, face contorted in a grimace.

"Oh, Archie, I didn't mean to hurt, Archie —"

"You did not," he groaned. "It's. I ain't never been. Loved. I just can't hardly STAND IT —" And he began to blubber "Feel like I been shot," pulling her into his arms, rolling half over so that the salty tears and his saliva wet her embroidered shirtwaist, calling her his little birdeen, and at that moment she would have walked into a furnace for him.

On the days he was away she would hack at the garden. She shot a hawk that was after her three laying hens, plucked and cleaned it, and threw it in the soup pot with a handful of wild onions and some pepper. Another day she gathered two quarts of wild strawberries, her fingers stained a deep red that would not wash away.

"Look like you killed and skinned a griz bear by hand," he said. "It could be a bear might come down for his berries, so don't you go pickin no more."

The second winter came on and Bunk Peck laid off all the men, including Archie. Cowhands rode the circuit, moving from ranch to ranch, doing odd jobs in return for a place in the bunkhouse and three squares. Down on the Little Weed, Archie and Rose were ready for the cold. He had waited for good tracking snow and shot two elk and two deer in November when the weather chilled, swapping a share of the meat with Tom Ackler for his help, for it could take a lone man several days to pack a big elk out, with bears, lions, and wolves, coyotes, ravens, and eagles gorging as much of the unattended carcass as they could. The meat house was full. They had a barrel of flour and enough baking powder and sugar for the city of Chicago. Some mornings the wind stirred the snow into a scrim that bleached the mountains and made opaline dawn skies. Once the sun below the horizon threw savage red onto the bottom of the cloud that hung over Barrel Mountain, and Archie glanced up and saw Rose in the doorway burning an unearthly color in the lurid glow.

By spring both of them were tired of elk and venison, tired of bumping into each other in the little cabin. Rose was pregnant. Her vitality seemed to have ebbed away, her good humor with it. Archie carried her water buckets from the river and swore he would dig a well the coming summer. It was hot in the cabin, the April sun like an oven door ajar.

"You better get somebody knows about well diggin," she said sourly, slapping the bowls on the table for the everlasting elk stew, nothing more than meat, water, and salt, simmered to chewability, then reheated for days. "Remember how Mr. Town got killed when his well caved in and him in it?"

"A well can damn cave in and *I* won't be in it," he said. "I got in mind not diggin a deep killin well but clearin out that little seep east a the meat house. Could make a good spring, and I'd build a springhouse, put up some shelves, and maybe git a cow. Butter-and-cream cow. Hell, I'm goin a dig out that spring today." He was short but muscular, and his shoulders had broadened, his chest filled out with the work. He started to sing, "Got to bring along my shovel if I got to dig a spring," ending with one of Tom's yo-heave-hos, but his jokey song did not soothe her irritation. An older woman would have seen that although they were little more than children, they were shifting out of the days of clutching love and into the long haul of married life.

"Cows cost money, specially butter-and-cream cows. We ain't got enough for a butter dish even. And I'd need a churn. Long as we are dreamin, might as well dream a pig too, give the skim and have the pork in the fall. Sick a deer meat. It's too bad you spent all your money on this land. Should a saved some out."

"Still think it was the right way to do, but we sure need some chink. I'm ridin to talk with Bunk in a few days, see can I get hired on again." He pulled on his dirty digging pants, still spattered with mud from the three-day job of the privy pit. "Don't git me no dinner. I'll dig until noon and come in for coffee. We got coffee yet?"

Bunk Peck took pleasure in saying there was no job for him. Nor was there anything at the other ranches. Eight or ten Texas cowhands left over from last fall's Montana drive had stayed in the country and taken all the work.

He tried to make a joke out of it for Rose, but the way he breathed through his teeth showed it wasn't funny. After a few minutes she said in a low voice, "At the station they used a say they pay a hunderd a month up in Butte."

"Missus McLaverty, I wouldn't work in no mine. You married you a cowboy." And he sang, "I'm just a lonesome cowboy who loves a gal named Rose, I don't care if my hat gets wet or if I freeze my toes, but I won't work no copper mine, so put that up your nose." He picked a piece of turnip from the frying pan on the stove and ate it. "I'll ride over Cheyenne way an see what I can find. There's some big ranches over there and they probly need hands. Stop by Tom's place on my way an ask him to look in on you."

Despite the strong April sun, there was still deep snow under the lodgepoles and in the north hollows around Tom Ackler's cabin; the place had a deserted feeling to it, something more than if Tom had gone off for the day. His cat, Gold Dust, came purring up onto the steps, but when Archie tried to pet her she tore his hand and with flattened ears raced into the pines. Inside the cabin he found the stub of a pencil and wrote a note on the edge of an old newspaper, and left it on the table.

Tom I looking for werk arond Shyanne.
Check on Rose now & than, ok?

Karok's Cows

In a saloon on a Cheyenne street packed with whiskey mills and gambling snaps, he heard that a rancher up on Rawhide Creek was looking for spring roundup hands. The whiskey bottles glittered as the swinging doors let in planks of light — Kellogg's Old Bourbon, Squirrel, Great Gun, G. G. Booz, Day Dream. He bought his informant a drink. The thing was, the man said, a big-mustached smiler showing rotten nutcrackers, putting on the sideboards by wrapping his thumb and forefinger around the shot glass to gain another inch of fullness, that although Karok paid well and he didn't hardly lay off men in the fall, he would not hire married men, because they had the bad habit of running off home to see wife and kiddies while Karok's cows fell in mud holes, were victimized by mountain lions and rustlers, drifted down the draw, and suffered the hundred other ills that could befall untended cattle. The bartender, half listening, sucked a draft of Wheatley's Spanish Pain Destroyer from a small bottle near the cash register.

"Stomach," he said to no one, belching.

Big Mustache knocked back his brimming shot of Squirrel and went on. "He's a foreigner from back East, and the only thing counts to him is cows. He learned that fast when he come here back in the early days, cows is the only thing. Grub's pretty poor too. There ain't no chicken in the chicken soup."

"Yeah, and no horse in the horseradish," said Archie, who'd heard all the feeble bunkhouse jokes.

"Huh. Well, he rubs some the wrong way. Most a them quit. What

I done. Some law dog come out there once with his hand hoverin over his shooter, and I could see he was itchin to dabble in gore. I felt like it was a awful good place a put behind me. But there's a few like Karok's ways. Maybe you are one a them. Men rides for him gets plenty practice night ropin. See, his herd grows like a son of a bitch, if you take my meanin. But I'll give you some advice: one a these days there'll be some trouble there. That's how come that law was nosin round."

Archie rode up through country as yellow and flat as an old newspaper and went to see Karok. There was a big sign on the gate: NO MaRIED MEN. When the dour rancher asked him, Archie lied himself single, and said that he had to fetch his gear and would be back in six days.

"Five," said the kingpin, looking at him suspiciously. "Other fellas look for work, they carry their fixins. They don't have to go home and git it."

Archie worked up some story about visiting Cheyenne and not knowing he'd been laid off until one of the old outfit's boys showed up and said they were all on the bum.

"Yeah? Get goin, then. Roundup started two days ago."

Back on the Little Weed with Rose, he half explained the situation, said she would not be able to send him letters or messages until he worked something out, said he had to get back to Karok's outfit fast and would be gone for months and that she had better get her mother to come down from the station to help with the baby, expected in late September.

"She can't stand a make that trip. You know how sick she is. Won't you come back for the baby?" Even in the few days he had been gone, he seemed changed. She touched him and sat very close, waiting for the familiar oneness to lock them together.

"If I can git loose I will. But this is a real good job, good money, fifty-five a month, almost twice what Bunk Peck pays, and I'm goin a save ever nickel. And if she can't come down, you better go up there, be around womenfolk. Maybe I can git Tom to bring you up, say in July or August? Or sooner?" He was fidgety, as though he wanted to leave that minute. "He been around? His place was closed up when I stopped there before. I'll stop again on my way."

Rose said that if she had to go to the station, early September was soon enough. She did not want to be where she would have to tend her sick mother and put up with her drunk father, to see the telegraph man's face like an eroded cliff, to suffer Mrs. Dorgan's supercilious comments about "some people" directed at Queeda but meant for Rose to hear. She did not want to show up rough and distended and abandoned, without the husband they had prophesied would skedaddle. September was five months away, and she would worry about it when it came. Together they added up what a year's pay might come to, working for Karok.

"If you save everthing it will be six hundred fifty dollars. We'll be rich, won't we?" she asked in a mournful tone he chose not to notice.

He spoke enthusiastically. "And that's not countin what I maybe can pick up in wolf bounties. Possible another hunderd. Enough to git us started. I'll quit this feller's ranch after a year an git back here."

"How do I get news to you — about the baby?"

"I don't know yet. But I'll work somethin out. You know what? I feel like I need my hair combed some. You want a comb my hair?"

"Yes," she said, and laughed just when he'd thought she was going to cry. But for the first time she recognized that they were not two cleaving halves of one person but two separate people, and that because he was a man he could leave any time he wanted, and because she was a woman she could not. The cabin reeked of desertion and betrayal.

Archie and Sink

Men raised from infancy with horses could identify salient differences with a glance, but some had a keener talent for understanding equine temperament than others. Sink Gartrell was one of those, the polar opposite of Montana bronc-buster Wally Finch, who used a secret ghost cord and made unrideable outlaws of the horses he was breaking. Sink gave off a hard air of competence.

Sink thought the new kid might make a top hand with horses if he got over being a showoff. The second or third morning after he joined the roundup, Archie had woken early, sat up in his bedroll, and let loose a getting-up holler decorated with some rattlesnake yodels, startling old cookie Hel, who dropped the coffeepot in the fire, earning curses from the scattered bedrolls. The black smell of scorched coffee knocked the day over on the wrong side. The foreman, Alonzo Lago, who had barely noticed him before, stared hard at the curly-haired new hand who'd made all the noise. Sink saw him looking.

Later, Sink took the kid aside and put the boo on him, told him the facts of life, said that the leathery old foreman was well known for bareback riding of new young hires. Archie, who'd seen it all at Peck's bunkhouse, gave him a look as though he suspected Sink of the same base design, said that he could take care of himself and that if anyone tried anything on him he'd clean his plow good. He moved off. When Sink came in from watch at the past-midnight hour, he walked past the foreman's bedroll but there was only a solitary head sticking out from under the tarpaulin; the kid was somewhere far away in the sage with the coyotes.

For Archie the work was the usual ranch hand's luck — hard, dirty, long, and dull. There was no time for anything but saddle up, ride, rope, cut, herd, unsaddle, eat, sleep, and do it again. On clear, dry nights, coyote voices seemed to emanate each from a single point in a straight line, the calls crisscrossing like taut wires. When cloud cover moved in, the howls spread out in a different geometry, overlapping like concentric circles from a handful of pebbles thrown into water. But most often the wind surging over the plain sanded the cries into a kind of coyote dust, fractioned into particles of sound. He longed to be back on his own sweet place, fencing his horse pastures, happy with Rose. He thought about the coming child, imagined a boy half grown and helping him build wild-horse traps in the desert, capturing the mustangs. He could not quite conjure up a baby.

As the late summer folded, Sink saw that Archie sat straight up in the saddle, was quiet and even-tempered, good with horses. The kid was one of the kind horses liked, calm and steady. No more morning hollers, and the only songs he sang were after supper when somebody else started one, where his voice was appreciated but never mentioned. He kept to himself pretty much, often staring into the distance, but every man had something of value beyond the horizon. Despite his ease with horses, the kid had been bucked off an oily bronc that had been ruined beyond redemption by Wally Finch, and, instinctively putting out one hand to break his fall, had snapped his wrist. He spent weeks with his arm strapped to his body, rode and did everything else one-handed. Alonzo Lago fired Wally Finch, refused to pay him for ruined horses, even if they were mustangs from the wild herds, and sent him walking north to Montana.

"Kid, there's a way you fall so's you don't get hurt," Sink said. "Fold your arms, see, git one shoulder up and your head down. You give a little twist while you're fallin so's you hit the ground with your shoulder and you just roll right on over and onto your feet." He didn't know why he was telling Archie this and grouched up. "Hell, figure it out yourself."

Rose and the Coyotes

July was hot, the air vibrating, the dry land like a scraped sheep hoof. The sun drew the color from everything and the Little Weed trickled through dull stones. In a month even that trickle would be dried by the hot river rocks, the grass parched white, and preachers praying for rain. Rose could not sleep in the cabin, which was as hot as the inside of a black hatbox. Once she carried her pillow to the big stone doorstep and lay on its chill until mosquitoes drove her back inside.

She woke one morning exhausted and sweaty, and went down to the Little Weed hoping for night-cooled water. There was a dark cloud to the south, and she was glad to hear the distant rumble of thunder. In anticipation, she set out the big kettle and two buckets to catch rainwater. The advance wind came in, thrashing tree branches and ripping leaves. The grass went sidewise. Lightning danced on the crest of Barrel Mountain, and then a burst of hail swallowed up the landscape in a chattering, roaring sweep. She ran inside and watched the ice pellets flail the river rocks and slowly give way to thrumming rain. The rocks disappeared in the foam of rising water. Almost as quickly as it had started the rain stopped, a few last hailstones fell, and against the moving cloud the arc of a double rainbow promised everything. Her buckets were full of sweet water and floating hailstones. She stripped and poured dippers of goose-bump water over her head again and again until one bucket was nearly empty and she was shaking. The air was as cool and fresh as September, the heat broken. Around midnight the rain began again, slow and steady. Half awake, she could hear it dripping on the stone doorstep.

The next morning it was cold and sleety and her back ached; she wished for the heat of summer to return. She staggered when she walked, and making coffee didn't seem worth it. She drank water and stared at the icy spicules sliding down the window glass. Around midmorning the backache increased, working itself into a slow rhythm. It dawned on her very slowly that the baby was not waiting for September. By afternoon the backache was an encircling python and she could do nothing but pant and whimper, the steady rattle of rain dampening her moaning call for succor. She wriggled out of her heavy dress and put on her oldest nightgown. The pain increased to waves of cramping agony that left her gasping for breath, on and on, the day fading into night, the rain torn away by wind, the dark choking hours eternal. Another dawn came, sticky with the return of heat, and still her raw loins could not deliver the child. On the fourth day, when Rose was voiceless from calling for Archie, her mother, Tom Ackler, Tom Ackler's cat, from screaming imprecations at all of them, at God, any god, then at the river ducks and the weasel, to any entity that might hear, the python relaxed its grip and slid off the bloody bed, leaving her spiraling down in plum-colored mist.

It seemed to be late afternoon. She was glued to the bed, and at the slightest movement felt a hot surge that she knew was blood. She got up on her elbows and saw the clotted child, stiff and gray, the barley-rope cord, and the afterbirth. She did not weep, but, filled with an ancient rage, knelt on the floor, ignoring the hot blood seeping from her, and rolled the infant up in the rough sheet. It was a bulky mass, and she felt the loss of the sheet as another tragedy. When she tried to stand, the blood poured, but she was driven to bury the child, to end the horror of the event. She crept to the cupboard, got a dishtowel, and rewrapped the baby in a smaller bundle. Her hand closed on the silver spoon, her mother's wedding present, and she thrust it into the placket neck of her nightgown, the cool metal like balm.

Clenching the knot of the dishtowel in her teeth, she crawled out the door and toward the sandy soil near the river, where, still on hands and knees, she dug a shallow hole with the silver spoon and laid the child in it, heaping it with sand and piling on top whatever river stones were within reach. It took more than an hour to follow her blood trail back to the cabin, the twilight deep by the time she reached the doorstep.

The bloody sheet lay bunched on the floor and the bare mattress showed a black stain like the map of South America. She lay on the floor, for the bed was miles away, a cliff only birds could reach. Everything seemed to swell and shrink, the twitching bed leg, a dank clout swooning over the edge of the dishpan, the wall itself bulging forward, the chair flying viciously — all pulsing with the rhythm of her hot, pumping blood. Barrel Mountain, bringing darkness, squashed its bulk against the window, and owls crashed through, wings like iron bars. Struggling through the syrup of subconsciousness in the last hour, she heard the coyotes outside and knew what they were doing.

The Line Shack

As the September nights cooled, Archie got nervous, went into town as often as he could, called at the post office, but no one saw him come out with any letters or packages. Alonzo Lago sent Sink and Archie to check some distant draws, ostensibly for old renegade cows too wily or a few mavericks too young to be caught in any roundup.

"What's eatin you?" said Sink as they rode out, but the kid shook his head. Half an hour later he opened his mouth as if he were going to say something, looked away from Sink, and gave a half shrug.

"Got somethin you want a say," Sink said, "Chrissake say it. I got my head on backwards or what? You didn't know we was goin a smudge brands? Goin a get all holy about it, are you?"

Archie looked around.

"I'm married," he said. "She is havin a baby. Pretty soon."

"Well, I'm damned. How old are you?"

"Seventeen. Old enough to do what's got a be did. Anyway, how old are you?"

"Thirty-two. Old enough a be your daddy." There was a half-hour silence, then Sink started again. "You know old Karok don't keep married fellers. Finds out, he'll fire you."

"He ain't goin a find out from me. And it's more money than I can git on the Little Weed. But I got a find a way Rose can let me know. About things."

"Well, I ain't no wet nurse."

"I know that."

"Long as you know it." Damn fool kid, he thought, his life already too complicated to live. He said aloud, "Me, I wouldn't never git hitched to no fell-on-a-hatchet female."

The next week half the crew went into town and Archie spent an hour on the bench outside the post office writing on some brown wrapping paper, and addressed the tortured missive to Rose at the stage station where he believed her to be. What about the baby? he wrote. Is he born? But inside the post office the walleyed clerk with fingernails like yellow chisels told him the postage had gone up.

"First time in a hunderd year. Cost you two cents a send a letter now." He smirked with satisfaction. Archie, who had only one cent, tore up his letter and threw the pieces in the street. The wind dealt them to the prairie, its chill promising a tight-clenched winter.

Rose's parents moved to Omaha in November, seeking a cure for Mrs. Mealor's declining health.

"You think you can stay sober long enough to ride down and let Rosie and Archie know we are going?" the sick woman whispered to Sundown.

"Why, I am goin right now soon as I find my other boot. Just you don't worry, I got it covered."

A full bottle of whiskey took him as far as the river crossing. Dazedly drunk, he rode to the little cabin on the river but found the place silent, the door closed. Swaying, feeling the landscape slide around, he called out three or four times but was unable to get off his horse, and knew well enough that if he did he could never get back on.

"They're not there," he reported to his wife. "Not there."

"Where could they be? Did you put a note on the table?"

"Didn't think of it. Anyway, not there."

"I'll write her from Omaha," she whispered.

Within a week of their departure a replacement freighter arrived, Buck Roy, with his heavyset wife and a raft of children. The Mealors, who had failed even to be buried in the stage station's cemetery, were forgotten.

*

There were no cattle as bad as Karok's to stray, and ranchers said it was a curious thing the way his cows turned up in distant locations. December was miserable, one storm after another bouncing in like a handful of hurled poker chips, and January turned cold enough to freeze flying birds dead. Alonzo Lago sent Archie out alone to gather any bovine wanderers he could find in a certain washout area, swampy in June but now made up of hundreds of deep holes and snaky little streams smoothly covered with snow.

"Keep your eyes peeled for any Wing-Cross leather-pounders. Better take some sticks and a cinch ring." So Archie knew he was looking for Wing-Cross cows, to doctor their brands. But the Wing-Cross had its own little ways with brand reworkings, so he guessed it was more or less an even exchange.

The horse did not want to go into the swamp maze. It was one of the warm days between storms, and the snow was soft. Archie dismounted and led his horse, keeping to the edge of the bog, wading through wet snow for hours. The exercise sweated him up. Only two cows allowed themselves to be driven out into the open, the others scattering far back into the coyote willows behind the swamp. In the murky, half-frozen world of stream slop and trampled stems there was no way a man alone could fix brands. He watched the cows circle around to the backcountry. The wind dived, pulling cold air with it. The weather was changing. When he reached the bunkhouse, four hours after dark, the thermometer had fallen to zero. His boots were frozen, and, chilled to the liver, he fell asleep without eating or undressing beyond his boots.

"Git back and git them cows," hissed Alonzo Lago two hours later, leaning over his face. "Git up and on it. Rat now! Mr. Karok wants them cows."

"Goddamn short nights on this goddamn ranch," Archie muttered, pulling on his wet boots.

Back in the swamp it was just coming light, like gray polish on the cold world, the air so still that Archie could see the tiny breath cloud of a finch on a willow twig. Beneath the hardened crust the snow was wallowy. His fresh horse was Poco, who did not know any swamps. Poco blundered along, stumbled in an invisible sinkhole, and took Archie deep with him. The snow shot down his neck, up his sleeves, into his boots, filled eyes, ears, nose, matted his hair. Poco, in getting up, rammed Archie's hat deep into the bog. The snow in contact with his body heat melted, and as he climbed back into the saddle the wind that accompanied the pale sunlight froze his clothes. Somehow he managed to push eight Wing-Cross strays out of the swamp and back toward the high ground, but his matches would not light, and while he struggled to make a fire the cows scattered. He could barely move, and when he got back to the bunkhouse he was frozen into the saddle and had to be pried off the horse by two men. He heard cloth rip.

Sink thought the kid had plenty of sand and, muttering that he wasn't no wet nurse, pulled off the icy boots, unbuttoned coat and shirt, half hauled him stumbling to his bunk, and brought two hot rocks from under the stove to warm him up. John Tank, a Texas drifter, said he had an extra pair of overalls Archie could have — old and mended but still with some wear in them.

"Hell, better'n ridin around bare-ass in January."

But the next morning when Archie tried to get up he was overcome by dizziness. Boiling heat surged through him, his cheeks flamed red, his hands burned, and he had a dry, constant cough. The bunkhouse slopped back and forth as if on rockers.

Sink looked at him and thought, Pneumonia. "You look pretty bad. I'll go see what Karok says."

When he came back half an hour later, Archie was on fire.

"Karok says to git you out a here, but the bastard won't let me take the wagon. He says he's got a cancer in his leg and he needs that wagon for hisself to have the doc at the fort cut it out. Lon's fixin up a kind a travois. His ma had some Indan kin so he knows how to fix it. Sometimes he ain't so bad. We'll git you down to Cheyenne and you can ride the train a where your mother is, your folks, Rawlins, whatever. Karok says. And he says you are fired. I had a tell him you was married so he would let you loose. He was all set a have you die in the bunkhouse. We'll get a doc, beat this down. It's only pneumony. I had it twice."

Archie tried to say his mother was long gone and that he needed to get to Rose down on the Little Weed, tried to say that it was sixty-odd miles from Rawlins to their cabin, but he couldn't get out a word because of the wheezing, breath-sucking cough. Sink shook his head and got some biscuits and bacon from the cook.

Alonzo Lago had trimmed out two long poles and laced a steer hide to them. Sink wrapped the legs of a horse named Preacher in burlap to keep the crust from cutting them and lashed the travois poles to his saddle, a tricky business to get the balance right. The small ends projected beyond the horse's ears, but the foreman said that was to accommodate wear on the drag ends. They rolled Archie and his bedroll in a buffalo robe, and Sink began to drag him to Cheyenne, a hundred miles south. With the wagon it would have been easy. Sink thought the travois was not as good a contraption as Indians claimed. The wind, which had dropped a little overnight, came up again, pushing a lofty bank of cloud. After four hours they had covered nine miles. The snow began, increasing in intensity until they were traveling blind.

"Kid, I can't see nothin," Sink called. He stopped and dismounted, went to Archie. The earlier snow had melted as fast as it touched that red, feverish face, but gradually, just a fraction of an inch above the surface of the hot flesh, a mask of ice now formed a gray glaze.

"Better hole up. There's a line shack somewheres around here could we find it. I was there all summer couple years back. Down a little from the top of a hogback."

The horse had also spent that summer at the line camp and he went straight to it now. It was on the lee side of the hogback, a little below the crest. The wind had dumped an immense amount of snow on the tiny cabin, but Sink found the door to the lean-to entryway, and that would do to shelter Preacher. A shovel with a broken handle leaned against the side of the stall. Inside the cabin there was a table and a backless chair and a plank bunk about twenty inches wide. The stove was heaped with snow and the stovepipe lay on the floor. Sink recognized the chipped enamel plate and cup on the table.

He wrestled Archie inside and got him and the buffalo robe onto the plank bunk, then put the stovepipe together and jammed it up through the roof hole. Neither inside nor in the entryway could he see any chunk wood, but he remembered where the old chip pile had been and, using the broken shovel, scraped up enough snow-welded chips to get the fire going. While the chips were steaming and sizzling in the stove he unsaddled Preacher, removed the gunnysacks from his legs, and rubbed him down. He checked the lean-to's shallow loft, hoping for hay, but there was nothing.

"God damn," he said, and tore some of the loft floorboards loose to burn in the stove. Back outside, he dug through the snow with the broken shovel until he hit ground, got out his knife, and sawed off the sun-cured grass until he had two or three hatfuls.

"Best I can do, Preacher," he said, tossing it down for the horse.

It was almost warm inside the shack. From his saddlebag he took a small handful of the coffee beans he always carried. The old coffee grinder was still on the wall, but a mouse had built a nest in it, and, unwilling to drink boiled mouse shit, he crushed the beans on the table with the flat of his knife. He looked around for the coffeepot that belonged to the cabin but did not see it. There was a five-gallon coal-oil tin near the bunk. He sniffed at it, but could detect no noisome odors. It was while he was outside scraping up snow to melt on the stove that the edge of the coal-oil can hit the coffeepot, which, for some unfathomable reason, had been tossed into the front yard. That too he packed with snow. It looked to him as though the last occupant of the shack had been someone with a grudge, showing his hatred of Karok by throwing coffeepots and burning all the wood. Maybe a Wing-Cross rider.

The coffee was hot and black, but when he brought the cup to Archie the kid swallowed one mouthful, then coughed, and finally puked it up. Sink drank the rest himself and ate one of the biscuits.

It was a bad night. The bunk was too narrow and the kid so hot and twitchy that Sink, swooning in and out of forty-wink snaps of sleep, finally got up and slept in the chair with his head on the table. A serious blizzard and fatal cold began to slide down from the Canadian plains that night, and when it broke twelve days later the herds were decimated, cows packed ten deep against barbed-wire fences, pronghorn congealed into statues, trains stalled for three weeks by forty-foot drifts, and two cowpunchers in a line shack frozen together in a buffalo robe.

The Stage Station

It was May before Tom Ackler rode up from Taos, where he had spent the fall and winter. Despite the beating sunshine, the snow was still deep around his cabin. Patches of bare ground showed bright green with a host of thrusting thistles. He wondered if Gold Dust had made it through. He could see no cat tracks. He lit a fire using an old newspaper on the table, and, just before the flame swallowed it, glimpsed a few penciled words and the signature "Archie."

"Lost whatever it was. I'll go down tomorrow and see how they are doin." And he unpacked his saddlebags and pulled his blankets out of the sack hanging from a rafter where they were safe from mice.

In the morning, Gold Dust pranced out of the trees, her coat thick. Tom let her in, threw her a choice piece of bacon.

"Look like you kept pretty good," Tom said. But the cat sniffed at the bacon, went to the door, and, when Tom opened it, returned to the woods. "Probly shacked up with a bobcat," he said. "Got the taste for wild meat." Around noon he saddled the horse and headed for the McLaverty cabin.

No smoke rose from the chimney. A slope of snow lay against the woodpile. He noticed that very little wood had been burned. The weasel's tracks were everywhere, right up into the eaves. Clear enough the weasel had gotten inside. "Damn sight more comfortable than a woodpile." As Tom squinted at the tracks, the weasel suddenly squirted out of a hole in the eaves and looked at him. It was whiter than the rotting snow, and its black-tipped tail twitched. It was the largest, handsomest weasel he had ever seen, with shining eyes and a lustrous coat. He thought of his cat and it came to him that wild creatures managed well through the winter. He wondered if Gold Dust could breed with a bobcat, and recalled then that Rose had been expecting. "Must be they went to the station." But he opened the door and looked inside, calling, "Rose? Archie?" What he found sent him galloping for the stage station.

At the station everything was in an uproar, all of them standing in the dusty road in front of the Dorgans' house, Mrs. Dorgan crying, Queeda with her mouth agape, and Robert F. Dorgan shouting at his wife, accusing her of betraying him with a human wreck. They paid little attention to Tom Ackler when he slid in on his lathered horse calling that Rose McLaverty was raped and murdered and mutilated by Utes, sometime in the winter, God knew when. Only Mrs. Buck Roy, the new freighter's wife, who was terrified of Indians, paid him much attention. The Dorgans continued to scream at each other. The more urgent event to them was the suicide that morning of the old bachelor telegraph operator, who had swallowed lye after weeks of scribbling a four-hundred-page letter addressed to Robert Dorgan and outlining his hopeless adoration of Mrs. Dorgan, the wadded pages fulsomely riddled with references to "ivory thighs," "the Adam and Eve dance," "her secret slit," and the like. What Tom Ackler had thought was an old saddle and a pile of grain sacks on the station porch was the corpse.

"Where there's smoke there's fire!" bellowed Robert F. Dorgan. "I took you out a that Omaha cathouse and made you a decent woman, give you everthing, and here's how you reward me, you drippin bitch! How many times you snuck over there? How many times you took his warty old cock?"

"I never! I didn't! That filthy old brute," sobbed Mrs. Dorgan, suffused with rage that the vile man had fastened his attentions on her, had dared to write down his lascivious thoughts as real events, putting in the details of her pink-threaded camisole, the red mole on her left buttock, and, finally, vomiting black blood all over the telegraph shack and the front porch of the Dorgans' house, where he had dragged himself to die, the bundle of lies stuffed in his shirt. For years she had struggled to make herself into a genteel specimen of womanhood, grateful that Robert F. Dorgan had saved her from economic sexuality and determined to erase that past. Now, if Dorgan forced her away, she would have to go back on the game, for she could think of no other way to make a living. And maybe Queeda too, whom she'd brought up as a lady! Her sense of personal worth faltered, then flared up as if doused with kerosene.

"Why, you dirty old rum-neck," she said in a hoarse voice, "what gives you the idea that you got a right to a beautiful wife and daughter? What gives you the idea we would stay with you? Look at you — you want a be the territory surveyor, but without me and Queeda to talk up the important political men you couldn't catch a cold."

Dorgan knew it was true and gnawed at his untrimmed mustache. He turned and melodramatically strode into his house, slamming the door so hard the report killed mice. Mrs. Dorgan had won, and she followed him in for a reconciliation.

Tom Ackler looked at Queeda, who was tracing an arc in the dirt with the toe of her kid-leather boot. They heard the rattle of a stove lid inside the house — Mrs. Dorgan making up a fire to warm the bedroom.

"Rose McLaverty —" he said, but Queeda shrugged. A tongue of wind lapped the dust, creating a miniature whirl that caught up straws, horsehairs, minute mica fragments, and a feather. Queeda walked away around the shaded back of the Dorgan house. Tom Ackler stood holding the reins, then remounted and started back.

On the way he thought of the whiskey in his cupboard, then of Rose, and decided he would get drunk that night and bury her the next day. It was the best he could do for her. He thought too that perhaps it hadn't been Utes who killed her but her young husband, berserk and raving, and now fled to distant ports. He remembered the burned newspaper with Archie's message consumed before it could be read and thought it unlikely that if Archie had killed his young wife in a frenzy he would stop by a neighbor's place and leave a signed note. Unless maybe it was a confession. There was no way to know what had happened. The more he thought about Archie, the more he remembered his clear, hard voice and his singing. He thought about Gold Dust's rampant vigor and rich fur, about the sleek weasel at the McLaverty cabin. Some lived and some died, and that's how it was.

He buried Rose in front of the cabin and for a tombstone wrestled the sandstone doorstep upright. He wanted to chisel her name on it but put it off until the snows started. By then it was too late, time for him to head back to Taos.

The following spring, as he rode past the cabin, he saw that frost heaves had tipped the stone over and that the ridgepole of the roof had broken under a heavy weight of snow. He rode on, singing, "When the green grass comes, and the wild rose blooms," one of Archie's songs, and wondering if Gold Dust had made it through again.

RON RASH

Into the Gorge

FROM *The Southern Review*

HIS GREAT-AUNT had been born on this land, lived on it eight decades and knew it as well as she knew her husband and children. That was what she'd always claimed, and could tell you to the week when the first dogwood blossom would brighten the ridge, the first blackberry darken and swell enough to harvest. Then her mind had wandered into a place she could not follow, taking with it all the people she knew, their names and connections, whether they still lived or whether they'd died. But her body lingered, shed of an inner being, empty as a cicada husk.

Knowledge of the land was the one memory that refused to dissolve. During her last year, Jesse would step off the school bus and see his great-aunt hoeing a field behind her farmhouse, breaking ground for a crop she never sowed, but the rows were always straight, right-depthed. Her nephew, Jesse's father, worked in an adjoining field. The first few times, he had taken the hoe from her hands and led her back to her house, but she'd soon be back in the field. After a while neighbors and kin just let her hoe. They brought meals and checked on her as often as they could. Jesse always walked rapidly past her field. His great-aunt never looked up, her gaze fixed on the hoe blade and the dark soil it churned, but he had always feared she'd raise her eyes and acknowledge him, though what she might want to convey Jesse could not say.

Then one March day she disappeared. The men in the community searched all afternoon and into evening as the temperature dropped, sleet crackled and hissed like static. The men rippled outward as they lit lanterns and moved into the gorge. Jesse watched from his family's pasture as the held flames grew smaller, soon disappearing and reappearing like foxfire, crossing the creek and then on past the ginseng patch Jesse helped his father harvest. Going deeper into land that had been in the family almost two hundred years, toward the original homestead, the place she'd been born.

They found his great-aunt at dawn, her back against a tree as if waiting for the searchers to arrive. But that was not the strangest thing. She'd taken off her shoes, her dress, and her underclothes. Years later Jesse read in a magazine that people dying of hypothermia did such a thing believing that heat, not cold, was killing them. Back then the woods had been communal, NO TRESPASSING signs an affront, but after her death neighbors soon found places other than the gorge to hunt and fish, gather blackberries and galax. Her ghost was still down there, many believed, including Jesse's own father, who never returned to harvest the ginseng he'd planted. When the Park Service made an offer on the homestead, Jesse's father and aunts sold. That was in 1959, and the government paid sixty dollars an acre. Now, five decades later, Jesse stood on his porch and looked east toward Sampson Ridge, where bulldozers razed woods and pastureland for another gated community. He wondered how much those sixty acres were worth today. Easily a million dollars.

Not that he needed that much money. His house and twenty acres were paid for, as was his truck. The tobacco allotment earned less each year but still enough for a widower with grown children. Enough as long as he didn't have to go to the hospital or his truck didn't throw a rod. He needed some extra money put away for that. Not a million, but some.

So two autumns ago Jesse had gone into the gorge, following the creek to the old homestead, then up the ridge's shadowy north face where his father had seeded and harvested his ginseng patch. The crop was there, evidently untouched for half a century. Some of the plants rose above Jesse's kneecaps, and there was more ginseng than his father could have dreamed of, a hillside spangled with bright yellow leaves, enough roots to bulge Jesse's knapsack. Afterward, he'd carefully replanted the seeds, done it just as his father had done, then walked out of the gorge, past the iron gate that kept vehicles off the logging road. A yellow tin marker nailed to a nearby tree said U.S. PARK SERVICE.

Now another autumn had come. A wet autumn, which was good

for the plants, as Jesse had verified three days ago when he'd checked them. Once again he gathered the knapsack and trowel from the woodshed. He also took the .32-20 Colt from his bedroom drawer. Late in the year for snakes, but after days of rain the afternoon was warm enough to bring a rattler or copperhead out to sun.

He followed the old logging road, the green backpack slung over his shoulder and the pistol in the outside pouch. Jesse's arthritic knees ached as he made the descent. They would ache more that night, even after rubbing liniment on them. He wondered how many more autumns he'd be able to make this trip. Till I'm seventy, Jesse figured, giving himself two more years. The ground was slippery from all the rain, and he walked slowly. A broken ankle or leg would be a serious thing this far from help, but it was more than that. He wanted to enter the gorge respectfully.

When he got in sight of the homestead, the land leveled out, but the ground grew soggier, especially where the creek ran close to the logging road. Jesse saw boot prints from three days earlier. Then he saw another set, coming up the logging road from the other direction. Boot prints as well, but smaller. Jesse looked down the logging road but saw no hiker or fisherman. He kneeled, his joints creaking.

The prints appeared at least a day old, maybe more. They stopped on the road when they met Jesse's, then also veered toward the homestead. Jesse got up and looked around again before walking through the withered broom sedge and joe-pye weed. He passed a cairn of stones that once had been a chimney, a dry well covered with a slab of tin so rusty it served as more warning than safeguard. The boot prints were no longer discernible but he knew where they'd end. Led the son of a bitch right to it, he told himself, and wondered how he could have been stupid enough to walk the road on a rainy morning. But when he got to the ridge, the plants were still there, the soil around them undisturbed. Probably just a hiker, or a bird watcher, Jesse figured, that or some punk kid looking to poach someone's marijuana, not knowing the ginseng was worth even more. Either way, he'd been damn lucky.

Jesse lifted the trowel from the backpack and got on his knees. He smelled the rich dark earth that always reminded him of coffee. The plants had more color than three days ago, the berries a deeper red, the leaves bright as polished gold. It always amazed him that such radiance could grow in soil the sun rarely touched, like finding rubies and sapphires on the gloamy walls of a cave. He worked with care but also haste. The first time he'd returned here, two years earlier, he'd felt a sudden coolness, a slight lessening of light, as if a cloud had passed over the sun. Imagination, he'd told himself then, but it had made him work faster, with no pauses to rest.

Jesse jabbed the trowel into the loamy soil, probing inward with care so as not to cut the root, slowly bringing it to light. The root was a big one, six inches long, tendrils sprouting from the core like clay renderings of human limbs. Jesse scraped away the dirt and placed the root in the backpack, just as carefully buried the seeds to ensure another harvest. As he crawled a few feet left to unearth another plant, he felt the moist dirt seeping its way through the knees of his blue jeans. He liked being this close to the earth, smelling it, feeling it on his hands and under his nails, the same as when he planted tobacco sprigs in the spring. A song he'd heard on the radio drifted into his head, a woman wanting to burn down a whole town. He let the tune play in his head and tried to fill in the refrain as he pressed the trowel into the earth.

"You can lay that trowel down," a voice behind Jesse said. "Then raise your hands."

Jesse turned and saw a man in a gray shirt and green khakis, a gold badge on his chest and a U.S. Park Service patch on his shoulder. Short blond hair, dark eyes. A young man, probably not even thirty. A pistol was holstered on his right hip, the safety strap off.

"Don't get up," the younger man said again, louder this time.

Jesse did as he was told. The park ranger came closer, picked up the backpack, and stepped away. Jesse watched as he opened the compartment with the ginseng root, then the smaller pouch. The ranger took out the .32-20 and held it in his palm. The gun had belonged to Jesse's grandfather and father before being passed on to Jesse. The ranger inspected it as he might an arrowhead or spear point he'd found.

"That's just for the snakes," Jesse said.

"Possession of a firearm is illegal in the park," the ranger said. "You've broken two laws, federal laws. You'll be getting some jail time for this."

The younger man looked like he might say more, then seemed to decide against it.

"This ain't right," Jesse said. "My daddy planted the seeds for this patch. That ginseng wouldn't even be here if it wasn't for him. And that gun, if I was poaching I'd have a rifle or shotgun."

What was happening didn't seem quite real. The world, the very ground he stood on, felt like it was evaporating beneath him. Jesse almost expected somebody, though he couldn't say who, to come out of the woods laughing about the joke just played on him. The ranger placed the pistol in the backpack. He unclipped the walkie-talkie from his belt, pressed a button, and spoke.

"He did come back and I've got him."

A staticky voice responded, the words indiscernible to Jesse.

"No, he's too old to be much trouble. We'll be waiting on the logging road."

The ranger pressed a button and placed the walkie-talkie back on his belt. Jesse read the name on the silver nametag. *Barry Wilson.*

"You any kin to the Wilsons over on Balsam Mountain?"

"No," the younger man said. "I grew up in Charlotte."

The walkie-talkie crackled and the ranger picked it up, said okay, and clipped it back on his belt.

"Call Sheriff Arrowood," Jesse said. "He'll tell you I've never been in any trouble before. Never, not even a speeding ticket."

"Let's go."

"Can't you just forget this?" Jesse said. "It ain't like I was growing marijuana. There's plenty that do in this park. I know that for a fact. That's worse than what I done."

The ranger smiled.

"We'll get them eventually, old fellow, but their bulbs burn brighter than yours. They're not big enough fools to leave us footprints to follow."

The ranger slung the backpack over his shoulder.

"You've got no right to talk to me like that," Jesse said.

There was still plenty of distance between them, but the ranger looked like he contemplated another step back.

"If you're going to give me trouble, I'll just go ahead and cuff you now."

Jesse almost told the younger man to come on and try, but he made himself look at the ground, get himself under control before he spoke.

"No, I ain't going to give you any trouble," he finally said, raising his eyes.

The ranger nodded toward the logging road.

"After you, then."

Jesse moved past the ranger, stepping through the broom sedge and past the ruined chimney, the ranger to his right, two steps behind. Jesse veered slightly to his left, moving so he'd pass close to the old well. He paused and glanced back at the ranger.

"That trowel of mine, I ought to get it."

The ranger paused too and was about to reply when Jesse took a quick step and shoved the ranger with two hands toward the well. The ranger didn't fall until one foot went through the rotten tin, then the other. As he did, the backpack dropped from his hand. He didn't go all the way through, just up to his arms, his fingernails scraping the tin for leverage, looking like a man caught in muddy ice. The ranger's hands found purchase, one on a hank of broom sedge, the other on the metal's firmer edging. He began pulling himself out, wincing as the rusty tin tore cloth and skin. He looked at Jesse, who stood above him.

"You've really screwed up now," the ranger gasped.

Jesse bent down and reached not for the younger man's hand but for his shoulder. He pushed hard, the ranger's hands clutching only air as he fell through the rotten metal, a thump and simultaneous snap of bone as he hit the well's dry floor. Seconds passed but no other sound rose from the darkness.

The backpack lay at the edge and Jesse snatched it up. He ran, not toward his farmhouse but into the woods. He didn't look back again but bear-crawled through the ginseng patch and up the ridge, his breaths loud pants. Trees thickened around him, oaks and poplars, some hemlocks. The soil was thin and moist, and he slipped several times. Halfway up the ridge he paused, his heart battering his chest. When it finally calmed, Jesse heard a vehicle coming up the logging road and saw a pale-green Park Service jeep. A man and a woman got out.

Jesse went on, passing through another patch of ginseng, probable descendents from his father's original seedlings. The sooner he got to the ridge crest, the sooner he could make his way across it toward the gorge head. His legs were leaden now, and he couldn't catch his breath. The extra pounds he'd put on the last few years draped over his belt, gave him more to haul. His mind went dizzy and he slipped and skidded a few yards downhill. For a while he lay still, his body sprawled on the slanted earth, arms and legs flung outward. Jesse felt the leaves cushioning the back of his head, an acorn nudged against a shoulder blade. Above him, oak branches pierced a darkening sky. He remembered the fairy tale about a giant beanstalk and imagined how convenient it would be simply to climb off into the clouds.

Jesse shifted his body so his face turned downhill, one ear to the ground as if listening for the faintest footfall. It seemed so wrong to be sixty-eight years old and running from someone. Old age was supposed to give a person dignity, respect. He remembered the night the searchers brought his great-aunt out of the gorge. The men had stripped off their heavy coats to cover her body and had taken turns carrying her. They had been silent and somber as they came into the yard. Even after the women had taken the corpse into the farmhouse to be washed and dressed, the men had stayed on his great-aunt's porch. Some had smoked hand-rolled cigarettes, others had bulged their jaws with tobacco. Jesse had sat on the lowest porch step and listened, knowing the men had quickly forgotten he was there. They did not talk of how they'd found his great-aunt or the times she'd wandered from her house to the garden. Instead, the men spoke of a woman who could tell you tomorrow's weather by looking at the evening sky, a godly woman who'd taught Sunday school into her seventies. They told stories about her, and every story was spoken in a reverent way, as if now that his great-aunt was dead, she'd once more been transformed back to her true self.

Jesse rose slowly. He hadn't twisted an ankle or broken an arm, and that seemed his first bit of luck since walking into the gorge. When Jesse reached the crest, his legs were so weak he clutched a maple sapling to ease himself to the ground. He looked down through the cascading trees. An orange-and-white rescue squad van had now arrived. Workers huddled around the well, and Jesse couldn't see much of what they were doing, but before long a stretcher was carried to the van. He was too far away to tell the ranger's condition, even if the man was alive.

At the least a broken arm or leg, Jesse knew, and tried to think of an injury that would make things all right, like a concussion to make the ranger forget what had happened, or the ranger hurting bad enough that shock made him forget. Jesse tried not to think about the snapped bone being in the back or neck.

The van's back doors closed from within, and the vehicle turned onto the logging road. The siren was off but the beacon drenched the woods red. The woman ranger scoured the hillside with binoculars, sweeping without pause over where Jesse sat. Another green Park Service truck drove up, two more rangers spilling out. Then Sheriff Arrowood's car, silent as the ambulance.

The sun lay behind Clingman's Dome now, and Jesse knew waiting any longer would only make it harder. He moved in a stupor of exhaustion, feet stumbling over roots and rocks, swaying like a drunk. When he got far enough, he'd be able to come down the ridge, ascend the narrow gorge mouth. But Jesse was so tired he didn't know how he could go any farther without resting. His knees grated bone on bone, popping and crackling each time they bent or twisted. He panted and wheezed and imagined his lungs an accordion that never unfolded enough.

Old and *a fool.* That's what the ranger had called Jesse. An old man, no doubt. His body told him so every morning when he awoke. The liniment he applied to his joints and muscles each morning and night made him think of himself as a creaky rust-corroded machine that must be oiled and warmed up before it could sputter to life. Maybe a fool as well, he acknowledged, for who other than a fool could have gotten into such a fix?

Jesse found a felled oak and sat down, a mistake, because he couldn't imagine summoning the energy to rise. He looked through the trees. Sheriff Arrowood's car was gone, but the truck and jeep were still there. He didn't see but one person and knew the others searched the woods for him. A crow cawed once farther up the ridge. Then no other sound, not even the wind. Jesse took the backpack and pitched it into the thick woods below, watched it tumble out of sight. A waste, but he couldn't risk their searching his house. He thought about tossing the pistol as well, but the gun had belonged to his father, his father's father before that. Besides, if they found it in his house, that was no proof it was the pistol the ranger had seen. They had no proof of anything, really. Even his being in the gorge was just the ranger's word against his. If he could get back to the house.

Night fell fast now, darkness webbing the gaps between tree trunks and branches. Below, high-beam flashlights flickered on. Jesse remembered two weeks after his great-aunt's burial. Graham Sutherland had come out of the gorge shaking and chalk-faced, not able to tell what had happened until Jesse's father gave him a draft of whiskey. Graham had been fishing near the old homestead and glimpsed something on the far bank, there for just a moment. Though a sunny spring afternoon, the weather in the gorge had suddenly turned cold and damp. Graham had seen her then, moving through the trees toward him, her arms outstretched. *Beseeching me to come to her,* Graham had told them. *Not speaking, but letting that cold and damp touch my very bones so I'd feel what she felt. She didn't say it out loud, maybe couldn't, but she wanted me to stay down there with her. She didn't want to be alone.*

Jesse walked on, not stopping until he found a place where he could make his descent. A flashlight moved below him, its holder merged with the dark. The light bobbed as if on a river's current, a river running uphill all the way to the iron gate that marked the end of Park Service land. Then the light swung around, made its swaying way back down the logging road. Someone shouted and the disparate lights gathered like sparks returning to their source. Headlights and engines came to life, and two sets of red taillights dimmed and soon disappeared.

Jesse made his way down the slope, his body slantways, one hand close to the ground in case he slipped. Low branches slapped his face. Once on level land he let minutes pass, listening for footsteps or a cough on the logging road, someone left behind to trick him into coming out. No moon shone but a few stars had settled overhead, enough light for him to make out a human form.

Jesse moved quietly up the logging road. Get back in the house and you'll be all right, he told himself. He came to the iron gate and slipped under. It struck him only then that someone might be waiting at his house. He went to the left and stopped where a barbed-wire fence marked the pasture edge. The house lights were still off, the way he'd left them. Jesse's hand touched a strand of sagging barbed wire and he felt a vague reassurance in its being there, its familiarity. He was about to move closer when he heard a truck, soon saw its yellow beams crossing Sampson Ridge. As soon as the pickup pulled into the driveway, the porch light came on. Sheriff Arrowood appeared on the porch, one of Jesse's shirts in his hand. Two men got out of the pickup and opened the tailgate. Bloodhounds leaped and tumbled from the truck bed, whining as the men gathered their leashes. He had to get back into the gorge, and quick, but his legs were suddenly stiff and unyielding as iron stobs. It's just the fear, Jesse told himself. He clasped one of the fence's rusty barbs and squeezed until pain reconnected his mind and body.

Jesse followed the land's downward tilt, crossed back under the gate. The logging road leveled out and Jesse saw the outline of the homestead's ruined chimney. As he came closer, the chimney solidified, grew darker than the dark around it, as if an unlit passageway into some greater darkness.

Jesse took the .32-20 from his pocket and let the pistol's weight settle in his hand. If they caught him with it, that was just more trouble. Throw it so far they won't find it, he told himself, because there's prints on it. He turned toward the woods and heaved the pistol, almost falling with the effort. The gun went only a few feet before thunking solidly against a tree, landing close to the logging road, if not on it. There was no time to find the pistol, because the hounds were at the gorge head now, flashlights dipping and rising behind them. He could tell by the hounds' cries that they were already on his trail.

Jesse stepped into the creek, hoping that doing so might cause the dogs to lose his scent. If it worked, he could circle back and find the gun. What sparse light the stars had offered was snuffed out as the creek left the road and entered the woods. Jesse bumped against the banks, stumbled into deeper pockets of water that drenched his pants as well as his boots and socks. He fell and something tore in his shoulder.

But it worked. There was soon a confusion of barks and howls, the flashlights no longer following him but instead sweeping the woods from one still point.

Jesse stepped out of the creek and sat down. He was shivering, his mind off plumb, every thought tilting toward panic. As he poured water from the boots, Jesse remembered that his boot prints led directly from his house to the ginseng patch. They had ways of matching boots and their prints, and not just a certain foot size and make. He'd seen on a TV show how they could even match the worn part of the sole to a print. Jesse stuffed the socks inside the boots and threw them at the dark. Like the pistol, they didn't go far before hitting something solid.

It took him a long time to find the old logging road, and even when he was finally on it he was so disoriented that he wasn't sure which direction to go in. Jesse walked a while and came to a park campground, which meant he'd guessed wrong. He turned around and walked the other way. It felt like years had passed before he finally made it back to the homestead. A campfire now glowed and sparked between the homestead and the iron gate, the men hunting Jesse huddled around it. The pistol lay somewhere near the men, perhaps found already. Several of the hounds barked, impatient to get back onto the trail, but the searchers had evidently decided to wait till morning to continue. Though Jesse was too far away to hear them, he knew they talked to help pass the time. They probably had food with them, perhaps coffee as well. Jesse realized he was thirsty and thought about going back to the creek for some water, but he was too tired.

Dew wet his bare feet as he passed the far edge of the homestead and then to the woods' edge where the ginseng was. He sat down and in a few minutes felt the night's chill envelop him. A frost warning, the radio had said. He thought of how his great-aunt had taken off her clothes and how, despite the scientific explanation, it seemed to Jesse a final abdication of everything she had once been.

He looked toward the eastern sky. It seemed he'd been running a week's worth of nights, but he saw the stars hadn't begun to pale. The first pink smudges on the far ridge line were a while away, perhaps hours. The night would linger long enough for what would or would not come. He waited.

ALEX ROSE

Ostracon

FROM *Ploughshares*

KATYA IS SEARCHING for her glasses. They were just here. One minute ago, on the counter, the big brown glasses. Without them, everything is waxy. She lays her hand on the cool Formica and makes a brushing motion. Keys, coffee mug, phone book. Two different pens. Why are there so many pens? She has never bought even a single pen.

Katya squints to see the table, pats various spots. The sisal placemats are crusty with stale crumbs. The Shabbos candles are dribbly stumps. Another pen.

She's had these glasses for so long. Decades probably. They are chestnut brown and shiny like a stone you pluck from the shore. They fit her face just right.

Now Katya is in the den. She is overturning newspapers and envelopes. She would like to throw them out, but what if they are new? Without her glasses, the headlines are smudgy glyphs.

When Joe comes home from work he finds his wife crouched on the floor, her sweater frosted with lint. She looks up and smiles.

Workmen have cut a hole in the living room ceiling. Apparently there was a leak in the roof which Joe said was causing some kind of damage. The men are short and brown and smell like the inside of a taxi. They smile at Katya, but she is suspicious. She is protectful of her space, this home she has spent half a century grooming and curating. Clods of who knows what are caked to the treads of their boots. One of them is smoking outside. *A choleryeh ahf dir.* He had better not leave the butt on the porch.

*

Writes the Russian neurologist, Alexander Luria: "I shall never forget a case in which a man wounded in the temporal region could easily read his surname 'Levsky' written on an envelope addressed to him, but was completely unable to read the much simpler word 'lev' (lion), which was not fixed to the same degree in his memory."

Joe is becoming impatient. He is inspecting a spoon Katya has scrubbed — she is certain she scrubbed — and making angry whispery grunts. He grabs a fistful of silverware from the drawer and hastily examines each utensil. He is shaking his head, glowering. He dumps them in the sink, which makes an explosive clang, and walks away. The ringing lingers in his ears like a tuning fork all the way back down to his office.

The workmen have left for the weekend. They said they needed to order a special tool to refasten something to something else, and that they would be back on Monday. In the meantime, there is a jagged half-moon gouge in the ceiling which looks into the dark crawlspace above. Katya is uneasy. She dislikes all that translucent tarp over everything, the little flakes of paint and plaster clustered in its folds. Will the men remember to wash off their dirty fingerprints from the ceiling once they've sealed it up?

Katya appraises her teeth in the bathroom mirror. How did they get like this? Each tooth is a pale, caramelized beige and emplaqued with creamy filament like dried-up caulk. Her lips are crackly and sallow. Is someone playing a trick? *A farshlepteh krenk.* She touches her hand to her face but it too has gone bad. Her flesh is slack and splotched with moles. Her fingers are too small, the veins too big. She traces the brittle etchings in her hand, remembering briefly the tender pink palm of a monkey that grasped her finger through its cage during a childhood trip to the zoo.

The noun *reflex* made its way into the medical vocabulary during the seventeenth century, having derived from *reflexion.* It was believed at the time that spirits in the nervous system were "reflected" into the muscles in the manner of light bouncing off a mirror.

As a younger woman, Katya illustrated books of Jewish folktales. One tells of a young student who has been traveling with his rabbi for many days. Each day they roam the land, study the Talmud, and sleep at a village inn. Tired of spending all his time with the rabbi, the student one night decides to continue his travels alone. He instructs the innkeeper to wake him extra early, so that he may take the first train before the rabbi wakes. The next morning the student stealthily gropes around in the dark for his clothes and, in his haste, dresses himself in the black robes of the rabbi. He rushes to the station, buys the ticket, boards the train, but is startled when he sees his reflection in the compartment mirror. "What a fool that innkeeper was," he says. "I ask him to wake me and instead he wakes the rabbi!"

During the Han Dynasty, Chinese soldiers wore mirrors over their breastplates to ward off wicked spirits. If these mirrors broke, the warriors would grind up the shattered glass and ingest it, so that its magic would protect them from within.

The men are back today. Katya is surprised at how glad she is to see them. Why shouldn't she be? The men are friendly. They smile and call her "meesez."

The living room is even less recognizable than it was last week. Thick orange cords, navy blue sound blankets, pails, toolboxes. It's like a crime scene, or a fabrication shop. The men are wearing thick gloves and gauze masks.

The sound of the drilling is savage but also fascinating. It's like a dentist's drill, high-pitched, metallic, and loud enough to be inside your mouth. It growls through the resounding crawlspace, sending specks of fiberglass across the rafters in jangling spurts.

What are the men doing in there? They've set up a yellow-caged lamp so they can see their way around. Katya is curious to look, but something seems perverse about the open cavity. Too intimate. Like looking into somebody's guts.

Of particular concern is the fate of the armoire. As a piece of furniture, it is not much to speak of — a clunky oak display case enswirled with scratch marks — but its contents are delicate and irreplaceable, protected only by a thin sheet of glass. Atop each of the four dimly lit shelves sits a selection of rare items Katya and Joe have collected over their many travels.

Fragments of pre-Columbian textiles, a beetle entombed in a

bulb of amber, a lock of Madame Curie's hair. There is a vial of perfume recovered from a sunken barge, an opened letter postmarked to a Ukrainian village that no longer exists. On the top shelf, a jar of gallstones sits beside a splinter of Katya's coccyx salvaged from the surgery last year — as foreign as an ancient mollusk.

Each year at Passover, the grandchildren ask Katya to identify these curiosities, and each year she enchants them with tales of adventure and magic. A bullet casing from one of the revolvers used to shoot Grigori Rasputin. A diamond smuggled from Kiev in the stomach of a boy who'd swallowed it in a ball of wax.

As the children grow older, they become more skeptical of Katya's stories, though the objects remain radioactive with mystery.

In 1873 a young Italian anatomist named Camillo Golgi discovered a revolutionary method for viewing nerve cells. He'd converted a small hospital kitchen into a makeshift laboratory where, in the evenings, by candlelight, he would carefully impregnate microscopic samples of neuronal tissue with silver nitrate. Laboriously he experimented with various chemical baths and exposure times until one night he observed what he called *la reazione nera,* or "black reaction." The silvery black clusters of neurons were suddenly crisp and vivid, the gossamer stain sharply articulated by the luminous yellow slide.

Thirty-three years later, the German physician Alois Alzheimer used this same technique to investigate the neurological roots of senile dementia. What he found was an almost literal correspondence between the pathology of the disease and the resulting affliction: nerve fibers were gnarled and pasty, synapses were clogged with proteins like a grimy sink drain.

It was about this time last year that Joe found the checkbook. The bank had called asking all sorts of questions. Why hadn't the amounts on the deposit slips matched those on the checks? Whom had number 3601 been made out to? Why hadn't these four been endorsed? Joe was flummoxed. Katya had always handled the money. She was good with numbers, with the planning and organizing. Her parents had run a textile business back in Poland, and had trained her to run the accounts since the age of nine.

Joe went to the study and fished through the drawers. Already something was off. Calculators, envelopes, typewriter ribbons — all were piled into heaps. Loose staples were scattered about. Had the maid carelessly dumped everything together? When he finally discovered the mint-green checkbook with its marble saddle stitch, two thoughts entered his mind at once. The first was the hope, the fantasy: *clearly one of the grandchildren defaced it.* The second was the fear, the reality: *clearly my wife has lost her mind.*

The carbons were ablaze with gibberish. The penmanship was a dance of curlicues, like a roll of barbed wire. But the scribbles were neither childish nor methodical. They were discernibly Katya's, hers alone; they contained both the impulsive, half-cursive jabs and drags of her handwriting and the needlepoint slopes and slashes of her drawings.

In World War I, fighter jets were first becoming equipped with machine guns. They were initially crude and imprecise. A tail gunner needed the flexibility to swivel his gun along a 360-degree axis in order to follow a moving target, yet this increased the odds of accidentally shooting his own propeller. Bulletproof propeller blades were no solution — they simply deflected the bullets back toward the gunner. Finally, in 1915, an ingenious instrument was engineered by Anthony Fokker which synchronized the rate of the machine gun with the oscillation of the propeller, such that the trajectory of each consecutive bullet would be interleaved between the microsecond windows in the spinning blades, like a beam of light through a movie projector.

On the bottom shelf of the armoire is a shattered limestone ostracon, each segment propped up with small Lucite sawhorses. The paint is pale and chalky, the accompanying text jagged and pocked. There is a narrative of some sort running across the grid of panels, though the events aren't clear, not with so many sections missing. A czar, a bride, a lake. Rust-colored figures strafe this way and that. Bare-breasted women carry baskets through fields of maize. A fire. A dance. A gift.

Katya is at the osteopath for her hip. She has been coming here ever since she fell down the front steps and shattered her coccyx.

Dr. Mallah is a short, gym-built man almost exactly half her age, with furry black forearms and slow walnut eyes. He is, of course, Jewish. She would never think to trust a gentile with her health.

On the walls are laminated pictures of skeletons and organs, the same ones that adorn every doctor's office. Such a mess the insides of bodies are. All that cartilage, all those valves and wires.

The term *synapse* was introduced by Charles Scott Sherrington in 1897. He'd taken it from the Greek verb *synapsis,* meaning "to clasp." Synapses, the connection points between neurons, were essential to Sherrington's conception of the brain. They were like docking stations in a vast network of stockyards, transferring or withholding cargo from one freight to another.

It is dusk and Katya is inexplicably agitated. She is getting up and sitting down. She is licking her finger and rubbing away tiny stains on the glass coffee table. Joe is demanding to know what's wrong.

A gesheft hob nicht, she keeps muttering. *What do I care.*

In 1963 a peculiar article appeared in the medical journal *Brain,* authored by a former student of Sherrington's named Wilder Penfield. Entitled "The Brain's Record of Auditory and Visual Experience," it described a series of intracranial experiments Penfield and his colleague, Phanor Perot, had performed on patients with severe epilepsy. Before operating, the surgeons applied local anesthesia and stimulated the exposed brain areas with tiny charges of electricity while the patients remained awake and fully conscious on the operating table. The results were startling: subjects reported sudden flashes of dreamlike imagery, many of them accompanied by a deep sense of familiarity. Some spoke of nightmarish visions, like being chased by robbers, while others reported quotidian episodes from the past, such as hanging up a coat or boarding a train. One claimed to hear voices in the dark, coming from "around the carnival somewhere — some sort of a traveling circus."

Where is the camera? The Seder is tomorrow evening. Her grandchildren will be there. Everyone is counting on her to capture the event like she always does. They are expecting her to develop the pictures and send them to each family. The precedent has been set by years of tradition. She can't let them down.

What will happen if there are no pictures? No one will remember the party. They won't remember the laughter and the children's games and the magnificent feast she is preparing.

Without a document, who will remember?

One of the men descends the red ladder holding a slender, forearm-length strip of wire. He shows it to the other men like he has just caught a great fish! It is warped and steel and strangely sculptural, with rusty perpendicular brackets clamped to the ridges like vertebrae. Was this the problem? Have the men solved the problem? Katya is excited. She would like to keep the metal wire for the armoire but worries it may be impolite to ask. After all, they were the ones who excavated it.

Joe stares up at the ceiling as Katya sleeps beside him. He is thinking of Matisse. *My lines are not crazy,* the artist claimed, *for they contain an implicit verticality.* The words loop in Joe's mind like an incantation, half soothing, half maddening.

Katya's parents were moderately wealthy, enough so to buy their daughter a ride overseas just before the occupation. There is a slightly overexposed picture of Katya boarding the ship in a gray peacoat with big white buttons and white gloves, looking not unlike Anne Frank.

A maidel mit a klaidel is the name Joe has given this photograph. A Yiddish expression meaning, approximately, "a pretty maiden showing off her fancy clothes." He has a name for all his favorite pictures of Katya.

Who could know what was going on inside her at that moment? Children never appear traumatized. Here is the thirteen-year-old refugee, buoyant and alert, her shoulders angled into a sort of lopsided shrug, like she is concealing some private joke.

"There are no specific recollections in the brain," writes Israel Rosenfield, "there are only the means for reorganizing past impressions, for giving the incoherent, dreamlike world of memory a concrete reality. Memories are not fixed but are constantly evolving generalizations — recreations — of the past, which give us a sense of continuity . . ."

*

New York was strangely welcoming to the fourteen-year-old Katya. Her wizened and soft-spoken uncle, who had taken residence in the Prospect Heights section of Brooklyn a decade earlier, converted his attic into a small bedroom. A single window, diamond-shaped, sepia-stained, faced the bustling intersection of Washington Avenue and St. John's. The vaulted ceilings and exposed beams in the space were both rustic and cathedral-like, hidden and holy. On her first day of school, Katya was shocked to receive a compliment from her homeroom teacher. *That's a pretty dress,* said the woman. Katya assumed it was a trick — friendly language between teachers and students was unthinkable back home.

It is Tuesday and the men are still working on the ceiling. Katya is growing anxious. What if they do not finish in time for Passover? The possibility quickly forks off into a host of attendant worries. Is there time to reschedule? Could one of her children host the Seder this year? How hard would it be to serve dinner outdoors? She's overwhelmed. There are too many fires to stamp out. She is pacing about the house, tending to various minor tasks without actually committing to any of them. *A foiler tut in tsveyen.* She sweeps the dust from the kitchen floor into fluffy gray islands but forgets to collect them with the dustpan. She scrubs the bathroom but leaves the filthy sponge in the tub.

Again the glasses are missing. Every spot of light is plied out into fuzzy radial threads.

"I sit at my worktable, a still world around me, and stare at the wall, empty of decoration," writes the gardener Thomas DeBaggio in *Losing My Mind.* "I become lost in the vocabulary of silence. Thoughts squiggle and writhe into sentences that disappear before they can be acknowledged."

A mighty storm had lashed the roof in the spring of 1940, causing a smattering of leaks in the attic ceiling. Within hours the beams were soggy and dripping. Katya was at school while her few belongings were soaked. Her pretty white dresses, which hung from an iron dowel, were jaundiced about the shoulders; her shoebox full of letters from home became a cloudy palimpsest of multicolored inks. Katya's uncle had managed to rescue three of her paintings, but most were soiled beyond recognition.

Of the three, one has survived the intervening decades. It is a humble yet darkly evocative composition, a capricious earth-tone sketch of bustling shoppers and vendors cramped in the Prospect Heights thoroughfare.

Something in its hasty, boyish contours suggests an immediacy, an urgency, held at arm's length. There is also a murky, gauzed quality, a faint glow smeared into the weathered flax canvas reminiscent not of fallen tears but of a world seen through misting eyes.

In her adult life, Katya has now and then returned to this painting, adding texture, dynamism, gradually threshing the implicit verticality from the adolescent craziness.

There are moments when Katya's youthful beauty reveals itself. The mid-April light casts a sudden sheen to her pewter hair; an impromptu smirk betrays a girlish sneakiness otherwise lost.

Katya is dusting the piano keys with the feather brush. She swipes in gentle curls up the octaves — *plink-tink-dink? piddi-tunk-tonk?*

The piano has not been played in a while. It must be clean for the Seder, when the grandchildren will stage a little recital as they do every year. She bends over the bridge to dust the strings like a mechanic under the hood. Each swish sends a thrum of crystalline whispers through the birch chamber.

The party is under way. Children are performing handstands in the den. Katya's nephew is showing off copies of his latest book to the in-laws. Rain-flecked peacoats and scarves are piling up on the guest-room bed.

Katya is thankful that no one has noticed, or at least commented on, the hole in the ceiling, which has been sealed with a makeshift slab of cardboard. She makes an effort not to look up, fearing that the duct tape might peel under the weight of her fretful gaze. She is not normally superstitious, but why push her luck?

Soon the Seder will begin. The family will take their seats at the long oak table. Katya's son, Ben, who is now twice the age she was when she married Joe, will read from the Haggadah with his nicotine baritone. Her nieces will serve the salty parsley, the bitter herbs. The youngest children, Jennifer and Rebecca, will skitter about the house, searching for the *aficomen.* After the Seder, they will beg their grandmother to read one of her books to them, either *The Train to Kiev* or *The Czar's Magic Mirror.*

Dusk is early to arrive this year. The windows are foggy and lusterless in the waning violet light. The muted scent of frost and peat leaks into the living room from the thawing backyard garden.

Who will remember?

ETHAN RUTHERFORD

The Peripatetic Coffin

FROM *American Short Fiction*

THE SOUND OF IRON WALLS adjusting to the underwater pressure around you was like the sound of improbability announcing itself: a broad, deep, awake-you-from-your-stupor kind of salvo. The first time we heard it, we thought we were dead; the second time we heard it, we realized we were. The third time wiped clean away any concern we had regarding our well-being and we whooped like madmen in our sealed iron tub, hands at the crank, hunched at our stations like crippled industrial workers. Frank yelled like a siren without taking a breath. Abel hooted like a screech owl. The walls pinged and groaned, but held their seams. We screamed for more.

My name is Ward Lumpkin, and I man the second crank station aboard the "fish boat" *H. L. Hunley,* the first underwater vessel commissioned for combat by the Confederate States of America. There are seven of us aboard, not including our captain, Lieutenant Dixon, and in navigating the submarine murk of Charleston Harbor we make up the third volunteer crew in as many months. Mechanical failure; flooding ballast tanks; human error; bad luck: conventional wisdom around Battery Marshall has the survival rate aboard the *Hunley* hovering near zero, and that's without ever having engaged an enemy ship. Cannon probability, Abel calls it, as in stuff yourself inside a cannon and see what happens. But there's probability, and there's certainty. Antietam was a washout. Gettysburg was worse. Crescent City folded like the house of cards it was and we lost the Mississippi.

And now? In Richmond war widows have begun rioting over

bread. Railways in our control are being blown at such a rate you'd think it was some kind of competition.

One thing, at least, is clear to everyone: the Union naval blockade encircling Charleston must be broken if we are to continue aggression with the North, and if things are ever going to roll our way it'll be by doing the unexpected. General to germ-soaker, we fold our hats and stand in awe before the ingenuity of this machine: a cylindrical steam boiler, lengthened and tapered at the ends, outfitted with conning towers, a propeller, and diving fins. Affixed to our bow is a seventeen-foot-long iron spar torpedo that carries one hundred and thirty-five pounds of gunpowder that Frank has taken to calling the Demoralizer. We are the unheard-of: an instrument of destruction that maneuvers *under* the waves. If we survive our test dives, if we make it past Breach Inlet without rolling in the tide, if we crank undetected the three miles from the mouth of Charleston Harbor, it's enough ordnance to send any ship we happen to greet to the bottom of the ocean.

"Desperation breeds invention," Arnold has begun saying each time he seals the hatch.

"May wonders never cease," Frank says back.

Arnold Becker, Carleton J. F. Carlson, Frank Collins, James Wicks, Abel Miller, Joseph Ridgaway. Before the *Hunley* arrived in Charleston, before we volunteered our way underwater, all of us were stationed on the receiving ship *Indian Chief* off of Battery Marshall. The Sloop of Invalids, we called it. The CSS *Not Much to Report*. Everyone aboard had either been shot, trampled, shell-shocked, maimed, amputated, or otherwise shellacked on various campaigns. We suffered from swamp foot, dysentery, low morale, and general incompetence. We've proven unreliable in combat. Frank had been at Bull Run, seen his best friend ribboned by shrapnel, and had dreams like you wouldn't believe. Abel had stepped on his bayonet while cleaning his rifle and severed a tendon. I was born with a hip irregularity and moved so herky-jerky it made *other* people wince. "Well, I guess we all know why *you're* here," Frank said when I introduced myself. In response I told a joke about a three-legged plow horse, which either no one heard or no one got.

Standing on deck, we had an unobstructed view of what Abel had dubbed our Tableau of Lessening Odds. The Federal blockade was stupefyingly effective. Union cannon ships patrolled the mouth of the harbor, just out of range, and sank anything we tried to send through with the insouciance of a bull swatting black flies. At night they resumed bombardment of the city. High, arching incendiaries, numbering in the thousands, painted the sky. You felt the concussion in your chest.

Damage reports read like the end of the world. Houses, churches, and hotels were demolished. Everything south of Calhoun Street was rubble. Stray dogs ran in packs down the boulevard and looked at whoever was sifting through the wreckage like, What are you doing here?

On our receiving ship, we sat back, dumbfounded, and familiarized ourselves with new definitions of inadequacy. Supplies were running low. Reinforcements, always coming, never showed. Larger attempts at mobilization had been catastrophic. We practiced knots and evacuation drills, memorized flag signals, and wondered how much longer the city would hold. We'd stand watch, scan the horizon for runners, and return below with a tally of the gulls we'd counted. Downtime was spent staring at cleats.

"I can't say I'm proud of our efforts," Abel said one day as hundreds of pounds of artillery whistled into Charleston.

"I've addressed the firmament," Frank, watching the bombardment with his head in his hands, said back. "And it remains uninterested in your evaluation."

Half our guns had been offloaded and sent to the front. Those that remained sported the dust of the museum pieces they were. Our defense seemed to consist of getting — and staying — out of range. "If we're not going to actually be *receiving* anything, couldn't we be of more use somewhere else?" Frank said one day when Lieutenant Joosten was aboard checking inventory.

"Your enthusiasm," Lieutenant Joosten said, looking around as if seeing us for the first time, "is admirable."

After he'd left, Abel kicked a Dalgren and broke his toe. Frank counted the picket ships just outside Battery Marshall's cannon line and cursed all fourteen vessels and himself with surprising combinations of colorful language. "We're just going to sit here in the pluff mud, watching, until they destroy everything?" Arnold said. "That a rhetorical question?" someone said back.

Two weeks later the *Hunley* was brought in over rail on a flatcar, transferred to dry dock, and, with the help of thirty-five men and an elaborate pulley system, lowered into the water. We crowded the gunwales. We jostled for a view. The August heat shimmered the air above her like a mirage.

"Cure for what ails you," someone said. "Our secret weapon's an iron pecker."

"For the record," Lieutenant Joosten said, clearing his throat, "that's an underwater iron pecker."

The crowd that had gathered by the dock parted to make room for a group of six non-uniformed men carrying a long boom with a charge and spar at one end. Even from where I was standing I could see they were less than comfortable handling the load. They attached it gingerly to the bow of the vessel and backed away.

There were no speeches, no explanations. But who needed one? Just by looking at the thing you knew what it was built for. "You getting emotional?" Frank said.

"I believe I might be," Abel said. "I believe it may be so."

How unfamiliar are we with what we are capable of? As a child I was Gimpy the Lump Foot, One-Legged Ward, Vomit the Hobbler. The one-room schoolhouse I attended in Columbia was an exercise in controlled explosions. Before school, groups of kids would taunt me until I chased them, then laugh at the shit-show. During school, balled pieces of paper were bounced off the back of my head with Swiss-clock regularity. After school were the fights. My sisters were no help. My father shrugged at my bloody noses and torn shirts and said I had to learn how to stand up for myself sometime. I pointed to my leg. "You know what I mean," he said.

My mother was more sympathetic, taking me, on occasion, in her arms to muffle my sobs. "You have to know your strengths," she said.

As far as I could tell, my only strength consisted of taking heroic portions of abuse and folding them into broods so unyielding that no one in my family would approach me for days. I was accused of being inconsolable. I was chastised for my inability to see beyond myself. Sunday sermons exhorted us to forgive and forget, but even then I knew forgiveness was the province of the healthy, of the unbeaten, and that no help was coming. My parents were treated with sympathy for their blessing in disguise. "Pretty good disguise," my father was fond of saying back.

The *Hunley*'s first crew was gathered from an elite corps of older seamen none of us, until the moment they filed down the dock, had seen before. They threaded through the assembled crowd, accepting slaps on the back from enlisted men. There was a speech at the water by her captain, Lieutenant Payne, of which only fragments of intoned heroism drifted to my ears. Once everyone was below, Lieutenant Payne waved, then saluted, and turned to board. As he lowered himself into the hatch, he inadvertently stepped on the lever controlling the diving plane and the *Hunley*, with startling speed, dove, submerging her while the hatches were still open. Lieutenant Payne, treading water amidst a soup of roiling air bubbles, wore a look so far beyond stricken it resembled paralysis. He was relieved of his command and the *Hunley* fished from the bottom of the harbor. Five men drowned. She hadn't traveled more than fifty feet from the dock.

A second crew volunteered, and Horace Hunley himself was brought in from Mobile to assume command. A short man with a square-cut beard, Hunley comported himself with the forbearance and austere regality of the general he had always wanted to be. We lined the shore as dive after successful dive was completed. Mud and milfoil, churned to the surface by her propeller, marked the vessel's underwater progress. It was like watching a monster patrol a pond.

Fifteen minutes; twenty-three minutes; an hour. We bet rations on how long she'd stay down. One day she'd ventured only into the shoals. The next she'd explored the deepest part of the harbor, and surfaced to applause.

After three weeks of successful practice dives, we waited one afternoon as an excruciating eighty-two submerged minutes ticked by. Abel paced the gangway. Carleton tied line in and out of Turk's-head knots. I scanned the harbor for milfoil. Nothing. We upped our times and doubled our bets in a show of solidarity until finally even we had to concede it was a lost cause. Word was sent to General Beauregard that the crew had drowned and a salvage operation would begin in the morning.

Half an hour later, a yell from the harbor sent us topside. "What's the time on that one?" Hunley shouted, half out of the hatch, clothing soaked, voice quavering.

It had been two hours and fifteen minutes. The *Hunley* bobbed fifteen feet from the dock like a fishing buoy. We cheered as though we'd won the war.

Abel'd had the highest guess when we'd stopped. "What am I going to do with all this hardtack?" he said, looking at the pile in front of him.

"Rebuild Fort Sumter?" Frank, fanning the heat off his face, said. "Shove it up your ass? Be grateful?"

Two days before she was scheduled to engage the picket ships, the *Hunley* failed to surface. Three days later she was found nine fathoms down, her bow augured into the mud, with her ballast tanks open and her cabin flooded. Eight men died, including Horace Hunley. The service was brief. The bloated deaths of these men was a fact we had difficulty assimilating.

The blockade, as if relieved to have dodged this particular assault, sank two of our runners and shelled a cathedral in celebration.

What kind of person signs up for duty aboard a self-sabotaging vessel that has failed — spectacularly — every test it's been given? Who willingly mans the underwater equivalent of a bicycle strapped to a bomb with the intention of pedaling it four miles through hostile waters to engage an infinitely better equipped enemy? After a two-week hiatus, the *Hunley* was reluctantly returned to active duty, and her new skipper, Lieutenant Dixon, asked for volunteers. We stepped forward. He was visibly touched. We were touched ourselves. He wondered why, out of over four hundred people, only seven had signed up. We shrugged. He asked if we knew how unlikely a successful mission would be. We nodded. And might he ask why we volunteered?

"You *could,*" Frank said, and offered nothing else.

The *Hunley* is thirty-nine feet long with a beam of three feet, ten inches. The entry hatches that cap the conning towers are fourteen by fifteen and a half inches; we swivel our hips diagonally, and even then it's like threading a cannonball through a needle. Below is a roomy four feet of total darkness that gets so hot we wring our clothes into buckets when we surface. Abel, generally the first below, has taken to greeting us as we file past. "The CSS *Steam Boiler* welcomes you aboard," he says.

The seven of us sit on the starboard side, shoulders chafing, hands on the propeller crank. Our legs, if extended, span the beam and come up short on the hull. Lieutenant Dixon perches in the bow, head in the conning tower, levers at the ready. On his signal we turn the propeller. He lights a candle, checks the manometer mounted above his head, and floods the ballast tanks. As we dive, the iron walls sweat and groan like old wood. The air goes from stale to rank. "Yo ho ho," someone says.

Every day we board a contraption that has killed thirteen men, including its inventor, on test runs alone. Every night we sight the picket ships, set a course, and practice maneuvers. Our purpose is comically straightforward: steer undetected to the mouth of the harbor, sink the largest Union frigate we can ram, hope we are not destroyed in the explosion, and crank ourselves back to shore. To call us brave would imply that we've thought this through. To call us a suicide outfit would be missing the point. How many men have been underwater for hours at a time? How many men have sat, crumpled, candlelit, and submerged, and been sure of themselves? Frank hums a marching song softly in time with the propeller. Carleton taps the crank handle with his ring finger.

On the hull, rivets have been countersunk to minimize drag. If the tide is with us, if the sea is calm, if we are cranking to absolute capacity, our top speed is four knots. If the water's against us, we have a cruising speed of one knot and are in danger of capsizing. On the rear conning tower Frank's painted *1863* and below it, *Speed Matters Little.* Someone else (not one of us) has painted, in smaller letters, *Also: Reason.* It shows a basic lack of understanding. As far as we can tell, our Confederacy is on the verge of collapse. What's so unreasonable about wanting to give some of it back?

October and November pass without improvement around Battery Marshall, the focused attention of our war effort shifting from one losing front to another, and enthusiasm regarding our new weapon seems to have tapered from the top down. In the absence of any clear directive, our dives become endurance tests. How deep can we go? How fast can we pump air back into the ballast tanks? We turn tight circles underwater. We set the *Hunley* down on the harbor floor and practice shallow breathing. We dive and surface, acquainting ourselves with immersion. We memorize instrument placement. Attached to the outer hull is extra ballast, iron platelets eyebolted through the floor, which, in case of an emergency, can be unscrewed and dropped. We practice locating them in the dark. Lieutenant Dixon studies tidal charts. Given that we are hand-powered, whenever we are scheduled to engage the blockade we will need to leave on the ebb tide and return with the flood. We will need the cover of darkness.

"Darkness, darkness, darkness," Frank has taken to saying before Lieutenant Dixon blows out the candle.

"Light, light, light," we say back, once the candle's extinguished. We're fond of the reversal.

There are moments of panic. Episodes of self-doubt that buffet our overall submarine elation. We've come to know our time underwater as a dampened and foggy silence punctuated by flashes of distress so immediately visceral it takes us days to stop shaking. During one dive, Lieutenant Dixon forgets to light the candle before setting the diving planes and accidentally floods the ballast tanks before the rear hatch is sealed. Another dive, we reverse into a pylon and break the flywheel that houses our propeller. While depth testing, Abel succumbs to a brief hysteria, and in our rush to surface we almost roll to port. "Pardon that," he says, shaking. He'd almost kicked a hole in the hull. "Pardoned," Frank says.

At the dock we heave ourselves out of the hatch and stretch out flat on our backs, letting the unreality of what we've just done sink in. The almost-morning sun, the gray-before-dawn light, warms our uniforms. The men puttering around Battery Marshall shake their heads and keep a distance that signals discomfort. We give them hard looks in return. They've taken to calling us Pickett's Charge, only without the charge. They place bets on the time it will take us to sink ourselves. The odds are on in under a week. We resent the implication.

"Whatever happened to patriotism?" Abel says. "Don't they know a war hero when they see one?"

"Apparently not," Carleton, watching the latest bombardment, says back.

One day, following up an idea we had the night before, Abel rigs a dummy spar and we knock it into the hull of the *Indian Chief.* We're pulled from the water for a week for having a detrimental effect on morale. "So it wasn't the best way to illustrate our potential," Frank says. "But morale? Half of me wishes it'd been a live load."

"Half of you?" someone says back.

Frank and James disappear in a reverie of letter writing. Lieutenant Dixon takes a leave of absence to visit his fiancée. Carleton and I spend the week sitting near the water, throwing pebbles at sticks. When Abel comes back, he tells us our comrades in arms have a new name for the *Hunley:* the peripatetic coffin.

I tell him I like the sound of it. Abel shrugs. "Incapacitation is as incapacitation does," he says.

"For our parade," Carleton calls over his shoulder to Lieutenant Joosten, who's running an inspection on the torpedo, "how about a full band and seven of South Carolina's finest untouched beauties?"

"We'll see about a celebration," Lieutenant Joosten, who has a beauty of his own, says, "when you guys actually do something."

Our first chance actually to do something comes in December. As we make our preparations, the thump of artillery sounds in the distance. We're under orders to engage the USS *Camden,* a sloop of war just arrived in the harbor. It has also come down from General Beauregard that, for our own safety, we are not to use the *Hunley* as a submersible, but to remain surfaced, using the night as camouflage. When this news reaches us, Abel says nothing. Carleton says nothing. I say nothing.

"Doesn't that defeat the whole purpose of this thing?" Frank says.

"You're looking at me like I have a reassuring answer to that," Lieutenant Dixon says.

We retrieve the torpedo from the armory and carry it the three hundred yards to the dock. My hands are sweating, and twice Carleton asks us to stop so he can get a better grip. We fasten the boom to the bow, sit on the dock, and listen to the waves lap the iron sides of the hull. The night is moonless, and very dark.

Without a word, we lower ourselves into the *Hunley.* Infantrymen line the dock wearing expressions caught somewhere between skepticism and disbelief. As we cast off, one of them, a kid, slowly waves. I close and secure the hatch without waving back.

Lieutenant Dixon sights the *Camden* and calls for a rotational speed of three quarters. He floods the front ballast tank and then gives the signal for Carleton to flood the rear. Beside me, Frank whispers a Hail Mary. Abel triple checks the eyebolt at his feet. We dive until only the conning towers are surface-visible and then secure the tanks. Two minutes in, the *Hunley*'s a hothouse. Six minutes in, Lieutenant Dixon blows out the candle, and we're moving in a darkness so complete I feel outside of myself.

It takes us an hour to get to the mouth of the harbor. It takes us another hour to get within half a mile of the *Camden*. Lieutenant Dixon calls for a lower speed, and we're surprised at the sound of his voice. My body's aching from sitting in the same position for so long. My shoulders are on fire. Sweat pools in my boots.

When we're what must be a hundred yards from the ship, Lieutenant Dixon orders us to stop. We take our hands off the propeller, and everything goes silent. We can hear the water breaking in wavelets over the conning towers as we glide forward. We can hear voices, indistinct. Laughter. Shouting. Part of a song. It sounds infinitely far away. For a moment we wonder if we're prepared to do what we came out here for — it seems, suddenly, ungraspable and remote — and then Lieutenant Dixon hisses, "Stop. Reverse."

We do nothing at first. "Reverse," he says again. "It's not the *Camden,* it's just a picket ship."

"What's the difference?" Frank says.

"The difference is that we only have orders to engage the *Camden,*" Lieutenant Dixon says. "Reverse."

"Why don't we just ram it?" I say. "We're out here."

"Reverse."

Because the tide is against us, it takes us four hours to get back. By the time we reach the dock, morning has broken. We sit at our stations, cold with sweat, furious with humiliation. No one wants to get out. Finally Lieutenant Dixon unscrews the hatch. As he heaves himself out, he shakes like he has a palsy. "It wasn't the *Camden,*" he says to someone at the dock.

"Well, I'll be," the voice comes back.

Opportunities come, opportunities go. We set out to engage the *Hoboken,* but the weather turns us back. We try the next night, but a seam opens for no apparent reason and we turn back. A week later we get caught in the tide at the mouth of Breach Inlet and are rolled around so violently Frank doesn't eat for two days.

The war drags — slogs — on. On New Year's Day two runners break the blockade and we're all grins and whoops until their cargo's revealed to be molasses and women's clothing. The ships we try to send through, carrying cotton and rice, are caught by the blockade and send up smoke in dark columns that travel so high before dissipating the horizon appears jailed. The shelling of Charleston continues unabated, the Federals launching shell after shell into the abandoned city from Morris Island and the harbor as if they have nothing better to do with the afternoon.

To the north of us, General Grant has begun what's promised to be a march of attrition and scorched earth, aimed at Richmond, and we seem unable to muster any sort of resistance. But how could we? We build an iron ship, they build one of theirs. We mobilize for Washington, and they cut us in half in Virginia. We shoot our best general in the back, and even he isn't that surprised about it. "You'd think, standing at a distance," Frank says, "that we're *trying* to lose."

"You'd also think," Carleton, who's sitting next to him, says, "that your emotional response would clock in somewhere above where it apparently is."

Reports place our dead in the tens of thousands. In January, Battery Marshall becomes a way station for casualties. Throughout the night we hear the screams of the newly wounded. Outside our makeshift hospital, amputated legs are stacked like wood until someone complains and they're covered up. "At least now you'll have some company in the hobble department," Abel says to me. I key my laughter to such a pitch that Lieutenant Joosten's dogs answer from across the encampment and Abel rapidly excuses himself from the table.

A letter from my mother informs me they've left our property in the face of the advancing Union army and plan to head east. *What I pray for now,* it reads, *is a swift end to this conflict, so we can be together again.*

I start a letter back and give up halfway through.

During a test dive in February we spring a leak, and the *Hunley* is pulled for repairs. A bolt had come loose, and seawater erupted through the hull in a tiny stream that came up between Carleton's legs in such a way that even Lieutenant Dixon, once safely on the dock, found it amusing. We're told we'll be back in the harbor in four days.

"What's the point?" Carleton says as we secure the torpedo in the armory.

"Of what?" Frank says back.

"Of practice dives? Of *any* of this?"

Frank secures the padlock and turns. He shrugs, palms out as if checking for rain. "Are you looking for the ontological explanation or something more accessible?" he says, shutting down the conversation.

In the harbor, the picket ships list around their newest arrival: the USS *Housatonic,* a twelve-cannoned sloop of war, measuring sixty-five feet without counting her sprit. She's a thing of fierce beauty. Her appearance is the cause of general concern around Battery Marshall. For us alone it's encouraging.

Lieutenant Dixon, for the first time in weeks, visits us in our barracks. He's smaller than I am, and is wearing what Abel has taken to calling his Look of Officiousness. He stands in the entry, silent, until Frank makes it clear that he either comes out with it or bids us goodnight. He smiles nervously, fishes in his pocket, and emerges with a twenty-dollar gold piece, dented in the middle.

"My fiancée gave this to me," he begins, and tells his story.

We listen as the thing unfolds. His inaugural morning of combat was at Shiloh, where he was a rifleman in a first-wave offensive blown back so quickly it was held up as a textbook "don't" in subsequent battles. Bullets whizzed by and lodged in the bodies of the men behind him. The sound of it, he said, was like apples exploding on the side of a barn. Cannon fire shredded his line. As he marched, unsure of himself — standing, so he felt, alone — the gold piece in his pocket caught a musket ball and sent him to the ground. He spent three weeks in the hospital but kept his leg. "It seems like luck," he says. "But it's not."

He passes it around. It's heavier than I imagined, and gleams in the lamplight. On one side there's an engraving: *Shiloh April 6 1862 My life Preserver G. E. D.*

"Where was this at Vicksburg?" Carleton says, when it's passed to him.

Lieutenant Dixon pockets the gold piece and tugs at his beard. "We engage the *Housatonic,*" he says. "As soon as we're repaired." He turns and leaves.

"As long as this is inspirational story hour," Arnold says from his bunk, and cuts wind. His point: coincidence, pluck, promises, talismans — what does any of that have to do with us? We know what we see and what we've always seen: a campaign of indiscriminate shelling, economic paralysis, and relentless destruction. The strategy of the more powerful and better equipped. The Union giant's footsteps thundered down our hallway the instant we struck our flints on Fort Sumter, and their response has so far outstripped the ethereal bonds of brotherhood that we blanch at our capacity for self-regard. How will we explain that we brought this on ourselves? How do you meet halfway a hammer blow that's larger than anything you can imagine? And how long can you do nothing before you begin to feel you deserve it?

Frank takes one of Arnold's boots and pulls the laces clean off. Arnold puts up his fists and Frank apologizes. "It was my intention," he says, "to unlace both."

"Intentions, intentions," Abel says. "Never the follow-through."

Frank shrugs. He leans over, finds Arnold's other boot, yanks the laces, and ties the boot closed. We have our fish boat. We have our bomb. We possess what the less observant might call an indifference to plausibility, which is matched only by our private desire to transfer this thing back to a human scale. We have what Abel calls our Stab at Enlargement. Everything else hovers in a constant state somewhere just beyond recognition.

Before going to sleep, Carleton convinces Abel to tell his balloon corps story. It's one of our favorites; we know it by heart. Before stepping on his bayonet, Abel had fought in Virginia with Beauregard. Things hadn't been going well. They were being outmaneuvered; any flank operation they'd attempted was spotted far ahead of time by the Union Balloon Corps, literally men in balloons, sweeping the ground from the air and reporting on their formations. These balloons were something to see. They hung in the sky like inverted bulbs, tethered to the ground. You kept waiting for them to sprout. The night before their planned mobilization, Abel volunteered to accompany Lieutenant Bingay beyond the frontlines to fire on the corps. No one in the balloon would be armed, and there would be minimal protection on the ground. Abel and Lieutenant Bingay had three muskets each. They ran like Indians through the forest, ducking branches, kneeling in the brush. It took them two hours to get within range. As Abel lined his shot, he caught a glimpse of the man in the basket. He was small and bespectacled. He looked completely at peace.

It took two shots to puncture the balloon. Beset by a sudden bolt of conscience — what Abel calls one of his finer moments of not connecting the dots — he'd been careful to aim well above the bespectacled man. The basket fell. The man plummeted in silence and hit a patch of rocks. The sound was like a melon breaking. The musket reports brought the Union soldiers out of their tents, but by the time they figured out what had happened, Abel and Lieutenant Bingay were streaking back to camp, congratulating each other on their marksmanship.

Confident he'd dismantled the enemy's ability to undercut his formations, General Beauregard drafted his plans and slept the sleep of the satisfied.

The next day thousands of men died, including Lieutenant Bingay and the man Abel had posed with, expressions stern and full of disdain, in a tintype four days earlier.

"Turns out," Abel says, "balloons weren't the problem."

Two nights later the repairs have been made. We move through the darkness and secure the torpedo with care, triple-checking the firing mechanism. Lieutenant Dixon is in full regalia, his pistols crossed below his bandolier. The tassels of his shoulder ensigns sweep with his movement like grass in the wind. A gibbous moon hangs suspended over Breach Inlet, mirror-reflected in the water. We lower ourselves into the *Hunley* barely aware of each other. No one sees us off. As we go hands on the propeller and prepare to flood the ballast tanks, Carleton remarks on the thorough pleasantness of the evening. It hadn't occurred to any of us that the shelling had stopped.

The *Housatonic* sits two and a half miles outside of Battery Marshall, sails reefed, becalmed. On Lieutenant Dixon's orders, we crank slowly, a monster of complete silence.

Fifty yards from the ship, Lieutenant Dixon calls for maximum speed and we oblige. Thirty-five yards away we are spotted and some sort of bell aboard the *Housatonic* peals alarm. Musket balls ricochet off our iron deck, the sound amplified between us. There is shouting, and I'm not sure if it's coming from us or somewhere else.

The hollow *thunk* of iron embedding itself in wood jolts us forward and we scramble to regain ourselves. Lieutenant Dixon yells for reverse. It takes us a second to remember which direction to crank until Frank says "Away from you" and we put it together. I'm aware that we're moving at an angle, our stern dipping low, leading the bow below the surface. We glide in reverse for just long enough to wonder whether we'd attached the line to the firing mechanism correctly, and then there's an explosion so deafening it's like tasting sound.

We take our hands off the crank and stare at the iron wall two feet in front of us. I can feel an arm on my shoulder, applying pressure. I'm vaguely aware of a hand on my leg. My feet are cold.

Lieutenant Dixon lights his candle and swivels in his seat. His expression is unreadable. He asks Carleton to check the ballast tank. He tells Frank to resecure the rear hatch. When they tell him all is as expected, three-quarters full, secured, he closes his eyes and lets his chin fall to his chest. I look down. We're sitting shin-deep in water.

Battery Marshall is two and a half miles away. No one says anything. The swell bobs us back and forth, gently sloshing the water we've taken, now at our knees, as if in a basin. Lieutenant Dixon tells us that out the porthole he can see the *Housatonic* in flames, listing to port. Lifeboats are being lowered. Men are in the water. We remain at our stations as he unscrews the front hatch and fires a magnesium flare, signaling success. Then he secures the hatch and returns to his seat without a word.

The *Hunley* fills fast. We stop moving in the swell, and I have the sensation of diving without diving. When the water's at my waist, I wonder if we'll make it to the bottom of the harbor before we drown. I imagine a gentle cessation, silt and mud pillowing out and up, then settling. I imagine rust and algae, inquisitive fish. When the water's at chest level, Frank mumbles something and puts his head under. No one restrains him.

When the water's at my neck, my father appears. He asks me if I know that one hundred years from now the *Hunley* will be found and fished out of the harbor by an expedition costing millions of dollars and, once salvaged, will be paraded around the streets of Charleston by young men dressed in gray uniforms. He asks me if I know that they will find a boot and a button and verify that Arnold had been one of the men aboard. That, eventually, they will find Lieutenant Dixon's gold coin, dented in the middle, and a great effort will go into finding out what happened to his fiancée — whose name, it turns out, was Queenie — after the war, and it will appear as if she went down with the submarine. He asks me if I know that despite sustaining over seven million pounds of artillery, Charleston will never succumb to Union occupation.

"Did you," he says, "ever wonder at this?"

I tell him that at every turn our understanding of what was happening around us had been mitigated by such a clanging abashment that we'd become rocklike as far as expectations go. It was pick-up sticks in the middle of a hurricane. It had never occurred to us to wonder about much of anything.

He tells me that we will be remembered mostly for our optimism. I tell him it isn't optimism that gets you aboard something like this. He says, Still.

I ask him what we've done beyond proving our own uselessness? What were we but a spectacle of self-defeat? He answers that we are an expression of an intangible truth that has plagued victors for thousands of years. That immolation as a form of confrontation holds irreducible power.

I tell him he has it backwards, and if it had been approval we were looking for, we would've kept diaries.

There is another explosion above us, the keel of the *Housatonic* seizing in on itself, collapsing, splintering, and my father disappears. Through the darkness I feel the iron hull on my back. I feel for the crank handle and grasp it. Carleton is frantic. Abel is standing so his head is in the small hollow of the conning tower, which will be the last place to fill. Someone is screaming at a pitch both familiar and thoroughly distant, a keening that only stops, and briefly, in surprise when our stern hits the floor of the harbor and our bow follows, scrapes a rock of some kind, and rests.

NAMWALI SERPELL

Muzungu

FROM *Callaloo*

ISABELLA WAS NINE YEARS OLD before she knew what *white* meant. White in the sense of being a thing, as opposed to not being a thing. It wasn't that Isa didn't know her parents were white, although with her mother, this was largely a matter of conjecture. A layer of thick dark hair kept Sibilla's face a mystery. And even though as she aged this blanket of hair turned gray, then silver, then white, a definite movement toward translucence, Isa never could properly make out her mother's features. More distinct were Sibilla's legs, tufts of fur running like a mane down each thick shin, and her strange laugh, like large sheets of paper being ripped and crumpled. Isa's father, the Colonel, was white, but it often seemed as if pink and gray were battling it out on his face. Especially when he drank.

Her parents had settled into life in Zambia the way most expats do. They drank a lot. Every weekend was another house party, that never-ending expatriate house party that has been swatting mosquitoes and swimming in gin and quinine for more than a century. Sibilla floated around in a billowy Senegalese boubou, sending servants for refills and dropping in on every conversation, distributing laughter and ease among her guests. Purple-skinned peanuts had been soaked in salt water and roasted in a pan until they were gray; they cooled and shifted with a whispery sound in wooden bowls. There were Tropic beer bottles scattered around the veranda, marking the table and the concrete floor with their damp semicircular hoof prints. Full or empty? Once the top is off a Tropic bottle, you can't tell, because the amber glass is so dark. You have to lift it to check its weight. Cigars and tobacco pipes puffed their foul sweetness into the air. Darts and croquet balls went in loopy circles around their targets, loopier as the day wore on.

The Colonel sat in his permanent chair just beyond the shade of the veranda, dampening with gin the thatch protruding from his nostrils, occasionally snorting at some private or overheard joke. His skin was creased like trousers that had been worn too long. Budding from his arms were moles so large and detached they looked ready to tumble off and roll away into the night. And as though his wife's hairiness had become contagious, his ears had been taken over — the calyx whorl of each had sprouted a bouquet of whiskers. The Colonel liked to drink from the same glass the entire day, always his favorite glass, decorated with the red, white, and green hexagons of a football. As his drunkenness progressed, the glass got misty from being so close to his open mouth, then slimy as his saliva glands loosened, then muddy as dirt and sweat mixed on his hand. At the end of the evening, when Isa was sent to fetch her father's glass, she often found it beneath his chair under a swarm of giddy ants, the football spattered like it had been used for a rainy day match.

Isa had no siblings, and when the other expatriate children were around she was frantic and listless in turns. Today she began with frantic. Leaving the grownups outside propping their feet on wooden stools and scratching at their sunburns, Isa marched three of the more hapless children inside the house and down the long corridor to her bedroom. There she introduced them to her things. First to her favorite book, *D'Aulaires' Book of Greek Myths.* Second to the live, broken-winged bird she'd found in the driveway. Third, and finally, to Doll.

"And this is my doll. She comes from America. She has an Amurrican accent. Her name is Doll."

Bird and Doll lived together in an open cardboard box. Isabella stood next to the box with her chin lifted, her hand pointing down to them. Due to the scarcity of imported goods in Lusaka, Isa was allowed only one doll at a time, and this one had gone the way of all dolls: tangled-haired–patchy–bald. Forever smiling Doll, denied a more original name by her fastidious owner, sat with her legs extended, her right knee bent at an obtuse and alluring angle. From Doll's arched left foot a tiny plastic pink stiletto dangled. Her perforated rubber head tilted to one side. She seemed interested and pleasant. Bird, also on its way to bald, cowered as far away from Doll as possible, looking defeated. Isa poked at it with her finger. The bird skittered lopsidedly around the box until, cornered, it uttered a vague chirp. Alex and Stephie, prompted by Isabella, applauded this effort.

But Emma, the littlest, thinking that the doll rather than the bird had made the sound, burst into startled tears. She had to be soothed (by Stephie) and corrected (by Isa). Isa was annoyed. So she sat them down in a row on her bed and taught them things that she knew. About fractions and about why Athena was better than Aphrodite. About the sun and how it wasn't moving, we were. But soon enough Emma's knotted forehead and Alex's fidgeting began to drive Isa to distraction. Then came the inevitable tantrum, followed by a dark sullen lull. The other three children hastened from the room in a kind of daze. Isa sat next to the cardboard box and cried a little, alternately stroking Doll's smiling head and Bird's weary one.

When she'd tired of self-pity, Isa walked to the bathroom and carefully closed and locked the door. She took off her shoes and climbed onto the edge of the bathtub, which faced a wall about two feet away. Only by standing on the edge of the tub could she see herself in the mirror on the wall, which hung at adult height. She examined her gray eyes, closing each of them in turn to see how she looked when blinking. She checked her face for hair (an endless, inevitable paranoia) and with a cruel finger pushed the tip of her nose up. She felt it hung too close to her upper lip. Then Isa let herself fall into the mirror, her own face rushing toward her, her eyes expanding with fear and perspective. At the last minute, she reached out her hands and stopped herself. She stayed in this position for a moment, angled across the room, arms rigid, hands pressed against the mirror, nose centimeters from it. Then, bored with her face, she jumped down and explored the floor. She unraveled the last few squares of toilet paper from its roll and wrapped them around her neck. Then she opened the cardboard cylinder from the toilet paper roll into a loose brown curlicue — a bracelet. She discovered some of her mother's torn OB wrappers, which twisted at each end like candy wrappers. She stood them on their twists to make goblets for Doll.

Eventually drunken guests started lining up outside the bathroom, knocking at the door with tentative knuckles and then flat palms and then clenched fists. Isa emerged, head high and neck at full extension, her OB goblets balanced on an outstretched hand like a tray. Bejeweled with toilet paper, she strolled past the line of full-bladdered guests. She gave Doll the goblets, modeled the jewelry for Bird. But Isa's heavily curtained bedroom was too cold to play in alone.

Reluctantly she removed her makeshift jewelry — too childish for her mother to see — and rejoined the party outside. As she marched outside in her marigold dress, she glanced at the other children running around making pointless circles and meaningless noises in the garden. She avoided them, choosing instead to be pointedly polite to their parents, who were still sitting in a half-circle on the veranda, insulting each other. There was something excessive about her attentiveness as she shoved snack platters under the noses of perfectly satiated guests and refilled their mostly full beer glasses, tilting both bottle and glass to minimize the foam, just like the Colonel had taught her.

Finally her mother told her to sit down over by Ba Simon, the gardener. He was standing at the far end of the veranda, slapping varieties of dead animal onto the smoking brai. He reached down to pat Isa on the head, but she ducked away from his hand, ignoring his eyes and his chuckle. The saccharine smell of the soap he used mingled with the smell of burned meat.

Ba Simon was singing softly under his breath. He'd probably picked up some nasty song from the shabeen, Isa thought emphatically, repeating in her head a condemnation that she'd heard a thousand times from Ba Gertrude, the maid. There are three kinds of people in the world: people who unconsciously sing along when they hear someone else singing, people who remain respectfully or irritably silent, and people who start to sing something else. Isa began singing the Zambian national anthem. Stand and sing of Zambia, proud and free. Land of work and joy and unity. Ba Simon gave up on his quiet song, smiling down at Isa and shaking his head while he flipped steaks he wouldn't get to eat. Ashes from the brai drifted and spun like the children playing in the garden.

Isa watched the other children with a detached revulsion, her elbows on her knees, cheeks cradled in her hands, ashes melting imperceptibly onto the pale shins below the hem of her marigold dress. Stephie was sitting in a chair, depriving a grownup of a seat, reading a book. Isa was scandalized. It was her mythology book! She stared at Stephie for a while and then decided to forgive her because her nose had a perfect slope. Unlike Winifred, whose nose was enormous and freckled, almost as disgusting as the snot bubbling from Ahmed's little brown one. The two of them were trying to play croquet under the not-so-watchful eye of Aunt Kathy. Younger than most of the adults at the party, Aunt Kathy always spent the day chain-smoking and downing watery Pimm's cups and looking through everyone, endlessly making and unmaking some terribly important decision. Isa found her beautiful, but looking at her for too long sometimes made her feel like there were too many things that she didn't know yet.

Emma, who had cried about Doll, was all smiles now, sitting cross-legged by herself and watching something, probably a ladybug, crawl along her hand. Emma was so small. Isa tried to remember being that small, but the weight of her own elbows on her knees made it hard to imagine. The ladybug was even smaller. What was it like to be that small? But anyway, how could Emma have been so afraid of Doll when she clearly wasn't afraid of insects, which everyone knew could bite and were much more disgusting? Isa had once retched at the sight of a stray cockroach in the sink, but it had been a pretend retch because she'd heard at school that cockroaches were supposed to be disgusting. Horribly, Isa's pretend retch had become real and had burned her throat and she'd felt ashamed at having been so promptly punished by her body for lying. But enough time had passed to transform the feeling of disgust at herself into disgust about small crawling creatures. She watched as Emma turned her cupped hand slowly like the Queen of England waving at everyone on the television. The ladybug spiraled down her wrist, seeking edges, finding curves. Emma giggled. Isa swallowed and looked away.

Far off in the corner of the garden, there was a huddle of boys crouching, playing with worms or cards or something. Isa watched them. Every once in a while the four boys would stand up and move a little further away and then crouch down again, like they were following a trail. They were inching this way along the garden wall, toward where it broke off by the corner of the house. Around that corner was the guava tree Isa climbed every afternoon after school.

Isa got curious. And then she got suspicious. She stood up, absently brushing ashes from her dress instead of shaking them off and accidentally streaking the yellow with gray. She noticed and bit her lip and squeezed her left hand with her right, caught between her resolve to do good and her need to change her dress. But the adults were roaring with laughter and slumping with drunkenness. Whatever inappropriate behavior was taking place in the garden, it was up to her to fix. She started running across the garden, looking behind her to make sure no one followed. When she was close, she stopped herself and began stalking the boys, holding her breath.

She tiptoed right up to their backs and peered over their shoulders. At first she couldn't see much of anything, but then she realized that they were huddled around a thick-looking puddle. It was mostly clear, but, as Jumani pointed out in a hushed whisper, there were spots of blood in it. Isa's eyes widened. Blood in her own garden? She winced a little and looked back at the party: Emma was interrupting Stephie's quiet read; Winifred's freckles were pooling into an orange stain in the middle of her forehead as she concentrated on the next croquet hoop; Ahmed, snot dripping dangerously close to his open mouth, stared back at Isa, but he seemed sun-struck rather than curious.

She glared warningly at him and turned back around. The boys, oblivious to her presence, had disappeared around the corner. She followed and found them squatting at the foot of the guava tree, her guava tree, with its gently soughing leaves, its gently sloughing bark. She circled the mysterious puddle and walked toward them with purpose, abandoning all efforts at being sneaky. But the boys were too fascinated with whatever they saw to notice her. A whining and a rustling from under the tree drowned the sounds of her approach. Isa looked between their shoulders, her throat tight.

Lying on its side, surrounded by the four boys, was Ba Simon's dog. She was a ridgeback, named thus because of a tufted line down the back where the hairs that grew upward on either side of the spine confronted each other. At the bottom of this tiny mane, just above the tail, was a little cul-de-sac of a cowlick. Ba Simon had named the dog Cassava because of her color, though Isa thought Cassava's yellowish white fur was closer to the color of the ivory horn that her father had hung on the living room wall. But today her fur was crusted over with rust. Her belly, usually a gray suedish vest buttoned with black teats, was streaked dark red.

Isa's first thought was that these boys had poisoned Cassava and were now watching her die a slow miserable death under the guava tree. But then she saw that the side of Cassava's head was pivoting back and forth along the ground. Isa stepped to the left and saw an oblong mass quivering under the eager strokes of Cassava's long pink tongue. The thing was the color of ice at the top of milk bottles from the fridge, cloudy and clear. From the way it wobbled, it seemed like it was made of jelly, maybe more like the consistency of gravy that had been in the fridge too long. It was connected by a pink cord to a slimy greenish black lump.

The boys were whispering to each other, and just then Jumani made to touch the lump with a stick. Isa jumped forward and said, "No!" in a hushed shout. Cassava whined a little and licked faster, her tail sweeping weakly in the dust. The boys turned to Isa, but before she could say anything, the oblong thing jerked a little and Isa inhaled sharply. She pointed at it, her eyes and mouth wide open. The boys turned back to look. Where Cassava was insistently licking, there was a patch along the oily surface through which they could just glimpse a gray triangle. It was an ear. Isa took her place beside the boys, sitting in the dust, her precious marigold dress forgotten.

Perhaps out of fear, perhaps out of reverence, the boys didn't touch Cassava until she had burst the wobbling sac and licked away all of the clear fluid inside it. Occasionally there was a tobacco-tainted breeze from around the corner. Sometimes laughter would flare up, crackling down to Sibilla's chortle. But the grownups didn't come. At first the children whispered their speculations, but soon they were all watching in silence, gasping only once when the outer skin finally burst, releasing a pool that crept slowly along the ground.

There it was, lying in a patch of damp dirt, trembling as Cassava's tongue grazed along its sticky body. It was the size of a rat; it was hairy and pink; its face was a skull with skin. Below its half-closed pink eyelids, the eyes were blue-black and seemed almost see-through. But that was just the sunlight dappling through the guava leaves and reflecting off their shiny surface; the children looked closer and saw the eyes were opaque and dead.

The boys became restless. Cassava was still licking but nothing was happening; the mystery was revealed, the thing was dead, what else was there to see? They got up and left, already knocking about for other ways to pass the long afternoon. Awed and resolved to maintain her dignity and her difference from the boys, Isa decided to stay, silently shaking her head when Jumani offered her a hand up. She was so absorbed in watching that hypnotic tongue rocking the corpse back and forth that she didn't notice the girl until she spoke.

"He et oh the bebbies? Eh-eh, he et them," the girl asked and answered.

Isa looked around and saw nothing. Laughter fell from the sky. Isa looked up into the tree and saw Ba Simon's daughter sitting in a wide crook, her little head hanging to one side as she smirked down upon the world. Chanda was about six or seven, close enough to Isa's age, but they weren't allowed to play together because of an unspoken agreement between Ba Simon and Sibilla. The two girls had been caught making mud pies together once when they were younger and had been so thoroughly scolded by their respective parents that even to look at each other felt like reaching a hand toward an open flame. Isa's entrance into primary school had made their mutual avoidance easier, as had her innate preference for adult conversation and her recently acquired but deeply held feelings about the stained man's T-shirt that Chanda wore every day as a dress.

Isa glared at Chanda's laughing face.

"He ate what? Anyway, it's a her," she replied with hesitant indignation. She gathered some strength in her voice. "Obviously," she said. Chanda was expertly descending from the crook of the tree, flashing a pair of baggy but clean pink panties on the way down. Isa abruptly decided that Chanda had been secretly climbing the guava tree during school hours and that she had stolen the panties off the clothesline.

As she carefully lowered herself to the ground, Chanda said, "His stomach has been very row. And then pa yesterday? He was just cryingcrying the ho day. Manje ona, jast look: he et the bebby."

Isa was horrified, then dubious. "How do you know?"

Chanda, now standing with her feet planted a little apart, her hands resting on her haunches in imitation of Ba Gertrude, nodded knowingly.

"Oh-oh? Jast watch." Her voice trembled nevertheless.

Cassava hadn't stopped licking the stillborn. Her tongue maintained its rhythm and her mouth appeared to have moved closer to the dead-eyed skull. Isa shuddered and scrambled to her feet. Suddenly, mustering all her courage, she stretched her leg out and with her bare foot kicked the dead puppy as hard as she could away from Cassava. It tumbled away into the dust, a guava leaf trailing from it like an extra tail. Cassava growled ominously.

"Did she do that yesterday too?" Isa demanded, reaching behind her for Chanda's hand. Chanda was silent. Cassava scudded her distended torso across the ground toward the puppy. Isa quickly glanced back at Chanda's face, which, in reflecting her own fear, terrified her even more. Cassava wheezed and growled at the same time. Her legs twitched.

"Let's go," Isa suggested breathlessly.

Their hands still clasped, the two girls ran away, Cassava baying behind them. Isa felt buoyed by her fear, like it had released something in her, and she let her legs run as fast as they wanted, relishing the pounding of her feet on the dusty path to the servants' quarters. It had been a long time since Isa had visited this concrete building at the back of the garden. When she had been a very little girl, like Emma, there had been an emergency when her father had drunk too much from his bleary glass. There hadn't been anyone among the expats to take care of her when the Colonel had tumbled to the ground, football stein clutched unbroken in his hand. So that night, while her mother veiled up and drove the Colonel to the hospital, Isa had gone with Ba Simon to his home for supper.

They'd eaten nshima and delele, the slimy okra dish that reminded her of the shimmery snail trails on the garden wall. Ba Simon had been as kind and as chatty as usual, but it had gotten cold and the servants' quarters had been very dark and cold. Isa had been grateful to hear the soft shuffle of her mother's hair on the floor when she came to fetch her that night.

Isa stopped running abruptly. Her left foot had stepped on a small but sharp rock. Her halt jolted Chanda, who still held her hand. With the pain in her foot, Isa suddenly felt an arrow of real fear piercing her exhilaration, deflating her back into her sulky self. The vegetable patch behind the servants' quarters was just visible beyond the avocado tree. She lifted her foot and examined the sole. It wasn't bleeding, but there was a purple dot where the rock had dented it. As she put her foot down, she remembered Cassava and turned to see how far they'd run. The garden was huge and encompassed a small maize field, which Isa could glimpse just beyond the mulberry trees with their slight branches and their stained roots. She really ought to go and tell Mummy about the dog.

When she turned back to tell Chanda exactly that in her most grown-up voice, Isa found herself surrounded by three other small children. There was a little boy who looked just like Chanda and two slightly younger girls, toddlers, who looked just like each other. Isa stared at them. She'd never seen twins before. They stood with their hands clasped behind their back, their bellies sticking forward like they were pretending to be pregnant. Isa sometimes played this game in the bath herself, pushing her belly out as far as it could go until her breath ran out, but this did not seem to be what the little girls were doing. A picture of Cassava's low stomach from the previous week flashed through Isa's head.

One of the girls was probing around her mouth with her tongue and the other was making stuttery noises that Chanda apparently understood because she replied, pointing at Isa and shaking her head. The little boy was staring at Isa and smiling broadly. He stepped forward and held out his hand, making the same upward-turned tray that Isa had made for Doll's goblets. Isa shook her head and stepped back, unsure. Chanda implored, "Bwela. Come. Come." She pointed at the servants' quarters to show where Isa was meant to come. There was blue smoke and the sound of splashing water coming from around back. Isa relented.

They walked together toward the building, which was low to the ground and had no door, just a gap in the facade. There were also no windows, just square grids drilled into the concrete here and there for ventilation. As they approached, the little boy ran to the back shouting something. A young woman whom Isa had never seen before appeared from around the corner carrying a metal pot, her wrists and hands wet. She wore a green chitenge and an old white shirt, but Isa immediately noticed that she wasn't wearing a bra: you could see the shape of her breasts and the dark outline of her nipples. The woman smiled at Isa and waved and as she approached said, "Muli bwanji?" Isa knew this greeting and replied in an automatic whisper, without smiling, "Bwino."

The woman shook Isa's hand, and Isa noticed that she didn't

bend at the knee or touch her right elbow with her left hand as blacks usually did with her. Halfway through the handshake, Isa suddenly realized that she herself was supposed to be deferential. She hurried to bend her knees, but they seemed to be locked and she managed only a jerky wobble. The woman lifted her head, sniffing the air imperiously. Then she looked at Chanda and demanded something. Chanda shrugged and ran up the three stairs into the servants' quarters, dribbling a forced giggle behind her. "Ach," the woman said and sucked her teeth. She walked back to the rear of the house to finish her washing. Halfway there she turned and gestured to Isa that she should follow Chanda into the quarters.

Isa gingerly made her way up the steps and into the velvet darkness beyond the doorway. The concrete floor wasn't dirty — it was polished to a slippery shine — but the dust on her bare feet rasped as she stepped inside. The place had a strong coppery smell of fried kapenta mixed with a tinge of wood smoke. As Isa moved further in, the smell took on an acrid note that she dimly recognized as pee. It was so dark that she couldn't see anything except for the gold grid on the floor where the sunlight had squeezed through the ventilation grill. The fuzzy squares seemed more radiant for having been through that concrete sieve. Isa walked toward them. The patch of latticed light traveled up her body as she moved into it and eventually glowed on her stomach. It was like being in church or on Cairo Road. She held her hand in front of it and the light made her hand glow like the orange road lamps . . .

A chuckle from the corner interrupted her reverie. Isa looked around, her heart thudding, but she still couldn't see anything. She stood still and concentrated her eyes on the darkness, willing them to adapt.

She could just make out three figures sitting in the corner. There was a young woman, younger than the one outside, an old woman, and Chanda, who sat cross-legged, fiddling with an ancient cloth doll with a vaguely familiar shape. Isa worked out that it was the faceless ghost of the Doll who had preceded Doll; she felt a little shocked that it should be here and then even more shocked that she should have forgotten it to such a fate.

She walked toward the women, who were mumbling to each other. Only then did Isa notice the baby sitting on the young woman's lap. In fact — she moved closer — the child was sucking on the woman's breast. Isa knew about breastfeeding but she'd never seen it before. She couldn't tell whether the baby was a boy or a girl; it had short hair and was naked except for a cloth diaper. She wanted to turn away but she couldn't stop looking at the way the child's lips moved and the way the breast hung, oblong and pleated like a rotten pawpaw. The women continued to deliberate while Chanda, who was responsible for this intrusion, for this straying, sat staring at Isa, absently twisting the doll's dirty arm as though to detach it.

The child started crying: not the wailing of a newborn, but an intelligent sobbing. Isa stared at it and then realized that it was staring back. Its mother lifted it and began bouncing it up and down on her lap. After a moment the old woman began laughing, a rattling laugh that devolved into coughing and then rose back up again to the heights of gratified amusement. She said something. Then the young woman began to laugh too, and finally Chanda joined in with a high-pitched trill.

"What?" Isa asked. "What?" she demanded.

But they kept on laughing, and then the woman stood up and held the baby in front of her. Isa stared at its sobbing face, distorted with wet concentric wrinkles like its nose was a dropped stone rippling a dark pool. The child began to scream, wriggling its little body as its legs kicked. Was she supposed to take the child in her arms? The room echoed with laughter and wailing.

Isa shouted "What? What?" again.

The laughing woman kept shoving the child at Isa's face in jerks until their noses suddenly touched.

"Muzungu," the woman said.

As though at the flip of a switch, Isa began to cry. Her breath hitching on every corner of her young-girl chest, she turned and ran out of the room, tripping down the steps in her haste. As she ran past the mulberry trees, the beat of her feet released a flock of birds from their boughs. They fluttered past her and flickered above her bobbing head, their wings a jumble of parentheses writing themselves across the sky.

The night brought the breeze and the mosquitoes. The guests waned in number and spirit. When she'd had enough, Sibilla planted bristling kisses upon their cheeks and sent them to navigate the intricacies of Lusaka's geography and their drunken dramas on their own. Colonel Corsale was still in the garden, dozing on his chair, one hairy hand holding his football glass clasped to his belly, the other dangling from the armrest, swaying like a hanging man. In the early days Sibilla used to drag her husband to bed herself. But over the years his boozing had swollen more than just his ankles. These days she told Ba Simon to do it.

"A-ta! I'm not carrying the cornuto to bed. The man's earlobes are fat," she'd grumble, leaving her husband to the night, the breeze, and the mosquitoes.

Isa wandered around the yard, yawning, picking up Tropic bottles of various weight under Ba Simon's direction. She hadn't told anyone about the dog yet, or about all the inhabitants of the servants' quarters — did they realize how many people lived there? — or about the laughing. She felt tired and immensely old, old in a different way from the times she played teacher to the other children. Old like her father was old, a shaggy shambling old, an old where you'd lost the order of things and felt so sad that you simply had to embrace the loss, reassuring yourself with the lie that you hadn't really wanted all that order to begin with.

Ba Simon was singing something spiritual, not in English, but Isa could barely muster the energy to gainsay his song with her own. She only got halfway through "Baby you can drive my car" before she collapsed on the grass beside her father's chair. The wicker creaked in rhythm with his snoring. She put her fingers in his dangling hand and he muttered something.

"Papa?" she asked softly. "Dormendo?"

She only spoke Italian to him when she was very, very tired. The international school she attended had compressed all her thoughts into English, but some of her feelings remained in the simple Italian her parents had used on her as a toddler.

"I went to the servants' quarters," she said.

The Colonel's whiffling snore continued. Isa slapped a mosquito away from her shin. She stood up and walked over to Ba Simon, who was vigorously scrubbing the grill.

"What does *muzungu* mean?" she asked, sitting on her stool.

He kept humming for a second. "Where did you hear that word?" he asked.

Isa didn't reply. Ba Simon hesitated. Then he made a face and said, "Ghost!" He waved his hands about. "Whoooo! Like that katooni you are always watching." He smiled and moved closer to her with his hands still waving. "Caspah Caspah the shani-shani ghost," he sang in the wrong key.

"Whoooo!" she giggled back at Ba Simon in spite of herself, and they chatted about nothing for a few minutes. Ba Simon wasn't very bright, she thought and then forgot. But Ba Simon noticed her thought even though she hadn't said it, and soon enough he told her to go to bed. When she looked back from the doorway to the house, Ba Simon was just getting ready to carry her father to bed. His body was pitched awkwardly over the Colonel, his face contorted, his long stringy arms planted beneath the Colonel's neck and knees. But when he saw Isa turn back, the strain on Ba Simon's face dissolved instantly into a smile.

"Go," he whispered, and she did.

Contributors' Notes

100 Other Distinguished Stories of 2008

Editorial Addresses

Contributors' Notes

DANIEL ALARCÓN is associate editor of *Etiqueta Negra,* an award-winning monthly magazine published in his native Lima, Peru. His novel *Lost City Radio* won the 2008 PEN USA Fiction Award, and his most recent book, a story collection entitled *El rey siempre está por encima del pueblo,* has just been published in Mexico.

▪ The novel I'm currently writing has a lot to do with theater, and in the course of researching, I've been reading all kinds of plays. Somewhere in the process I came upon a handful of scripts a friend, the Peruvian playwright Walter Ventosilla, had given me many years ago, among them a one-act called *El Mariscal Idiota.* I found Walter's play so funny, so startling, that I knew immediately I would use it. I started writing around this script, in conversation with it, and though my version of the play is different from Walter's original in several key ways, without that initial spark, I simply couldn't have written the story. I renamed Septiembre, Walter's theater company, and tried to capture a bit of that world as it was told to me by Walter and Gustavo Lora, another friend and theater veteran, known, perhaps only to me, as Patalarga. This story is dedicated to the two of them. What is now "The Idiot President" was originally part of my novel, but as is often the case, it took on a life of its own, and though it still shares a narrator with that longer text, it no longer fits within that unfinished book. The climactic image of the miners' headlamps is based on an anecdote, possibly apocryphal, told to me by Khalid Abdalla, an actor I met last year in Palestine. I seem to recall that he set it in a Brazilian copper mine, though I could be mistaken. For months after that trip, I was unable to escape the image, and these two ideas began to coalesce around Nelson, a character I've been happily getting to know for the last two years.

SARAH SHUN-LIEN BYNUM is the author of *Ms. Hempel Chronicles,* a finalist for the 2009 PEN/Faulkner Award, and *Madeleine Is Sleeping,* a finalist for the 2004 National Book Award. Her stories have appeared in *The New Yorker, Tin House, The Georgia Review,* and *The Best American Short Stories 2004.* She directs the MFA Program in Writing at the University of California, San Diego, and lives in Los Angeles with her family.

▪ I don't drink a lot of alcohol, mostly because I've never learned to like the taste of it, and this story began with me trying to remember the times I have really enjoyed getting drunk. That train of thought led me back to Mooney's Irish Pub, a neighborhood bar on Flatbush Avenue in Brooklyn, where I used to drink and dance on Friday afternoons with the other teachers from my school. This all happened a long time ago, more than ten years ago, and thinking about Mooney's made me feel how much I missed those friends. I missed them enough to start writing about them, and one in particular. I'd never written a story where so many of the details about the focal character were borrowed from a real person, and I struggled with the ethics of this as I was working on the first draft. I kept promising myself that I would go back through on the second round and change all the identifying markers — a log cabin in place of the yurt, tennis shoes for clogs — but once I finished the story I couldn't do it. Yemen, yurts, subway poems, the Meat Puppets: I realized too late that these details were neither incidental nor replaceable. Is there an old saying that a story lives in its details? I think there must be, and finishing the first draft of "Yurt" was the moment when I fully understood the truth of this. A different constellation of details could not conjure up the qualities that I associated with my friend and needed for the character of Ms. Duffy: inventiveness as a teacher, a sense of adventure, curiosity about other parts of the world, a readiness to completely reimagine one's life. Log cabins and tennis shoes were not up to the task. Fortunately, among my friend's other qualities is generosity of spirit. I didn't realize how anxious I had been about her reading the story until she responded with the graciousness and humor and warmth that she did; my sense of relief was enormous. I am grateful to her, and also to Carin Besser and the fiction department at *The New Yorker,* from whom I learned so much during the editing of this story.

STEVE DE JARNATT grew up in Longview, Washington, where he briefly held the state high school track record in the quarter mile. He attended Occidental College, graduated from the Evergreen State College, and has just completed the creative writing MFA program at Antioch University in Los Angeles. He currently lives in Los Angeles and wrote and directed the indie feature *Miracle Mile,* among many other film and television credits. He will be moving to Port Townsend, Washington, in the near future to live and write. This is the first fiction he ever sent out and his first published story.

▪ The tale was spawned from an exercise given to me: write about a man in a room with a plant. Its purpose was to encourage me to write more sparingly, and in this story at least I probably failed to do so, but it sparked a great way for me to vent about the all-time clusterfuck of the Katrina aftermath. I doubt any words can really do justice to that weeklong bombardment of images of monumental suffering, so I decided to focus on the predicament of a single broken man, trapped with his memories, not at all sure his accursed life will make it through the day. I know I have a tendency to be drawn to primal survival stories, and if things can get down to the absolute raw necessities of life — food, water, air (and, yes, companionship) — all the better. I now feel considerable remorse for the misfortune I put my poor Rubiaux character through, and I am certain he's doing swell today — addiction-free, happily married, with state-of-the-art prosthetics, even a job — though probably still living in a FEMA trailer.

The plant in the story has its seeds in the huge, misshapen heirloom tomatoes my grandfather grew next to his outhouse in southern Indiana, and I can still remember how their intense, wild flavor and that fetid breeze would wrestle for your senses.

Being brand-new to this fiction racket, I must give props to a few: all my recent MFA program teachers and fellow students for greatly accelerating my learning curve in this craft I have come to late in life, and on this story, mentors Jim Krusoe and Susan Taylor Chehak in particular, who shaped this story; my hometown lit buds Flavia Loeb and Chas Hansen for their notes; my friend Glen Pitre for vetting some Cajun verisimilitude I attempted; Andrew Tonkovich, who first published something I wrote; and I will be forever indebted to Heidi Pitlor and Alice Sebold for the validation that comes with inclusion here.

JOSEPH EPSTEIN is the author, most recently, of *Fred Astaire*, published by Yale University Press. He hopes soon to bring out his third collection of short stories.

▪ "Beyond the Pale" is the result of fairly lengthy observation on my part of the behavior of literary widows, behavior that is often unreasonable, often unjust, often quite nutty, but beyond all that often immensely admirable. In my story I tried to create a character that comprised all these passionate qualities — a heroine not necessarily likable but genuinely heroic.

ALICE FULTON's first book of fiction, *The Nightingales of Troy*, was published in 2008. "A Shadow Table" is from this linked collection, which follows a single family for one hundred years. Other stories have appeared in

The Best American Short Stories and the Pushcart Prize anthology. Fulton's eight books include *Cascade Experiment: Selected Poems* and *Felt: Poems.* She has been honored with the Bobbitt National Prize for Poetry from the Library of Congress, the Editors' Prize in Fiction, and a MacArthur fellowship. She lives in Ithaca, New York, and teaches at Cornell.

▪ "A Shadow Table" is one of ten fictions set in each decade of the twentieth century. I knew the 1920s story would focus on Charlotte Garrahan's romance with a wealthy boy of a different class and religion. My first attempt was full of jaunty dialogue and period details that somehow rang false. I tried to revise that story for the longest time, but the problem was tonal, and tone is the soul of prose, infusing every aspect. After years of static revisions, I decided to discard what I'd written and start again, keeping only the characters and basic conflict.

This time I thought it'd be interesting to show people in the 1920s suffering from what we'd call "eating disorders" today. Then, while doing research, I lucked upon *A Daughter of the Samurai,* a 1920s memoir by Etsu Inagaki Sugimoto, and the book's delicate phrasing helped me find a nuanced, reticent tone. I further realized that Charlotte might have more in common with the world of the samurai than with the culture she experiences in Connecticut. The opening of King Tut's tomb in the 1920s triggered a huge craze for exoticism, so the trope of Nipponophilia also seemed right for the decade.

The actual Charlotte's thwarted romance was a family mystery. No one knew exactly what happened, and "A Shadow Table" is an imagined answer. I wrote the story slowly, trusting the gathering narrative to suggest the next move. And to my relief, it did.

Karl Taro Greenfeld is the author of four nonfiction books, *Speed Tribes, Standard Deviations, China Syndrome,* and *Boy Alone: A Brother's Memoir,* about his autistic brother, Noah. His writing has previously been published in *The Best American Travel Writing, The Best American Sports Writing,* and *The Best American Nonrequired Reading* anthologies. His fiction has appeared in *The Paris Review, American Short Fiction, Cream City Review, New York Tyrant, Asia Literary Review,* and *Evergreen Review.* His journalism has appeared in *Time, Sports Illustrated,* the *New York Times, GQ, Condé Nast Traveler,* and *Vogue,* among other publications.

▪ In 2006 I was going back and forth from New York to Beijing, working on the launch of *Sports Illustrated* China. I had run a magazine in Hong Kong, *Time*'s Asia Edition, but working on a magazine in mainland China was a new experience for me. *Sports Illustrated*'s U.S. edition, where I was editor at large, was supposed to have equal say in who the editor of the Chinese edition would be. But in reality all I did was sit in meetings and agree to hire whoever our Chinese partners wanted. The man they chose to serve as both editor and publisher of *SI* China was a legend in that he had once run a great newspaper in southern China that had dared to expose corruption and had even occasionally taken on the government; yet he had ended up getting arrested on phony charges and serving time in jail. This position, at a sports magazine, was far less controversial, and I could see that this formerly aggressive editor had decided that he was going to play the game a little differently now. So he was answering a question I had: how do you have a career as a journalist or a writer in a society where certain subjects are only written about at great personal risk?

Also, as part of launching *SI* China, I saw that the magazine business in China, which was then booming, was very different from in America. They were making it up as they went along, and operating under some strange ground rules, such as the one requiring a *kanha,* or publishing permit, which were like New York City taxi medallions, issued in small quantities by the General Administration of Press and Periodicals for specific titles; new magazines were forced to purchase them from existing or defunct magazines, whose names had to remain on the cover somewhere. (This made for some weird arrangements, such as the Chinese edition of *Rolling Stone* being published with the Chinese name, in small letters, saying something like *Shanghai Audio Equipment and Instrument Review.*) At one point, on a flight back to New York, thinking about the murky transactions that were going on — I sometimes couldn't figure out which way the money was flowing — the sentence "Who pays who?" began to rattle around in my head, sort of to the tune of the AC/DC song "Who Made Who," and I thought, That should be the first line of something. (It ended not being in "NowTrends," but the idea is certainly there.) During the same period, I was asked by the *Washington Post* to review a nonfiction book by John Pomfret about China, a really good book called *Chinese Lessons,* about his experiences going to an elite college in Beijing, his classmates and what happened to them. I definitely felt that there was something in that milieu that would be interesting combined with the stuff I was seeing firsthand. I owe a debt to that book.

I started with that idea — who pays who — and then came upon the starlet. I don't know where she came from, but vaguely, in my mind, I could discern the facial features of the Taiwanese actress Shu Qi. The whole police station and the dealing with officialdom were familiar to me from working in China, researching a previous book I wrote, about the SARS virus.

ELEANOR HENDERSON received her MFA from the University of Virginia in 2005. Her fiction has appeared in journals including *North Ameri-*

can Review, Indiana Review, and *Ninth Letter;* her nonfiction has appeared in *Poets & Writers,* where she was a contributing editor, and *Virginia Quarterly Review,* where she is the chair of the fiction board. An assistant professor at James Madison University, she lives outside Charlottesville with her husband and son.

▪ When we first moved to Charlottesville, my husband and I lived in a new-construction, vinyl-sided townhouse complex, and among our neighbors were two young black girls who routinely locked themselves out. One afternoon while they sat on their stoop in their parkas, my husband invited them inside, where we dug up everything we owned that might appeal to children: board games, cartoons, a tin of hot chocolate with a polar bear on the label. Over the few hours I spent with them, I felt more aware of my race than I ever had before, and I probably shouldn't have been surprised that the girls seemed to as well. At one point, while watching a doll commercial, the younger sister exclaimed to the older, "Look, a little black girl, like us!" My husband and I were amused, but her sister was not. Neither was their mother, a woman who wore military fatigues and who avoided our eyes every day after.

I tried several times to write about those girls, at first from the perspective of a young white couple, but I didn't get far. I knew in a vague way that I wanted to address the feeling I'd had and wasn't very proud of — the feeling of wanting to be praised for my beneficence and to forge a connection with my neighbors who seemed so unlike me. It wasn't until I tried that feeling on a thirteen-year-old narrator that it felt right. In an earlier story, "The Kissing Disease," I'd already introduced Meg, then twelve. I hadn't intended to return to her character, but once I started thinking about her life after her brother's death, it made sense to me that her innocence and grief would make her ripe for this experience. I'd like to thank David Keeling and Anna Solomon for their help in shaping the story, as well as Sven Birkerts and Bill Pierce at *Agni* for giving it a home.

The week after we moved out of the apartment complex, the serial rapist who had terrified our city for a decade made one of our neighbors his final victim before he was caught. I only knew that she was a black woman, and I've since wondered if she was the girls' mother. Now, when I think about their family, my adolescent sympathy has a darker edge. But my imagination is probably getting the best of me.

GREG HRBEK is a graduate of the Iowa Writers' Workshop and the author of a novel, *The Hindenburg Crashes Nightly.* His short fiction has appeared in *Harper's Magazine, Salmagundi, Black Warrior Review,* and *The 2007 Robert Olen Butler Prize Stories.* He teaches fiction at Skidmore College in New York.

▪ When I was working on this story about parenthood, my own son was about nine months old. I was writing in Baja, Mexico, for a month, and I'd brought two wallet-sized photos of him. I hadn't brought the pictures for inspiration, but I found myself looking at them a lot and carrying feelings about him into the writing.

The first version of the story was rejected by about fifteen magazines and journals. I later rewrote it, adding the older brother and his point of view, and his character led me to the idea of the car crash. I'm thankful now for the failure of the first version, because this final one is much better.

ADAM JOHNSON is a senior Jones Lecturer in creative writing at Stanford University. His fiction has appeared in *Esquire, Harper's Magazine, Tin House,* and *The Paris Review.* He is the author of *Emporium,* a short story collection, and the novel *Parasites Like Us,* which won a California Book Award.

▪ I lived in Lake Charles, Louisiana, for three years while I earned an MFA from Robert Olen Butler at McNeese State University. A mixture of lush wetlands and petrochemical plants, the area was both a rare ecological treasure and an apocalypse in progress. I'd come from the sprawling suburbs of Phoenix and had never lived in a close-knit community. But in Lake Charles, when I'd generically say "How's it going" to folks in Abe's Grocery, they'd tell me about the corns on their feet, a bass boat they were thinking of buying, how I really needed to attend their church. Strangers invited me to dances, festivals, crab boils, and gumbo feasts. They spoke openly of cancer, of incarcerated family members, and let me know when they got a whiff of the Devil near me. With regularity, folks would impart upon me hilarious, strange, or chilling accounts of what they thought was the meaning of life. When people got drunk, they always told me the reason. As a fiction writer, I'd spent my time trying to depict people via suggestion, subtlety, and subtext. Here were emotional and vibrant people who were the opposite of fiction, and they made me rethink the kinds of stories I was trying to tell.

My wife and I had been in New Orleans just before Hurricane Katrina struck on August 29, 2005, and we followed the aftermath closely. Thousands of evacuees from New Orleans were given shelter in Lake Charles, only to be battered again when Hurricane Rita struck twenty-six days later. The most powerful hurricane to ever make landfall from the Gulf, Rita harrowed southwest Louisiana. The thought of people hit twice by massive hurricanes gripped me, and I decided to try to give voice to that. I am indebted to UPS for allowing me to ride along with their wonderful drivers Sharon Guillory and Mary Ann Jaunet and for allowing me to interview Yoval "Yogi" Villaso. Thanks also to Calcasieu Parish Sheriff Tony Mancuso, Assistant Chief Deputy Buba Mayeaux, and Nelson Robles of their Homeland Security Division. Thanks to Calcasieu Parish Deputy Coroner Zeb Johnson, Clyde Mitchell of Entergy, and John Williams of the Beer Industry League of Louisiana. The Louisiana Department of Wildlife and Fisheries was very helpful, especially Captain Jubal Marceaux, Lieutenant Remy Broussard, Sergeant David Sanford, and Senior Agent Sean Moreau. I'm indebted to Arthur "V-Ray" Guidry, Carolyn Harper, Carolyn Shelton, Carlotta "Tu Tu" Savoie, Jacob Blevins, Arnold Jones, Jr., and the many others who shared their stories with me. Special thanks to Neil Connelly and Skip Horack.

VICTORIA LANCELOTTA was born and raised in Baltimore, Maryland. She is the author of *Here in the World: Thirteen Stories* and the novel *Far.* Her fiction has appeared in *Mississippi Review, The Threepenny Review, Nerve.com, McSweeney's,* and other magazines, both print and electronic. She has been a fellow at the Fine Arts Work Center, the Djerassi Foundation, and the MacDowell Colony. She lives in Nashville with her husband, Steven Conti.

▪ There were a few years during which my husband and I had the great good fortune to be able to spend time, frequently, in Paris, and what was particularly fantastic about this opportunity was the fact that we didn't feel compelled to try to *do* things — we didn't race from museum to cemetery to cathedral, we didn't make schedules or buy souvenirs. We slept in, and wandered, and ate and drank, and even as I was acutely aware of the luxuriousness of our situation, I was also aware of how transitory and artificial it was. The more comfortable I felt in the city itself, the more unsettled I became by my own presence there — it began to be difficult to stay focused on where I was at any given moment; my mind would spin out to the life that I'd left in a sort of suspended animation back in the States. I began to feel ghostly, almost.

I wrote a version of the first paragraph of "The Anniversary Trip" in a small bedroom on the rue St.-Placide. It was before dawn, and my husband was sleeping but I was awake and close to frantic — it was suddenly incredibly important to me to know how we would remember this strange charmed time in our lives when it was over. I wrote the rest of it months later, at our house in Nashville, right before a typically hectic holiday season, before that annual round of family visits and the accompanying marathon of taxis and airports, boarding gates and baggage claims, and when I finished it I felt an overwhelming sadness for Monica, not because I knew she'd never go back to Paris, but because I thought she'd always remember it as a place where she didn't belong.

YIYUN LI grew up in Beijing and came to the United States in 1996. Her stories and essays have been published in *The New Yorker, The Best American*

Short Stories, The O. Henry Prize Stories, and elsewhere. She has received fellowships and awards from the Lannan Foundation and the Whiting Foundation. She is the author of a collection of stories, *A Thousand Years of Good Prayers,* which won the Frank O'Connor International Short Story Award, the PEN/Hemingway Award, and the Guardian First Book Award, and *The Vagrants,* a novel. She was selected by *Granta* as one of the twenty-one Best Young American Novelists under thirty-five. She lives in Oakland, California, with her husband and their two sons and teaches at University of California, Davis.

▪ A few years ago I read in the news that a young woman in China sued her father because she thought he was having an affair, and she asked that he, as a member of the Communist Party, be put in prison. I followed the case for a few months and then decided to write a story with a character who was equally fascinated by the case, though for a different reason.

REBECCA MAKKAI's stories have appeared in *The Best American Short Stories 2008* and in journals including *New England Review, The Threepenny Review, Shenandoah,* and *The Iowa Review.* She lives near Chicago with her husband and daughter and is completing a novel.

▪ Here's the ending I wanted: The woman walks into the post office, sees the man, and recognizes him as her husband. And now that he thinks about it, yes, he actually has become the professor; he remembers this woman and their life together. But I'm not Marquez, and so I couldn't pull it off.

Two minor points of origin: Steve Martin's wonderful play *Picasso at the Lapin Agile,* in which the character Einstein states that the reason the sun does not revolve around the earth is that the proof for a geocentric universe wouldn't be beautiful enough, and a painting of a half-peeled apple on the wall of the coffee shop where I write.

And one major point of origin: During World War II, a distant family member, a university professor, was grabbed and forced into a line of prisoners when the count came up short, and was never seen again. I don't feel quite right having appropriated this story from those closer to that man, and I suppose that's why this so quickly became a story about guilt — and perhaps why I couldn't quite bring myself to write that tidier ending.

JILL MCCORKLE is the author of five novels — *The Cheer Leader, July 7th, Tending to Virginia, Ferris Beach,* and *Carolina Moon* — and three story collections, *Crash Diet, Final Vinyl Days,* and *Creatures of Habit.* Her new collection, *Going Away Shoes,* will be published this fall. Her work has appeared in *The Atlantic Monthly, Ploughshares, The Best American Short Stories,* and *New Stories from the South,* among other publications. The recipient of the New England Book Award, the John Dos Passos Prize, and the North Carolina

Award for Literature, she has taught creative writing at the University of North Carolina at Chapel Hill, Tufts, Harvard, Brandeis, and Bennington College. She is currently on the faculty at North Carolina State University.

▪ The whole idea for "Magic Words" came out of my own thinking about the way these words are often taken for granted and spouted without any sense of what is really going on. I was struck by the weird extremes in usage from the polite superficial "please" versus someone pleading for his or her life, or the polite superficial "thank you" versus an honest sense of gratefulness. So that's where I started — a sense of the surface action being completely out of balance with what is being thought, felt, known below it all. The various characters are in such a place, their actions masking their real desires and needs. I consciously placed them all in what felt like a minefield, threatening turns all around them. When Paula looks out and makes eye contact with the coyote and acknowledges that everyone wants something, she is speaking to the whole cast, each one having come to a place of needing a kind of acceptance. That's a common enough story, but I was surprised where I wound up when their lives began to intersect. I had fully intended that Paula would make it all the way to the motel and consummate the relationship she has been flirting with and that the boy *would* intentionally hurt Agnes and that the cat would likely never come home. For whatever reason, as soon as Paula made the decision not to go, the volume turned way down on all the others, and I found myself more focused on the fragility of both their lives and the moment. The image from reality that fed this story was my own moment of being surprised by a coyote in my backyard. There was about one second when I thought it was a dog and then just as quickly knew it was *not* a dog. We made eye contact, both of us frozen in place, and I remember taking note of where my children and pets were and thinking the word *please.* Please go away. Please don't come closer. And needless to say, I was thankful when he turned and darted back into the woods. I could only imagine that he was feeling the same.

KEVIN MOFFETT is the author of the story collection *Permanent Visitors.* His short fiction has appeared in *McSweeney's, New Stories from the South, Tin House, Harvard Review, The Best American Short Stories 2006,* and elsewhere. He has received the Pushcart Prize, the Nelson Algren Award, and a grant from the National Endowment for the Arts. He teaches in the MFA program at California State University, San Bernardino.

▪ I grew up in Ormond Beach, Florida, a few miles from the Casements, John D. Rockefeller's modest gray-and-brown winter home on the Halifax River. I used to go there for school field trips and once, unless I dreamed this, a birthday party. There were rumors of an underground tunnel connecting Rockefeller's house to the Ormond Hotel — then big and stately and crumbling, now gone — across the street. I had a hard time squaring my admittedly distorted view of Rockefeller — gold-plated top hat, walking cane made from the shinbones of adversaries — with my hometown, and with a house that was so . . . ordinary.

A while ago, looking for something else, I found a copy of the amazing *WPA Guide to Florida* in a used bookstore. In it was a brief sketch of a grandfatherly Rockefeller wintering in Florida. Conserving energy, golfing, giving away his money, enjoying auto races, trying to make it to his hundredth birthday. (He died about two years shy of it.) "Rockefeller had his first airplane ride here in Ormond Beach," it said. "The plane taxied up and down the beach, but did not leave the ground."

Unlike most stories I've written, this one began with a clear view of the ending, but with no idea how to get there. Maybe an underground tunnel? While working on it I called the Casements to ask about the tunnel, and the woman who answered the phone laughed a little before telling me that there were no underground tunnels or secret rooms. I nixed the tunnel, but I invented details elsewhere, choosing plausibility over historicity in hopes of letting the story reveal itself through trial and error, as I wrote it.

RICHARD POWERS is the author of ten novels, most recently *Generosity.*

▪ The story "Modulation" was born out of years of fascination with the German word *Ohrwurm.* When the playlist of my portable music player was temporarily hijacked by forces beyond my understanding, that virus or a word was released in my mind, and a couple of weeks later I had my SATB quartet.

ANNIE PROULX lives and writes in Wyoming and New Mexico.

▪ The story was written as part of a final collection of stories set in rural Wyoming. It is a bit of an ironic wink at the collection title, for things are often *not* fine the way they are, and was offered as an antidote to the mythological Founding-of-the-Big-Happy-Ranch story. Many times in the state's early history people started out bravely homesteading and failed through adverse circumstances. I have long appreciated the old cowboy songs and wanted to write a story that was built around them.

RON RASH is the author of four novels, three books of poetry, and three collections of stories. He has won NEA fellowships in poetry and fiction and is a former O. Henry Award winner. His collection of short stories *Chemistry* was a finalist for the 2007 PEN/Faulkner Award and winner of the Thomas Wolfe Award. *Serena,* his most recent book, was a finalist for the 2008 PEN/Faulkner Award. He teaches at Western Carolina University.

▪ "Into the Gorge" came to me first as an image. A man was running from something. He was too old to be running, yet he was running nevertheless. At first I didn't know what he ran from, but soon I began to understand that he was, at least in part, running from a world he no longer understood. I live in a region that has undergone rapid change in the last few years. Such change has brought gains but also losses. This story emphasizes what one man has lost.

ALEX ROSE grew up in Providence, Rhode Island, and graduated in 1998 from Hampshire College, where he studied creative writing and film production. Since then he has published stories and essays in the *New York Times, The Reading Room, North American Review,* the *Providence Journal,* the *Forward, Ploughshares, Diagram,* and others. He is the author of *Synapse,* a novella in hypertext, and *The Musical Illusionist and Other Tales,* a collection of short fiction.

As a filmmaker, Rose has directed a number of short films, videos, and animations, which have appeared on HBO, MTV, Comedy Central, Showtime, and the BBC as well as in over two dozen festivals worldwide. His latest film, *Call It Fiction,* a fourteen-minute comic drama starring Ron Silver, can be viewed on iTunes.

In 2006 Rose designed and helped launch Hotel St. George Press, an online arts quarterly and literary press with national distribution. HSG has since published four critically acclaimed titles, including the handcrafted, limited-edition release *Correspondences,* by Ben Greenman. Currently Rose resides in Brooklyn, New York.

▪ Ostraca were flat slabs of limestone on whose surfaces ancient artists would depict narratives in pictorial (or occasionally textual) form, as an alternative to papyrus or vellum. Etymologically, the term also carries a hint of the slabs' brief use as ballots, which the Greeks used to mark the names of those voted to be exiled — hence the modern term *ostracize.*

The idea of the object and its various ghostly connotations seemed to me an appropriate metaphor for the character of Katya. My grandmother, on whom she was based, had been suffering from senile dementia for over a decade, and her many stories — indeed, her identity itself — had gradually become transfigured, like something beautiful and mysterious but also shattered and bleached into abstraction. There was also the additional layer of meaning that resonated with her experience as a refugee, having fled Nazi-occupied Europe to New York as a young girl.

I wrote this piece over several weeks in late 2007, during which time I submerged myself in my grandmother's writings — her enchanting folktales, her sophisticated grown-up fictions, and her heartbreaking autobiographical novel, *Refugee.* She died nine months later, on the same day "Ostracon" first appeared in print.

ETHAN RUTHERFORD's fiction has appeared in *Esopus, New York Tyrant, Verb, Faultline, American Short Fiction,* and *Fiction on a Stick: New Stories by Minnesota Writers.* His work received special mention in the 2009 Pushcart Prize anthology, and he is the recent recipient of a SASE/Jerome Foundation grant for emerging writers. In 2009 he received his MFA in creative writing from the University of Minnesota.

▪ I've always loved submarines — they seem to appear, unbidden, in a lot of my work (you hit that point in a story where you go, You know what would make this better? A submarine!) — but I'd never heard of the *Hunley* before visiting Charleston. One afternoon, while walking with a friend, we passed a replica of it, and she briefed me on its history. Looking at this thing and then hearing what it was built for, it's hard to keep yourself from thinking, Well, what'd they expect? It's a hand-cranked death trap. It's the fever-dream of a claustrophobe. There is no way I would've set foot anywhere near this boat. But some people, even after watching the invention drown its inventor, did.

A few months later I found myself stuck on two separate stories — one about suicide bombers, one about a submarine locked under ice in the Arctic — and the *Hunley* came up in conversation and jarred something loose. So "The Peripatetic Coffin" is sort of a thematic meet-cute between those two stories, neither of which were going anywhere on their own, propelled by my desire to contextualize the experience of its third unlucky crew. The question I struggled with, the question that kept me interested, was what gets someone — voluntarily — aboard an invention like this? Another friend told me about the bombardment of the city, and it was the relentlessness of this bombardment that allowed me into the story.

Of great help to me during the writing of this story was a book called *Confederates Courageous,* by Gerald F. Teaster. A number of facts in this story are off — some accidental, some purposefully. It's fiction. Enduring gratitude to Paul Yoon, Jim Shepard, and the fine folks at *American Short Fiction* — Jill Meyers and Stacey Swann — for publishing the story to begin with.

NAMWALI SERPELL was born in Lusaka, Zambia, in 1980 and moved to the United States when she was nine. She has a BA from Yale, a PhD from Harvard, and a job as an assistant professor at the University of California, Berkeley — all three in English. "Muzungu" is her first published short story. She has contributed nonfiction to *Bidoun* and *The Believer.*

▪ I wrote "Muzungu" — untitled at first — one long, sunny afternoon in my old apartment on Washington Street in Somerville, Massachusetts. I sat in my sticky pleather desk chair; there was a bar of sunlight coming from the left -tych of my bay window; I was suddenly, unaccountably awake.

The story is, as always, a clutter of real things. Isa is not me, but as a child, I too intentionally scared myself with mirrors, climbed guava trees, and tried to save a broken-winged bird. My father, who is white, once told me about being used as a sort of game to scare children in a rural village in Zambia. It struck me then as an uncanny reversal of what I'd gathered — from reading and living — about being called out as black. Our dog Benjy gave birth to a premature litter and, as many animals are wont, destroyed the evidence. I once set off a flutter of birds running out of a sketchy neighbor's house in the suburbs of Baltimore.

I can't explain exactly what made me put these converted memories together in this way, in this order, with this or that connective tissue. What others have said about the story helps me understand some of what I wanted to capture: the sadness and exhaustion of race; how events can press against each other; the disruption of the solipsism of childhood, a breaking out into being seen by others but also into being with them.

I like the ending best, both of the story and of the process. My friend Case Q. Kerns helped me clean it up to submit to *Callaloo*. After it was accepted, my friends Margaret Miller and Michael Vazquez and my sister Zewelanji Serpell all edited the story with me with generosity. That the story could be the occasion for conversations is my pleasure in it and my continued hope for it.

100 Other Distinguished Stories of 2008

SELECTED BY HEIDI PITLOR

ADICHIE, CHIMAMANDA NGOZI
The Headstrong Historian. *The New Yorker,* June 30, 2008.

ALLIO, KIRSTIN
The Other Woman. *Alaska Quarterly Review,* vol. 25, nos. 1 & 2.

ALMOND, STEVE
First Date Back. *New England Review,* vol. 29, no. 1.

ANTRIM, DONALD
Another Manhattan. *The New Yorker,* Dec. 22 & 29, 2008.

AUSUBEL, RAMONA
Safe Passage. *One Story,* Issue 106.

BAKKEN, KERY NEVILLE
Indignity. *Gettysburg Review,* vol. 21, issue 1.

BASSETT, COLIN
This Is So We Don't Start Fighting. *Mississippi Review,* vol. 36, nos. 1 & 2.

BENDER, KAREN E.
What the Cat Said. *Harvard Review,* no. 34.

BERRY, WENDELL
A Desirable Woman. *Hudson Review,* vol. 61, no. 2.

BISSELL, TOM
Punishment. *Normal School,* vol. 1, issue 1.

BOYLE, T. C.
Ash Monday. *The New Yorker,* Jan. 21, 2008.
The Lie. *The New Yorker,* April 14, 2008.

BRAZAITIS, MARK
The Incurables. *Ploughshares,* vol. 34, nos. 2 & 3.

CAMPBELL, BONNIE JO
The Inventor, 1972. *Southern Review,* vol. 44, no. 1.

CARLSON, RON
At the Broken Ridge. *Tin House,* vol. 9, no. 3.

CASEY, MAUD
Fugueur. *Bellevue Literary Review,* vol. 8, no. 1.

CLARK, GEORGE MAKANA
Half Night. *Tin House,* vol. 9, no. 3.

DAUGHERTY, TRACY
Bern. *Georgia Review,* vol. 62, no. 1.

DIAZ, NATALIE
The Hooferman. *Bellingham Review,* vol. 31, issue 60.
DOVEY, CERIDWEN
The Family Friend. *n + 1,* no. 7.
DURDEN, E. A.
Mr. Dabydeen. *Glimmer Train,* issue 69.

ENBERG, SUSAN
Time's Body. *Sewanee Review,* vol. 116, no. 2.
ENGLANDER, NATHAN
Everything I Know About My Family on My Mother's Side. *Esquire,* July 2008.
EUGENIDES, JEFFREY
Great Experiment. *The New Yorker,* March 31, 2008.

FERRIS, JOSHUA
The Dinner Party. *The New Yorker,* August 11 & 18, 2008.
FORD, RICHARD
Leaving for Kenosha. *The New Yorker,* March 3, 2008.

GAITSKILL, MARY
Description. *Threepenny Review,* no. 116.
GALCHEN, RIVKA
The Region of Unlikeness. *The New Yorker,* March 24, 2008.
GILLS, MICHAEL
How Jesus Comes. *McSweeney's,* no. 26.
GIUSTA, MICHAEL
The Good Guy. *American Short Fiction,* issue 40.
GOODMAN, THEA
Evidence. *New England Review,* vol. 29, no. 4.
GORDON, MARY
Au Pair. *Salmagundi,* nos. 158 & 159.
GROFF, LAUREN
Sir Fleeting. *One Story,* issue 112.

HALL, SANDS
Hide & Go Seek. *Iowa Review,* vol. 38, no. 3.
HALLMAN, J. C.
Ethan: A Love Story. *Tin House,* vol. 10, no. 1.
HARPER, BAIRD
Yellowstone. *Cutbank,* issue 68.
HARRISON, WAYNE
Charity. *McSweeney's,* no. 26.
HARUN, ADRIENNE
Pearl Diving. *Colorado Review,* vol. 35, no. 1.
HAVAZELET, EHUD
Law of Return. *Ploughshares,* vol. 33, no. 4.
HAWLEY, MICHAEL
Diptych. *Alaska Quarterly Review,* vol. 25, nos. 1 & 2.
HEMON, ALEKSANDAR
The Noble Truths of Suffering. *The New Yorker,* September 22, 2008.
HOLLADAY, CARY
The Runaway Stagecoach. *Southern Review,* vol. 44, no. 3.
HUDDLE, DAVID
Wages of Love. *Conjunctions,* issue 51.

JEFFERS, HONOREE FANONNE
Easter Lilies in the West Room. *Poem Memoir Story,* no. 8.
JHABVALA, RUTH PRAWER
The Teacher. *The New Yorker,* July 28, 2008.
JIN, HA
The House Behind a Weeping Cherry. *The New Yorker,* April 7, 2008.
JOLLETT, MIKEL
The Crack. *McSweeney's,* no. 27.

KARDOS, MICHAEL
Maximum Security. *Southern Review,* vol. 44, no. 1.
KOCHIS, MARIA
Coral. *Pigsah Review,* vol. 3, issue 1.

KOHLER, SHEILA
Portrait of an Artist. *Boulevard*, vol. 23, nos. 2 & 3.

KOLDYS, SAYZIE
Mona, Yehya, Basma. *New England Review*, vol. 29, no. 1.

KRASIKOV, SANA
The Repatriates. *The New Yorker*, April 21, 2008.
Debt. *A Public Space*, issue 6.

LASALLE, PETER
What I Found Out About Her. *Antioch Review*, vol. 66, no. 1.

LE, NAM
The Boat. *Conjunctions*, issue 50.

LEE, ANDREA
Three. *The New Yorker*, September 29, 2008.

LI, YIYUN
A Thousand Years of Good Prayers. *Zoetrope*, vol. 12, no. 1.

LONGSTREET, KATHERINE
The Waters of Xochimilco. *Antioch Review*, vol. 66, no. 4.

LUNSTRUM, KIRSTEN SUNDBERG
Familial Kindness. *One Story*, issue 101.

LYCHACK, WILLIAM
Solpestad. *Ploughshares*, vol. 14, no. 1.

MCCANN, COLUM
Phreak. *Paris Review*, no. 186.

MCCRACKEN, ELIZABETH
Something Amazing. *Zoetrope*, vol. 12, no. 1.

MCGAHAN, JERRY
Reclamations. *Georgia Review*, vol. 62, no. 1.

MCILVAIN, RYAN
Keep It Bible. *Paris Review*, no. 184.

MEANS, DAVID
The Botch. *Harper's Magazine*, November 2008.

MELOY, MAILE
Liliana. *Paris Review*, no. 187.

MILLHAUSER, STEVEN
The Next Thing. *Harper's Magazine*, May 2008.

MOFFETT, KEVIN
In the Pines. *Harvard Review*, no. 34.

MUNRO, ALICE
Face. *The New Yorker*, September 8, 2008.
Free Radicals. *The New Yorker*, February 11 & 18, 2008.
Some Women. *The New Yorker*, December 22 & 29, 2008.

OATES, JOYCE CAROL
The Glazers. *American Short Fiction*, vol. 11, issue 40.

O'NEILL, JOSEPH
The World of Cheese. *Harper's Magazine*, February 2009.

PARKER, MICHAEL
Let Me Explain. *Columbia*, issue 46.

PATTERSON, VICTORIA
Johnny Hitman. *Santa Monica Review*, vol. 20, no. 1.

PEARLMAN, EDITH
Snoop. *Lake Effect*, vol. 12.

PECK, DALE
St. Anthony of the Vine. *Threepenny Review*, no. 114.

PERCY, BENJAMIN
The Killing. *Salt Hill*, no. 20.

PERRY, MARISSA
Trespassing. *Tin House*, vol. 9, no. 3.

PHILLIPS, ARTHUR
Note from a Previous Denizen. *Ecotone*, vol. 4, nos. 1 & 2.

PROULX, ANNIE
Tits-up in a Ditch. *The New Yorker*, June 9 & 16, 2008.

RASH, RON
Burning Bright. *Ecotone*, vol. 4, nos. 1 & 2.

SARTOR, COLETTE
Lamb. *Prairie Schooner*, vol. 81, no. 1.

SCHUMACHER, JULIE
Patient, Female. *Atlantic Monthly,* fiction issue.

SORRENTINO, CHRISTOPHER
Ever Again. *Tin House,* vol. 10, no. 3.

SPENCER, ELIZABETH
Sightings. *Hudson Review,* vol. 61, no. 1.

STUCKEY-FRENCH, ELIZABETH
Interview with a Moron. *Narrative Magazine.*

TEL, JONATHAN
The Beijing of Possibilities. *Zoetrope,* vol. 12, no. 3.

THOMPSON, JEAN
Wilderness. *One Story,* issue 105.

THRAPP, DAN
Ancient Remedies. *Colorado Review,* vol. 35, no. 1.

TOWER, WELLS
Leopard. *The New Yorker,* November 10, 2008.

TUCK, LILY
My Flame. *Yale Review,* vol. 96, no. 4.

VALLIANTOS, CORINNA
My Escapee. *Tin House,* vol. 9, no. 3.

VESTAL, SHAWN
Gulls. *Tin House,* vol. 10, no. 3.

WEIL, JOSH
Mirza. *Narrative Magazine.*

WHITE, JACOB
The Days Down Here. *Georgia Review,* vol. 62, no. 3.

WILLIAMS, NAOMI J.
Welcome to Our Shinkansen. *Gettysburg Review,* vol. 21, no. 1.

WOODREL, DANIEL
Black Step. *New Letters,* vol. 74, no. 4.

YODER, RACHEL
I Want to Forgive Everyone, Trousers. *The Sun,* May 2008.

ZENTNER, ALEXI
Trapline. *Narrative Magazine.*

Editorial Addresses of American and Canadian Magazines Publishing Short Stories

African American Review
St. Louis University
Humanities 317
3800 Lindell Boulevard
St. Louis, MO 63108
$40, Joycelyn Moody

Agni Magazine
Boston University Writing Program
Boston University
236 Bay State Road
Boston, MA 02115
$20 Sven Birkerts

Alaska Quarterly Review
University of Alaska, Anchorage
3211 Providence Drive
Anchorage, AK 99508
$20, Ronald Spatz

Alimentum
P.O. Box 776
New York, NY 10163
$18, Paulette Licitra

Alligator Juniper
Prescott College
220 Grove Avenue
Prescott, AZ 86301
$15, Melanie Bishop

American Letters and Commentary
Department of English
University of Texas at San Antonio
One UTSA Boulevard
San Antonio, TX 78249
$10, David Ray Vance, Catherine Kasper

American Short Fiction
P.O. Box 301209
Austin, TX 78703
$30, the editors

Antioch Review
Antioch University
150 East South College Street
Yellow Springs, OH 45387
$40, Robert S. Fogerty

Apalachee Review
P.O. Box 10469
Tallahassee, FL 32302
$15, Michael Trammell

Arkansas Review
Department of English and Philosophy
P.O. Box 1890
Arkansas State University
State University, AR 72467
$20, Tom Williams

Ascent
English Department
Concordia College
901 Eighth Street

Moorhead, MN 56562
$12, W. Scott Olsen

Atlantic Monthly
600 NH Avenue NW
Washington, DC 20037
$39.95, C. Michael Curtis

Baltimore Review
P.O. Box 36418
Towson, MD 21286
$15, Barbara Westwood Diehl

Bamboo Ridge
P.O. Box 61781
Honolulu, HI 96839
Eric Chock, Darrell H. Y. Lum

Barrelhouse
barrelhousemagazine.com
the editors

Bat City Review
Department of English
University of Texas at Austin
1 University Station B5000
Austin, TX 78712
$14, Ryan P. Young

Bayou
Department of English
University of New Orleans
2000 Lakeshore Drive
New Orleans, LA 70148
$15, Joanna Leake

Bellevue Literary Review
Department of Medicine
New York University School of Medicine
550 First Avenue
New York, NY 10016
$15, Danielle Ofri

Bellingham Review
MS-9053
Western Washington University
Bellingham, WA 98225
$14, Brenda Miller

Bellowing Ark
P.O. Box 55564
Shoreline, WA 98155
$18, Robert Ward

Big Sky Journal
P.O. Box 1069
Bozeman, MT 59771
Brian Schott

Blackbird
Department of English
Virginia Commonwealth University
P.O. Box 843082
Richmond, VA 23284-3082
Anna Journey

Black Clock
California Institute of the Arts
24700 McBean Parkway
Valencia, CA 91355
$20, Steve Erickson

Black Warrior Review
P.O. Box 862936
Tuscaloosa, AL 35486-0027
$14, Laura Hendrix

Bomb
New Art Publications
80 Hanson Place
Brooklyn, NY 11217
$25, Betsy Sussler

Boston Review
35 Medford Street, Suite 302
Somerville, MA 02143
$25, Joshua Cohen, Deborah Chasman

Boulevard
PMB 325
6614 Clayton Road
Richmond Heights, MO 63117
$20, Richard Burgin

Brain, Child: The Magazine for Thinking Mothers
P.O. Box 714
Lexington, VA 24450-0714
$19.95, Jennifer Niesslein, Stephanie Wilkinson

Briar Cliff Review
3303 Rebecca Street

P.O. Box 2100
Sioux City, IA 51104-2100
$10, Tricia Currans-Sheehan

Callaloo
MS 4212
Texas A&M University
College Station, TX 77843-4212
$48, Charles H. Rowell

Calyx
P.O. Box B
Corvallis, OR 97339
$23, Margarita Donnelly and collective

Canteen
70 Washington Street, Suite 1214
Brooklyn, NY 11201
$35, Stephen Pierson

Carolina Quarterly
Greenlaw Hall CB 3520
University of North Carolina
Chapel Hill, NC 27599-3520
$18, Matthew Luter

Chattahoochee Review
Georgia Perimeter College
2101 Womack Road
Dunwoody, GA 30338-4497
$20, Marc Fitten

Chicago Review
5801 South Kenwood
University of Chicago
Chicago, IL 60637
$25, V. Joshua Adams

Cimarron Review
205 Morrill Hall
Oklahoma State University
Stillwater, OK 74078-4069
$24, E. P. Walkiewicz

Cincinnati Review
Department of English
McMicken Hall, Room 369
P.O. Box 210069
Cincinnati, OH 45221
$15, Brock Clarke

Colorado Review
Department of English
Colorado State University
Fort Collins, CO 80523
$24, Stephanie G'Schwind

Columbia
Columbia University
415 Dodge Hall
2960 Broadway
New York, NY 10027
$15, Kristin Vukovic

Commentary
165 East 56th Street
New York, NY 10022
$45, Neal Kozody

Confrontation
English Department
C. W. Post College of Long Island University
Greenvale, NY 11548
$10, Martin Tucker

Conjunctions
21 East 10th Street, Suite 3E
New York, NY 10003
$18, Bradford Morrow

Crab Orchard Review
Department of English
Southern Illinois University at Carbondale
Carbondale, IL 62901
$20, Carolyn Alessio

Crazyhorse
Department of English
College of Charleston
66 George Street
Charleston, SC 29424
$16, Carol Ann Davis

Cutbank
Department of English
University of Montana
Missoula, MT 59812
$12, Anne-Marie Inge

Daedalus
136 Irving Street, Suite 100

Cambridge, MA 02138
$40, James Miller

Denver Quarterly
University of Denver
Denver, CO 80208
$20, Bin Ramke

Descant
P.O. Box 314
Station P
Toronto, Ontario M5S 2S8
$28, Karen Mulhallen

Dossier
244 Dekalb Ave.
Brooklyn, NY 11205
Thomas Yagoda

Doublethink
1001 Connecticut Ave. NW, Suite 1250
Washington, D.C. 20036
Cheryl Miller

Ecotone
Department of Creative Writing
University of North Carolina, Wilmington
601 South College Road
Wilmington, NC 28403
$18, David Gessner

Eleven Eleven
California College of the Arts
1111 Eighth Street
San Francisco, CA 94107
Hugh Behm-Steinberg

Epoch
251 Goldwin Smith Hall
Cornell University
Ithaca, NY 14853-3201
$11, Michael Koch

Esquire
300 West 57th St., 21st Floor
New York, NY 10019
$17.94, fiction editor

Event
Douglas College
P.O. Box 2503
New Westminster, British Columbia V3L 5B2
$24.95, Rick Maddocks

Fantasy and Science Fiction
P.O. Box 3447
Hoboken, NJ 07030
$50.99, Gordon Van Gelder

The Farallon Review
1017 L Street
No. 348
Sacramento, CA 95814
$7, the editors

Fiction
Department of English
City College of New York
Convent Ave. at 138th Street
New York, NY 10031
$38, Mark Jay Mirsky

Fiction International
Department of English and Comparative Literature
San Diego State University
San Diego, CA 92182
$18, Harold Jaffe

The Fiddlehead
Campus House
11 Garland Court
UNB P.O. Box 4400
Fredericton, New Brunswick E3B 5A3
$40, Mark Anthony Jarman

First City Review
editors@firstcityreview.com
Michael Pollack

Five Points
Georgia State University
P.O. Box 3999
Atlanta, GA 30302
$21, David Bottoms and Megan Sexton

The Florida Review
Department of English

P.O. Box 161346
University of Central Florida
Orlando, FL 32816
$15, Susan E. Fallows

Flyway
206 Rose Hall
Department of English
Iowa State University
Ames, IA 50011
$24, David DeFina

Fourteen Hills
Department of Creative Writing
San Francisco State University
1600 Halloway Ave.
San Francisco, CA 94132-1722
$17, Charles Rech

Fugue
Department of English
378 Brink Hall 200
University of Idaho
Moscow, ID 83844-1102
$14, Michael Lewis, Kendall Sand

Gargoyle
3819 North 13th Street
Arlington, VA 22201
$30, Lucinda Ebersole, Richard Peabody

Georgia Review
Gilbert Hall
University of Georgia
Athens, GA 30602
$30, Stephen Corey

Gettysburg Review
Gettysburg College
300 N. Washington Street
Gettysburg, PA 17325
$24, Peter Stitt

Glimmer Train Stories
1211 NW Glisan Street, Suite 207
Portland, OR 97209
$36, Susan Burmeister-Brown, Linda Swanson-Davies

Good Housekeeping
300 W. 57th Street
New York, NY 10019
Laura Mathews

Grain
Box 67
Saskatoon, Saskatchewan 57K 3K9
$26.95, Kent Bruyneel

Granta
1755 Broadway, 5th Floor
New York, NY 10019-3780
$39.95, Ian Jack

Green Mountains Review
Box A58
Johnson State College
Johnson, VT 05656
$15, Leslie Daniels

Greensboro Review
3302 Hall for Humanities
and Research Administration
University of North Carolina
Greensboro, NC 27402
$10, Jim Clark

Grist
University of Tennessee
English Department
301 McClung Tower
Knoxville, TN 37996
$29.95, Bradford Tice

Gulf Coast
Department of English
University of Houston
4800 Calhoun Road
Houston, TX 77204-3012
$16, Nick Flynn

Gulf Stream
English Department
Florida International University
Biscayne Bay Campus
3000 NE 151st Street
North Miami, FL 33181
$15, John Dufresne, Joe Clifford

Hanging Loose
231 Wyckoff Street

Brooklyn, NY 11217
$22, group

Harper's Magazine
666 Broadway
New York, NY 10012
$21, Ben Metcalf

Harpur Palate
Department of English
Binghamton University
P.O. Box 6000
Binghamton, NY 13902
$16, Sarah Klenbort, Eve Rutherford, Kim Vose

Harvard Review
Lamont Library
Harvard University
Cambridge, MA 02138
$16, Christina Thompson

Hawaii Review
Department of English
University of Hawaii at Manoa
1733 Donagho Road
Honolulu, HI 96822
$20, Che S. Ng

Hawk & Handsaw
Unity College
90 Quaker Hill Road
Unity, NE 04988
$10, Kathryn Miles

Hayden's Ferry Review
Box 875002
Arizona State University
Tempe, AZ 85287
$14, Cameron Fielder

High Desert Journal
P.O. Box 7647
Bend, OR 97708
$16, Elizabeth Quinn

Hobart
P.O. Box 1658
Ann Arbor, MI 48106
$20, Aaron Burch

Hotel Amerika
Columbia College
English Department
600 S. Michigan Avenue
Chicago, IL 60657
$18, David Lazar

H.O.W.
Helping Orphans Worldwide
112 Franklin Street, 4th floor
New York, NY 10013
$25, Alison Weaver, Natasha Radojcic

Hudson Review
684 Park Avenue
New York, NY 10065
$32, Paula Deitz

Hyphen
17 Walter U. Lum Place
San Francisco, CA 94108
$18, Harry Mok

Idaho Review
Boise State University
1910 University Drive
Boise, ID 83725
$10, Mitch Wieland

Image
Center for Religious Humanism
3307 Third Avenue West
Seattle, WA 98119
$39.95, Gregory Wolfe

Indiana Review
Ballantine Hall 465
1020 East Kirkwood Avenue
Bloomington, IN 47405-7103
$17, Jenny Burge

Inkwell
Manhattanville College
2900 Purchase Street
Purchase, NY 10577
$10, Autumn Kindelspire

Iowa Review
Department of English
University of Iowa
308 EPB

Iowa City, IA 52242
$25, David Hamilton

Iron Horse Literary Review
Department of English
Texas Tech University
Box 43091
Lubbock, TX 79409-3091
$12, Leslie Jill Patterson

Isotope
Utah State University
3200 Old Main Hill
Logan, UT 84322
$10, the editors

Italian Americana
University of Rhode Island
Providence Campus
80 Washington Street
Providence, RI 02903
$20, Carol Bonomo Albright

Jabberwock Review
Department of English
Drawer E
Mississippi State University
Mississippi State, MS 39762
$12, Joy Murphy

Jewish Currents
45 East 33rd Street
New York, NY 10016-5335
$30, editorial board

Juked
110 Westridge Drive
Tallahassee, FL 32304
$10, J. W. Wang

Kalliope
Florida Community College
3939 Roosevelt Boulevard
Jacksonville, FL 32205
$12.50, Margaret L. Clark

Kenyon Review
Finn House
102 W. Wiggin Street
Kenyon College
Gambier, OH 43022
$30, David H. Lynn

Lady Churchill's Rosebud Wristlet
Small Beer Press
150 Pleasant Street
Easthampton, MA 01027
$20, Kelly Link

Lake Effect
Penn State Erie
4951 College Drive
Erie, PA 16563-1501
$6, George Looney

Lilies and Cannonballs Review
P.O. Box 702
Bowling Green Station
New York, NY 10274
$23, Daniel Conner

Lilith
250 W. 57th Street, #2432
New York, NY 10107
$25.97, Yona Zeldis McDonough

The Literary Review
Fairleigh Dickinson University
285 Madison Avenue
Madison, NJ 07940
$18, René Steinke

Louisville Review
Spalding University
851 South Fourth Street
Louisville, KY 40203
$14, Sena Jeter Naslund

Lumina
Sarah Lawrence College
Slonim House
One Mead Way
Bronxville, NY 10708
$8, Michael Wolman

Madison Review
University of Wisconsin
Department of English
H. C. White Hall
600 North Park Street

Madison, WI 53706
$25, Miles Johnson

Mānoa
English Department
University of Hawaii
Honolulu, HI 96822
$22, Frank Stewart

Massachusetts Review
South College
University of Massachusetts
Amherst, MA 01003
$37, David Lenson, Ellen Dore Watson

McSweeney's
826 Valencia Street
San Francisco, CA 94110
$55, Dave Eggers

Meridian
Department of English
P.O. Box 400145
University of Virginia
Charlottesville, VA 22904-4145
$12, Julia Hansen

Michigan Quarterly Review
3574 Rackham Building
915 East Washington Street
University of Michigan
Ann Arbor, MI 48109
$25, Laurence Goldstein

Mid-American Review
Department of English
Bowling Green State University
Bowling Green, OH 43403
$12, Michael Czyzniejewski

Minnesota Review
Department of English
Carnegie Mellon University
Pittsburgh, PA 15213
$30, Jeffrey Williams

Mississippi Review
University of Southern Mississippi
18 College Drive, #5144
Hattiesburg, MS 39406-5144
$15, Frederick Barthelme

Missouri Review
357 McReynolds Hall
University of Missouri
Columbia, MO 65211
$24, Speer Morgan

Ms.
433 South Beverly Drive
Beverly Hills, CA 90212
$45, Amy Bloom

n + 1
68 Joy Street, #405
Brooklyn, NY 11201
$20, Keith Gessen, Mark Greif

Narrative Magazine
narrativemagazine.com
the editors

Natural Bridge
Department of English
University of Missouri, St. Louis
St. Louis, MO 63121
$15, Steven Schreiner

New Delta Review
English Department
15 Allen Hall
Louisiana State University
Baton Rouge, LA
$30, Craig Brandhorst

New England Review
Middlebury College
Middlebury, VT 05753
$25, Stephen Donadio

New Letters
University of Missouri
5100 Rockhill Road
Kansas City, MO 64110
$22, Robert Stewart

New Madrid
Department of English and Philosophy
Murray State University
7C Faculty Hall
Murray, KY 42071
$15, the editors

New Ohio Review
English Department
360 Ellis Hall
Ohio University
Athens, OH 45701
$20, John Bullock

New Orleans Review
P.O. Box 195
Loyola University
New Orleans, LA 70118
$14, Christopher Chambers

New Orphic Review
706 Mill Street
Nelson, British Columbia V1L 4S5
$30, Ernest Hekkanen

New Quarterly
Saint Jerome's University
290 Westmount Road
N. Waterloo, Ontario N2L 3G3
$36, Kim Jernigan

New Renaissance
16 Heath Road
Arlington, MA 02474
$38, Louise T. Reynolds

The New Yorker
4 Times Square
New York, NY 10036
$46, Deborah Treisman

Nimrod International Journal
Arts and Humanities Council of Tulsa
600 South College Avenue
Tulsa, OK 74104
$17.50, Francine Ringold

Ninth Letter
Department of English
University of Illinois
608 South Wright Street
Urbana, IL 61801
$21.95, Jodee Rubins

Noon
1324 Lexington Avenue
PMB 298
New York, NY 10128
$12, Diane Williams

The Normal School
5245 North Backer Ave.
M/S PB 98
California State University
Fresno, CA 93470
$5, David Durham, Alex Espinoza

North American Review
University of Northern Iowa
1222 West 27th Street
Cedar Falls, IA 50614
$22, Grant Tracey

North Carolina Literary Review
Department of English
2201 Bate Building
East Carolina University
Greenville, NC 27858-4353
$20, Margaret Bauer

North Dakota Quarterly
University of North Dakota
Merrifield Hall, Room 110
276 Centennial Drive Stop 27209
Grand Forks, ND 58202
$25, Robert Lewis

Northwest Review
1286 University of Oregon
Eugene, OR 97403
$22, John Witte

Notre Dame Review
840 Flanner Hall
Department of English
University of Notre Dame
Notre Dame, IN 46556
$15, John Matthias, William O'Rourke

One Story
232 Third Street, #A111
Brooklyn, NY 11215
$21, Maribeth Batcha, Hannah Tinti

Open City
270 Lafayette Street, Suite 1412
New York, NY 10012
$30, Thomas Beller, Joanna Yas

Oxford American
201 Donaghey Avenue, Main 107
Conway, AR 72035
$24.95, Marc Smirnoff

Pak N Treger
National Yiddish Book Center
Harry and Jeanette Weinberg Bldg.
1021 West Street
Amherst, MA 01002
$36, Aaron Lansky

Paris Review
62 White Street
New York, NY 10013
$34, Philip Gourevitch

PEN America
PEN America Center
588 Broadway, Suite 303
New York, NY 10012
$10, M Mark

Phantasmagoria
English Department
Century Community and Technical College
3300 Century Avenue North
White Bear Lake, MN 55110
$15, Abigail Allen

Phoebe
George Mason University
MSN 2C5
4400 University Drive
Fairfax, VA 22030-4444
$12, Lisa Ampleman

Pigsaw Review
Division of Humanities
Brevard College
400 N. Broad Street
Brevard, NC 28712
$12, Jubal Tiner

The Pinch
Department of English
University of Memphis
Memphis, TN 38152
$18, Kristen Iverson

Playboy
680 North Lake Shore Drive
Chicago, IL 60611
$12, Amy Grace Lloyd

Pleiades
Department of English and Philosophy
University of Central Missouri
Warrensburg, MO 64093
$12, Kevin Prufer

Ploughshares
Emerson College
120 Boylston Street
Boston, MA 02116
$24, Ladette Randolph

Poem Memoir Story
HB 217
1530 3rd Ave. South
Birmingham, AL 35294-1260
$7, Linda Frost

Post Road
P.O. Box 400951
Cambridge, MA 02420
$18, Mary Cotton

Potomac Review
Montgomery College
51 Mannakee Street
Rockville, MD 20850
$20, Julie Wakeman-Linn

Prairie Fire
423–100 Arthur Street
Winnipeg, Manitoba R3B 1H3
$30, Andris Taskans

Prairie Schooner
201 Andrews Hall
University of Nebraska
Lincoln, NE 68588-0334
$28, Hilda Raz

Prism International
Department of Creative Writing
University of British Columbia
Buchanan E-462

Vancouver, British Columbia V6T 1Z1
$25, Ben Hart

A Public Space
323 Dean Street
Brooklyn, NY 11217
Brigid Hughes

Puerto del Sol
MSC 3E
New Mexico State University
P.O. Box 30001
Las Cruces, NM 88003
$10, Kevin McIlvoy

Quarterly West
255 South Central Campus Drive
Department of English/LNCO 3500
University of Utah
Salt Lake City, Utah 84112
$14, Brenda Sieczkowski, Paul Ketzle

Redivider
Emerson College
120 Boylston Street
Boston, MA 02116
$10, Laura van den Berg

Red Rock Review
English Department, J2A
Community College of Southern Nevada
3200 East Cheyenne Avenue
North Las Vegas, NV 89030
$9.50, Richard Logsdon

Reed Magazine
Department of English
San José State University
One Washington Square
San José, CA 95192
$8, D. E. Kim

River Oak Review
Elmhurst College
190 Prospect Avenue
Box 2633
Elmhurst, IL 60126
$12, Ron Wiginton

River Styx
3547 Olive Street, Suite 107
St. Louis, MO 63103-1014
$20, Richard Newman

Room Magazine
P.O. Box 46160
Station D
Vancouver, British Columbia V6J 5G5
$25, Anna Torres

Ruminate
140 N. Roosevelt Ave.
Ft. Collins, CO 80521
$28, Brianna Van Dyke

Salamander
Suffolk University
English Department
41 Temple Street
Boston, MA 02114
$23, Jennifer Barber

Salmagundi
Skidmore College
Saratoga Springs, NY 12866
$20, Robert Boyers

Salt Flats Annual
P.O. Box 2381
Layton, UT 84041
$10, Dana Layton Sides

Salt Hill
Syracuse University
English Department
Syracuse, NY 13244
$20, Daniel Torday, Tara Warman

Santa Monica Review
1900 Pico Boulevard
Santa Monica, CA 90405
$12, Andrew Tonkovich

Sewanee Review
University of the South
Sewanee, TN 37375-4009
$25, George Core

Shenandoah
Mattingly House

2 Lee Avenue
Washington and Lee University
Lexington, VA 24450-2116
$22, R. T. Smith, Lynn Leech

Sonora Review
Department of English
University of Arizona
Tucson, AZ 85721
$16, PR Griffis, Amy P. Knight

South Dakota Review
University of South Dakota
414 E. Clark Street
Vermilion, SD 57069
$30, Brian Bedard

Southern California Review
3501 Trousdale Parkway
Mark Taper Hall
THH 355J
University of Southern California
Los Angeles, CA 90089
$20, Annlee Ellingson

Southern Humanities Review
9088 Haley Center
Auburn University
Auburn, AL 36849
$15, Dan R. Latimer, Virginia M. Kouidis

Southern Indiana Review
College of Liberal Arts
University of Southern Indiana
8600 University Blvd.
Evansville, IN 47712
$20, Ron Mitchell

Southern Review
43 Allen Hall
Louisiana State University
Baton Rouge, LA 70803
$25, Jeanne M. Leiby

Southwest Review
Southern Methodist University
P.O. Box 750374
Dallas, TX 75275
$24, Willard Spiegelman

Subtropics
Department of English
University of Florida
P.O. Box 112075
Gainesville, FL 32611-2075
$26, David Leavitt

The Summerset Review
25 Summerset Drive
Smithtown, NY 11787
$8, Joseph Levens

The Sun
107 North Roberson Street
Chapel Hill, NC 27516
$36, Sy Safransky

Sycamore Review
Department of English
500 Oval Drive
Purdue University
West Lafayette, IN 47907
$14, Mehdi Okasi

Talking River
Lewis-Clark State College
500 8th Ave.
Lewiston, ID 83501
$14, editor

Third Coast
Department of English
Western Michigan University
Kalamazoo, MI 49008
$16, Rachel Swearingen

Threepenny Review
2163 Vine Street
Berkeley, CA 94709
$25, Wendy Lesser

Timber Creek Review
P.O. Box 16542
Greensboro, NC 27416
$17, John Freiermuth

Tin House
P.O. Box 10500
Portland, OR 97296-0500
$29.90, Rob Spillman

Transition
69 Dunster Street
Harvard University
Cambridge, MA 02138
$28, Kwame Anthony Appiah, Henry Louis Gates, Jr., Michael Vazquez

TriQuarterly
629 Noyes Street
Evanston, IL 60208
$24, Susan Firestone Hahn

Upstreet
P.O. Box 105
Richmond, MA 01254
$10, Vivian Dorsel

Virginia Quarterly Review
One West Range
P.O. Box 400223
Charlottesville, VA 22903
$32, Ted Genoways

War, Literature, and the Arts
Department of English and Fine Arts
2354 Fairchild Drive, Suite 6D45
USAF Academy, CO 80840-6242
$10, Donald Anderson

Weber Studies
Weber State University
1214 University Circle
Ogden, UT 84408-1214
$20, Brad Roghaar

West Branch
Bucknell Hall
Bucknell University
Lewisburg, PA 17837
$10, Paula Closson Buck

Western Humanities Review
University of Utah
255 South Central Campus Drive
Room 3500
Salt Lake City, UT 84112
$16, Barry Weller

Whitefish Review
708 Lupfer Ave.
Whitcfish, MT 59937
$24, Brian Scott

Willow Springs
Eastern Washington University
705 West First Avenue
Spokane, WA 99201
$18, Samuel Ligon

Yale Review
P.O. Box 208243
New Haven, CT 06520-8243
$31, J. D. McClatchy

Zoetrope
Sentinel Building
916 Kearney Street
San Francisco, CA 94133
$24, Michael Ray